A SUDDEN CRASH CAUGHT LIEUTENANT TOM PARIS BY SURPRISE . . .

He spun around to see B'Elanna Torres lifting a large, curly-haired alien off the dance floor. "Son of a *targ!*" Torres roared, and hurled the man physically into the air. He came flying at the dance floor, a cry of alarm escaping his wide open mouth. Paris ducked at the last minute, and the B'Elanna-propelled alien slammed into another.

They crashed to the floor, landing in a tangle of limbs that threatened the vertical stability of every couple dancing nearby. The alien's angry curses mixed with the other man's groans, spoiling the romantic mood music.

Captain Janeway wouldn't be happy about this turn of events, Paris decided. Perhaps it was time for the *Voyager* crew members to excuse themselves from the party.

STAR TREK®
VOYAGER™

THE BLACK SHORE

Greg Cox

POCKET BOOKS

New York   London   Toronto   Sydney   Tokyo   Singapore

An *Original* Publication of POCKET BOOKS

POCKET BOOKS, a division of Simon & Schuster Inc.
1230 Avenue of the Americas, New York, NY 10020

This book is published by Pocket Books, a division of
Simon & Schuster Inc., under exclusive license from
Paramount Pictures.

ISBN: 0-671-56061-1

First Pocket Books printing May 1997

10 9 8 7 6 5 4 3 2 1

POCKET and colophon are registered trademarks of
Simon & Schuster Inc.

Printed in the U.S.A.

For Alex,
who wanted to play kitty games instead

CHAPTER
1

Captain's log, stardate 491750.0

We are continuing our travels through what appears to be an unusually barren and desolate sector of the Delta Quadrant. Little has interrupted *Voyager*'s daily routines for several weeks now—a mixed blessing, to be sure. With no new dangers or discoveries to command my attention, I find my thoughts drifting increasingly toward Earth, and the people and lives that we have left behind. The Federation seems especially far away, and I suspect that I am not the only person aboard this ship that feels that way. . . .

"C'MON, DOC! I DON'T HAVE TIME FOR THIS."

First Officer Chakotay heard Harry Kim's heated complaint the moment he entered the sickbay. He was struck by the note of genuine irritation in Kim's

1

voice; the young ensign had always impressed Chakotay as being relatively even-tempered. *I wonder what's got under his skin,* he thought.

The doors slid shut silently behind him. The air in the sickbay had a medicinal odor that Chakotay associated with disinfectants and sterilization fields. He saw Kim struggling to rise from the medical biobed on which he was none too happily lying. His upper body was propped up on both elbows, and his legs were swinging toward the edge of the bed. The Doctor placed a restraining hand against Kim's chest. "Yes, I'm sure you must have an urgent appointment to play pool in that seedy holographic bar—or something equally compelling." Although holographic himself, The Doctor's hand was evidently solid enough to keep the impatient ensign on the bed. "Regular checkups are an essential part of a proper health regimen for most humanoid species. As the sole medical officer on this improvised expedition through parts unknown, it is my thankless task to ensure that every member of this luckless crew gets all the preventive care they require, whether they appreciate it or not." The Doctor sighed theatrically. "Now, would you *please* lie back so I can finish recording your vitals?"

Chakotay glanced at the monitor above the biobed. Kim's readings looked normal enough, although his blood pressure seemed slightly elevated. Kes stood a few centimeters behind The Doctor, holding a medical tricorder. The Ocampa acknowledged Chakotay's arrival with a nod and a friendly smile. Intent on his reluctant patient, The Doctor seemed oblivious to the first officer's presence.

"Okay, okay," Kim said, lowering his head onto the cushioned surface of the bed. "Let's just get this over with. I haven't got all day."

"You're seventy-five years away from civilization as

we know it," The Doctor observed. "How much of a rush can you be in?"

Kim glared at The Doctor with anger in his eyes; The Doctor's tart remark had apparently struck a nerve. "That's it!" he said, sitting up abruptly. "I may be stuck out here, light-years from anywhere, but I have better things to do than listen to a holographic lecture on health care." His boots smacked against the floor as he hopped off the bed, ignoring The Doctor's protests. Chakotay was surprised by the intensity of Kim's reaction; over the last few years, the crew had largely overcome the homesickness that had afflicted them at the beginning of their sojourn in the Delta Quadrant. What could have happened to provoke such a response from Kim now?

"Now wait just one second," The Doctor said indignantly. He laid a hand upon the ensign's shoulder. "This examination is over when I say it is."

"Please, Harry," Kes added. "This will just take a moment or two." Her tone was softer and more conciliatory than The Doctor's.

Kim disregarded the young woman's attempt at peacemaking. "No, *you* wait," he told The Doctor. "Computer, deactivate emergency medical program. Command priority gamma."

The Doctor's jaw dropped and a look of surprise came over his face a heartbeat before he blinked out of existence. "What do you—"

Kes appeared both stunned and disappointed by Kim's preemptory dismissal of The Doctor. "Harry, how could you?" she asked. She glanced upward at the ceiling as she addressed the ship itself. "Computer, restore medical program immediately."

"—think you are doing?" The Doctor rematerialized between Kes and Kim, his hand still holding on to the ensign's right shoulder, his voice picking up exactly where he had been cut off only seconds before.

A puzzled expression crossed his features. His eyes looked slightly more unfocused than usual. "Excuse me, was I gone for an instant there?"

"Not for long enough," Kim said. He shoved The Doctor's hand away and started to shoulder his way past Kes and The Doctor. "I'm out of here."

Chakotay decided he had seen enough. "Ensign!" he barked. Kim suddenly became aware of the first officer's presence. He snapped to attention, a look of embarrassment melting the angry set of his expression. Kes and The Doctor stepped aside to let Chakotay approach Kim. Body stiff, Kim stared past Chakotay, unable to meet the first officer's gaze. Chakotay let him stew for a couple of seconds before speaking again.

"The Doctor's bedside manner may leave something to be desired," Chakotay stated. He heard The Doctor make a harrumphing sound behind him. "But that's no excuse for insubordination and incivility, nor for abusing your command priority privileges."

"I apologize, sir," Kim said, still looking straight ahead. Chakotay guessed that the ensign would sooner face an entire Kazon warrior sect than prolong this encounter one more minute. "I'm afraid I just, well, lost my temper."

"That's not enough of an explanation," Chakotay said. "I know you, Harry; you're not usually a hothead. What's this all about?"

Kim blushed, his face turning almost as red as Chakotay's crimson Starfleet uniform. He lowered his voice, perhaps hoping that neither The Doctor nor Kes would hear his sheepish confession. "I'm sorry, sir. It's just that, I guess, today is my birthday and I'm used to spending it with my family, not going through an annual checkup somewhere in the Delta Quadrant." His eyes finally met Chakotay's. His voice remained admirably even, despite his humiliation.

"That's no excuse, I know, but it probably has something to do with my—reaction—a few moments ago."

"I see," Chakotay said. Kim's emotional display made a little more sense now; despite the crew's improved attitude, it stood to reason that birthdays and anniversaries and such would inevitably remind crew members of the loved ones they'd left behind. "Very well. For today, you are excused from completing this exam, but I expect you to reschedule a new appointment with The Doctor sometime in the next seventy-two hours. And no more taking out your bad moods on your fellow officers and crew members. Do you understand me, Ensign?"

"Yes, sir," Kim said, visibly struggling to conceal his relief. *What did he expect,* Chakotay wondered, *that I'd have him confined to quarters for blowing off a little steam?* "Thank you, Commander."

"At ease, Ensign. You may go now." Kim murmured a few more apologies in the direction of The Doctor and his assistant, then hurried for the door as quickly as decorum allowed. "And, Harry," Chakotay called out as Kim stepped out the door, "have a happy birthday."

The sickbay doors slid shut, but not before Chakotay spotted a grin on the ensign's face. Turning away from the exit, Chakotay faced Kes and The Doctor. "I thought you handled that very well," Kes commented. "I'm sure Harry didn't mean to cause a disturbance."

"Easy for you to say," The Doctor groused. "You're not the one who was switched off like a light bulb." He reached over and deactivated the sensor screen above the now-vacant biobed. Chakotay wondered if it reassured The Doctor to be able to turn off his own equipment at will, asserting his position on *Voyager*'s technological pecking order, or if it only reminded him of the transitory nature of his own artificially maintained existence? "Now then, Commander, what can I do for you?"

Chakotay contemplated the events of the last few minutes. "Actually," he said, "it may have everything to do with what I just witnessed."

"A morale problem?" Captain Kathryn Janeway asked.

"Exactly," Chakotay said. They were having a private conference in the captain's ready room, located off the bridge. A porcelain mug full of steaming coffee sat on Janeway's desk in front of her. Due to energy restrictions on the ship's replicators, she rationed herself one fresh coffee every other morning. Janeway took a sip of the hot java, savoring the bracing bitterness of its taste, while Chakotay described a recent episode in the sickbay. Her first officer sat opposite her in a sturdy duranium chair. According to *Voyager*'s daily schedule, it was still morning. Janeway treated herself to another swallow of the precious coffee, anticipating a much-needed kick from the caffeine.

"Harry Kim, you say?" she echoed Chakotay. "That is disturbing. Without casting too many aspersions on others in the crew, I wouldn't find it quite so remarkable to hear that B'Elanna or Neelix or even Tom Paris had thrown a tantrum. But Harry? That's not like him at all."

Chakotay nodded gravely. "The incident with Ensign Kim is just a symptom of a larger problem. The Doctor confirmed my own observations. Most of the crew are showing signs of stress and fatigue. Nerves are frayed. Tempers are short. Just the other day, I had to stop B'Elanna from force-feeding Neelix some particularly unappetizing Talaxian delicacy."

"How odd," Janeway stated. "I was under the impression that the crew's attitude had improved since we left Kazon space." *And none too soon,* she thought. Certainly, her own sense of adventure had grown since they left the Kazon and their dire intrigues behind. It troubled her that her first officer thought the crew's morale was slipping again.

"In general, the mood had lightened until recently," Chakotay explained, "but now we're flying through what appears to be the Delta Quadrant equivalent to Death Valley. Adventure and exploration are great antidotes for homesickness, but day after day spent traversing dead, lifeless space would get anybody down."

"I see," Janeway said. She had to admit she'd been feeling a bit bored herself lately. "So what do you suggest we do about this outbreak of sour spirits?"

"My own diagnosis," Chakotay said, "is that a bad case of cabin fever is spreading through *Voyager.* There's not much we can do about the root causes of any homesickness, but I strongly recommend shore leave for the crew as soon as a suitable site is found."

"That's an excellent idea," Janeway said. "As you say, the crew's been stuck aboard the ship for weeks now, without any break." A circular porthole behind her head offered a view of the surrounding space. Janeway glanced out the window at the stars streaking by. "Unfortunately, we don't seem to be near any prime vacation spots at present."

"True enough," Chakotay began. "Still—" The commbadges on their uniforms beeped in unison, interrupting the first officer's comment. Janeway tapped her badge in response while Chakotay listened in.

"Captain here," she said. "What is it?"

Harry Kim's voice emerged from her badge. "Ensign Kim. I think you and Commander Chakotay should come to the bridge. We've detected a transmission coming from a nearby solar system."

A transmission? Janeway experienced the same

thrill she always felt at the prospect of encountering a new civilization and life-form. *This is what Starfleet is all about,* she thought, *even when we're in the Delta Quadrant.* "Understood, Mr. Kim. We're on our way."

Chakotay was already rising from his chair. He waited by the closed door for her to join him, then they entered the bridge together.

An almost palpable aura of excitement suffused the bridge, emanating from the eager expressions and alert body language of the officers on duty. Lieutenant Tom Paris had the conn, while Harry Kim was stationed at Ops. Both men looked more upbeat and alive than they had in weeks. Ensign Susan Tukwila, a promising young officer recently transferred from stellar cartography to the bridge, manned the port forward science console; like Chakotay, Tukwila was a Native American who had served among the Maquis renegades before ending up on *Voyager.* Tukwila appeared just as energized as Paris and Kim by the discovery of the alien transmission. Only Lieutenant Commander Tuvok, stationed at the security/tactical console at aft starboard, seemed immune to the urgency and impatience on display throughout the bridge; his face maintained its customary expression of Vulcan detachment.

Taking her seat in the command area, Janeway glanced toward the starboard engineering station. She did not see B'Elanna Torres at her usual post. Janeway assumed that Torres was hard at work down in the main engineering core. Chakotay sat down beside Janeway, a few meters to her left. "Very well," the captain said. "Let's hear this transmission."

"We have visual as well as audio, Captain," Kim informed her.

"Even better," Janeway said. "Put it on the Main Viewer, Mr. Kim."

The large viewscreen at the front of the bridge lit up. Janeway expected to see the person or persons responsible for the transmission. Instead the screen offered a panoramic look at an alien landscape. "Oh my," Janeway said, caught off guard by the breathtaking beauty of the view.

It was a beach scene, actually, but like none that she had ever seen before. The peaceful shore bore little resemblance to, say, the surging swells that crashed against the rocky coastline beneath Burleigh Manor in her favorite holo-novel. Instead sparkling golden water rippled beneath a red-hued sky. Saffron foam crested the gentle waves that broke upon an ebony shore, while small puffy clouds drifted slowly through the air, doing little to obscure the warm crimson sunlight that illuminated the entire scene. The beach itself seemed composed of millions of glossy black pebbles the size of small beads. Every pebble shined like polished obsidian, worn smooth by the ceaseless caress of the waves, so that the shore glittered with countless dark mirrors. Janeway imagined walking her long-lost dog upon the beach, then chided herself for daydreaming on duty. She searched in vain for footprints or any other sign of habitation; the beach looked pristine, untouched.

Rosy sunshine glinted off the gleaming pebbles, but here and there looming trees provided shade from the sun. Deep purple fronds, streaked with veins of pink, sprouted from the top of each tree, casting shifting shadows upon the beach as the trees swayed leisurely in response to an unseen breeze. Their slender trunks were covered by coppery metallic bark. Smaller vegetation grew abundantly along the rim of the beach; a hundred different shades of green, they resembled sea anemones and living coral, as though underwater plant life had taken root on dry land. Delicate purple tendrils danced in the breeze, adding a touch of alien beauty to the idyllic tableau. "It's lovely," Ensign Tukwila said out loud. "Just gorgeous." Janeway had to agree.

At first, she could hear only the waves lapping at the shore and the soft rustling of the fronds in the wind. Then a disembodied voice accompanied the postcard-pretty scenery. The Universal Translator gave the unseen speaker a deep masculine voice with a distinct but unfamiliar accent.

"Behold Ryolanov," came the voice, "whomever you are. We welcome the opportunity to meet you and your people. Please consider yourself wholeheartedly invited to share the beauty and hospitality of our world for as long as you care to visit. Come to Ryolanov. We await you with open arms."

The voice fell silent, leaving only the natural splendor of the alien beach to speak for the source of the transmission. Janeway tore her gaze away from the ever-so-inviting view and glanced back over her left shoulder at Harry Kim. "Is that it?" she asked.

"Yes, Captain," Kim answered. "The invitation simply repeats itself at regular intervals, about every five minutes."

"How long has it been running?" Chakotay asked Kim.

"Uncertain." Kim said. "We detected the transmission as soon as we came within range. For all we can tell, it's been broadcast continuously for years."

"Is there anyway to respond?" Janeway inquired. She was anxious to establish a dialogue with the mysterious inhabitants of—what was that name again? She retrieved the unfamiliar word from her memory. *Ryolanov,* she repeated silently. The name had a pleasingly exotic sound.

Kim shook his head. "I'm afraid not, Captain. It's strictly a one-way transmission. The signal wasn't even aimed at us specifically; *Voyager* just happened to be in the right place at the right time." The voice from Ryolanov began to deliver its invitation once more. Kim cut off the audio transmission, leaving the visuals up on the screen.

"In other words," Janeway concluded, turning back toward the screen, "what we're dealing with is the subspace equivalent of a message in a bottle."

"Not unlike Earth's SETI program in the late twentieth century," Tuvok commented, referring to the historic Search for Extra-Terrestrial Intelligence. "Intriguing."

Janeway swung around in her chair to look at the Vulcan. "What's your take on this, Mr. Tuvok?" She had known Tuvok longer than any other member of her crew and valued his judgment. Indeed, it often occurred to her that, given the Vulcan's longer-than-human lifespan, Tuvok would probably be in command of *Voyager* if and when the misplaced starship found its way home several decades from now. She found this thought both comforting and, on a personal level, disturbing.

"From a security standpoint," Tuvok said, "it concerns me that our would-be hosts seem unwilling to show themselves."

"Perhaps they do not wish to be judged by their appearance," Chakotay said. "Given the wide variety of physical forms throughout the galaxy, this strikes me as a reasonable precaution. After all, not all spacefaring peoples are as accepting of diversity as the Federation."

And even Starfleet, Janeway thought, *has occasionally been known to misjudge an alien species on account of its appearance.* She recalled humanity's tragic first encounter with the Hortas of Janus VI close to a century ago, not to mention that ugly Romulan witch hunt aboard the *Enterprise* a few years back.

"You may be correct, Commander," Tuvok conceded. "Still, I would prefer more data before accepting Ryolanov's extraordinary hospitality at face value."

"As would we all," Janeway said, "but the advantages of pursuing this invitation further seem to outweigh the risks involved. As a Starfleet vessel, our fundamental duty must be to seek out unknown alien cultures and increase the total knowledge of our collective peoples. Someday we *will* get back to the Federation, and when we do, we will be the modern-day Marco Polos of the Delta Quadrant, bringing back vital information about new territory that no human—and no Vulcan—has ever explored."

With luck, she thought, *that little pep talk will help perk up the bridge crew's sagging morale.* It was nothing she hadn't said before, but it couldn't hurt to reinforce the higher purpose of their journey every so often. "Besides," she said, feasting her eyes once more on the spectacular beauty of that unearthly beach, "this might be just what the doctor ordered."

She shared a sideways glance, and a conspiratorial smile, with Chakotay. "You know," he said, "it might be at that."

"Mr. Kim," Janeway said firmly. "I assume we can trace the transmission back to its place of origin?"

The young ensign looked up from the monitor at the operations console. "Easily, Captain."

"Transmit the necessary coordinates to the conn," she ordered. "Mr. Paris, set a course for Ryolanov. Warp factor five."

"Yes, ma'am!" Paris said with enthusiasm. His fingers raced deftly over the controls of the navigation station. He seemed eager to plant his feet upon that glistening jet-black sand and dive perhaps into that shimmering golden foam. Janeway could hardly blame him.

"Er, Captain?" Kim asked. "Shall I take the visual transmission off the main viewer?"

Janeway sank back into the cushioned padding of the captain's chair. She watched the violet palm trees away hypnotically above the sunlit beach. "Not just yet, Mr. Kim," she decided. "Leave it up a little while longer."

She couldn't imagine a more enchanting locale for a shore leave.

CHAPTER

2

"So you know nothing about this Ryolanov?" Janeway asked Neelix as she, Tuvok, Tom Paris, and Neelix stepped onto the transporter pads. Tuvok had argued, quite properly, against the captain joining the first mission to the planet's surface, but she had decided to overrule his objections in this instance. So far, the Ryol had greeted *Voyager*'s initial hails with nothing but peaceful and friendly overtures, nor had they demonstrated any sign of hostility toward the visitors from the Federation. They had readily agreed to a meeting between representatives of *Voyager* and their own leader and even provided coordinates for a location on the planet's surface.

"Frankly, Captain," Neelix replied, taking his place upon the transporter platform, "I'm more amazed than any of you to find a flourishing people and planet in the middle of this interstellar wasteland. Every reputable explorer and trader, and most of the less reputable ones, wrote off this entire region generations ago. 'Creation's garbage heap,' the early Haakonian cartographers used to call it. 'Here there lies . . . nothing,' they inscribed on their maps. Not even the Kazon considered it worth claiming. There weren't supposed to be any valuable resources or populations anywhere in this sector." Neelix laughed heartily, shaking the wiry bristles along his jawline. "Who would have ever guessed that a veritable paradise was hiding amid all this lifeless desolation?"

"Indeed," Tuvok said. "It defies probability that your vaunted familiarity with the Delta Quadrant should prove incomplete once more."

"That's right!" Neelix cheerfully seconded Tuvok, then mulled over the Vulcan's statement a few more moments. "Hey, wait, what exactly did you mean by that?"

"No more than what I said," Tuvok replied. His phaser was affixed to the right side of his gold-and-black Starfleet uniform. At the Vulcan's insistence, both he and Tom Paris carried side arms. Janeway suspected that Neelix probably had a weapon concealed on his person as well; the little Talaxian was too much of a wily survivor to go into an unknown environment unarmed. She had left her own phaser in her quarters, largely as a symbolic gesture of good faith. *At present,* she thought, *the Ryol appear to have no ulterior motives—and little in the way of a military.* Preliminary sensor readings taken from orbit had revealed Ryolanov to be exactly what it appeared to be: an M-class class planet inhabited by a peaceful and orderly society. *Voyager's* sensors hadn't even detected the presence of a single prison installation, let alone any battlefields or weapons systems. *The Ryol probably have more reason to fear us than we have to distrust them.*

"It's time," she announced, silencing the banter. "Prepare to beam down. B'Elanna?"

Lieutenant B'Elanna Torres had volunteered to personally man the transporter controls, just in case something went wrong. Although the Ryol appeared friendly, first impressions could be deceptive—as in the case of the Trabe convoy who had betrayed *Voyager* a year ago. "The first sign of trouble," the half-Klingon engineer said grimly, "and I'm beaming you back onto the ship faster than a Cardassian can violate a treaty agreement."

"I appreciate your concern," Janeway replied. "Trust me, if they start boiling us in cooking pots, you'll be the first to know."

If Torres was amused by Janeway's quip, she didn't show it. She glowered at the controls as she activated the transporter. Both Torres and the transporter room itself seemed to fade from view as a wall of cascading yellow sparks obscured Janeway's vision. In fact, the captain knew, it was she who was really dissolving into a coruscating pillar of pure energy. Janeway experienced a momentary chill, then the sparkling distortion cleared from her eyes and she found herself standing, along with the rest of the away team, on the surface of Ryolanov.

They were outdoors, in the very setting whose beckoning image the Ryol had broadcast to the stars. *Let's hear it for truth in advertising,* Janeway thought. The beach was even more breathtaking in reality. The waves, which she now saw belonged to a spacious harbor, looked like overlapping sheets of molten gold. There were, if anything, even fewer clouds in the crimson sky. The air was warmer than *Voyager*'s, but not uncomfortably so, and fragrant with the aroma of blooming flowers. Janeway took a deep breath, enjoying the sweetly perfumed air. A breeze blew in from the harbor, carrying the scent of, no, not salt, but ginger. She could almost taste the spice upon her lips.

The gravity, as suggested by the planet's size and density, felt perceptibly lighter than Earth's. She could feel a little extra spring in her step.

They stood upon a level pathway that looked as though it had been created by fusing together hundreds of the tiny black pellets. A boardwalk of sorts, Janeway guessed, formed from the basic stuff of the beach itself. From where they now assembled, she could see that the obsidian beach bordered a well-trimmed garden that eventually gave way to a group of graceful opalescent buildings less than a kilometer away. A trio of humanoid figures waited in front of a topiary arch. The stems and leaves of the plants, she noted, were as purple as the drooping fronds of the trees upon the beach. The blooms themselves displayed every shade of green, from chartreuse to jade. *The botanists aboard* Voyager *will have a field day here,* she guessed.

The Ryol delegation approached them, consisting of two men and one woman. As they came closer into view, Janeway saw that all three Ryol were extremely attractive by humanoid standards. Their skin was a uniform reddish brown, almost maroon, while their pale green eyes shone like malachite. Both men had tawny yellow manes like a lion's, while only a thin layer of blond fur covered the female's scalp. Janeway noted that Tom Paris's eyes widened significantly as his gaze fell upon the Ryol woman. "My, oh, my," Paris said, too quietly to be heard by the oncoming aliens, "I think I'm going to like it here."

Well suited to the tropical environment, the clothing of the Ryol was both lightweight and brief. All three wore embroidered vests and short skirts that fell to just above their knees. The men's vests were open in front, exposing hairless chests, while the woman's was tied shut by three scarlet ribbons. Both vests and skirts seemed made from a thin gauzy fabric that resembled silk. Aside from the fur upon their heads, the Ryol displayed little hair upon their bodies. Sandals protected the soles of their feet; Janeway noted that their nails were dark brown and slightly pointed. Delicate pieces of silver jewelry adorned their fingers and ears. At a quick glance, the craftsmanship appeared exquisite.

"Welcome!" one of the men declared. Janeway recognized his voice and accent from the transmission she had heard aboard *Voyager*. "I am Varathael, Eldest of the Ryol." He in fact looked older and more mature than either of his companions. His mane was fuller and streaked with gray, giving him the look of an Old Testament patriarch, although he seemed far from infirm. His back was straight, his bearing proud and dignified. He reminded Janeway a little of Lord Burleigh, the highborn hero of her holodeck adventures. A silver medallion hung from a chain around his neck. A translucent red gem, its multifaceted surface reflecting the sunlight, rested at the center of a shining metal disk. A symbol of his authority?

The Ryol appeared unfazed by the away team's sudden materialization on their beach, which Janeway took as a good sign. She had warned the inhabitants of the planet of what to expect during their preliminary discussions regarding this meeting, but less technologically advanced cultures sometimes reacted with surprise and alarm anyway. Perhaps Ryolanov was more scientifically advanced than it appeared on first glance. After all, she reminded herself, they knew enough to transmit an invitation out to the stars.

Varathael gestured toward his younger associates. "This is Laazia, my daughter and heir, and Naxor, my personal aide."

"I am delighted to make your acquaintance," Laazia said warmly. Her voice, surprisingly deep, had a slight vibrato quality. A wide smile revealed rows of pearly white teeth. Long black lashes curled above exotic green eyes. "Your arrival is the most exciting thing to happen on this planet in ages."

"Most stimulating, yes," Naxor agreed, although he seemed to be controlling his ebullience easily enough. The young Ryol male struck Janeway as aloof and a bit full of himself. A thin white scar, running from the corner of his mouth to below his chin, marked his handsome features. Janeway wondered how he had obtained the scar, even as Naxor declined to establish eye contact with her when he spoke. Still, she reminded herself, compared to a typical Kazon warrior or Vidiian organ snatcher, Naxor was practically overflowing with hospitality. *In the Delta Quadrant,* she thought, *I'll take whatever friends I can find.*

"I want to thank you all for your gracious invitation to visit this extraordinarily beautiful world," she said, "I'm Captain Kathryn Janeway of the Federation *Starship Voyager.*" She introduced each member of the away team by name. "We look forward to learning more about you and your people."

"No more than we wish to share our blessings with you," Varathael said. "We have been radiating our message of welcome out into the ether for many years now, but yours is the first vessel to respond." He eyed the away team with unconcealed fascination. "So many shapes and colors," he marveled. "From whence, Captain, did you say your ship originated?"

"The United Federation of Planets," she explained, "which represents many races and worlds working together in cooperation and harmony. Mr. Paris and I both come from a planet known as Earth, while Mr. Tuvok is a Vulcan. Only Mr. Neelix is a native of this region of space, which we call the Delta Quadrant. He is a Talaxian."

"No doubt you have heard of us," Neelix said. He puffed out his chest, preening in his garish motley attire. "We Talaxians are descended from a noble breed of explorers and adventurers."

"Alas, no," Varathael answered, "although I am sure your people are quite remarkable in their own way." He returned his attention to Janeway. "Earth, Vulcan . . . your Federation sounds most colorful and intriguing. I hope I shall have the opportunity to visit it myself someday, and behold your people in all their rich variety."

Janeway shook her head sadly. "I'm afraid the Federation is very far away." *Much too far from here,* she thought.

"But surely your magnificent starship, your *Voyager,* can traverse such distances in a twinkling?" Varathael said. "After all, look how far you have come."

"That was something of a fluke," Janeway stated. She looked for a way to broach the subject gracefully. "I am curious, Elder," she said. "You have not encountered the Talaxians before, yet the Ryol are clearly comfortable with the concept of other worlds and other forms of intelligent life. How far have your own people traveled beyond this planet?"

He looked up at the beckoning heavens. "To be honest, we have devoted few resources to the exploration of space. Look around you: why ever would we want to leave such a natural paradise? It always seemed easier, I suppose, to invite other races to visit us here."

Janeway could see why crossing the void to explore worthless and unexciting lumps of dirt might end up a low priority for the Ryol. *If humanity had not been born with some sort of incurable wanderlust hardwired into our genetic makeup,* she thought, *then we might have grown discouraged as well by the harsh conditions we encountered throughout Earth's solar system.* Janeway felt a tiny surge of pride at humanity's stubborn persistence in the face of a seemingly hostile universe, although she diplomatically kept such sentiments to herself.

"This is undeniably a beautiful world," she said. "I

can readily see why you love it so." She hoped it would be possible to allow her crew some shore leave here. She wouldn't mind a little vacation herself.

"Excuse me, Captain," Tuvok interrupted. The Vulcan security chief joined her beside Varathael and his entourage. "Commander Chakotay is awaiting a report on the status of the away team."

"Tell him that everything is fine," she instructed, "and that we will be staying a little while longer." She looked at Varathael. "Assuming that is acceptable to you, of course."

"Absolutely!" Varathael said, beaming, bright green eyes welcoming them. His smile was as bright and flawless as his daughter's. "Why, you haven't even seen our city yet. Come, let us stroll through this public garden. I confess, we are quite proud of our lovely flora."

Sure beats crawling through the mud during a firefight, Janeway thought, *or trying to hold a collapsing warp core together.* "On behalf of the *U.S.S. Voyager* and the United Federation of Planets, I accept your most appealing offer."

The heady aroma of the lush green blossoms was almost overwhelming as Varathael led them through an intricate floral maze composed of coral-like bushes that rose well above their heads. Tuvok kept close to Janeway, his somber features unmoved by the beauty and tranquillity of the garden. Predictably, Paris dropped back to mingle with Laazia, while Neelix attached himself to Naxor, who looked none too pleased by this turn of events. "You have really never met a Talaxian before?" she heard Neelix say. "How astounding! Let me tell you all about us. . . ."

Small birds, looking much like sparrows, chirped in the spreading branches of the coral-bushes, Janeway observed, while carefully avoiding the waving tendrils of the anemone-plants. Hundreds of shiny black pebbles paved the path beneath her feet, and the sun was warm upon her face. *I could get used to this,* she thought.

Laazia spoke softly behind Janeway, laughing at some joke of Paris's. *Watch it, Lieutenant,* Janeway thought sternly, wishing she were telepathic. *Let's not charm the locals too much.* She still recalled the trouble Paris's wandering eye had gotten him into on the Banean homeworld. What had that young woman's name been again? *Ah, yes,* she remembered. *Lidell.* She glanced back over her shoulder. Laazia was already holding on to Paris's arm as they shared another laugh. Not far away, Naxor glared at the couple with a scowl on his face while Neelix babbled on, oblivious to the Ryol male's apparent anger. Janeway wondered what exactly Naxor's relationship to Laazia was. *This could be a problem,* she thought.

"Is anything wrong?" Varathael asked.

"Not at all," she lied, looking away from the simmering triangle behind her. "I was merely admiring your daughter. She is quite charming. You must be very proud of her."

Varathael nodded. "Laazia possesses a keen mind and laudable ambition. She is already a skilled arbitrator, adept at mediating whatever small disputes arise among my fellow Ryol. I fully expect her to lead our people when I have grown too old to look out for our welfare."

Janeway noted the lines upon his face. He seemed only a few years older than she. "Surely that day must be far way," she said.

"Quite," he agreed. "Ours is a very long-lived race."

She wondered how a Ryol's lifespan compared to that of a human or a Vulcan. By Ocampa standards, she remembered, ten years was an unbelievably long time to live. In any event, the Elder appeared healthy enough. He walked at a vigorous pace through the garden. Janeway had to hurry to keep up with him, grateful for the slightly diminished gravity.

She gave up trying to figure out the maze herself, content to follow Varathael's lead. In the unlikely event that she found herself stranded in the maze later on, she could always be beamed back to the ship from any point within the maze. Laazia and Paris spoke to each other too softly to be overheard, but Janeway caught snatches of Neelix's ongoing monologue.

"The really astounding thing," he told the unfortunate Naxor, "about Talaxian hair pasta is the way a true gourmet can tell in just one bite what year the hair was cut and during what phase of the moon. Why, I remember one time I was dining at an asteroid colony outside the Revodro System when the proprietor actually had the nerve to insist he was serving full-moon follicles even though the fibers were stringy and the texture was as coarse as the hide of a Lapinkan gorzehop deep in the grip of rigor mortis! I mean, really! Can you believe it?"

"I suppose I must," Naxor said coldly. Janeway thought she overheard a trace of irritation in the younger Ryol's tone.

Neelix appeared oblivious to his escort's surly manner, or perhaps, Janeway speculated, he was simply determined to improve Naxor's mood through sheer force of personality. She suspected the latter, although she feared that her morale officer may have, in this particular instance, overestimated the capabilities of his distinctive charisma.

"I say, this is a spectacular garden, Mr. Naxor," he said, pausing to contemplate an immense anemone whose swaying violet tendrils stretched well above Neelix's head. "What sort of plant nutrients do you use? My Kes is quite a gardener in her own right. You should see some of the floral masterpieces she's caused to bloom in *Voyager*'s hydroponics labs. She has what the humans call a 'green thumb,' not that she's literally green of course, not like the Emerald Priestesses of Msyamysa. Now those are really green! My Kes, on the other hand, is more of a pinkish shade. . . ."

"I'm sure she is," Naxor said curtly, his fraying patience too obvious to be missed. "Perhaps you would prefer to contemplate the splendors of our garden *in silence.*" Janeway hoped that Neelix would take this none-too-subtle hint and leave Naxor alone. Was there anyway she could signal Neelix without attracting undue attention from Varathael?

Neelix seemed to regard Neelix's ill temper as a challenge to be overcome. "Well, enough about me and my travels, fascinating though they may be to some. I want to know all about Ryolanov. Tell me about everything! How's the cuisine around here. I fancy myself something of a gourmet, but I'm always open to new culinary experiences. Tell me all about your food. What's the planetary specialty? What sort of exotic repast really whets your appetite?"

"Silence!" Naxor snapped at Neelix. The pupils of his eyes expanded dramatically. "Must you prattle on endlessly?" He raised his hand above his head, his fist clenched as if to strike the Talaxian.

Amid the diplomatic pleasantries of the Ryol's meeting with the away team, Naxor's angry words erupted like a thunderclap out of a clear blue sky. Other conversations hushed abruptly as all eyes turned toward the ugly scene. Paris dropped Laazia's arm as his hand drifted toward his phaser. Janeway started to intervene, but Varathael spoke first. "Naxor!" he barked. Janeway heard a harshness in the Elder's tone that had not been there before. His own pupils seemed to expand somewhat. *A sign of anger,* Janeway speculated, *or simply strong emotion?*

His leader's voice seemed to cool Naxor's fury by several degrees. His raised arm drooped limply to his side. His pupils shrank to mere pinpricks in the malachite brilliance of his eyes. "Elder," he said. "I am sorry. I did not mean—"

"These people are our guests," Varathael declared, "and they have not traveled so far to be insulted by such as you. Apologize to them, not me."

Tension descended over the garden. Even the chirping birds seemed to have fallen silent. Naxor glowered at Paris through half-lowered lids. Laazia reclaimed Paris's arm, making a bad situation worse. Varathael stood stiffly beside Janeway, impaling Naxor upon a icy stare.

"Really, there's no harm done," Neelix insisted, clearly hoping to defuse the crisis. "It's all my fault. I always talk too much. Sometimes even I get tired of listening to me. . . ."

"That's enough, Mr. Neelix," Janeway said quietly. As nearly as she could tell, this was an internal matter now, something for the Ryol to work out among themselves. The best thing they could do now was stay out of it—and hope that this awkward incident did not permanently sour their relations with the Ryol. *So much for shore leave,* she thought, glancing over at Tuvok. The Vulcan stood by attentively, one hand poised above his commbadge, ready to have the entire team beamed back to *Voyager* if the situation got out of hand. She exchanged a meaningful look with Tuvok, shaking her head slightly. *Not just yet,* she signaled. *Let's see how this plays out.*

"Well?" Varathael demanded. "Apologize!"

Naxor clenched his fists at his side, his sharp nails digging into his palms. Janeway was surprised to see an inky black fluid drip from his hands onto the walkway. Blood? She noted again the scar upon his face. The legacy, she wondered, of some past battle or brawl? The imperious young Ryol seemed capable of violence. Even now, he seemed only slightly cowed by Varathael's displeasure.

He looked away from Paris and Laazia, staring instead at the fused black paving. "I apologize, Captain Janeway," he said, hesitating a beat before including the bewhiskered Talaxian, "and to you as well, Mr. Neelix."

He did not, Janeway noted, offer any explanation for his behavior. Still, it appeared the situation could be salvaged after all. "I accept your apology," she said, stepping forward. "First contact with representatives from another civilization is always stressful. I'm just glad we can put this little misunderstanding behind us."

"Yes, of course! My sentiments exactly," Neelix added. "I promise not to bore you again—unless I can't help it."

"Frankly, I'd put my money on the latter," Paris joked. He extended a friendly hand toward Naxor. "Trust me on this, I've known Neelix a lot longer than you have."

Janeway admired Paris's initiative, but questioned his timing, especially since Laazia was still beaming her incandescent smile in the young lieutenant's direction. Naxor peered disdainfully at Paris's proffered hand. His gaze slid sideways to lock with Varathael's. The Elder nodded. Naxor shook Paris's hands. Janeway saw Paris wince slightly as the Ryol squeezed his hand; she guessed Naxor's grip was none too gentle.

"I can tell you are a sociable sort, Mr. Paris," Naxor said. He glared at Laazia. "Very sociable."

The Elder's daughter ignored Naxor's pointed remark. She kept her malachite eyes focused on Paris as she spoke. "I do hope you will all be able to stay with us a while. There is so much I want to learn about you." Letting go of Paris's arm, she stepped between Naxor and Neelix. "About all of you," she added diplomatically. "I couldn't help overhearing your remarks about the hair pasta, Mr. Neelix. It sounds quite extraordinary. As much as I revere our society and its traditions, I have often thought that we might benefit from an infusion of new blood and new ideas—not to mention some new recipes!" Her laughter acted as a salve over the raw feelings exposed a few moments before. Janeway recalled the Elder's praise for his daughter's skills as a mediator.

"Yes," Varathael seconded his heir. "Perhaps we can arrange an program of social and cultural exchange."

Sounds like shore leave to me, Janeway thought. "I would like nothing better," she said sincerely. *So why do I feel so uneasy about this whole thing?*

CHAPTER

3

"So what do you think of our city, Commander?"

Chakotay strolled down a spacious thoroughfare lined on both sides by swaying purple palms. High in the sky, a crescent moon adorned the night. Through the trees, he glimpsed pyramidal structures constructed out of a marblelike substance of various colors and textures. Few of the pyramids were more than two or three times taller than the nearby trees; the Ryol, it appeared, did not go in for skyscrapers. The grounds between the pyramids were attractively landscaped. A fuzzy violet moss spread over neatly trimmed lawns. Evidence of advanced technology was discernible, but nonintrusive, such as the artificial lighting that cast a diffuse white glow around the entrances and exits of the pyramids, or the decorative lanterns that, rising at regular intervals along the way, illuminated the road on which he walked beside a charming Ryol functionary named Boracca. Occasionally a pair of Ryol zoomed past them on lightweight air-cycles that levitated several centimeters above the road. Judging from their lack of noise or visible exhaust, Chakotay guessed that the vehicles employed some form of magnetic suspension. As nearly as he could tell, the Ryol lived a peaceful existence in harmony with their environment. Chakotay found himself pleasantly reminded of the traditional Native American colony where he had grown up.

"It's very scenic," he told Boracca. "Is all of Ryolanov this idyllic?"

"Mostly," Boracca said. She was an athletic-looking woman about the same height as Chakotay. "Of course, I like to think that Ryolaler is the most beautiful city on the planet—it is the capital, after all—but every city has something to recommend it. The poles are cold and uninhabitable, but most of the population lives on islands north and south of the equator. The climate here is so agreeable that I can't imagine living anywhere else."

"I can appreciate that," Chakotay agreed. Captain Janeway, he decided, had not exaggerated the planet's natural blessings. Although the sun had descended several hours ago, the temperature was still warm. He was quite comfortable wearing nothing more than his red Starfleet uniform. The night was still and serene with the scent of exotic spices in the air.

Boracca led him to an imposing pyramid at the end of the avenue. A warm glow escaped the open doorway of the pyramid, beneath the graceful curve of a marble arch. "Here we are, sir," Boracca said. "Speaking for the rest of my people, we are honored that you agreed to attend this reception. I know many who are looking forward to meeting you."

"Likewise," Chakotay replied, "and thanks for letting me take a stroll around your city first. After spending several weeks on a starship, it's nice to spend some time outdoors."

"I suppose that must be so, Commander," Boracca said. Her malachite eyes seemed to glow with excitement, further enhancing her already stunning good looks.

Is everyone on this planet this attractive? Chakotay thought. It certainly seemed that way.

"To me, life on a starship sounds absolutely fascinating and adventurous," Boracca continued. "I hope I shall have the opportunity to actually visit your ship."

"Perhaps," Chakotay said, being politely noncommittal. Concerned about the Prime Directive, Captain Janeway wanted to get a better sense of the Ryol's technological level before inviting them aboard *Voyager*. His own impression so far was that a tour of the bridge and living quarters could do little harm to Ryol society, although it might be wise to keep them away from the engine rooms, at least until they knew a little bit more about their hosts.

He entered the pyramid to find a spacious ballroom filled with Ryol and Starfleet personnel mingling freely. Hanging lamps spun far overhead, throwing shifting waves of light and shadow upon the chamber below. Incense, thick and musky, scented the air. A trio of Ryol musicians occupied a raised stage in the center of the ballroom. Chakotay did not recognize their instruments, but the music was bright and lively. *Sort of a cross,* he thought, *between Terran calypso tunes and a Bolian wedding jig.* Glancing around the room, he spotted B'Elanna Torres standing in the corner, glumly sipping from a crystal goblet. She looked singularly out of place and uncomfortable. *Poor B'Elanna,* he thought. Mingling was not one of her strong points. That was one advantage the Maquis had over Starfleet, he mused. The Maquis never expected you to make small talk at a diplomatic reception.

A movement near his elbow distracted Chakotay. He looked down to see an unusual creature standing only centimeters away. It was a primate of some sort, its naked body covered by a thick coat of bristling red hair. The coarse fur concealed the creature's gender, as well as most of its face. The creature was less than half the first officer's height and more than a little scrawny-looking; its spindly arms trembled beneath the weight of a triangular serving tray containing several fresh goblets filled with a bubbling orange liquid. Large black eyes peered out of a hairy face, watching Chakotay expectantly.

"Would you care for a drink, Commander?" Boracca asked. She reached down and lifted two goblets off the creature's tray. The tiny primate held on to its burden as if its life depended on it, its skinny fingers curled around two edges of the tray. Chakotay noticed that the creature had six fingers on each hand. "*Sucrusso* elixir," Boracca volunteered. "It's a carbonated fruit juice, and quite refreshing."

"Er, thank you," Chakotay said, accepting a goblet. The little creature scurried away, winding its way through the crowd where more guests removed drinks from its tray. He waited for Boracca to say something about the creature, but no explanation appeared to be forthcoming. "Excuse me," he said, "but that being that just brought us these cups, who or what was that?"

"Being?" Boracca looked puzzled for a second. "Oh, you mean the neffaler."

"Neffaler?" he prompted her.

"A useful animal," she said. "They can be trained to perform simple, menial tasks. Not very aesthetic, I admit, it's all we can do to keep them bathed and groomed."

Chakotay frowned. "Are they sentient?"

"Hardly!" Boracca laughed at the very notion. "If not for us, they'd still be gibbering in the trees."

"I see," Chakotay said diplomatically, uncertain how to respond. He glanced around the ballroom. Now that he knew what to look for, he spotted maybe half a dozen neffaler at work throughout the crowd, their shaggy heads bobbing at waist-level for the assembled Ryol and Starfleet humanoids. Some of the neffaler carried trays of food and drink; others cleaned up after the guests at the reception, picking up empty goblets and discarded napkins and such. They looked more like servants than pets, he thought.

Then again, he remembered, humans had employed animal labor for millennia, as had most sentient species at some point in their history, so he was reluctant to pass summary judgment on another culture. Who was he to tell the Ryol how to deal with their fellow life-forms, especially after they had gone out of their way to make the crew of *Voyager* feel welcome?

Still, Boracca seemed a lot less alluring all of a sudden. He glanced again at B'Elanna Torres. The ship's engineer remained stranded at the edge of the reception. "If you'll excuse me," he said, "I see a member of my crew that I need to have a brief conference with."

"Certainly," Boracca said. "Try not to work too much, though. Our nights are far too beautiful to waste on business." Goblet in hand, she wandered off into the depths of the crowd. Chakotay watched her go, then skirted around the borders of the reception to join Torres. She was still nursing her glass of elixir and all but pacing the floor in impatience. He thought he spotted a visible trace of relief in her expression as she saw him approaching her. Chakotay could sympathize; during his days as a Starfleet officer, before abandoning his commission to join the Maquis, he had ended up stuck at more than one boring reception, forced to hang around with no one to talk to. *No wonder the Captain delegated this party to me,* he thought.

"Good evening, Lieutenant," he said. "Enjoying your drink?"

Torres made a face. "Too sweet," she said.

Chakotay sipped from his own goblet. Actually, the bubbly elixir was quite tangy and delicious, but Torres's palate, he suspected, was more Klingon than she would want to admit. He knew better than to say as much. "The Ryol certainly know how to throw a party, don't they?"

"If you say so," Torres said. "Frankly, I'd much rather get a look at one of their power generators. Our supply of dilithium crystals is running lower than I like. Ideally, we should refill *Voyager*'s primary dilithium chamber before we leave this system. If the Ryol use any form of matter/antimatter reactor to power this city, then maybe we can work out some sort of trade."

Chakotay nodded. He knew how important dilithium was to the proper functioning of the warp engines—and how rare it was in the Delta Quadrant. "I thought you were using the theta-matrix compositing system to recrystallize the used dilithium?"

"We have been," Torres told him, "but with mixed results. The compositing system's been operating at less than fifty-percent efficiency ever since that last battle with the Kazon, plus we burnt out another crystal escaping from that quantum singularity. We've managed to recrystallize some of our original dilithium, but not enough to give us a comfortable margin of safety."

A neffaler ambled past them carrying a tray stacked with discarded glasses. Torres added her own glass, still full, to the creature's tray. Chakotay watched the neffaler disappear into the crowd, quietly impressed at its ability to navigate through the throng of Ryol and Starfleet merrymakers.

"Hard to imagine running out of dilithium," he said. Back in the Alpha Quadrant, the vital crystals were manufactured in quantity. Even the Maquis had little trouble getting their hands on black-market crystals. "It's like living back in the twenty-third century, when the stuff was worth more than gold-pressed latinum."

"A pretty primitive state of affairs," Torres agreed. "We have barely enough crystals to tune the harmonics of the antimatter reaction, and we can't even take full advantage of the dilithium we do have, what with the damage to the theta-matrix."

"Damn," Chakotay said. "I knew we were running short, but I didn't realize it was quite that serious." Beneath his ceremonial tattoo, his face was somber. "B'Elanna, you're as entitled to some shore leave as anyone else in the crew, but I'd appreciate it if you'd pursue this dilithium matter while we're here. I don't want *Voyager* stalling out the next time we're being chased across the Delta Quadrant."

"Shore leave. Right," Torres said, rolling her eyes. Apparently, shore leave was up there with sugared fruit drinks in her affections. Chakotay wondered if that was the Klingon or the engineer in her speaking. "I've been trying to get some of these Ryol to open up about their power systems, but none of them wants to talk shop. They keep inviting me to look at the stars instead!"

Chakotay smiled. He could see where the friendly and effusive natives might get on Torres's nerves. "This is a party, not a seminar," he reminded her. "Now may not be the right time to exchange technical data."

"I guess so," Torres said grudgingly.

A single neffaler approached them. For all Chakotay knew, it might have been the same creature he met before; he wasn't sure he could tell them apart. This one was pushing a cart on which were stacked several empty plates and goblets. Chakotay finished off his drink and handed the glass to the neffaler. "Thank you," he said.

The neffaler did not respond. It merely pushed its cart past Torres, heading for the next cluster of partygoers. *Was it mute?* he wondered, watching the dwarfish creature struggle with its cart, which seemed to weigh much more than it did. The neffaler was breathing hard, clearly exhausted by its task. Chakotay hoped that *Voyager's* arrival had not added to the burden of all the neffaler. The more he saw of their sorry state, the less he liked it.

"Maybe one of these things can tell me about their technology," Torres said. Her tone suggested that she was already tempted to give up on the Ryol themselves.

"I doubt it," Chakotay said. "They don't seem very talkative."

"You wanted to see me, Captain?" Tom Paris asked, slightly apprehensively. He was scheduled to start his shore leave in approximately thirty minutes, and the last thing he wanted now was a last-minute emergency assignment. *What's this all about?* he wondered.

Janeway sat behind the desk in her ready room, a serious expression on her face. "Come on in, Lieutenant," she said. "This won't take long."

I sure hope not, he thought. He and Harry had already made plans to check out the night life on Ryol. From what he'd seen earlier, there were women on Ryol who made even the Delany sisters look like Ferengi.

Captain Janeway waited for the door to slide shut behind Paris before she continued. "Ordinarily, I like to stay out of my crew's personal lives. What you do when you're off-duty is none of my concern, as long as it doesn't endanger the ship or its reputation. However—"

Uh-oh, Paris thought.

"As awkward as this is, I have to ask you to be careful around the Elder's daughter, Laazia. We don't want to have another episode like what almost happened the other day in the garden."

Paris knew exactly what Janeway was referring to. He remembered Laazia, all right, and the murderous hate in Naxor's green eyes. "But, Captain," he protested, "that wasn't my fault. Neelix provoked that guy."

Janeway eyed him skeptically. "I don't believe that and neither do you. We both know what that was really about."

Paris couldn't deny it. He knew a jealous boyfriend when he saw one. "Laazia, right?"

"Look, Tom, no one is saying you did anything wrong . . . yet." Janeway gave him a wry smile. "But you appear to have wandered into the middle of a volatile situation, and I'd like to avoid any unnecessary complications while we're visiting this planet. Do we understand each other, Lieutenant?"

"Yes, ma'am," Paris said. *Oh well,* he thought. *Easy come, easy go.* Laazia had undeniable appeal, but it wasn't like he was planning to settle down on Ryol forever. "Just one question: what if the Elder's daughter won't take no for an answer?"

"You're a Starfleet officer," Janeway said, smiling. "I trust you can defend yourself."

CHAPTER
4

"OH, NEELIX, ISN'T THIS GLORIOUS?"

The sun hovered directly overhead as Kes waded into the golden surf. Warm water swirled around her legs, more water than she had ever seen in her short life. In the underground city where she had been born, water was carefully rationed by the Caretaker. Small wonder then that a mere day at the beach seemed so miraculous to her. *To think,* she thought, *the Ryol can go swimming here every day!*

"I'm not sure I'd go so far as 'glorious,'" Neelix said, splashing through the waves behind her. "The Flaming Falls of Fortunata Five . . . now those are glorious. But this is certainly nice, I must admit. It sure beats some of the ghastly places we've visited on this voyage. Planet Hell, for instance."

Kes didn't want to think about Planet Hell or anything else hellish for that matter. She dug her bare feet into the sand beneath the surf, letting the tiny beads run between her toes. The sparkling water rose above her waist as she slowly waded away from the shore. She could smell the spice in the air, taste the spray upon her lips. Her fingers trailed behind her, breaking the surface of the harbor. *Is there a beach program stored in the memory banks of* Voyager's *holodeck,* Kes wondered. She resolved to find out at the first opportunity.

"Careful," Neelix called out. "Don't go too far." He charged through the water, eager to catch up with her, splashing more water with every step. His arms and legs emerged from a striped blue-and-orange bathing suit that covered his entire torso. Soggy, shaggy fur was plastered along the lengths of his arms. Plowing awkwardly through the waves, he stumbled and fell face-first into the water.

"Neelix!" Kes cried out, momentarily alarmed, but her companion quickly scrambled back onto his feet. He coughed and sputtered, spewing golden sea water from his mouth. Soaked bristles hung limply on his head. Kes couldn't help laughing; he looked so ridiculous. "Are you all right?" she asked.

"Never better," he insisted, expelling one last mouthful of fluid. "Nothing like a refreshing dip to invigorate oneself. Why, I remember one time when I walked across the entire length of the Great Kanspo Desert just to swim in the Sea of Semi-Sentient Soap." He drew closer to her, moving somewhat more carefully than before.

Voyager's replicators had provided them both with swimming attire, based on designs found in the computer's capacious memory. Kes wore a simple one-piece garment whose pale green coloring matched her eyes. It was rather more, she noted, than the Ryol themselves wore, but Neelix had blanched at the very idea of her wearing anything more revealing, especially in front of the young Ryol males. He seemed to regard the local men with suspicion, no matter how friendly and attentive they were. Indeed, the more hospitable they were, the more Neelix appeared to distrust them. Kes sighed inwardly. She loved Neelix, but sometimes she wished he wasn't so jealous all the time.

She glanced back at the shore, where a handful of *Voyager* personnel shared the sunlit beach with a few of their Ryol hosts. She spotted Susan Tukwila chasing after an inflatable plastic ball that bounced along the beach. A pair of Ryol also pursued the ball, but Ryolanov's lesser gravity gave the human woman an edge. Bounding high above the sand, she snatched the sphere out of the air moments before it would have landed in the waiting hands of a tall Ryol man whom Kes did not recognize. Laughing heartily, all the nearby Ryol applauded Tukwila's spectacular catch.

This is the way it should be, Kes thought. Too often *Voyager*'s encounters with alien races had been fraught with uncertainty and conflict. How joyous it was to get to know another culture without shields being raised and phaser banks armed. The overflowing trust and generosity of the Ryol was a blessing to them all.

"Isn't this wonderful, Neelix?" she said. "It's opportunities like this that make me so glad we decided to join *Voyager*'s journey." She strode farther into the shimmering water, immersing herself up to her neck in the warm welcoming liquid. "I've seen so much more than I ever expected to, done so many things I could never have done back home."

"I'm glad you're enjoying this," Neelix said. A centimeter or two shorter than Kes, he had to paddle with his hands to keep his head above the waves. "But maybe you ought to think about turning back. After all, we don't know how deep this water gets."

He was probably right, Kes conceded. Neelix had traveled far more extensively than she had and knew infinitely more about the dangers of the worlds beyond her own. Still, she didn't want to retreat just yet, not with so much harbor left to explore. "I want to swim," she announced impulsively. "Teach me how to swim, Neelix."

"Swim?" he said, sounding rather unsure. For a second, Kes wondered if Neelix actually knew how to swim. *Of course he does,* she thought. *Neelix has been everywhere and done just about everything.* She watched him paddling to stay afloat. *Why, he's practically swimming already.*

Her companion mulled the idea over for a few moments, then an exuberant grin broke out over his face. "Well, why not?" he declared. "First things first, though. Before you can swim, you have to learn how to float."

That made sense, she thought. "All right. How do we begin?"

"Nothing to it." He paddled backward until his feet were resting securely on the sandy floor of the harbor. "Come over here." Kes walked toward him. "Okay," he said. "Now just turn around and lean backward into the water. Don't worry, I'll hold you up."

It took her several tries to get it right. The first time she was startled by a stray wave washing over her face and sank, splashing wildly, beneath the water. Neelix kept her from sinking too far, though; as promised, she felt his arms beneath her, supporting her. "Just relax," he murmured. "Let the water carry you." It was no use, she thought, extending her arms and legs out as far as she could. Her muscles tensed automatically the moment her feet left the ground. She felt as stiff and solid as an anchor—and just as quick to sink toward the sea floor. "Relax," Neelix repeated over and over. "Don't worry about getting your face wet. It's just water . . . I think."

Gradually, she got the hang of it. *Relax,* she

thought, letting her limbs drift limply atop the surface of the water, feeling the liquid's natural buoyancy carry her along with the waves. It was like one of the meditation exercises Tuvok had taught her to help her hone her nascent telepathic abilities; the trick to emptying her mind was not to think about not thinking. She closed her eyes, feeling the warm sunlight upon her face. The gentle rhythm of the waves murmured in her ears, drowning out all other sounds. She heard Neelix's voice, but only dimly. He seemed to be speaking from far away. The trick to floating was not to think about floating. She simply drifted with the tide, letting the warm soothing water carry her loose and careless body whichever way it chose. Neelix's arms fell away. Only the sea supported her now, rocking her gently with its waves, lulling her into a restful, meditative, almost trancelike state.

She floated aimlessly for some time, savoring the silence and the peace. The crimson sunshine suffused her being with warmth; she could sense its radiance even through shut eyelids. Then she heard a voice, so softly at first that she thought she was imagining it, but the voice persisted, steadily increasing in volume. *Neelix?* she wondered, but the faint whispering noise she heard did not come from above, but from somewhere deep beneath her. At first she thought there was only one voice, but as the sound grew louder, she realized that there were many voices, calling out in unison. The whisper turned into sobs which rose into a heart-rending cry of fear and despair. There was no mistaking the anguish in that awful keening, the torment and terror in the screaming that went on and on. *Stop,* she thought desperately, unable to bear the wailing any longer. *Please, please stop.*

But the scream only grew louder, until Kes thought her ears would burst. A shadow fell over her face, blocking out the sun. Her eyes snapped open, but, to her horror, the darkness remained. The sun and sky were gone; there was only blackness all around her, an all-encompassing blackness that blotted out every point of light in her universe. Where was Neelix? Where was everything? She tried to move, but her limbs would not respond. The darkness lay upon her like a heavy weight, holding her down, pinning her fast. There was no more water, no more warmth, only the blackness holding her tightly in its cold and paralyzing grip. And still the scream was all she heard, frantic and hopeless and unending, and finally she realized that she was the one who was screaming, but she still couldn't make it stop. She kept on screaming, adding to her fear and panic. She was trapped. She couldn't move. She couldn't breathe . . .

The crimson sun was high in the sky, but the leafy Ryol tree provided Harry Kim with plenty of shade in which to practice his clarinet. His Starfleet-issue boots sat empty upon the lawn a few meters away from him, his bare feet cushioned by the purple moss that carpeted the fragrant ground. Wide violet fronds rustled in the cooling breeze as Kim relaxed, resting his back against the copper-colored bark of the tree, and ran once more through the jazzy melody of "Nightbird" by the famed Betazed composer DuZoinn. It was a tricky piece, with lots of high notes, but Kim thought he was starting to get the hang of it. Certainly this idyllic garden park, one of many scattered throughout the city, provided a lot more inspiration than the all-too-familiar confines of his quarters back on *Voyager*.

His fingers danced over the slender black instrument that transformed his vigorous exhalations into a string of rich musical notes. As always, he found it impossible to play the clarinet without thinking of his family back on Earth. Mom and Dad had always encouraged his musical talents, as had Libby, his long-lost fiancée. He wondered what they all were doing now, wishing there was some way to let them know he was okay.

If I have to be far from home, he thought, looking around the peaceful garden and breathing in the subtle floral scent all about him, *there are worse places to be.* Indeed, that homesick feeling didn't seem to hurt quite so much today; his yearning for home felt more bittersweet than heartbreaking. *Nothing like a taste of paradise,* he mused, *to ease those Delta Quadrant blues.*

Deftly manipulating the tiny silver valves adorning the woodwind, he reached for another high note— and produced an alarming squeak instead. *Ouch,* Harry thought, wincing at the high-pitched squeal. *Where did that come from?* He removed the mouthpiece from his lips and inspected the business end of the clarinet. As he feared, the thin wooden reed was cracked and fraying around the edges, looking badly in need of replacement. Harry scowled at the broken reed. *There goes another replicator coupon. . . .*

His gaze traveled upward toward the drooping tree branches above him, weighed down by pink and purple leaves. He wondered if he could carve a new reed from the oddly metallic wood of these Ryol trees. *It might work,* he thought.

Suddenly he became aware of two large black eyes, the size of Terran sand dollars, peering down at him from the boughs overhead. Another neffaler, he realized, although he could barely see the rest of the animal through the lush canopy of leaves. The neffaler stared at him with obvious curiosity.

"C'mon here, little guy," Kim called, keeping his voice mild and unthreatening. "Come on. I won't bite."

The neffaler kept watching him, but showed no signs of budging from his perch. Kim considered the clarinet resting in his hands. Maybe the neffaler was attracted by the music? Kim lifted the mouthpiece to his lips and experimentally ran through some of the easier passages of "Nightbird." The battered reed gave him some trouble, but held together enough to produce a passable tune.

The music had the desired effect. Slowly, hesitantly, the diminutive primate descended toward Kim one branch at a time. As the neffaler drew nearer, Kim saw that the furry little music lover was smaller and younger-looking than any of the other neffaler he had seen running errands for the Ryol. It was painfully thin, like the rest of its species, but it also had an amazed wide-eyed quality that Kim associated with children and baby animals. He guessed that this particular neffaler was far from fully grown.

As Kim kept playing, the neffaler eventually ended up hanging from the lowest branch on the tree, its six-toed feet dangling in the air only a few meters above Kim's face. Kim took pains not to make any sudden moves, and to keep the music coming, and, sure enough, the tiny neffaler soon dropped onto the manicured lawn in front of Kim. Its shaggy red bristles standing out against the violet moss, the neffaler advanced cautiously toward Kim. It was actually kind of cute, he thought, deciding that the small neffaler reminded him of some baby chimps he and Libby had seen at a wildlife preserve near Starfleet Academy.

It came to a halt about a meter and a half away from Kim. For several minutes the human and the young neffaler watched each other, the only sound in the park being the music of the clarinet and the rustling of the leaves overhead. Finally Kim decided that he couldn't bear to play the easy parts of "Nightbird" one more time. He stopped blowing into the mouthpiece and slowly lowered the instrument onto his lap, half expecting the skittish animal to run away the moment the music stopped.

To his surprise and delight, the creature stayed, eyeing the shiny black clarinet with undisguised fascination. "Is this what you're interested in?" Kim asked softly. He offered the instrument to the neffaler, turning the mouthpiece toward the creature's small hands.

The neffaler glanced quickly from side to side, as if afraid of being caught doing something it shouldn't, then snatched the clarinet from Kim's fingers.

It blew into the wrong end first, producing a noisy *blat* that made the neffaler jump in surprise. Then it got the idea and blew enthusiastically into the mouthpiece, visibly excited by the sounds it made. In fact, to Kim's amusement, the neffaler appeared just as pleased by the occasional raucous squeak as by the more euphonious notes.

The squeaks became fewer and fewer, though, as the neffaler caught on with ridiculous speed. Kim listened in growing astonishment, his jaw dropping steadily toward the ground. He could have sworn that the scrawny, shaggy, little animal was actually starting to produce something resembling a melody. It was a simple tune, hardly more complicated than "Mary Had a Little Lamb," but Kim thought he heard a sad, almost plaintive quality to the sounds emerging from the far end of his clarinet. *I wish I could play with that much feeling,* he lamented silently. The neffaler displayed more than merely a natural aptitude for music, he decided; it was a veritable prodigy.

Caught up in the animal's astounding performance, Kim was unaware of anyone else entering the garden until the neffaler spotted something—or someone— coming up behind him. A panicky expression rushed over the neffaler's face. The clarinet dropped from its fingers, and the tiny creature turned and fled before the woodwind even hit the ground. The neffaler scurried away as fast as its skinny legs could carry it, heading for the safety of a nearby row of aquatic-looking shrubs.

"Wait!" Harry called out to the animal. "What's the matter?" He looked back over his shoulder to see what had spooked the neffaler.

All he saw was an attractive Ryol woman standing a few centimeters behind him. A saffron robe fell to just above her knees, the gauzelike fabric clinging to her body as the breeze blew against her. "Was that beast bothering you?" she asked. Her voice was melodious, with a faintly exotic accent. "I'm so sorry. It must not have been trained properly. We do our best to educate them, but"—she shrugged her shoulders, one thin strap of her gown slipping down onto her upper arm—"well, there are limits to what they can be taught."

"But it wasn't bothering me," Kim began. "You should have heard it play! It was unbelievable. If I hadn't heard it myself—"

"Is that a musical instrument?" she asked brightly, interrupting his chain of thought. She knelt beside him and lifted his clarinet from the ground, brushing away the bits and pieces of moss that hung on to the discarded instrument. Her fingers were long and graceful, with neatly pointed tips. "I would love to hear you play."

"Oh," Kim said. He took one last look at the shrubs beyond, but the young neffaler was long gone. *Too bad,* he thought, *the little fellow really seemed excited by the clarinet.* Kim would have liked to learn more about the creature's musical abilities. Shrugging, he turned his attention back to the lovely Ryol woman. He couldn't resist showing off for such an appreciative audience. "I guess I can play a little more." He smoothed down the splintered edges of the wooden reed with his thumb and hoped for the best.

"It's called 'Nightbird,'" he said.

"Kes!" Something grabbed on to her shoulders, shaking her violently amid the suffocating darkness that had ensnared her. Her mind felt like it was being turned inside out, and suddenly the blackness was gone and so was the scream. Neelix stared down at her, his face only centimeters away from her own, his expression filled with concern. "Kes! What's the matter? Are you all right?"

She tried to speak, but her mouth was full of water. For one long second, she wished desperately that she had never donated one of her lungs to Neelix a few years ago. She still couldn't breathe. The golden fluid gushed from her mouth as a fit of agonized coughing shook her body. It seemed like hours before she could breathe again. "The scream," she said finally. "I heard screaming."

"What scream?" Neelix asked, holding on to her tightly. Her feet touched the floor of the harbor and she weakly struggled to assume a standing position. Neelix propped her up while she regained her strength and attempted to reorient herself.

Everything was back to normal. The blackness was gone, replaced by sky and sea and sun. She listened for the scream but heard only her own ragged breathing. "Didn't you hear it?" she asked.

"Hear what?" Neelix examined her apprehensively. "I don't understand. What happened to you?"

A Ryol male came running through the surf toward them. A lifeguard, Kes guessed; Neelix had explained the concept to her earlier. "Is there a problem here?" he asked. Like most Ryol swimmers, he was taller than either Neelix or Kes, and he wore only a skimpy loincloth of delicate fabric.

"I'm not sure," Neelix said. His eyes scanned the

Ryol's exposed physique and he drew Kes even closer against him. For once, she did not object to his overprotectiveness; at the moment, she could use the support. "We were having a little swimming lesson, that's all. Everything was going fine until she had some sort of panic attack and swallowed a lot of water. Is that all that happened, darling? Did something frighten you?"

"I don't know," she said hesitantly. "I heard something, or I thought I did." The tall lifeguard watched her avidly. She looked back and forth between the two men, searching their faces for some sign that they, too, had experienced what she'd endured. But Neelix only seemed worried about her, while the lifeguard appeared only curious and alert. "There was no screaming?" she asked. "No shadow?"

Neelix shook his head. "Just me and you and the sea. Maybe some fish, too, but no screams from you or anyone else. To be honest, you were too busy inhaling water to scream or shout. Gave me quite a scare, you did."

"I don't understand," she said, clinging to her companion's soggy frame. His wet bristles were plastered to his skull. "It seemed so real."

"Perhaps you had a nightmare," the lifeguard suggested. "Could you have fallen asleep for a moment or two?"

A nightmare? Kes supposed it was possible. Floating upon the waves had been incredibly relaxing for a while. She could easily imagine herself drifting off to sleep beneath the sun. "But I opened my eyes," she recalled aloud, "and there was blackness everywhere. And I still heard the screams, at least until Neelix shook me out of it." Lifting her head off Neelix's chest, she looked around her, taking in the seemingly tranquil atmosphere of the beach. "Surely I couldn't have dreamed all of that, could I?"

The lifeguard looked skeptical. "Some people claim

to hear voices in the roar of the surf, but it's merely a trick of the waves," he said. "In any event, I think you've had enough swimming for today. Perhaps you'll feel more comfortable aboard your ship?" He stepped forward, stretching out his arm to escort her back to the shore.

Neelix stepped between Kes and the lifeguard, as if terrified that the tall Ryol might attempt mouth-to-mouth resuscitation. Kes would have been amused if she were not still shaken by her . . . what? Dream? Hallucination? Kes couldn't begin to explain what she had just experienced.

"Probably not a bad idea," Neelix said. "How about it, sweetheart? Ready to call it a day?"

Kes nodded absently. The memory of her so-called nightmare was proving harder to dispel than the darkness itself. Was it just her imagination, or could she still hear that terrible screaming, echoing faintly in the furthest corners of her mind? Perhaps The Doctor would have an answer that would satisfy her, she hoped, or maybe Tuvok. Despite the brilliant sunlight, Kes felt a chill come over her. As miraculous as the Ryol beach was, suddenly she couldn't wait to get back to the safety of the ship.

I did hear something, she thought, gaining strength from her faith in her resources. *I know I did.*

Accompanied by both Neelix and the Ryol, Kes waded back to shore. While Neelix retrieved their commbadges and towels from a sunny stretch of beach, she turned around to take one more look at the gleaming surface of the harbor. Golden waves surged over the beach, then gently receded. The seascape was idyllic, its beauty and apparent serenity betraying none of the unquenchable anguish she had sensed within its depths.

Somehow she knew she would be coming back to this place.

CHAPTER
5

IT WAS WARM OUTSIDE, BUT EVEN HOTTER INDOORS. Fragrant smoke rose from the incense burner lodged in the center of every table. Raucous music, heavy on the percussive side, made conversation impossible at distances greater than ten centimeters. The low tables, surrounded by comfortable cushions, ringed a thriving dance floor where inhabitants of both Ryolanov and *Voyager* enthusiastically worked up a sweat to the pounding beat of drums and cymbals. The Prime Directive had been temporarily supplanted, for tonight at least, by an even more venerable imperative: *Party till you drop.*

Tom Paris approved.

"Not bad," he said, assessing the situation. "On the Official Tom Paris Scale for Nightclub Excellence, this place rates about a seven-plus."

"What rates a ten?" Harry Kim asked. "That seedy

French dive you installed in the holodeck?" Along with Paris and B'Elanna Torres, he was squatting around a table on the perimeter of the dance floor. His voice was hoarse from trying to talk over the music for the last fifteen minutes. Fortunately, the neffaler kept the drinks coming. Paris was developing a definite taste for Ryol wine.

"No," he said thoughtfully. "That particular dive loses one point for being a holographic simulation. The real Sandrine's, back on Earth, rates a ten." Taking a sip from his cup, he glanced around the local watering hole. "Doesn't seem to be much in the way of gambling, organized or otherwise, but otherwise . . . loud music, strong drinks, friendly natives. What else do we need?"

"Dilithium," Torres growled. She glared at Harry Kim. "I don't know why I let you drag me along on this idiocy, Starfleet. I need to find out if there are any available crystals on this miserable planet, but the Ryol are almost as good at wasting my time as you two are."

"Remind me never to take a Klingon to a dance hall," Paris said, then instantly regretted it. He saw the hurt expression on Torres's face. It was gone in an instant, hidden behind her usual fierce exterior, but he had seen it. *What the hell did I say that for?* he thought. He knew how conflicted B'Elanna was about the Klingon half of her ancestry. *I must have had too much to drink already.* "Er, nothing personal, Torres. It's just that all you engineering types never know how to have a good time. Take the night off, for pete's sake. You owe it to yourself."

Given a choice, he knew, Torres would rather be identified as an engineer than as a Klingon. He hoped that he'd helped her save a little face, and gotten himself off the hook.

"You try piloting *Voyager* with nothing but burnt-out crystals in your engines, Lieutenant, then tell me your idea of a good time." She drained her cup with one savage gulp, then threw the empty vessel onto the table. "I'm going to get some hard info out one of these overbred playboys or die trying." Rising from the table, she turned her back on Paris and nodded at Kim. "See you later, Starfleet. Don't let this pig get you into too much trouble."

Torres stalked away onto the crowded dance floor, leaving behind an empty place at the table and an awkward silence. "Tell me again," Kim said finally, "about your magic touch with women."

Ouch, Paris thought silently. "That was no woman," he said. "That's a warp drive with claws and a bad disposition." Kim gave him a knowing look, apparently unconvinced by his glib bravado. "Look, Harry, I'm sure she'll get over it."

"You better hope so," Kim said. "Remember what she did to that Vidiian?"

In excruciating detail, Paris thought. *Maybe the captain is right, and I shouldn't be let out without a leash. I wonder how I'm going to screw up next.* A neffaler shambled past their table. Paris grabbed it by a scrawny shoulder and pointed toward his cup. "Water," he said. "Plenty of it." The apelike creature displayed no sign of comprehension, but it scurried away toward the bar. Paris hoped his Universal Translator could overcome an evolutionary gap of several million years.

"Water?" Kim said, feigning disbelief. "Boy, are you turning over a new leaf."

"Hey, one of us has to keep a clear head down here." Paris scanned the smoky night club, wondering if there was any real reason for sticking around. Tiny clouds of multicolored incense hovered over every table. The blaring music sounded like sleigh bells being fed through an old-fashioned garbage disposal. Judging from the conspicuous absence of any visible musicians, Paris assumed that civilization on Ryolanov had achieved the vital techo-sociological equivalent of a jukebox. *Who knows?* he thought. *Maybe they've even invented Muzak.* "Good enough for me," he muttered. "Welcome to the Federation."

His roaming eyes locked on to a shapely pair of maroon legs that seemed to be coming his way. *Things are starting to look up,* he thought. His gaze strayed upward at a leisurely pace until he found himself staring into a familiar pair of malachite eyes. *Oh hell,* he thought. *I should have expected this.*

"Tom!" Laazia greeted him enthusiastically. "You wouldn't believe how happy I am to find you here." The Elder's gorgeous daughter had traded in her silk vest and skirt for a sheer togalike garment that hung loosely from one bronzed shoulder, leaving the other bare. The filmy fabric of her gown invited his eyes to probe its none-too-hidden mysteries.

Red alert, Paris thought. *All shields up and holding. Executing defensive maneuvers.* His mouth dried up, and he had to swallow a gulp of wine before he could speak. "Laazia. What an . . . amazing . . . stroke of luck." The powerful wine went straight to his head. *Where in blazes is that monkey with my water?*

"How goes your evening?" she asked, gazing pointedly at the empty cup and cushion left behind by Torres. Paris wondered if there was any diplomatic way to avoid inviting her to sit down. He couldn't think of one.

"Just as enjoyably as we've come to expect on Ryolanov," Paris said. Stalling shamelessly, he gestured toward Kim. "This is my friend, Ensign Harry Kim. Harry, this is Laazia. She's the one I was telling you about." He shot Kim a meaningful look. *Help me out here,* he thought. He had filled Kim in on the captain's warning regarding Laazia. Hopefully, Harry had not drunk enough wine to blot out their earlier conversation.

"Pleased to meet you," Kim told Laazia. To Paris's

relief, he did not say anything about taking Torres's place. *Maybe I can still get out of this alive,* he thought.

"Any friend of Tom's is mine as well," Laazia said. Her smile was bright enough to light up a nebula. B'Elanna shouldn't bother searching for dilithium, Paris mused; Laazia had enough charisma and sex appeal to power *Voyager* for a year. "You must tell me," she teased Kim, "what sort of scandalous rumors Tom has been spreading about me."

She showed no sign of leaving anytime soon. Paris looked around desperately for a way to escape, but nothing presented itself. Every excuse he could think of seemed ridiculously transparent. How was he supposed to discourage Laazia without offending her? *Damned if I do,* he thought, *and damned if I don't.*

Seconds ticked by remorselessly. Paris felt the uncomfortable silence stretching further every heartbeat. Laazia eyed him carefully, her tawny eyebrows arched. He saw an ugly diplomatic incident arising and surrendered to the inevitable. "Won't you join us?"

"I thought you'd never ask," she said. Her throaty voice dropped another octave even as she gently lowered herself onto the cushions, only microns away from Paris. She shifted her weight and he felt her warm thigh pressing against his. He took a deep breath and inhaled her perfume. The flowery scent seemed even more intoxicating than the wine. "This is one of my favorite places," she said. "You look like you belong here."

Shields down to fifty percent, Paris thought. *Requesting assistance.* Turning his face away from her, he silently mouthed an urgent plea to Kim. *Read my lips,* he prayed. *Whatever you do, don't leave me alone with her.*

Kim looked puzzled at first. *Small wonder,* Paris thought, repeating the message. Playing chaperon wasn't usually numbered among a Starfleet officer's duties. Then comprehension dawned on the young man's face. Kim nodded, trying and failing to suppress a grin. He was clearly amused by Paris's predicament. "Is it always so busy here?" Kim asked Laazia.

"It's a popular locale," she said, "but I can't deny that the arrival of you and your fellow travelers has added to the excitement tonight. After all, how often does one get to celebrate with beings from another star?" She laughed heartily. "The cosmological implications alone are staggering."

"That's one way to look at it, I guess," Paris said. Taking in the sights, he saw an exuberant group of mostly Maquis crew members teaching the Ryol the latest dances from Bajor. The Ryol men and women looked like they were quick learners. He couldn't hear the laughter over the pounding music, but a good time was obviously being had by all. Susan Tukwila, in particular, looked like she didn't have a care in the world as she hauled a good-looking Ryol male out onto the dance floor to demonstrate an acrobatic double dip that Paris would have sworn could only be performed in zero gravity. *I'm glad somebody's taking full advantage of their shore leave,* he thought.

B'Elanna Torres knew what her Klingon ancestors would think of this planet and these people. The Ryol were soft, indolent, spoiled, lacking any of the drive and determination of a more aggressive race. Growing flowers and throwing parties seemed all they were good for; nobody wanted to talk about warp drives, impulse engines, or anything practical. Torres struggled to overcome this innate prejudice against the Ryol, as she resisted all her more Klingon impulses, but it wasn't easy.

Especially when they refused to cooperate, like the one who was annoying her now. His name was Nimdir, and someone had said he was a technician, but he might as well have been a hair stylist for all the useful data she had managed to extract from him. Indeed, his yellow mane was more elaborately curled and coifed than that of any other Ryol she had encountered so far. A mass of golden ringlets framed his face, reminding her of the flowing wigs that had once been the fashion back on Earth, even though she couldn't remember precisely where or when. Pre-industrial England, maybe, or France? She didn't search her memory too hard; she was an engineer, not an historian, and she had more important things to find out.

"But do you use an electro-plasma system for power conduction," she asked for what felt like the tenth time, "or a microwave-based energy stream using individual station relays?"

Nimdir leaned against the wall of the nightclub, sipping from a half-filled goblet. He had discarded a green silk vest, the better to show off his manly chest. Torres was distinctly unimpressed, but that didn't stop the man from sucking in his gut and puffing up his chest as much as physically possible. "A little bit of this, a little bit of that," he said, shrugging his shoulders. "Microwaves, plasma . . . what difference does it make as long as the music keeps playing?"

Was he being evasive, she wondered, or was he just as stupid as he looked? Torres fought down an urge to grab him by his curls and knock some sense into him. The music was so loud that she had to stand only centimeters away from him, their faces practically touching, in order to hear him at all. She wondered if that was the idea behind the ear-splitting din.

"But when the music does break down," she pressed him, "then you have to know how it works in order to fix it, right? So what kind of technology do you need to repair?"

"What if I told you that nothing on our planet ever

breaks down?" Nimdir said with what he clearly considered an impish grin. "Would you believe me?"

"No," Torres said flatly. She was tempted to demonstrate the traditional Klingon punishment for lying, but figured the Captain would want him to keep his tongue. *It's odd,* she thought. The longer she stayed on this decadent playground of a planet, the closer she felt to her embarrassing Klingon roots. *Another good reason,* she thought, *for finding some dilithium and getting the hell out of here.*

"Ah, I should have known better than to try and fool such an intelligent, not to mention attractive, woman as yourself. Of course things malfunction occasionally," he admitted, "and some small labor is required to set things right, but it's such a boring topic of conversation that I can't imagine you're really interested in hearing all the tedious details." Nimdir dropped an overly familiar hand onto her shoulder. "What a shame, really, that the neffaler can't handle all the repairs themselves, but they just don't have the faculties to handle anything too complicated."

"Move the hand," Torres growled.

A timid neffaler, its body speckled with mangy clumps of hair, brought another round of drinks to the table. Paris groaned aloud as he observed that his request for water had somehow gotten lost in the transmission. "Just my luck," he muttered. "More wine."

"Don't you like our wine, Tom?" Laazia's long lashes fluttered above her pale green eyes. The motion of the lashes was almost hypnotic, he thought. He couldn't tear his gaze away from them. If he leaned in closer, he could see his own reflection in the gemlike depths of her eyes. The scented smoke hovering over the table did strange things to the light, the shadows moving sinuously over the elegant planes of her face.

"It's wonderful wine," he murmured, "almost too wonderful to resist." His lips hung above her ear. The downy fleece covering her scalp looked soft and inviting. "I don't trust myself." He edged even closer to her, feeling her warmth even through his Starfleet uniform.

Something jabbed him under the table. Hard.

Paris sat up straight. He turned his head to see Harry Kim sitting nearby, an innocent expression on his face. One of Kim's hands slid out from beneath the low table. Paris saw a fork gripped in Kim's fingers. He shook his head, trying to rescue his senses from Laazia's seductive allure. He didn't know whether to thank Harry or punch him.

"Is something wrong, Tom?" Laazia asked, giving Kim a suspicious look. It dawned on him that, aside from a few pleasantries, she had barely spoken to Kim since she sat down. Three was definitely a crowd, he guessed, at least as far as she was concerned. From where he was sitting, however, safety in numbers was the key. *I'm going to owe Harry big time,* he thought, *if I can get out of this mess with my reputation intact.*

A roar of laughter came from the dance floor, briefly overcoming the throbbing pulse of the music. Paris glanced at the revelers. Susan Tukwila was nowhere to be seen, having disappeared into the night with her handsome Ryol admirer, but Paris spotted Kellar, Felice, S'dbrg, Dembinski, and several other acquaintances from *Voyager* still dancing up a storm. He even thought he glimpsed B'Elanna Torres talking to a curly-headed Ryol on the other side of the club. *Poor guy,* he thought. Torres probably had him trapped in a discussion of inertial damping fields or something.

"So," he addressed Laazia, looking for a suitably safe topic for small talk, "the captain tells me you're an arbitrator. Is that like a lawyer or something?"

"More like a judge," she said, "or so I gather from what I've learned about your Federation legal practices. The judicious use of authority is a valuable skill to develop, especially for one in my position."

"Which is designated heir to your father?" Paris said. He tried to imagine Laazia draped in austere black robes. It wasn't easy.

"Precisely." Laazia shrugged modestly. "It is important that our people learn to accept my judgments."

"A pretty big responsibility," Paris commented, remembering his own struggles to live up to his father's lofty reputation. Maybe he and Laazia had more in common than he realized.

Harry Kim joined the conversation. "What sort of disputes do you mediate?" He had to raise his voice to be heard over the music.

"Nothing too interesting," she said. "We have a shockingly placid society. Why, I haven't had to execute anyone for days." She frowned for a moment, then broke out laughing at the Starfleet officers' shocked expressions. "You should see your faces!" Her green eyes sparkled with mischievous glee. "I was only joking!"

"Oh, right," Kim said sheepishly. He started to say something more, but Laazia held up her hand to cut him off.

"Please, no more shop talk," she insisted. "I come to this club to relax and forget about my duties." She grabbed on to Paris's wrist. "Come dancing with me, Tom. That looks like so much fun!"

He and Kim exchanged a stricken look. *Now what do we do?* he wondered. Laazia was halfway to her feet already. Paris felt the pointed tips of her nails digging into his skin. "Wait!" he said.

The Elder's daughter looked down on him, her full lips forming an unmistakable and irresistible pout.

Her pupils expanded until there was only a thin green outline around their beckoning darkness. "What's the matter now? Don't you want to dance with me?"

"I'd love to," he said, not entirely lying, "but what about Harry here? I can't just abandon him. What sort of friend would I be if I left my best buddy stranded at an empty table with nobody to talk to—and on an alien planet, no less!"

Laazia kept a tight hold on his wrist. Kim just rolled his eyes. "Oh brother," he muttered.

"I'm sure he'll do just fine," she insisted, tugging on his arm. Against his will, he found himself rising to his feet. *Wow,* he thought, *she's a lot stronger than she looks.*

"You don't know Harry," he said, lowering his voice to a stage whisper. "I shouldn't say this, but Harry . . . well, he's sort of socially challenged, if you know what I mean."

Kim groaned and buried his face in his hands. *He's going to kill me for this,* Paris thought, but it was the best he could do on the spur of the moment.

Laazia could not be dissuaded. "Don't worry," she said, "I can remedy that." She raised her voice and called out to the tightly packed throng filling the dance floor. "Romeela! Sitruua! Come to me!"

Like genies summoned from a magic lamp, or fantasies conjured up by a compliant holodeck, two stunning young women emerged from a crowd of dancers. Paris was impressed with how quickly they responded to Laazia's call. Were these women her friends or her subjects, he wondered, and exactly how much clout did an Elder's daughter have anyway?

Both women were, like all the Ryol, remarkably attractive by humanoid standards. Maybe not as breathtaking as Laazia herself, Paris decided, but beautiful enough to make a Dabo girl green with envy and an Orion belly dancer even greener. Fresh from the dance floor, their red-hued flesh gleamed with perspiration while their satiny gowns clung to their bodies. Kim lifted his head from the tabletop and his eyes looked ready to pop out of their sockets. His Adam's apple bobbed up and down.

"Ladies," Laazia said, pointing toward the table, "this is the eminently fascinating Ensign Harry Kim of the *U.S.S. Voyager.* He's been from one end of the universe to another. If you're nice to him, I'm sure he'll tell you all about it."

With an explosion of smiles and laughter, the women descended on Kim. Paris wasn't sure which one was Romeela and which was Sitruua, but they planted themselves on both sides of his friend, chattering merrily and holding on to his arms. Laazia tugged again on his own arm, and Paris looked down at Kim, suddenly unsure who was most in need of rescue. "Harry . . . ?" he began.

Kim's gaze swung back and forth between the beauties flanking him, then turned sheepishly toward Paris. He gave Paris a this-is-bigger-than-the-both-of-us sort of look. Paris nodded back. He had to concede that he had been hopelessly outmaneuvered. He was on his own. "See you later, Harry," he said as Laazia pulled him toward the music, "I hope."

"At last," she whispered into his ear, "I have you all to myself!"

Shields buckling, Captain, he thought. *We can't take much more of this.*

"The hand," Torres said again. "Move it now." It was a snarl, not a request.

Nimdir pretended he couldn't hear her. "What's that?" he said, cupping his free hand around his ear. "This music is really quite deafening, isn't it?"

Torres clenched her fists at her sides. In the old days, before *Voyager,* she would have already fed this preening idiot his own mane, curl by curl. Since signing on as the chief of Engineering, however, she had been doing her best to control her temper and justify both the captain's and Chakotay's faith in her. She was an officer now and she had to adhere to a higher standard of behavior, set a better example, than she had as an out-of-control rebel firebrand. *Give me strength,* she prayed to nobody in particular. *Let me stay in control.*

"I don't have time for these games," she said firmly. "Either talk to me about your technology or go away and leave me alone. It's your choice."

A wink and a smile, clearly intended by Nimdir to be ingratiating, had the opposite effect. Torres ground her teeth together while visions of bloodshed played on the viewscreen of her mind. Her blood came to a near boil, but she kept the beast within her at bay. *Focus on your primary objective,* she told herself. *Remember the dilithium.*

"Have I mentioned yet," Nimdir said, "how intriguing I find those ridges on your forehead? Do they have any special significance?"

It was exactly the wrong thing to say.

The music, which had been fast-paced and raucous all evening, slackened just as Paris and Laazia located an empty patch of floor. A languid romantic melody wound its way through the warm and smoky air. *Oh, terrific,* Paris thought. *A slow dance.* Things couldn't have gone more disastrously if he had planned them, which made him wonder if Laazia had done just that.

"Listen," she murmured, "they're playing our song."

Either my Universal Translator is getting lazy, he thought, *or some clichés stretch all the way to the Delta Quadrant.* He struggled to hang on to a snide sarcastic attitude; that was the only way, he decided, that he was going to keep from succumbing to the seductive web that seemed to be forming around him. *Good thing fate is throwing all this temptation at a cynical veteran like myself,* he thought. *Poor Harry wouldn't stand a chance.*

Laazia placed her hands upon his shoulders. Following her lead, he rested his own hands lightly upon her hips. Then they glided across the floor, crossing back and forth between various other couples, most consisting of one Ryol and one visitor from *Voyager.* Paris was relieved to see that he wasn't the only crew member fraternizing with the natives tonight, just the only one doing so against the explicit advice of the captain. *I can handle this,* he reassured himself. *All I have to do is keep cool.*

Easier said than done. Laazia's fingers danced beyond his shoulders, entwining themselves behind his neck. She pressed herself against him while the slow haunting melody seemed to go on and on. Paris couldn't believe how hot and sultry the club's interior had become. It was all he could do to keep his sweaty palms from sliding down Laazia's swaying hips.

"What are you thinking of?" she whispered huskily in his ear.

Exactly what I shouldn't, he thought. "Oh, gravity wells, wormholes, subspace anomalies . . . you know, all that starship stuff. I'm really a very boring person once you get to know me."

"I don't believe that," she said. Her fingertips traced circles on the back of his neck, tangling themselves in his hair. Her eyes were dark singularities, drawing him in. "And I intend to know you very well indeed."

Her open declaration unnerved him. He missed a step of the dance, inadvertently bumping into a Ryol male dancing nearby. "Sorry about that," Paris said to the man. "Would you believe I'm supposed to be a navigator?"

"You!" the man said angrily, letting go of his dance partner and turning around to confront Paris. "I should have known!"

Paris recognized the haughty indignant tone even before he spotted the thin white line running down Naxor's face. *Just my luck,* he thought bitterly. *Mr. Hospitality himself.*

Naxor's eyes grew wider when he saw Laazia standing beside Paris, clutching on to the lieutenant's arm. Behind him, a Bajoran ensign, whose name Paris could not recall, observed the scene with a puzzled expression on her face. "Laazia," Naxor said. "What are you doing here . . . with him?" He did not bother to explain or introduce his Bajoran companion; apparently, Paris guessed, the double standard was alive and well on Ryolanov.

"What does it look like?" Laazia replied defiantly, embracing Paris more tightly than he would have liked under the circumstances. He tried to gently disengage himself, but her arms again proved stronger than they appeared. Obviously, the Elder's daughter was not going to be any help in calming her jealous admirer.

"Look, I'm sorry I jostled you a moment ago," Paris said. "Two left feet and all that. How about I buy you a drink?"

Naxor sneered at him disdainfully. "I would sooner share wine with a neffaler, although, in truth, I see little difference between you and the lowliest of our servitors."

This guy is really getting on my nerves, Paris thought. Ordinarily, he wouldn't take this sort of abuse from anybody, let alone this scar-faced snob, but he knew the captain was counting on him to avoid any unpleasant encounters with the Ryol. *Let it go,* he thought, wondering if the ship's holodeck could whip up a punching bag that looked exactly like Naxor. *Something to check out later.*

Laazia showed no such restraint. "You go too far, Naxor," she told him, her sultry voice now cold and contemptuous. "Leave us at once or I will report your . . . lack of discretion . . . to my father."

But Naxor was too furious to heed Laazia's warning. "One less human will make no great difference in the end," he declared. His pupils grew slowly larger. He raised his hands in front of his chest, the sharp points of his brown nails extended toward Paris. *Is he planning to punch me or slash me,* Paris wondered, *and how in the world am I going to get out of this mess?*

"Lieutenant?" the Bajoran ensign asked nervously, apparently unsure where her duty lay.

"Stay out of this," Paris ordered. He saw no need for anyone else to get into trouble. "I don't want to do this," he told Naxor, clenching his fists just in case the Ryol proved impossible to reason with. Captain's orders or not, Paris didn't plan on turning the other cheek.

"Neffaler!" Naxor said and spit upon the floor. Paris guessed the term was not meant as a compliment. Naxor's saliva, pooled atop the black stone tiles, had a faintly orangish tint.

"Naxor, I forbid this!" Laazia said. Letting go of Paris, she stepped between the two men, but Naxor refused to give up. He dodged past Laazia, then marched toward Paris, his green eyes assuming a predatory gleam. *Sorry, Captain,* Paris thought, *I did my best.* He waited for Naxor to throw the first blow.

A sudden crash caught both men by surprise. Paris spun around to see B'Elanna Torres lifting a curly-haired Ryol off the floor. Blood, dark and watery, gushed from the man's crumpled nose. "Son of a *targ!*" Torres roared and hurled the man physically into the air. He came flying at the dance floor, a cry of alarm escaping his wide-open mouth. Paris ducked at the last minute and the B'Elanna-propelled Ryol slammed into Naxor, bowling the man over. They crashed to the floor, landing in a tangle of limbs that threatened the vertical stability of every couple dancing nearby. Naxor's angry curses mixed with the other man's groans, spoiling the romantic mood music.

Saved by the Klingon, Paris thought. The captain wouldn't be happy about this turn of events, but at least he wasn't to blame. Paris looked at Laazia. For the first time since he'd met her, the Elder's daughter appeared stunned and at a loss for words. Paris caught her gaze, shrugged his shoulders, and ran for the door. He grabbed Torres by the arm on his way. The sooner they both got out of there, the better.

"Thanks for the assist," he said as they fled into the warm tropical night. "Your timing was just about perfect."

She gave him a puzzled look. "I have no idea what you're talking about," she said.

CHAPTER

6

"I'M FINE. REALLY I AM," KES INSISTED.

"You nearly drowned!" Neelix said. "I've never been so frightened, except for maybe when the Kazon captured you, or when we were trapped inside that giant space creature, or when the Female Caretaker tried to destroy us. . . ."

Kes sat on the edge of a biobed in the sickbay while The Doctor scanned her with his medical tricorder. She would have liked to have changed out of her wet bathing suit, but Neelix had insisted that she be checked out by The Doctor the instant they returned to *Voyager*. Indeed, they had beamed directly to the sickbay from the planet's surface which made her feel slightly ridiculous. Aside from a slight cough and a bit of a chill, she felt fine.

Sort of.

"Tell me the truth, Doctor," Neelix said. His

striped bathing suit seemed equally out of place in the sickbay. "Is she going to be all right?"

"I certainly think so," The Doctor replied, "although I must admit that the appeal of immersing oneself in a large body of water eludes me. Neither of you are equipped with gills or fins; evolution clearly intended you to stay on dry land."

"Oh, it was marvelous," Kes said. She could still remember how exciting her first trip to the ocean had been. "At least, it was at first."

"And then?" The Doctor asked. He put his tricorder down on a counter and eyed her carefully.

Kes hesitated. Now that she was back in a familiar environment, her experience out in the harbor seemed unreal and ephemeral. Could she merely have imagined those despairing wails, that suffocating sense of entrapment? It didn't seem possible, but she could not think of a more plausible explanation, nor did she know what she could do about the voices even if they were real and not an auditory illusion created by the waves and her wandering thoughts. She could still hear those anguished voices echoing through her memory. She shivered involuntarily, feeling an icy chill that had nothing to do with her damp swimsuit and the temperature of the room. The Doctor noticed her trembling and produced a blanket of thermal insulation that he wrapped around her shoulders. "Tell me about it," he urged her. "What's the matter?"

Kes nodded, tugging the blanket tightly around her. "It seemed so real," she began, "and it started without warning. One moment I was floating blissfully on the waves, feeling the warmth of the sun above me and the cool water below, then I heard them whispering in my ear." She told The Doctor and Neelix everything she experienced, sparing no detail, while they looked on with concern and curiosity on their faces. "What do you think?" she asked them finally. "Did I just dream those voices?"

The Doctor looked thoughtful. "It's possible, I suppose. Back on Earth, human beings used to immerse themselves in sensory-deprivation tanks in order to stimulate similar illusions and hallucinations. It was regarded as an effective way to probe one's own unconscious mind, on the dubious assumption that there was something of worth to be found there." He shook his head disdainfully. "I know I've always managed perfectly well without an unconscious."

"You see," Neelix said, visibly relieved, "there's nothing to it."

"On the other hand," The Doctor continued, "there remains much we do not know about the latent psychic abilities of the Ocampa mind. I'm afraid I cannot rule out the possibility of a genuinely extrasensory experience."

"Oh," Neelix said. His face fell. He obviously wanted to dismiss her nightmare as an insubstantial daydream. Kes admired his stubborn optimism, but found herself unable to let the matter go so easily. She wasn't sure which option she preferred: that she could be frightened to near panic by the phantasms of her mind, or that she had inadvertently tapped into a very real cry for help? She tried to imagine what sort of extreme suffering could produce the anguished screams she had heard, feeling horrified at the ghastly implications of those hopeless shrieks and that inescapable darkness.

"It wasn't just voices," she pointed out. "There was something wrong with my eyes as well. Everything was black and close and confining. I felt like I was trapped, unable to breathe."

"Again," The Doctor said, "it is difficult to distinguish between hysterical blindness and a psychic invasion of some sort." He scowled, and Kes sympathized with his unhappiness. The Doctor prided himself, she knew, on his encyclopedic medical knowledge; she could imagine how frustrated he felt to be unable to produce a more definitive diagnosis. "Although, considering how each of you has only one lung apiece, you might want to reconsider any deepsea diving you may have on your vacation plans."

"Don't worry, Doctor," Neelix assured him. "Kes won't take any unnecessary risks while I'm around." He helped her down from the biobed. The duranium floor felt cold to her bare feet. "Maybe we should talk to Tuvok about what happened. He's the expert on telepathic powers."

That thought had already occurred to Kes. "Good idea," she said. She folded the silver thermal blanket and placed it on the biobed. Goosebumps covered her exposed arms and legs. "But can I *please* change into some dry clothes first?"

Chakotay dimmed the lights in his cabin. Kneeling on the floor, he spread out the contents of his medicine bundle before him: the feather of a blackbird, a polished stone, and the small electronic device known as an *akoonah*. He placed the device against his forehead and closed his eyes.

"Akoo-cheemoya," he chanted. "I remain far from the sacred places of my grandfathers, far from the bones of my people. We seem to have found a safe harbor, and yet my spirit is troubled. If it is permitted, lend me your guidance. Show me the truth of this place so that I can better help those who journey with me. Let me find the answers I seek."

Chakotay could not have told himself exactly why he could not fully accept *Voyager's* good fortune in chancing upon Ryolanov. Perhaps, he mused, too many years in the Maquis and the Delta Quadrant, too many betrayals by Seska and others, had left him slightly paranoid and slow to trust anyone and anything. Thank his ancestors, then, that there was still one place he could always turn to when his mind was clouded by doubt.

He activated the *akoonah*. Electrical impulses stimulated slumbering portions of his brain while drawing a veil over his sensory intake. Generations ago, his ancestors had used psychoactive herbs to induce a similar meditative state; the akoonah provided the same effect without polluting his blood with potent chemicals. The physical world receded from his consciousness, giving way to an inner realm of symbols and spirits. His breathing slowed. His heart beat in time with the eternal rhythms of creation. In his mind, if not in what he usually considered reality, Chakotay opened his eyes.

He found himself staring up at a barren mountaintop. No trees, moss, or other vegetation softened the grim forbidding aspect of this jagged peak. No snow had crowned the mountain, nor had any wind buffed its harsh edges. There was only the brutal black granite itself, thrusting up from the rocky ground like a spear of stone. The mountain was lifeless, colorless. He saw only the uniform gray solidity of the mountain, silhouetted against a dead white sky, and the impenetrable black shadows cast by its looming crags and canyons. The sun was a mere pinprick of light on the distant horizon, too cold and far away to do any good. An icy wind chilled his bones.

"Where am I?" Chakotay asked aloud. This desolate place looked like none of the metaphysical realms he had explored in the past. It was hard to imagine anything dwelling in such a bleak landscape, let alone the honored spirits of his ancestors. He looked for his spirit guide, the totem animal who acted as both his teacher and his twin in the world beyond, but saw no sign of his guide. He could not feel its presence anywhere, which filled his soul with dread. Never before had he felt so alone inside his own heart and mind. He considered opening his eyes for real, deactivating the *akoonah* and returning to the here and now of his cabin on *Voyager,* but shook his head. He had to believe the spirits had brought him here for a reason. He would not turn back until he had learned whatever there was to learned in this dead and discouraging land.

He stared again at the very peak of the mountain looming in front of him. He thought he saw something move at the top of the peak. For an instant, he glimpsed a glowing pair of eyes, flashing in the pale sunlight. His spirit guide, he wondered, or something far less benevolent? He looked and looked for another sign upon the mountain, but only the stone and shadows revealed themselves.

Very well, he thought. He began to climb the mountain. "Because it's there," he told himself, grinning despite his grim surroundings. He knew the answer, if there was an answer, waited for him at the end of the climb. The only alternative was to return to the waking world empty-handed, and that was not an option he was ready to accept. "Don't go away," he whispered to the presence lurking above. "Here I come."

The climb was hard and tiring. There was no trail, so he had to make his own way, clutching at handholds no larger than cracks, sometimes scrambling on all fours over the jagged rock face. The gray stone was freezing to the touch. The cold rock stung his fingertips until they began to grow numb. The higher he climbed, the more the wind blew against him, trying to toss him off the mountain. Gravity tugged at him as well, with far greater force than the slack pull of Ryolanov; Chakotay felt like he was back in basic training again, trying to complete one of Starfleet Academy's infamous heavy-G obstacle courses. His muscles ached from the strain. The wind blew in his face, burning his cheeks and forcing him to squint as he climbed. *Don't look down,* he told himself. *Keep on going.*

Finally the steep incline leveled out a little bit. Chakotay pulled himself over the edge of a cliff and rose to his feet on a rocky ledge only a few meters from the top of the mountain. He blew on his fingers in a futile attempt to warm them. His breath emerged in puffs of white fog. The persistent cold sapped his strength. An awful weariness descended upon him, and it took all his energy to keep standing. *What kind of stubborn fool am I?* he wondered. While the rest of the crew was enjoying a tropical pleasure planet, he was facing hypothermia in a chill joyless realm of his own creation. He had to assume, though, that there was some higher purpose to his ordeal, that a deeper truth awaited him.

Refusing to look back at the way he had come, he examined the grim scene before him. Two large boulders blocked his view, with only a narrow passageway between them. Beyond the boulders, the peak of the mountain lay shrouded in shadows. For a moment, peering through the crack separating the boulders, he thought he saw something, even blacker than the shadows, moving in the darkness ahead. He strained his ears to hear above the wind, catching the faint echoes of a low growl.

He stepped toward the boulders, determined to confront the entity on the other side of the huge rocks, but it moved faster than he, reaching the passageway first. Chakotay reached instinctively for his phaser, but came up empty-handed; his weapon and technology had not come with him on this spiritual journey. The entity filled up the passage with its ebony presence. Although Chakotay searched the darkness with his eyes, he could not make out any details concerning the growling creature. The darkness swallowed its form, concealing its identity. Chakotay realized that he would not be able to truly see the entity until it was too close to escape from. He sniffed the air. A musky odor, reeking of fur and fresh blood, suffused the atmosphere. He almost gagged at the foul aroma.

Something padded toward him on four legs. For a heartbeat, he thought it might be his spirit guide. Then he saw the brilliant green eyes, the first trace of color he had witnessed in this stark and monochromatic landscape, and rows of sharp white teeth. . . .

It looked like a cross between a wolf and a grizzly, flaunting the most savage aspects of both beasts. Chakotay caught a glimpse of its massive shaggy body and a snout full of ivory fangs. Steam rose from flaring nostrils, and its hot breath hit him like the heat from a fusion reactor. Five sharp talons extended from a hairy paw that took one step closer to Chakotay. An angry growl rumbled like thunder.

Chakotay glanced back over his shoulder. There was nowhere to run; behind him, the ledge gave way to a long drop to the rocks below. Besides, he had not climbed so far, and under such arduous conditions, to flee now. Despite its alarming appearance, this beast was a part of his vision, perhaps the essential part. He had to learn what all this meant.

"Greetings," he said. He regarded the beast with a steady gaze. "Although I cannot find my guide, I believe the spirits have brought me here. Are you their messenger?"

Green eyes glared at Chakotay as he waited for the creature's response. Foam dripped from the beast's jaws. Snarling, it lunged at Chakotay. He threw up his hands, but he could not overcome the beast's speed and strength. An immense fur-covered body slammed into him like an avalanche, knocking him to the ground. Powerful jaws clamped down on his throat. Fangs tore through his flesh. Chakotay screamed in pain as he felt the beast rip out his heart!

A safety circuit activated in his akoonah. Abruptly, with no sense of transition, he found himself sitting on the floor of his darkened cabin. He experienced a moment of disorientation. Where was the beast? The mountain? The freezing wind? He clutched his throat, only to find both his flesh and his uniform neatly intact.

Of course, he thought. It was only a vision. Usually he allowed himself a more gradual return to the waking world, but the safety override in the akoonah must have halted the spirit journey at the first sign of neurological distress. *And just in time,* he thought. His heart was still pounding. He took a deep breath to calm himself.

His quarters were just as he had left them, his medicine tools still laid on the floor in front of him. He glanced around the dimly lit cabin, half-expecting to see the dream-beast glowering at him from a shadowy corner. "Lights," he requested. The cabin responded instantly. Overhead lighting brightened, dispelling the shadows. Chakotay removed the akoonah from his forehead and placed it on the animal hide next to the feather and the stone. Slowly, methodically, he wrapped his medicine bundle, letting the familiar task soothe his jangled nerves even as his mind inspected the content of his disturbing vision.

What did it mean? he wondered. A hostile environment. A dangerous—and triumphant—predator. His own death beneath the hungry fangs of the beast. *Was this nightmarish fantasy merely a reflection of my own unspoken anxieties,* Chakotay thought, *or a desperate warning from the spirits of my ancestors?* His Starfleet training, and experiences among the Maquis, provided him with few clues with which to interpret his vision. Not for the first time, he wished his father were still alive and around to talk to. Kolopak had always possessed a greater understanding of the old ways than his occasionally wayward son. *How would my father react to such a terrifying omen?*

His commbadge beeped, startling him. "Chakotay here," he said, rising to his feet.

"I'm sorry to bother you, Commander," came The Doctor's voice, "but the computer reported a scream from your quarters. Is everything all right?"

"I don't know," Chakotay said, recalling the beast's feral green eyes. He could still feel the creature's fangs tearing into his throat. "I wish I knew."

The mess hall was not very crowded. Kes guessed that most crew members preferred to sample the exotic cuisine of the planet below. Still, Neelix was busy preparing a small buffet supper while she conversed with Tuvok. Kes wore a simple brown dress over a matching blouse and leggings; it felt good to get out of that wet swimsuit.

"There are many different sorts of telepathy," Tuvok observed. He sat opposite Kes, a plain green salad on his plate. "The Vulcan mind-meld requires profound concentration and involves a total blending of two minds, while Betazoids practice a more casual form of empathy; they are generally better at sensing emotional states rather than extracting factual information from others. Other races within the Federation can project illusions, while others exhibit various forms of clairvoyance. Some beings have claimed precognitive abilities, although this matter is open to question. Our current understanding of space-time makes genuine precognition unlikely, unless some manner of time travel is involved."

Tuvok paused to take a sip of water, then proceeded with his lecture. "Unfortunately, the full range of Ocampa telepathic abilities remains unknown, although our encounter with Tanis suggests that your latent psychic potential is considerable. That being the case, I must assume that your experience at the Ryol harbor is the result of some form of telepathic stimuli, although I cannot readily identify the precise nature of the telepathy involved."

Kes shuddered at the memory of those despairing voices. She remembered that awful sense of being buried alive. "But couldn't I have just imagined it all?" she asked.

"That is possible, but not probable," Tuvok declared. "In my experience, you are not prone to hallucinations or delusions of this sort, while your telepathic abilities are demonstrably real."

Kes was amazed at how calmly Tuvok could discuss her strange mental powers, especially considering that she had once nearly killed him with an uncontrolled burst of psychic energy. Tom Paris had told her that all Vulcans possessed Tuvok's extreme composure. She found it hard to imagine an entire planet filled with people like Tuvok, but she hoped she would have a chance to visit Vulcan someday, provided that *Voyager* could find a shortcut home. She had heard so much about the Federation from Tom and the others; she wanted to get there almost as much as the rest of the crew did.

Besides, she admitted, it was easier to fantasize about Earth and the Alpha Quadrant than to cope with whatever horror she had discovered on Ryolanov. Her own telepathic abilities frightened her sometimes because she knew so little about them. "But what am I supposed to do now?" she asked Tuvok.

He paused before answering. "The safest course would be to stay away from the beach for the time being. The mind is a powerful force and should not be underestimated. Unknown psychic phenomena should be approached with great caution, or dire consequences may result."

Kes felt her limbs growing weak. She held on to the

edge of the table for support. "What sort of consequences?"

"Madness," Tuvok stated flatly. His stoic expression never changed. "Psychic possession. Mental impairment. Coma. Death."

"Oh," Kes said. She glanced down at her plate. Her supper, hair pasta with a side order of fresh fruit, was largely untouched. Neelix would be disappointed, she knew, but all this talk of mysterious psychic forces had killed her appetite. "But what if those voices are trying to tell me something important?" she asked. "We can't just ignore them."

"If you wish," Tuvok volunteered, "I will also investigate the site of your experience, although I cannot guarantee that I will detect the same phenomenon. As I was explaining, telepathic abilities vary from species to species, and from individual to individual."

That's not enough, she thought, grateful that Tuvok could not read her mind without "profound concentration." As thrilling as it was to be rediscovering the ancient powers of her Ocampa ancestors, there were times she wished that she had never learned about her latent telepathy. This was definitely one of those times.

"Thank you," she said, even as she realized that, despite Tuvok's warning, she would have to return to the beach herself. In her heart, she had always known this, but she wanted Tuvok to confirm her fears. The prospect of being trapped in the dark once again, with only those terrible screams to keep her company, horrified her. Part of her knew, however, that she would never truly know peace until she had discovered the origin of the screaming.

I have to go back.

CHAPTER
7

"I MUST APOLOGIZE, ELDER," CAPTAIN JANEWAY BEGAN, "for the unfortunate incident at the dance club last night. I assure you that I have already reprimanded Lieutenant Torres for her part in the altercation."

Varathael's face occupied the small screen on her desk. Janeway sat alone in her ready room, taking advantage of her privacy to have a frank discussion with the Elder. She hoped the Ryol leader was not too upset about yesterday's brawl. The crew really needed some good shore leave. It would be a shame if she had to recall them all from the planet just because B'Elanna lost her temper.

Varathael shrugged. The ruby gem around his neck reflected the lights in his office. "Do not concern yourself about such a trivial disturbance," he insisted. "Young people are full of passion. The wine, the music . . . such things happen."

"Not with my officers," Janeway said firmly. "I wouldn't want you to think that this sort of behavior is typical of Starfleet officers. I can assure you it is not." She chose not to mention that time, years ago at the Academy, when she was the last person standing after a free-for-all that pretty much leveled an oyster bar in Seattle. That hadn't been a first-contact situation, after all. Besides, that Tellarite had insulted her dog.

"You mustn't be too hard on your Lieutenant Torres," Varathael said. "I know the Ryol youth involved. Nimdir can be most annoying. I have no doubt that he provoked Torres beyond endurance."

So I gathered, Janeway thought. To her credit, B'Elanna had informed the captain of the incident as soon as she had returned to the ship. Tom Paris had backed up B'Elanna's story, although Janeway suspected that Paris had played a larger role in the episode than he let on. She made a mental note to ask Harry Kim what really went on down on Ryolanov. If Paris was there, Harry probably hadn't been too far away.

"Well, I am greatly relieved that you are being so forgiving," she said. The Cardassians would have demanded Torres's immediate execution, she thought, while the Romulans would have used such a petty incident as an excuse to detain *Voyager* indefinitely, and the Ferengi would have hit the Federation with a truly enormous fine. Never mind how the Kazon or the Klingons would have reacted.

"Please, Captain," Varathael said. "I consider the matter closed." He smiled warmly on the viewscreen, his ingratiating charm reminding her somewhat of Gathorel Labin of Sikaris. So far, however, the Ryol had proven more sincerely generous than the hedonistic Sikarians. "Now then, let us discuss more pleasant matters: when might I expect to enjoy a tour of your starship?"

Janeway had given the matter a lot of thought, eventually agreeing with Chakotay's recommendations. Although the Ryol showed remarkably little interest in developing their own space program, perhaps not too surprising given the desolate and unpromising star systems surrounding their world, they displayed no sign of xenophobia or technological chauvinism. There was no evidence to suggest that their culture and worldview would be threatened by a mere visit to a starship. As long as key technical regions, such as the warp cores, were kept off-limits to the visitors, a friendly diplomatic tour seemed harmless.

"I look forward to having you aboard *Voyager* whenever is convenient," she told Varathael. "It's the least we can do after you and your people have been so very hospitable to us."

"Excellent," Varathael said. "You can't imagine how exciting your vessel sounds to us. An actual starship from the other side of the galaxy! My daughter Laazia can hardly wait to 'beam aboard,' as you say."

"We will be honored to receive her," Janeway said. *I had better warn Tom Paris,* she thought. The last thing she needed now was *another* diplomatic incident.

Me and my stupid temper, B'Elanna Torres cursed herself silently. She was mortified for having embarrassed the captain and for bungling her assignment from Chakotay. She went looking for dilithium and found trouble instead. *It's this damn Klingon blood,* she thought ferociously. *I can't help myself sometimes.* She wondered if the full humans and Vulcans on board realized how lucky they were, not having to constantly wrestle with a primitive barbarian inside them that was just waiting to erupt at the worst possible moment? Some people said that the Klingons were an honorable and civilized people. She knew better. They were animals, all of them, and so was she.

A small growl escaped her lips. Horrified at her slip, she bit down hard on her bottom lip to silence the growl, then looked around her furtively. Had anybody heard her?

Fortunately, the bridge was operating on a skeleton staff. The captain was in her ready room, behind closed doors, while a mixture of Starfleet and Maquis personnel were stationed at various consoles around the bridge. She wondered for a second where Chakotay was. Could he be down on the planet, perhaps romancing one or more of those shameless Ryol women? A pang of jealousy stabbed at her heart, adding to the shame and anger she felt for letting that idiot Nimdir unleash her Klingon fury. She fought back another snarl of frustration.

Stop it, she told herself. *You have a job to do.* She was determined to redeem herself by finding out, once and for all, if there was any dilithium to be had on this useless party planet. She stared at the glowing display screen in front of her face, searching the sensor readings for the telltale energy spike that would alert her to the presence of dilithium crystals. Ordinarily, she manned the starboard engineering station on the bridge, but for this mission she needed the sensors she could access at the port forward science console, on the other side of the bridge. *So much for the subtle approach,* she thought, tired of trying unsuccessfully to extract a straight answer from one of the planet's feckless inhabitants. The high-tech approach was more her style; she'd track down some dilithium if she had to scan every square meter of Ryolanov.

She took a few seconds to calibrate the planetary observation sensors to the specific energy signature of crystallized dilithium. There was no point in scanning for the uncrystallized forms, not as long as the theta-matrix compositing system remained on the blink. For about the thousandth time, she wished that there had been a chance to salvage some equipment from the Maquis ship that had originally carried her to the Delta Quadrant. She had personally kept the compositing system on that ship running in peak condition. Unfortunately, that ship—and all its technological resources—had been reduced to space dust above the Ocampa homeworld.

Still, *Voyager* had plenty of potential in her own right, as Torres had quickly learned. She focused the lateral sensor arrays on the planet's surface, starting at the equator and gradually working their way toward both poles. It only made sense to begin with the more populated regions of the planet, since that was where any power-generation facilities were likely to be located. Given Ryolanov's own rotation, and *Voyager's* steady orbit around the planet, it would take a while to scan each hemisphere, but Torres vowed to keep searching for as long as it took.

Four hours later she felt ready to explode. Patience was another quality that her half-Klingon heritage had shorted her on. How dare that planet spin so slowly! It would be faster, she decided, to blow the whole blasted planet apart and sift through the ashes rather than endure this slow plodding survey of the planet's unremarkable surface. Meter by meter, sector by sector, *Voyager* scanned Ryolanov, but without any success. If there was any dilithium on that planet, the inhabitants seemed to have gone out of their way to hide it. *Just to spite me,* Torres thought. As nearly as she could tell, the Ryol derived the bulk of their energy from such safe, sane, and unexciting sources as geothermal and hydroelectric power. *They probably have windmills, too,* she thought, disgusted. How was she supposed to find anything a starship could use on such a benign and backward little world?

She yawned loudly, drawing stares from the handful

of crew members staffing the bridge. Torres ignored the stares. All she cared about now was locating some dilithium so she could go and get a good night's sleep. The captain frowned on eating on the bridge, but she was sorely tempted to get a cup of coffee from the nearest replicator. *This is a waste of time,* she thought. *There's no dilithium here. There never was.*

She was about to give up when she noticed something odd about the readings from one small sector of the planet. The computer was reporting no available data from any of the various scans that had been directed at that region. Just a programming glitch, she wondered, or something more intriguing?

Torres interrupted the progress of the automatic mapping and survey scans and redirected the lateral sensor arrays at the area in question. Again, no new data was reported; the sensors declared themselves unable to complete the scans requested. *Interesting,* she thought, feeling a rush of excitement. She was definitely on to something here. She tried the active magnetic interferometry scanner, but to no avail. The high-energy proton spectrometry clusters flunked out, too, as did the gravimetric distortion mapping scanner, the fixed angle gamma frequency counter, the wide-angle EM radiation imaging scanner, the quark population analysis counter, the Z-range particulate spectrometry sensor, the low-frequency EM flux sensor, the localized subspace field stress sensor, the parametric subspace field stress sensor, the hydrogen-filter subspace flux scanner, the linear calibration subspace flux sensor, the variable band optical imagining cluster, the virtual aperture graviton flux spectrometer, the high-resolution graviton flux spectrometer, the very low energy graviton spin polarimeter, the passive imaging gamma interferometry sensor, the low-level imagining sensor, the virtual particle mapping camera, and even the life-form analysis instrument counter. *Give me a break,* she thought. She *knew* there were life-forms down there, even if she had doubts about their relative intelligence.

It was impossible that this was a system failure on *Voyager*'s part. That many discrete and differing sensors would not malfunction simultaneously unless a Q was involved. Besides, the sensor arrays were having no trouble scanning the rest of the planet. It was only one small portion of Ryolanov, roughly one square kilometer, that seemed impervious to her scans. *They're hiding something,* she concluded. The Ryol had to be using a sophisticated and highly effective system of force shields to protect this region from observation.

"Why?" Torres muttered aloud. What did the Ryol have on their tropical playground that was worth hiding? As nearly as their earlier scans could tell, they didn't have even a rudimentary planetary defense system, let alone any military installations worth defending. And if they were concerned enough about their privacy to erect this formidable a barrier, why shield only this single little sliver of their world? Thinking like both a Klingon and an engineer, it didn't make any sense to her—unless maybe the site had some bizarre religious significance to the Ryol. She considered notifying the captain or Chakotay about her discovery, but decided to wait until she had a firmer understanding of the facts involved. She'd made a fool of herself once already on this mission, and that was more than enough for one stardate. There was no need to disturb them just yet, not over a few anomalous readings.

"Excuse me, Lieutenant." Torres looked up. It was Ensign Erin Jourdan, a blond Terran assigned to the port aft Ops console when Harry Kim was off-duty. Jourdan watched her quizzically; Torres wondered if she'd been growling again. "Is there anything I can help you with?" Jourdan asked.

"Yes," Torres snapped. "Get me a raktajino. I'm going to be here for a while."

Dozing in the shade beneath the lush purple foliage of his favorite tree, Harry Kim could barely keep his eyes open. His memories of last night's activities were foggy, although he was pretty sure he had sampled too much Ryol wine. He wasn't even sure when he had returned to *Voyager* last night, just that he had woken up in his own bed sometime after noon, badly in need of a shower and fresh coffee. Searching his memory, he came up with vague images of watching a crimson sunrise in the company of two very friendly Ryol women. He couldn't recall their names at the moment, but he remembered their eyes: green at first, then darkening to midnight blackness. . . . He yawned loudly, then let his eyelids droop again. A nap was sounding better and better.

Something landed heavily a few centimeters away from him, rousing Kim from half-sleep. He saw a scruffy red figure shambling toward him and recognized the young neffaler he had met a few days ago in this very same park. "Hi there, little guy," he said. "I was hoping I'd run into you again."

The neffaler chirped in reply. It appeared to recognize Kim as well. There was no sign of the shyness or trepidation it had displayed during their first encounter. The neffaler plopped down in the grass beside Kim, its large eyes searching the Starfleet officer expectantly.

"Are you looking for the clarinet?" Kim guessed. "Is that it?"

The neffaler chirped again, but Kim could only guess what the small creature was trying to say. His Universal Translator had its limits, alas, and talking to animals was beyond it. The verbal translation algorithms needed an actual language to work with.

Still, Kim thought he had a pretty good idea what the neffaler wanted.

He stuck his hand into a pocket and withdrew a shiny white object. "Here," he said, offering the object to his visitor. It was a plastic flute, about five centimeters long, with twelve tiny holes drilled into the top of the instrument, one for each of the neffaler's twelve fingers. A thin white cord hung in a loop from one end of the flute. "I made this for you especially."

The neffaler grasped the flute eagerly. Kim smiled; the little whistle had cost him one replicator coupon, but it was worth it to see the little creature's obvious delight. The neffaler had a good memory, too. This time it did not waste any time blowing into the wrong end, but located the proper mouthpiece immediately. Its whiskered little cheeks swelled as it puffed energetically on the whistle, producing a string of loud toots. Kim let the creature improvise for a few minutes, then reached out slowly and rearranged the neffaler's fingers, showing it how it could produce different notes by covering one or more of the holes along the top of the instrument. He was amazed at how thin and fragile the little animal's fingers were. They were nothing but skin and bone and bristles. "Boy," he said, "I'm not sure they're feeding you guys enough."

Again, the neffaler caught on quickly, shifting its fingers along the length of the flute to vary the sounds its new toy emitted. Pretty soon it was coming shockingly close to playing something like an actual tune. Kim shook his head in amazed appreciation. "You're a little monkey Mozart," he said out loud. "Who would've guessed it?"

He wondered momentarily if teaching a domesticated primate to play the flute violated the Prime Directive in some manner, then decided not to worry about it. The Prime Directive concerned itself with sentient cultures, not their pets, and, judging from last night's busy dance floor, the Ryol already knew plenty about making music. Besides, he thought, watching the young neffaler play happily with his new flute, the little guy was just too cute to resist.

Yawning despite himself, Kim leaned back and rested his head against the trunk of the tree. He closed his eyes and drifted off, the sound of the neffaler's freshly invented music playing in his ears.

Kes heard the waves before she saw them. Night had fallen and the lamps illuminating the beachside path were not bright enough to cast their light all the way to the water's edge, but her shell-shaped ears detected the soothing susuration of the waves lapping against the shore. The breeze blowing off the harbor was just cool enough to be refreshing. She peered into the darkness, looking for the water and dreading whatever ghastly secrets it might hold. *How can such a peaceful setting,* she wondered, *hold such terror for me?*

Tuvok would not approve of this nocturnal expedition, Kes knew, but she could not forget the voices that had called out to her. She had felt a similar compulsion years ago, when the Ocampa Elders forbade her to leave their underground city and seek out the world above. She had ignored their warnings, as she now ignored Tuvok's sound advice, and encountered danger, yes, but also a universe of wonders that she had barely dared to dream about. She had no idea what awaited her beyond the black shore, but she knew she had to find out.

"You know," Neelix said, walking beside her, "the more I think about it, the more I think this beach would be the perfect site for a special on-location episode of *A Briefing with Neelix*." Because he deemed it too late to go swimming, he was wearing his usual motley-colored suit, just as she had donned her everyday attire. Only the commbadges pinned to their chests identified them as *Voyager* personnel. "Just think of the footage I could get if I came back tomorrow afternoon. Minute after minute of carefree crew members running and playing on the beach in their individually replicated swimsuits."

"I don't know," Kes said, grateful for a distraction from her worries. "Do you think anyone will really want to watch a full hour of nothing but beach scenes?"

Harry Kim awoke with a start in the now-darkened garden. He had been dreaming of a pair of irresistible Ryol women with eyes of ebony black, but was surprised to find that the sun had gone down while he slept. *How long was I out?* he wondered. *I must have been more exhausted than I realized.* The last thing he remembered was listening to his little neffaler friend playing with the toy flute.

He sat up and scanned his surrounding while his eyes struggled to adjust to the darkness. The leafy boughs above him blocked out whatever moonlight might have been available, although he could glimpse the bright lights of the city through the violet hedges to the east. He automatically checked to see if his commbadge was still in place, and was relieved to feel the cool metal insignia beneath his fingers.

Good thing Ryolanov is so safe and peaceful, he thought. A tourist who nodded off at *Deep Space Nine* or Risa was likely to wake up wearing nothing but his socks. Thank goodness the nearest Ferengi was several hundred light-years away. He was glad to discover he still had his phaser, too.

His eyes began to get used to the shadows. Glancing around, he spotted no sign of his newfound neffaler buddy and the toy flute. *Must have gotten bored and wandered off,* Kim decided, heartened that the little creature had thought enough of his gift to take the cheap plastic whistle with it. He stood up and stretched, then wiped bits of leafs and twigs off his trousers. *Now what?* he wondered. He wasn't due back on the bridge until tomorrow morning. Maybe he should hike into town and try to hook up with either Tom or B'Elanna. He wasn't quite sure where to find his friends, although he guessed that neither of them would return to the same dance club where they'd run into so much trouble the night before. Frankly, given B'Elanna's general opinion of the Ryol, he'd be surprised if she beamed back to the planet again.

A familiar chirp interrupted his contemplation. He looked up and saw a small shadowy figure nestled in the branches overhead. The shiny white whistle hung from the cord around the neffaler's neck. "Well, hello," Kim said. "I thought you were long gone."

The neffaler leaped onto the lawn beside Kim, chirping noisily. "I'm glad to see you, too," Kim said, crouching down on bended knees so he could talk to the little animal face to face, more or less. The neffaler lifted one scrawny hand toward Kim. In the dim light, he glimpsed a pale yellowish object clutched between the creature's fingers.

"What's that?" Kim asked. The neffaler waved the item in front of Kim's hand. "For me?"

The neffaler chirped once, which Kim took for a yes. He reached out and gently lifted the object out of the young creature's outstretched hand. It felt dry and brittle in his grasp, like old bone or sea shell. Deep grooves or scratches covered the surface of the artifact, although sections of it still felt smooth and polished.

He stepped away from the shade of the old tree in order to see the gift better. *The little neffaler must have gone and retrieved this,* he guessed, *while I was snoozing.* A moonbeam penetrated the leafy foliage overhead, illuminating one small portion of the garden. Kim held the artifact up to the moonlight.

It was bone all right, crescent-shaped and yellowed with age. Kim hoped the little neffaler had not lifted the artifact from some Ryol's private collection. It certainly looked old enough to be a museum piece. At one time, it appeared, some sort of symbols or inscription had been etched on the surface, but the ancient marks had been worn away until they were barely visible. The outer curve of the crescent was chipped and broken, while hairline fractures ran along the length of the object. He handled the artifact gingerly, turning it over in his hands while he tried to identify its function. The bone was lighter than it looked. Looking more closely, he saw that it had been hollowed out, leaving open slits, less than a millimeter wide, on both sides of the crescent. When he peered through the narrow gap inside the crescent, he could see a sliver of moonlight peeking through from the other side of the object. Five small holes had been poked in the top of the bone. There might have been six holes originally, but part of the upper layer had broken off over the years, making it hard to tell.

Less than a meter away, the neffaler tugged excitedly on its flute, pulling the thin white cord taut while the small creature chirped at Kim. An idea occurred to him. He raised the artifact in front of his mouth, holding the crescent parallel to the lawn beneath his feet. It was a tight fit—his jaw was much larger than any neffaler's—but he managed to place the inner curve of the crescent against his lips. He blew into the open slit.

Fine black dust sprayed from the outer curve of the artifact, raining down on the head of the neffaler, who coughed and sneezed and backed away a few meters. Obviously, no one had tried blowing on this instrument for a very long time, but a shrill piercing whistle escaped the cracked and crumbling artifact nonetheless. Kim clamped his fingers over the five surviving holes and heard the pitch of the whistle change in response. The little neffaler reacted to the harsh siren Kim produced. He placed both hands over his ears while his monkeylike features wrinkled comically.

Lifting the antique instrument away from his face, Kim laughed at the tiny creature's expression. So much for any Prime Directive worries, he thought. Clearly he wasn't the first person to introduce the concept of a whistle to a neffaler, although his little plastic flute had been a hit anyway. He wondered when was the last time any neffaler got a new toy to play with. A long time ago, probably. Despite their obvious warmth and generosity, the Ryol seemed to spare precious little affection or attention on their pets.

Must be some peculiar cultural thing, Kim guessed, shrugging his shoulders. Starfleet had taught him to expect a wide variety of attitudes from alien civilizations on almost every topic. One culture's beloved pet, he reminded himself, was another race's favorite hors d'oeuvre. He shouldn't be too quick to pass judgment on the apparent lack of concern of the Ryol for the neffaler.

Still, he thought, watching the cute little animal start to toot happily on its plastic flute, the Ryol don't know what they're missing. Handling the ancient bone instrument carefully, he followed the neffaler's lead, gradually discovering the range of sounds still available to the decrepit artifact.

Beneath the pale moonlight, accompanied by the faint rustling of the leaves and shrubs, the Starfleet officer and the naked inarticulate primate shared a private duet.

Kes and Neelix kept to the path as they approached the beach. Kes regretted that yesterday's nightmarish psychic experience had cast a shadow over this nocturnal stroll. What a lovely romantic walk they might have had otherwise. Looking into the night, listening to the waves, inhaling the spicy aroma of the sea, she was unsure how to employ her other, more mysterious senses. Part of her wanted to erect a firm psychic wall, just as Tuvok had taught her, against any invasive telepathic transmissions, while curiosity and a sense of responsibility compelled her to open herself up to whatever had contacted her before. Remembering those anguished voices, and the suffocating darkness that had enveloped her despite the warm Ryol sun, she braced herself for more of the same.

"Are you all right?" Neelix asked. Concern was written on his face as plainly as the lighted display on a padd. He placed a comforting arm around her. "You're trembling," he observed. "We can go back to the ship if you want. You don't have to do this."

"No," she said, shaking her head. "There was something here, something that called to me. I have to find out what it was. Who they are."

"For your sake?" he asked. "Or for theirs?"

"I don't know," she admitted. So far, she had not detected anything at all. She listened to the distant waves, spilling over the beach somewhere beyond the radiance of the lamps. "Perhaps we should get closer to the water," she suggested.

"Whatever you say," Neelix agreed. They stepped off the solid pathway, their boots sinking into the granular substance of the beach. Following the sound of the water, they paced away from the light. "Careful," he said, holding on to her arm. "Watch your step." The closer they got to the shore, the more the wet black spheres mixed with the sea water to form a slippery colloidal film beneath their boots.

They had only walked a few meters away from the path when a harsh white light greeted their faces, startling Kes. "What?" she exclaimed, her heart pounding. Neelix tightened his grip upon her arm.

The light sank below their faces, shining instead on the commbadges on their chests. Blinking her eyes to dispel the aftereffects of the sudden glare, Kes saw a brawny Ryol male standing on the other side of the light, which came, she saw, from a small crystal he held in his upraised palm. His green eyes reflected the light in his hand, giving his face an eerie inhuman look.

"Sorry to surprise you," the Ryol said. Aside from the shining eyes, he could have been the brother of the lifeguard who had come to her assistance the day before. "I'm going to have to ask you to turn around. The beach is restricted at night."

"Restricted?" Neelix asked. "Why?" Kes recognized the tone is his voice. Neelix had switched into his "investigative journalist" mode.

"Dangerous tides," the man replied. "It's not safe for wading, let alone swimming, when the tide is going out or coming in. An undertow can drag you out to sea before you can catch your breath." The Ryol smiled at them, his flawless white teeth gleaming. "The last thing we want is for you or any of our other guests to suffer a tragic accident."

His explanation sounded plausible enough to Kes, who knew next to nothing about tides and undertows. Still, she strained her extrasensory faculties in hopes of dredging up some answer from the mysterious depths of the unseen water. Was it merely a lingering memory, or could she hear the faint echo of yesterday's scream, still calling out to her with voices filled with wordless agony? A wave of shock and despair swept over her, dimming her vision and turning her legs to rubber. Her knees buckled, and she would have fallen if not for Neelix's support.

"Is something the matter?" The Ryol lifeguard eyed her suspiciously.

"Not at all," Neelix said heartily. "It's been a long and active day, that's all. There's so much to do on this wonderful planet of yours!" His grip on Kes relaxed as her head cleared and she secured her footing. "Thank you for your concern, but I guess we'll be on our way now. I assume that the beach will open again in the morning?"

"Of course," the Ryol said. Moving his hand, he shined the light toward the path. The fused black pellets glistened when the brilliant beam fell upon them. "Let me escort you back to the path."

"Oh, that's not necessary," Neelix objected. "We can find our own way."

"I insist," the Ryol said. His pupils expanded ominously. He swung the beam back and forth between the path and the two visitors from *Voyager*. "You are strangers on Ryolanov. It is the least I can do."

As he led them away, Kes looked back over her shoulder at the impenetrable darkness where the water hid. Her momentary weakness had passed, but not her determination to find the source of the disturbing sights and sounds that had assaulted her untapped psychic resources. Tides or no tides, she couldn't help feeling that the Ryol were hiding something here. She wondered if Neelix felt the same way.

I hear you, she thought to the bodiless voices that wailed on the periphery of her conscious mind. *I will stop your pain if I can. I promise.*

CHAPTER
8

CHAKOTAY GLANCED DOWN AT THE DIGITAL DISPLAY ON his padd. It was 20:11. Susan Tukwila was over ten minutes late for bridge duty. He frowned. This wasn't like her. Tukwila had been a good soldier when they had both served in the Maquis. Guerrilla operations in the Demilitarized Zone had often required split-second timing, and he had always been able to count on Susan to hold up her end of the operation. He remembered one occasion when they had been ambushed by an "unauthorized" Cardassian death squad; only Susan Tukwila's quick thinking had kept a close call from becoming a disaster.

So where in blazes is she now? he fumed. He tapped his fingers against the arm of the captain's chair. This was hardly an emergency situation, he admitted, but even routine bridge duty required discipline and diligence. He didn't anticipate any sort of crisis over the next few hours, just more time spent cruising in orbit above Ryolanov, but he took his responsibility to manage the bridge in the captain's absence very seriously, more so than Tukwila apparently. Besides, he thought, any misconduct on the part of one of his former comrades-in-arms reflected badly on all the Maquis now serving on *Voyager*. Chakotay considered himself personally responsible for the conduct of every Maquis aboard, and it was a burden that sometimes weighed heavily on him.

It hadn't been easy trying to integrate an ad-hoc army of rebels and freedom fighters into an efficiently run Starfleet organization. He had his success stories, most notably B'Elanna Torres, despite her recent clash with that Ryol male, but he'd had more than his share of failures, too. Seska. Michael Jonas. Lon Suder. All three of them had proved dangerous to *Voyager* and her crew; all had died violently. The names haunted his memory and plagued his conscience with recriminations of poor judgment and leadership. Was there something he could have done to avert Seska's treachery? Or Jonas's? Should he have done something about Lon Suder's homicidal tendencies before they ended in murder? At least, he recalled, Suder had redeemed himself somewhat before the Kazon killed him. Chakotay prayed that he would not be forced to add Susan Tukwila's name to his private list of shame.

Finally, at precisely 20:15, the turbolift doors slid open and Tukwila stepped hurriedly onto the bridge. Her sleek black hair was loose and uncombed in the back. Her commbadge was stuck upside down on the front of her black-and-yellow Starfleet uniform. Chakotay spotted dark circles under her eyes; she looked badly in need of a good night's sleep.

"You're late, Ensign," he announced. It still felt odd, sometimes, to address Maquis personnel by Starfleet ranks. At moments like this, he was acutely aware that very few Maquis crew members had actually completed the Academy. His frown deepened. He didn't like being embarrassed by his own people.

"Sorry, Commander," she blurted out, rushing to take her place at the port aft Ops console. Her voice sounded hoarser than usual. Too much time, Chakotay wondered, in loud and smoky Ryol clubs? He recalled that he had personally recommended her transfer from stellar cartography to the bridge. It didn't make him feel any better.

He rose slowly from the captain's chair, then marched over to where Tukwila was standing. Although the rest of the bridge crew kept their faces turned conspicuously toward the forward viewscreen, Chakotay knew that the entire bridge was holding its collective breath, waiting to see what he would do next. He milked the moment for maximum drama before reaching over and plucking the inverted commbadge from Tukwila's uniform. "Shore leave is no excuse for sloppiness, Ensign," he said, handing the shiny metal badge back to her.

For a long instant, Tukwila looked on the verge of saying something that Chakotay knew he didn't want to hear. Above the puffy shadows that sagged beneath her eyes, those familiar dark orbs flashed with anger and defiance. Chakotay had admired that rebellious spirit once, when it was directed at the Cardassian usurpers who had tried to drive Federation colonists from their homes. Now that it was directed at him, he didn't know how to feel. *Don't do it, Susan,* he thought.

At the last moment, she thought better of whatever retort had sprung to mind. Maintaining a stony silence, she took the badge and fixed it correctly to her chest. Standing so near to her, Chakotay saw that the collar of her uniform was badly wrinkled. The gray fabric looked like it hadn't been freshly replicated for a week. "This is a long trip," he said, frowning at this further evidence of Tukwila's sloppiness. "We can't afford to let our standards slip so soon."

"Like it really matters," she said, a smirk upon her face.

"What was that, Ensign?" Chakotay asked. "I didn't hear you."

She lifted her gaze from her feet. "With all due respect, sir, we're light-years from the Federation. What does all this Starfleet rigamarole really matter?" Her expression grew even more scornful. "It's not like we're due for an inspection anytime soon."

"That Starfleet 'rigamarole' is what's going to keep us alive on this voyage," Chakotay said, loud enough for the entire bridge to hear. "Here in the Delta Quadrant, far from the safety of the Federation, we need *more* discipline and dedication, not less. There's no room for error out here, nor for lax standards." Tukwila opened her mouth to reply, but he cut her off. "Now is not the time or the place to debate the captain's policies. I expect every crew member to execute their duties to the best of their abilities. That will be all, Ensign."

He turned his back on Tukwila and walked back to the captain's chair. A hush fell over the bridge; Chakotay heard only the humming of the machinery and the occasional rustle of someone shifting nervously in their seat. He resolved to talk to the captain about Tukwila's lapses as soon as possible; he didn't need to check with Neelix to know a morale problem when he saw one.

Days had passed, and hours of concentrated toil, but the enigmatic region beneath the shields had stubbornly refused to divulge its secrets to B'Elanna Torres. It was maddening. She could have reported the exact number of petals on any one flower anywhere else on Ryolanov, but this single piece of planet resisted all her efforts to probe its elusive mysteries.

Granted, she reminded herself, she had not been able to devote all her waking hours to the challenge. The day-to-day duties of heading Engineering, including keeping a close eye on their dwindling supply of crystallized dilithium, took up much of her time, as did her irritating requirements for food and exercise. *At least,* she thought, *no one is pressuring me anymore to "enjoy" some shore leave.* Her little tiff with Nimdir the Idiot had cured everybody of that particular misconception. The captain had not actually ordered her to stay on the ship, but Torres knew that her superiors would breathe a good deal easier if she kept her distance from the planet's surface.

Fine with me, she thought as she strode onto the bridge. She walked straight toward the port forward science console. A sullen-looking Susan Tukwila was at the conn, she noticed; Chakotay sat in the captain's seat. "Good morning, Lieutenant," he said as she passed him. She grunted a reply, intent on her mission.

Time to break out the big guns, she thought. She had given the problem a lot of consideration last night, when she was supposed to have been sleeping, and the long-range sensors seemed like her best bet. These sensors were the most powerful scientific instruments on *Voyager,* designed to monitor interstellar phenomena at a range of approximately five to seventeen light-years, depending on the degree of resolution required. Turning the long-range sensors on a planetary surface from an orbital location was akin to using an electron microscope to inspect one's fingernails, or like unleashing a full salvo of photon torpedoes to sterilize a tribble, but Torres could not imagine that any sort of ground-based shielding would be able to stand up against the sheer observational power of the long-range sensors.

With my luck, she thought, *this will turn out to be*

just a sacred burial site or something like that. Nothing to do with dilithium at all.

"Request permission to access the long-range sensors," she said to Chakotay. Ordinarily, these sensors were employed to detect potential flight hazards such as micrometeoroids or other debris. This function was less essential when the ship was locked in to a planetary orbit; short-range navigational sensors could watch out for stray satellites and space garbage when *Voyager* was traveling at significantly sub-light speeds. Still, Torres felt obliged to check with the commander before diverting the long-range sensors to another purpose.

Chakotay gave her a curious expression. Torres wondered if he knew how attractive he was. "Something up, Lieutenant?" he asked.

"Just an experiment," she answered, "relating to that supply problem we discussed a few days ago." She didn't want to admit how much time she had spent trying to probe one tiny corner of Ryolanov until she came up with some hard results. *Probably just the hidden vault of the Ryol crown jewels,* she thought, *or the Elder's private harem.* She had imagined every possible explanation for the secrecy surrounding this area; none of them had convinced her that the captain needed to be notified immediately— or that she would be better off abandoning the search. *Let's find out what you're hiding down there,* she thought, *once and for all.*

Her explanation satisfied Chakotay. "Proceed," he told her, then turned his attention to a padd resting on the arm of his chair. Torres called up the relevant coordinates from the ship's computer.

According to the overall map of Ryolanov now stored in *Voyager*'s neural gel-packs, the blacked-out region corresponded to a harbor area located near the capital city of Ryolaler. Probably the same beach, she thought, that Neelix was raving about on this morning's news broadcast. This knowledge only puzzled Torres more. Why shield from observation the very same stretch of sand and sea that *Voyager's* crew was frolicking upon daily? She had spent sleepless nights trying to figure that one out, but now, perhaps, the answer was finally within reach.

She transferred control of the long-range sensors to the science console, then focused the full array of sensors on the appropriate planetary coordinates. She opted for a low-resolution scan at first; the last thing she wanted was a subatomic analysis of a single pellet of sand.

The Ryol shields resisted the scans at first. Electronic static muddied the sensor readouts, making them difficult to determine, but she upped the power of the long-range sensors and the shields crumpled like tissue paper before phaser fire. *Success,* Torres thought jubilantly, experiencing a Klingon's savage joy at victory over a particularly hated foe. She crossed her fingers, an ancient Earth custom her human father had taught her, hoping to see the telltale energy spike that would announce the presence of dilithium crystals.

It wasn't there.

Disappointment nearly overwhelmed her. All that work with nothing to show for it! She felt like gutting the control panel with her bare hands, then she noticed something odd about the readings from the parametric subspace field stress sensor. It wasn't the energy spike she was looking for—that would have showed up on the data from the variable frequency EM flux sensor—but what could cause a subspace fluctuation of that sort on the planet's surface? Intrigued, she adjusted the main deflector emitter screen on the subspace scanner, then double-checked her findings against the input from the gravimetric distortion scanner. *Intriguing,* she thought as she inspected the new data, her anger and disappointment now forgotten. There was definitely something down there, and confined to one discrete location. *Not dilithium, not even uncrystallized, but maybe*—a rush of adrenaline raced through her body as she considered the possibilities—*could it possibly be . . . antimatter?*

What could be the Ryol be doing with antimatter, she wondered, and why only in one place on the entire planet? She had found the secret of the Ryol, she knew it, but she didn't want to alert the captain until she was sure she knew what it meant. Captain Janeway might think she was holding some sort of irrational Klingon grudge against the Ryol on account of that altercation at the dance club. Torres wanted to present a fair, unbiased, and totally incontrovertible report on the hidden stash of antimatter before finding the Ryol guilty of gross and doubtless malevolent intention. *Next time,* she thought vindictively at the planet below, *maybe you'll tell me what I want the first time I ask.*

"Let's take a closer look at you," she muttered to the display panel as she zoomed in on the region in question with the passive neutrino imaging scanner. A map of Ryolanov appeared on her screen, a flashing blue dot marking the location of the subspace irregularities. "Visual," she requested, and another image appeared in the lower left-hand corner of the screen. Torres saw waves crashing upon a beach; in the distance, she recognized the tips of several tall pyramids. One of them, she felt sure, was the very same dance club where she had disgraced herself on her first and only trip to the planet. She checked her memory against the computer's. Sure enough, just as she'd suspected, the minute subspace fluctuations were coming from the harbor outside Ryolaler.

Under the beach? Torres didn't understand. She couldn't be positive it was antimatter, not from this high in orbit, but if it was, then it couldn't possibly be a natural phenomenon. So why were the Ryol hoarding antimatter under the harbor? And if it was for some variety of matter-antimatter power station, then how were they managing to regulate the energy output without any dilithium?

"Find anything interesting, B'Elanna?" Chakotay asked. He walked over to glance over her shoulder, then looked vaguely surprised to find a pretty seascape occupying a portion of Torres's monitor.

"Maybe, sir," she answered. "Not dilithium, I'm afraid, but I am picking up some odd readings that I can't entirely account for."

"Anything I should report to the captain?" Chakotay asked.

"Not just yet, sir," Torres said. A full Klingon, she thought, would simply rush to judgment, heedless of the consequences; she prided herself on being more patient and exacting, at least most of the time. "I'll let you know after I get back from the surface."

Up until now, she had thought she'd had enough of shore leave and Ryolanov. Suddenly, though, the beach was sounding a lot more interesting.

"Thanks for seeing me right away, Doctor," Harry Kim said warmly. Kes guessed that Harry was trying to make up for his rude behavior the last time he visited the sickbay. He sat on the edge of a biobed while The Doctor scanned him with a medical tricorder. Kes stood nearby, only half watching the examination. Her mind was still filled with the menacing impressions she had picked up on the planet's surface. Were they the psychic residue of some long-ago catastrophe, she wondered, or presentiments of impending danger? If only she knew more about her own telepathic abilities!

"I have nothing but time, Ensign," The Doctor stated. "Aside from a few bad cases of sunburn, our visit to Ryolanov has provided me with little in the way of stimulating medical emergencies. Speaking of which"—he peered at the lightly browned tint of Kim's face—"I assume you have been assiduous in applying your Starfleet-issue protective solar radiation blocker?"

"Everyday, Doc, I promise," Kim said.

"Very good," The Doctor pronounced. "Now then, what exactly was the nature of your complaint?"

Kim shrugged. "It's nothing I can put my finger on. I've just been feeling kind of run-down and groggy." He covered his mouth while he yawned. "Sorry about that. I'm finding it hard to stay awake."

"I see," The Doctor said, inspecting the readings on his tricorder. "Well, your metabolism seems a little sluggish and you're a trifle anemic, but otherwise there doesn't appear to be anything seriously wrong with you. Too much strenuous recreational activity is my guess."

Harry blushed. "That's one way of putting it, I suppose." Kes wondered why he looked so embarrassed.

The Doctor rolled his eyes. "Frankly, I don't understand the incredible appeal of this particular planet. You're not the first crew member I've treated who has vacationed his or herself to the point of exhaustion. Why, Ensign Jourdan sprained her ankle dancing, then went out waterskiing the very next day! Against doctor's orders, I might add."

"Oh, you've got to see this place!" Harry Kim enthused. "The sun, the waves—" A sheepish look materialized on his face as he realized what he was saying. "Er, no offense, Doctor. That is, I mean—"

The Doctor dismissed Kim's apologies with a curt wave of his hand. "No need to stammer, Ensign," he said. "As a hologram, I am naturally obliged to take your word for it when it comes to the astonishing attractions of this apparently marvelous planet. Fortunately, my programming does not instill in me the same reckless susceptibility for foreign climes that seems to override the common sense of you organic beings."

Kes didn't believe a word of it. She knew The Doctor's physical limitations—his inability to exist outside a specially equipped holographic environment—frustrated him more than he would ever admit. One of her greatest fears was that one day the entire crew might be forced to abandon *Voyager*—leaving The Doctor behind. "What about you?" he asked her. "Are you equally enraptured with this veritable paradise?"

The Doctor had evidently forgotten, at least for the moment, her vague and intangible fears about the planet. "I don't know," she admitted. "It certainly seems beautiful." She inspected Kim more closely; Harry did seem more fatigued than usual. His tanned features looked drawn and tired, although his spirits were undeniably high. Was The Doctor right, she wondered. Had Harry simply overexerted himself on Ryolanov—or was something terrible happening to them all?

No, she thought, *that was ridiculous.* Harry was just having too much fun, like most everybody else on *Voyager*. She shook her head, chasing away her fears. It was all the voices' fault, she thought. The bodiless screams within her mind had her looking for horrors everywhere, and doubting her own instincts. She didn't know what she really felt anymore.

Everyone else is happy to be here, she thought. *What's wrong with me?*

"Morale again?" Janeway asked Chakotay. Her first officer had joined her in her ready room for a private briefing. He waited by her desk while she watered the decorative plants by the door. Thankfully, she thought, it had never been necessary to ration water aboard *Voyager;* otherwise her plants would hardly have stayed so green. "I don't understand," she said. "I thought Ryolanov was the solution to our morale problems."

"So did I," Chakotay conceded. "Certainly, the mood has improved among the crew, maybe too much so."

"What do you mean?" Janeway asked. She sat down behind her desk. It felt good to get off her feet. She had spent most of the last few days accompanying Varathael on an exhausting whirl of diplomatic functions. At times, she felt like she had personally met and greeted every Ryol on the continent, yet there always seemed to be another reception or welcoming ceremony. *What no one tells you,* she thought, *is that the key to a city can get awful heavy sometimes.* Still, if it meant better relations between *Voyager* and the Ryol, and a much-needed break for her crew, then she was determined to shake as many hands and attend as many banquets as necessary. It bothered her that Chakotay seemed to be suggesting that all her efforts might have produced precisely the opposite effect than the one she had hoped for. *Too bad,* she thought, *that Chakotay usually knows what he's talking about.*

He told her about his confrontation with Susan Tukwila on the bridge. "Unfortunately," he continued, "this is not an isolated incident, only an extreme example of a syndrome that seems to be overtaking much of the crew. According to Tuvok, whom I consulted before raising this matter with you, the scientific data collected by various away teams to the planet has been sloppy and incomplete. B'Elanna reports a slight rise in safety violations in engineering, while The Doctor confirms a rash of careless accidents among the crew, both aboard the ship and down on Ryolanov." He paused a moment before summing up. "On their own, none of these incidents amounts to much. Taken together, however, they point toward a general lack of discipline—and a possibly dangerous level of fatigue—all through the crew."

Myself included, Janeway thought. Certainly she felt badly in need of a nap. It was all she could do to keep her eyes open, despite an extra cup of coffee this morning. This was more than her usual midday drowsiness; she felt absolutely exhausted. "How serious is this?" she asked. "Surely, we're not looking at a 'Mutiny on the Bounty' type situation here?"

"You'll have to refresh my memory there," Chakotay admitted. "We didn't have much opportunity to brush up on history in the Demilitarized Zone."

"The *Bounty* was a British sailing vessel of the late eighteenth century," she explained, "whose crew succumbed to the exotic delights of Tahiti. When the captain tried to restore discipline and force the crew to sail back to England, they rebelled and took over the ship."

"I remember now," Chakotay said, nodding. "I think I played a holographic version of the story back at the Academy."

"For my sake, I hope you didn't cast yourself as Fletcher Christian," Janeway commented, recalling the *Bounty's* first officer—who ended up being the leader of the mutineers.

"I don't think so," Chakotay said with a grin.

"Good," she said. "I wasn't looking forward to playing Captain Bligh." Her voice acquired a more somber tone. "Seriously, how bad is it?"

Chakotay paused before answering. "I don't know," he said thoughtfully. "I'm not worried about an actual mutiny. Our crew's gone through too much together to think they'd turn on each other now. Still, there's no doubt in my mind that excess recreation on Ryolanov is undermining the crew's ability to perform their duties. I would be shirking my own responsibilities if I didn't call the matter to your attention."

"And I appreciate it," Janeway said. "This isn't the

first time, though, that we've dropped anchor at a very hospitable port. Remember the Sikarians? Not to mention the 37's." She recalled the flourishing human society formed by Amelia Earhart and other refugees from the Alpha Quadrant. If ever *Voyager* had been tempted to abandon its long trek back to the Federation, it had been there. "In the end," she reminded Chakotay, "this crew has always managed to stay focused on the journey home."

She gazed out the porthole behind her desk, contemplating the beckoning stars. Earth was out there somewhere, its blazing sun too distant to be seen. She wondered if she would ever see Earth again. "The crew has been under enormous pressures the last few years," she said. "Perhaps they deserve a chance to blow off some steam."

"As long as that's all that blows," Chakotay said. "I hate to sound like the voice of doom and gloom. That's usually Tuvok's job. But, well, there's something else you ought to know about."

"What?" Janeway asked, turning away from the window. She ignored his little dig at Tuvok; she knew that Chakotay and Tuvok were often at odds, just as she knew that neither of the two men would ever let their personal feelings about each other get in the way of their duties aboard the ship. But what was worrying Chakotay now? She could tell that her first officer felt slightly uncomfortable bringing up the subject, whatever it was.

"I was in my cabin," he began, "getting in touch with my spirit guide. . . ." Chakotay described the eerie nature of his recent vision-quest, including the malevolent beastlike presence that had attacked him within his own mind. "I can't tell you exactly what this vision means," he said, "but the spirits seemed determined to warn me about something."

"I see," Janeway responded. She didn't quite know what to make of Chakotay's experience. A scientist by training, she resisted mysticism, preferring data derived from the objective analysis of the physical world. On the other hand, she had to concede that many advanced cultures, from the Vulcans to the Bajorans, placed a good deal of faith in extrasensory revelations. She had worked beside Tuvok for too many years not to respect his psychic gifts, while Chakotay had personally introduced Janeway to her own spirit guide. But was the threat Chakotay had detected simply of a spiritual nature or was it something more concrete? *Where there's smoke, there's probably fire,* she thought, *but what kind of fire?*

A wave of weariness washed over her. There was too much to worry about and not enough hours in the day. *Seventy-five years to home,* she thought. The sheer enormity of her task crashed down on her spirits. She could never truly rest, she realized, until she had safely delivered the crew back to the lives and loved ones they had lost, but there was such a long, long way to go. . . .

"Captain," Chakotay said. For a second, she had forgotten he was in the room. "Are you all right?"

"I'm fine," she said, shaking off the malaise that had briefly descended on her. "My mind was wandering, I guess." She smiled ruefully. "Not unlike Ensign Tukwila and the others."

She leaned forward to address him, resting her elbows on the top of her desk. "Your point is well taken, Commander. Too much shore leave can be a dangerous thing. For now, however, I'm inclined to take a wait-and-see attitude toward the situation. The crew seems to be enjoying this temporary respite from our long trip home. The last thing I want to do is overreact and spoil their vacation. Nor do we want to offend the Ryol; they can hardly be blamed if their generosity is undercutting the crew's discipline. You and I should keep an eye on things, though."

"I agree," Chakotay said. "I just wanted you to be

aware of the problem." He rose from his seat and walked toward the exit. As the door slid open, he turned and looked at Janeway once more. "Are you sure you're okay, Captain?" he asked. "No offense intended, but you seemed to fade away there for a moment."

She smiled and shrugged her shoulders. "Thanks for asking, but it's nothing you need to worry about. I'm just tired."

Very tired, she thought.

CHAPTER
9

ANTIMATTER OR NO ANTIMATTER, SOME JOBS COULDN'T wait. Starfleet regulations required that the impulse engines be regularly inspected for routine wear and tear, and B'Elanna Torres had no intention of letting her curiosity get in the way of proper care and maintenance for the engines, not while she was the chief engineer. Ryolanov—and that annoyingly secretive beach—would just have to wait.

Torres stood on a metallic gray catwalk overlooking the fusion generators in the starboard wing. Three armored spheres, each approximately six meters in diameter, were linked in sequence. Each sphere was constructed of eight layers of dispersion-strengthened hafnium excelinide and was designed to contain the energy released in a conventional proton-proton fusion reaction. As usual, Torres prayed fervently that nothing unfixable turned up during the inspection. In theory, impulse reaction chambers such as the spheres below should be replaced completely every 8,500 flight hours, a massive undertaking that generally required the full resources of an active starbase. Given that the nearest Federation starbase was nearly a lifetime away, Torres had little choice but to tend to her engines like a mother hen and hope they lasted as long as possible.

As she looked on, Ensign Erin Jourdan climbed inside the forward sphere to inspect its inner lining for cracks and abrasions. Jourdan was a blonde pale-skinned humanoid fresh out of Starfleet Academy. Torres noticed that Jourdan walked with a slight limp; she recalled that the ensign had sprained her ankle during some ridiculous accident on the planet's surface.

While Jourdan inspected the impulse reaction chamber from the inside, Torres checked the readouts provided by the ship's internal monitoring system. The IPS command coordinator was performing a level-three diagnostic when a muffled cry of alarm came from the interior of the IRC. "Erin?" Torres called out.

The scream grew louder, full of fear and agony. Adrenaline rushed through Torres's body. Dropping her padd, she leaped off the catwalk onto the top of the IRC. The armored plating rung harshly as her boots connected with the huge metal sphere, almost drowning out the sound of Jourdan's cries. *What's happening,* she wondered. Had some idiot been stupid enough to initiate a fusion reaction while Jourdan was inside the IRC? *No,* she realized, that would have incinerated Jourdan instantly, leaving no one to scream. Yanking open the hatch, she thrust her head into the opening that the young ensign had climbed through to enter the chamber. Her eyes instantly took in the situation.

Ensign Jourdan was sprawled at the bottom of the

sphere, clutching her leg. A white porcelain glaze, which Torres knew to be crystallized gulium fluoride, covered the curving inner wall of the chamber, while a cascade of icy slush poured out of an open vent several centimeters above Jourdan's head. The semi-frozen liquid steamed as it came into contact with the woman. That was pure deuterium, Torres knew, super-cooled to at least fourteen degrees Kelvin. Jourdan thrashed spasmodically in a steaming puddle of slush, her shrieks of anguish echoing off the walls of the chamber.

"Damn it," Torres snarled. Someone had carelessly forgotten to flush out the fuel injection conduits before today's planned inspection. When Jourdan opened the vents to observe the seal, the frigid slush must have coming gushing into the chamber, knocking her to the floor of the IRC and, almost literally, freezing her flesh and bones. "Hold on!" she shouted, climbing down the ladder Jourdan had attached to the side of the chamber. She tried to stay clear of the deuterium spray. An icy fog filled the IRC, sapping her strength and obscuring her vision. "Grab my hand!" she yelled, reaching out for the endangered ensign while she kept her other hand on the ladder.

"I can't!" Jourdan cried. "I can't move my legs!" The puddle expanded, swallowing more of Jourdan. She could barely keep her face above the water. "Oh my god, help me! It's so cold!"

"I'm trying!" Torres shouted. She climbed lower on the ladder, leaning out as far as she could reach. Spray from the gushing fuel vents splashed against her arm. Torres had to bite down on her lip to keep from screaming. The slush was so cold it burned.

She could barely see Jourdan through the swirling mist now. Her outstretched fingers sought out the origin of the other woman's desperate cries, but grasped only the fog. "Reach for me!" she shouted. "Grab my hand!"

Torres heard a frantic splash beneath her, then felt five cold fingers brush against hers. Jourdan's fingers felt like ice. They were cold and brittle and cracked loudly as Torres squeezed them. The fingers began to slip away, but Torres reached out and grabbed Jourdan by the wrist. Still hanging on to the ladder, she began to pull the other woman out of the slush. Her energy exhausted, Jourdan was dead weight; for once, Torres felt grateful for the strength she had inherited from her Klingon ancestors. A normal human would have never managed to drag Jourdan up the ladder and out of the reaction chamber.

Not until they were both safely collapsed on top of the IRC, with the hatch thrown shut behind them, did Torres inspect her own wounds. Her right arm looked badly frostbitten; the exposed flesh was blue and lifeless. She used her other hand to activate her commbadge. "Torres here." She gasped, breathing heavily. "Two for Sickbay."

Just wait until I get my hands, she thought, *on the moron who forgot to flush out the system!*

The sun was shining, a cool breeze was blowing, and Laazia was nowhere in sight. Tom Paris felt that all was right with the world. Not that he minded the Elder's daughter's company all that much, but, as undeniably appealing as Laazia was, Paris didn't want to get into any more trouble with Naxor and/or the captain. For now he was content to stretch out on an isolated strip of beach and bake in the sun next to his buddy Harry. "Life doesn't get much better than this," he declared. "Isn't that right, Harry? Harry?"

A snore was his friend's only reply. Paris chuckled. He couldn't blame Harry for snoozing. Ryolanov seemed specially designed to encourage goofing off. *Too bad it's so far off the beaten track,* he thought. The Ryol could make a fortune in the tourist trade. He didn't care what the holodeck dealers said; there was still nothing like the real thing.

And, for now, they pretty much had the whole place to themselves. No doubt there were plenty of visitors from *Voyager* mingling with Ryol on the sands closer to the city, but he and Harry had, in hopes of staying out of trouble, deliberately hiked until they were out of sight of the other swimmers and sunbathers. Rolling dunes of pebbly black sand, interspersed with tufts of emerald foliage, obscured his view of the Ryol city with all its opportunities for ghastly social blunders. *This was better,* he thought. *Nothing but peace and quiet all around.*

He rolled over onto his back. One of the nicer aspects of this beach, he'd discovered, was that the polished black granules did not stick to your skin the way ordinary sand did, thus eradicating the need for beach towels. The tiny pellets rolled and shifted beneath him, adjusting themselves to the contours of his body. He blinked his eyes against the bright crimson sunlight.

"Tom! Harry!"

Raising his hand to shield his eyes, Paris spotted two figures approaching. One of the figures was unmistakably female; for a second, he feared that Laazia had caught up with him already. Then he noted the long black hair, quite unlike Laazia's short golden down, and recognized the woman calling his name.

It was Susan Tukwila, very much out of uniform. A typically emaciated neffaler trailed behind her, lugging a large wicker basket. Judging from the exhausted expression on the creature's face, the basket was full of something heavy. Paris gave the neffaler only a moment's glance. Instead his eyes widened as Tukwila grew nearer. He nudged Kim with his elbow. "Wake up, Harry," he whispered. "You don't want to miss this."

"Huh?" Kim said. He sat up and rubbed his eyes.

"What did you do that for? I was having the greatest dream," he grumbled sleepily.

"Look up," Paris said.

Kim did. "Oh my goodness," he whispered. "I think I'm still dreaming."

The object of their rapt attention came strolling across the beach, then sank down onto the black sand between them. Paris couldn't believe his eyes. While both he and Harry had donned fairly traditional bathing trunks for their trip to the beach, Susan Tukwila wore the embroidered vest and short loincloth that the Ryol themselves seemed accustomed to. Paris decided she had never looked better.

"Going native?" he asked her. Catching up with Tukwila, the neffaler deposited the picnic basket on the sand behind the three humans. His mission accomplished, the monkeylike creature took a moment to rest in the shade of the basket.

"And why not?" Susan Tukwila responded defiantly. Paris was surprised by the heat in her voice. "Anything's better than slaving away for that humorless stick-in-the-mud, Chakotay. He's so caught up in his holier-than-thou Starfleet attitude that it's hard to remember that he was ever Maquis."

"Hey," Kim protested, tearing his eyes away from Tukwila's undraped form, "there's nothing wrong with being part of Starfleet." Paris recalled that Harry was the only individual present at this little beach party who had never served among the Maquis. Not counting the neffaler, of course.

"No offense intended, Harry," Tukwila said. "It's just that I'm not sure why we have to keep pretending that we're on some sort of formal mission when, let's face it, none of us is ever likely to see the Alpha Quadrant again." She stretched out on the gleaming black sand, a bronzed arm draped over her face to shield her eyes from the sun. She snapped her fingers and the neffaler fetched her a slice of juicy purple fruit from the basket. "Frankly, I think we should thank our lucky stars that we stumbled onto a paradise like Ryolanov while we're still young enough to enjoy it."

Paris sympathized with Tukwila's sour feelings toward Chakotay; he'd had more than one run-in with *Voyager*'s strict first officer himself. Even still, he found something disturbing about the direction Tukwila's thoughts seemed to be heading. "You're not suggesting what I think you're suggesting?" he asked.

"Staying here?" she answered boldly. "Of course that's what I'm saying." Taking a bite from the fruit, she raised herself up onto her elbows so that she could look both Kim and Paris in the eyes. "Think about it, guys: why should we risk our lives to get back to the Federation, growing old in the process, when we have everything we'll ever want right here?"

"But we *have* to go home," Kim objected, a horrified expression on his face.

"Why?" she challenged him. A thin stream of violet juice ran down her chin, dripping onto her chest. "Maybe some of you Starfleet types have ties and careers waiting for you, but all we Maquis have to look forward to are court martials or criminal prosecution. Sorry, but I'm not thrilled by the idea of spending seventy-five years in space just to get arrested at the end of the voyage. That's assuming, of course, that we don't get blown to pieces by the Kazon in the meantime, or reduced to spare parts by the Vidiians."

The neffaler lingered near Tukwila, wringing its hands apprehensively. She reached out and stroked the tousled red bristles atop the primate's head. "Cute little guy, isn't he? Kind of nervous, though. I guess he's not used to humans yet." She glanced at the basket. "Either of you want a snack?"

"Sure," Kim said. Paris nodded as well, then watched as their furry little servitor passed out pieces of the fruit to all three humans. Paris took a deep bite out of the fruit, tearing through its purple skin to the succulent pulp inside. It was delicious, tart, and sweet at the same time. *Kind of like a cross between blueberry and watermelon,* he decided. *I could get used to this.* It was definitely better than Neelix's usual brand of gourmet cooking.

"Great, isn't it?" Tukwila said, her broad smile stained a deep purple. "The Ryol call it *sotul.* Another good reason for sticking around, at least as far as I'm concerned."

"What about the cause?" Paris asked. "The noble campaign against the Cardassians? I thought that's what the Maquis were all about?" He didn't have any particularly strong feelings on the subject himself—unlike Chakotay and the others, he had joined the Maquis largely for lack of anything better to do—but he wanted to know how and why Susan had managed to put the Maquis agenda behind her.

Sorrow transformed Tukwila's expression. He heard pain and regret in her voice. "I haven't forgotten the cause. I'd give everything I have, even all this," she said, her gaze sweeping over the sunlit beach, the gentle waves, and the cloudless sky, "for a chance to make a difference again. But I have to be honest with myself about the hard facts of our situation. By the time *Voyager* gets back to the Alpha Quadrant, the conflict in the Demilitarized Zone will have been resolved, one way or another. Like it or not, I'm out of that fight for good. All I can do now is get on with my life."

"And that means staying on Ryolanov?" Kim asked. The distress in his voice frightened the neffaler, who scurried away to the shelter of the picnic basket. Kim seemed surprisingly upset by the notion, almost as though he was protesting a bit too much. Could it be, Paris wondered, that even Harry, forever homesick for his family and fiancée back on Earth, found Ryolanov more tempting than he was ready to admit? Now that was a scary idea.

"Maybe," she replied. "And I'm not the only person who's feeling that way." She gave Kim a searching look. "Seventy-five years is a long time, Harry. Are you sure you want to spend it on a Federation starship?"

"Yes!" Harry insisted. "I mean, no, of course not. But maybe we'll find a wormhole or something. The other Caretaker could send us home tomorrow, if only we can find her again, or so could another highly advanced entity—like another Q, for instance. There are shortcuts out there. There have to be. But we're not going to find them staying here."

"I don't see you in any hurry to leave," Tukwila teased him. She grabbed the waistband of his swimming trunks and snapped it playfully against his suntanned skin.

"There's a difference between shore leave and desertion," Kim said, scooting across the sand until he was out of reach of Tukwila's fingers. "We don't have to find the shortcut right away."

"And we might never find it," she declared, tossing him another piece of *sotul*. "There's a difference between wishful thinking and a genuine plan, too. I don't know about you, but I don't feel like gambling the rest of my life on the long-shot possibility that we just might happen to chance upon a quicker way home. It's been three years already, Harry. How long are you willing to wait for your miracle?"

Kim looked like he was running low on arguments. "I don't know," he said weakly. "Long enough, I guess." His eyes sought out Paris, looking to his friend for support and reinforcement. *Sorry,* Paris thought. *She's got me stumped, too.*

He honestly wasn't sure whose side to take in this debate. A few years ago, he reflected, there wouldn't have been any question; he would have gladly gone AWOL on a pleasure planet like Ryolanov, hiding from his past failures and his father's crushing expectations amid a lifestyle of unabashed hedonism. But that was before Captain Janeway gave him a second chance to make something more of his life. Redemption wasn't an easy business, he had learned, but was he ready to throw his second chance away, even for all that paradise had to offer?

"I wouldn't make any hasty decisions," he advised Tukwila, amazed at his own words even as they escaped his mouth. *Look who's talking,* he thought. *The original seat-of-his-pants flyer.* "Ryolanov is a great place to visit, no one is denying that, but you have to take everything into consideration."

"Such as?" she asked, rolling onto her side to face him. Tiny dunes of black pellets shifted beneath her weight.

"Well, there's always . . . that is, we can't forget . . . something or another . . . I'm sure the captain would say . . ." He found himself momentarily incapable of making the case for *Voyager* versus Ryolanov. Racking his brain for a pithy and irrefutable argument for leaving the planet, he was caught off guard by the shadow that suddenly fell across him, cutting him off from the warmth of the sun. He looked up and saw looming over him the single most compelling reason to put Ryolanov far behind him.

Naxor.

"I am surprised you had the nerve to leave your ship once more," the hostile Ryol said, "after your cowardly performance at the dance a few nights ago." His sneering lips intersected with the scar running down his cheek. *How the hell did he find me?* Paris wondered. *The man is more persistent than a bloodhound.*

Nor had he come alone. Paris counted three more Ryol males standing behind Naxor. All were dressed for the beach, but none seemed to have swimming on the mind. *This looks bad,* Paris thought. Naturally, he had left his phaser back in his quarters and his commbadge in a dressing room at the other end of the beach. Ditto for Harry and Susan, he assumed. They were outnumbered and unarmed. The only bright side to their situation, as far as he could see, was that none of the Ryol appeared to be carrying weapons either.

"Back home we call that the better part of valor," Paris said, rising slowly to his feet. Kim and Tukwila also lifted themselves off the sand. Out of the corner of his eye, he saw their neffaler scamper away across the obsidian beach, his picnic basket and catering duties evidently abandoned. *Smart guy,* he thought. "But I don't suppose you care about that, do you?"

"No," Naxor said coldly. He stepped closer to Paris, raising his fists. The pupils of his malachite eyes shrunk to pinpricks of black.

"Everybody calm down," Kim said. "There's no need to fight."

"That's right," Tukwila agreed. "It's too beautiful a day to spoil with a lot of broken noses and split lips."

The Ryol males ignored the humans' attempts at peacemaking, except by snickering behind Naxor as he glared at Tom Paris with undisguised hatred in his eyes. *Thanks for trying,* he silently acknowledged his friends, *but I don't think that's going to work today.*

Paris felt a peculiar sense of relief as he mentally bowed to the inevitable. This smug Ryol had been giving him a hard time since almost the moment he first beamed down to the planet; Paris was tired of trying to stay out of his way. *Let's get this over with,* he thought. Eager to let the Ryol make the first move, he gave Naxor his most infuriating smirk.

It worked. Snarling like an enraged wolf, Naxor grabbed for Paris's throat with both hands. Paris efficiently blocked Naxor's lunge, thrusting his arms between Naxor's and spreading them apart while simultaneously kicking out at the Ryol's undefended kneecap. His bare foot slammed into Naxor's knee, staggering his opponent, who howled in pain as he clutched his leg. Naxor's companions surged forward, only to be met by Kim and Tukwila who took up defensive positions to the left and right of Paris.

Despite their recent disagreement, the trio from *Voyager* fought with discipline and teamwork. Paris saw Tukwila take out one Ryol with a deft chop to the neck. He fell face-first into the basket of *sotul,* producing a singularly squishy splash. Kim grappled with another attacker, eventually twisting his arm behind his back. Veins and tendons stood out on the Ryol's neck as he clenched his teeth in rage and growled with surprising ferocity. It took all Kim's effort to keep his foe immobilized.

That left one more Ryol for Paris to deal with, not counting Naxor, who, bent over at the waist, continued to writhe in agony, holding on to his injured knee. The remaining Ryol charged between Paris and Naxor, his golden mane streaming in the wind generated by his headlong dash. Paris aimed a solid punch at the Ryol's jaw, but the man proved more agile than expected; he ducked beneath the blow and barreled into Paris. Black sand went flying into the air as Paris was knocked off his feet, landing flat on his back upon the beach. The Ryol pounced on top of him, his sharpened nails digging into Paris's shoulders, his white teeth snapping at the human's face and throat.

Is he really trying to bite me? Paris didn't want to find out. He grabbed the Ryol by his forehead and chin and, extending his arms with all his strength, shoved the hate-crazed face away from his, at least for the moment. The Ryol had the superior position, though, not to mention gravity, on his side. His head and shoulders pressed against the force of Paris's arms, his gnashing teeth lowering second by second until they were only centimeters away from the Starfleet officer's exposed throat. The savage growl of his attacker roared in Paris's ears; he was suddenly reminded of the vicious dog that had attacked him on the Caretaker's array. "Hey," he said to the Ryol assaulting him, "let's not get carried away here!"

The Ryol merely snarled in reply. His teeth crashed together next to the human's neck. Paris felt the Ryol's hot breath upon his skin.

"Tom!" Susan Tukwila shouted. "Over here!" Yanking his gaze away from the enraged visage of his Ryol assailant, Paris risked a glance in his comrade's direction. She had dispatched her own opponent with commendable speed; as he watched, the fallen Ryol made a half-hearted attempt to rise from the shattered remains of the picnic basket, only to be driven back into the juicy purple mess by an emphatic kick from Tukwila's well-aimed leg. Paris spared a heartbeat to admire her technique and muscle tone. "Ready anytime you are," she called out to Paris.

"Got it," he acknowledged. Returning his attention to his own foe, he rocked backward, flipping the seemingly bloodthirsty Ryol over his shoulders. Caught off balance, the Ryol landed in a heap at Tukwila's feet, only a few meters away from the other dazed Ryol. She brought both fists down on his golden scalp. Paris heard them crash against the Ryol's skull. He dropped unconscious onto the sand before the sound of the blow ceased echoing in Paris's ears. *Let's hear it for Starfleet training,* he thought, *and Maquis enthusiasm.*

He peered over at Kim. Harry had both of "his" Ryol's arms locked behind his back now, but the captive Ryol was still kicking and thrashing himself into a frenzy. Kim looked like an old-time rodeo cowboy struggling to stay astride a bucking bronco. "C'mon, Harry!" he shouted. "Are you still dancing with that clown? What's your problem?"

"He's stronger than he looks," Kim said between

grunts. He tried to trip the Ryol, but the maroon-skinned alien refused to fall. His bare feet kicked up small storms of flying black sand, until Susan Tukwila strolled over and delivered a forceful karate chop to the man's abdomen. He instantly went limp in Kim's arms. Paris heard Kim breathe a sigh of relief.

"Tell me about it," Paris said. He climbed to his feet, leaving behind a shallow depression in the sand. His shoulders still stung where the maddened Ryol had dug his sharp brown nails into them. Inspecting his wounds, Paris saw that the man's claws had indeed broken the skin in several places. Small amounts of blood leaked from ten deep indentations in his flesh. *Ouch,* Paris thought, wondering if a trip to the sickbay was in order.

First, though, there was Naxor himself to deal with. Laazia's insanely jealous Ryol suitor was hunched over not far away, massaging his battered kneecap with both hands. He looked like he'd had the fight kicked out of him for now. Paris hoped that Naxor wouldn't give them any more trouble now that his buddies had been taken out of the picture. "You had enough?" he called to the persistently difficult Ryol.

Naxor lifted his head, his pale green eyes blazing with fury. "How dare you speak to me in that tone!" he barked. His voice was hoarse and husky and full of menace. "Animals. *Neffaler.* I will show you how little your feeble resistance means to me."

He limped toward the human trio, breathing heavily. His eyes grew wider, his pupils expanding until the green of their irises almost completely disappeared, leaving only two vacant black holes that seemed to suck in all light and hope from whatever they beheld. *Spooky,* Paris thought, working hard to maintain a cocksure attitude. It felt like whistling in a graveyard.

"I hate to break this to you, Naxor, old pal," Paris said. It was difficult not to flinch in the face of those empty black eyes. They looked darker than ordinary optics allowed, almost as if they had delved beyond mere blackness into some unnatural fuliginous hue beyond the outer reaches of the visible spectrum. They were more than dark; they were anti-light. "But the rest of your gang is down and out. You're on your own."

"So are you," Naxor whispered.

A gasp pushed its way past Tukwila's lips. Kim began to choke and cough. *What the devil?* Paris wondered. He spun around on his heels just in time to see both Kim and Tukwila clutching their throats as their eyes filled up with surprise and alarm. They staggered upon the beach, barely able to keep standing. Their faces looked pale and bloodless. "Tom," Tukwila croaked, her voice no more than a raspy squeak. "Help."

She dropped to her knees, then collapsed into the black sand. Kim managed to stay on his feet for a few more seconds before losing consciousness and falling only a meter or two away from Tukwila's prostrate form. Paris ran over and hastily checked the fallen bodies; he felt their pulses, listened to their shallow breathing. They were still alive, thank goodness, but out cold. *How?* he wondered. *What had Naxor done to them?*

He heard the Ryol laughing, and spun around to confront him. "Damn you," Paris said. "This was just between you and me." A new intensity gripped him. What had started out as just another brawl had suddenly turned deadly serious. He had to survive—and tell Captain Janeway about Naxor's mysterious assault on Kim and Tukwila.

"Precisely," the Ryol answered him. "Are you ready to face me alone, without your bodyguards and babysitters?"

I'll show you how ready I am, Paris thought. Dropping quickly onto one knee, he grabbed a handful of dark pellets and threw them in Naxor's face. The move caught Naxor by surprise. He stumbled backward, rubbing the tiny particles from his eyes, spitting the sand from his mouth. Paris took advantage of his foe's confusion by running forward and delivering a solid punch to Naxor's chin. The blow staggered Naxor, but didn't drop him. *That punch would have put a Klingon on his back,* Paris thought, disappointed. He remembered the surprising strength of Laazia's embrace. *Just how tough are these Ryol anyway?*

He wasn't too worried, though. From what he had seen so far, the Ryol might be strong but they were also sloppy fighters. *Time to use some of that Starfleet Academy training,* he thought, following his punch with a roundhouse kick to Naxor's jaw. Then he grabbed the arrogant Ryol by his blond mane and spun him around, letting go of Naxor only after he had built up enough momentum to send Naxor stumbling forward across the beach. Following in his opponent's wake, Paris rammed him in the small of the back. The impact served to knock Naxor into the surf. He threw out his hands to break his fall as the golden foam broke against his arms and legs.

Paris's bare feet splashed through the water after Naxor. The sun beat down upon his shoulders. He could taste the ginger in the air. *As long as I can keep him on the defensive,* he thought, *maybe he won't be able to do to me what he did to Harry and Susan.* Naxor was sprawled on all fours in front of him. He locked his arm around the Ryol's neck and dragged him backward toward the shore. "Come on," Paris grunted. "You're not going anywhere until you tell me what you did to my friends."

A shockingly feral growl emerged from Naxor. The sound sent a chill down Paris's spine; he had heard enraged tigers and *sehlats* that sounded more sentient. Naxor twisted in Paris's grasp. Paris tried to hold on to him, but he'd underestimated the Ryol's strength once more. Naxor wrenched his body around until Paris found himself looking into the twin black holes beneath Naxor's angry brows. *No,* Paris thought urgently. *Don't look in his eyes!*

Too late. Paris felt his own strength slipping away, sucked into the cavernous depths of Naxor's empty black eyes. His arms felt like heavy duranium weights. His legs felt as limp and rubbery as Neelix's infamous hair pasta. He struggled to hang on to Naxor, but there was no energy left in his fingers; they trailed away uselessly as Naxor pulled himself free. Paris tried to lift his head, to keep his enemy in view, but his eyelids kept drooping. It was no use; even when he succeeded in keeping his eyes open, the world grew dim and vague around the edges.

He had never felt so tired, not even after those grueling days of rehabilitative labor at the Federation penal settlement the captain had rescued him from. Even breathing was a strain. And he was cold. Every last bit of warmth seem to be fleeing his body; all he wanted to do was curl up into a ball in hopes of hanging on to whatever heat was left. The waves lapping at his shins felt like ice water. His toes were numb. *Is this what it's like to freeze to death?* he wondered.

A heavy blow struck him in the back. *Naxor,* he realized, but he was too weak to fight back. *No fair,* he thought, as a series of brutal jabs and punches hammered him relentlessly. He tried to strike out at his attacker, but his limbs did not respond to his increasingly hazy mental commands. He didn't even have enough energy to try to dodge the next blow. Naxor's fists smacked against his spine and Paris fell face-first into the surf.

The cold water shocked him back to partial alertness. He swallowed a mouthful of gingery sea water and started to lift his head out of the shallow water.

Then a remorseless hand pushed his head downward—into the golden brine and the slippery sand below the waves.

"Neffaler!" Naxor snarled in his ears.

Sharpened nails dug into the back of his scalp as Paris felt his face pressed deeper and deeper into the slurry. Wet sand clogged his nostrils and forced its way past his lips. He couldn't breathe! His enervated arms and legs thrashed weakly as he numbly fought to extricate himself from Naxor's grip. His cheeks swelled as he tried to hold on to his last gasp of air. Blinded by the sand, suffocating by the second, he knew he couldn't hold out much longer. He expected his life to pass before his eyes, but, to his surprise, the first thing he remembered was that time he broke the warp barrier and transformed into an amphibian. *Now would be a good time to get those gills back,* he mused.

Bubbles of carbon dioxide slipped out between his clenched teeth. He guessed he was only a heartbeat away from inhaling a couple lungfuls of water and sand. *The ship,* he thought desperately. *Someone has to warn her. . . .*

Without warning, the pressure on the back of his skull went away. Strong hands grabbed him by the shoulders and rolled him over so that his face was out of the water. He could breathe again. Sea and slurry running from his nose and mouth, Paris gratefully sucked in oxygenated air, taking one deep breath after another. Ryolanov's crimson sun warmed his face.

"Are you quite all right, Lieutenant?" came a familiar voice. Averting his eyes from the blinding glare of the sun, Paris saw Tuvok kneeling beside him. The Vulcan security officer was in uniform, but appeared unconcerned about the water soaking his boots and the cuffs of his trousers.

"I think so," Paris answered. He shook his head, throwing off tiny droplets of brine, and rubbed the water and sand out of his eyes. *That was a close call,* he thought, then remembered his adversary. "Naxor?" he asked.

"Neutralized for the moment," Tuvok stated. He called Paris's attention to the supine figure lying nearby. The homicidal Ryol lay flat on his back amid the surging spray of the tide. His eyes were closed— *good thing,* Paris thought—and his mouth hung open. "Interesting," Tuvok commented as he rose to his feet. "The Ryol have not been forthcoming with biological data about their species. I was unsure whether the Vulcan nerve pinch would have any effect on one of their kind."

Now that the battle was over, Paris felt his strength beginning to return. He still felt like he'd just run the Deltan Marathon, but he no longer seemed to be leaking energy faster than a cracked dilithium crystal. He stood up slowly, then helped Tuvok drag Naxor's insensate body onto dry land. The Vulcan kneeled again and applied what looked like a hypospray to the Ryol's exposed neck. "I suggest we attempt to rouse our comrades, then beam directly to *Voyager.* There is much that needs to be discussed with the captain."

"I'll say," Paris agreed. He glanced around the now-peaceful beach. Of the eight humanoids currently occupying this stretch of shore, only he and Tuvok remained upright, and only the Vulcan was not dressed for a day of idle sunbathing. In his neatly pressed (if slightly damp) Starfleet uniform, Tuvok looked very much out of place. For the first time, an odd question occurred to Paris:

What in blazes was Tuvok doing on the beach?

B'Elanna swore in Klingon as Kes applied an anesthetic to her arm. Since Torres usually disdained her Klingon heritage, Kes guessed that the pain had to be fairly intense. "Hang on," Kes said, "this should relieve the discomfort in a few seconds." She put the hypospray down on a counter. "You should feel your arm growing numb right away."

"Yes," Torres hissed through clenched teeth. "I can feel it starting to take effect." Her foot tapped impatiently on the floor of the sickbay. She had refused to lie down on a biobed, insisting that her injuries were minimal. Kes wondered if all Klingons were this stubborn; B'Elanna was the only Klingon she had met, possibly the only Klingon in the Delta Quadrant, but both Tom and Harry insisted that B'Elanna's legendary temper was typical of her species. Kes had asked The Doctor about Klingons once, only to receive a thirty-minute lecture on the intricacies of their auxiliary nervous system. Interesting enough, she conceded, but not exactly what she had hoped for. Ultimately she was more interested in the hearts and minds of each new race she encountered, not just the details of their respective anatomies.

The Doctor could not lecture now. All his attention was consumed by Ensign Jourdan who was flat on her back on the primary biobed, beneath a surgical support frame. Kes glanced at the sensor readings on the monitor suspended over the patient's head; despite the severity of her injuries, the young ensign's vital signs looked good. As Jourdan had received the most serious damage in the accident, The Doctor was concentrating on her, leaving Kes to care for Torres.

"You were very lucky," Kes said. She ran a dermal regenerator over Torres's arm. "This could have been a lot worse."

"I don't feel lucky," Torres grumbled. She glared at the ravaged flesh of her right arm. Beneath the healing influence of the regenerator, the cracked and blistered skin began to regain its normal appearance. "Is this going to take long?" she asked impatiently. "I have to get down to that damn beach."

"The beach?" Kes looked up from her work. A chill worked its way down her spine. Torres's interest in the beach seemed out of character. Kes seldom socialized with B'Elanna, but the half-Klingon engineer had never struck her as the type to enjoy sunbathing. Kes felt her psychic intuition tickling the back of her mind. *This is important,* she thought, taking a deep breath. "Why are you so interested in the beach?"

"Never mind," Torres responded brusquely. "Just fix my arm and let me get back to work."

"I thought you wanted to go to the beach," Kes pressed her. "Do you have work to do—at the beach? Please, B'Elanna, I really want to know."

The urgency of her tone got through to Torres. She gave Kes her full attention for the first time since entering the sickbay, eyeing her suspiciously. "Why do you ask? Is there any reason I shouldn't go to the beach?"

"Maybe," Kes confessed. Having shared her fears with both Tuvok and The Doctor, as well as with her beloved Neelix, she hardly considered them top secret. "I've been having some strange . . . feelings . . . about that beach. I think there's something there, something we haven't been told about."

She saw a spark of recognition in Torres's eyes. B'Elanna knew something about the beach, Kes realized. She had her own questions to answer, her own mystery to solve. "I think we should compare notes," Kes suggested.

Torres inspected Kes carefully before answering. The Ocampa imagined that she must look frail and unimpressive by Klingon standards. *I may be no warrior,* she thought, *but I can take care of myself.*

Finally Torres nodded her assent. "You may be right," she said. She rolled down her sleeve. Aside from some slight reddening, her arm looked good as new. She glanced at The Doctor, who was still busy repairing the damage to Erin Jourdan's vulnerable human shell. The ensign appeared unconscious but alive. "He could probably use some help," Torres said. "Meet me at Transporter Room Two at sixteen hundred hours."

"I'll be there," Kes said. She couldn't wait to find out what Torres had learned about the zealously guarded secret of the beach. She knew she was zeroing in on the answer.

CHAPTER
10

CAPTAIN JANEWAY WOULD HAVE FOUGHT AN ENTIRE HIVE of Borg for a strong cup of black coffee. She had not felt so exhausted for a long time, nor spent so much time in her best dress uniform. *I'm going to need a week's rest in a holodeck just to recover from this "vacation" on Ryolanov,* she thought. Still, it was worth all this endless diplomatic chitchat if it meant some much-needed relief for her valiant-yet-homesick crew. Janeway felt personally responsible for ensuring that each and every crew member, Starfleet or Maquis, did not suffer more than necessary from the consequences of her decisions. *If that means another banquet or reception,* she thought, *so be it.*

Right now sunset was approaching and she was already late for her next appointment with Varathael. Her weary legs protested with annoying aches and pains as she quickened her pace through a maze of corridors within one of Ryolaler's many pyramids. She needed no Ryol functionary to guide her; at this point she practically knew all their government offices by heart. Turquoise carpeting, decorated with intricate swirls of gold and red, cushioned the path beneath her boots. Satiny rainbow-colored tapestries hung from smooth marble walls while an elegant arrangement of mirrors and windows brought the scarlet sunlight indoors. As she rounded yet another corner, Janeway spotted an elderly neffaler diligently polishing a reflective plate in the ceiling with a brush attached to a long pole. The dwarfish creature did not look at her as she walked past him; he kept his large black eyes on his job.

Janeway frowned. Despite the apparent generosity and good natures of the Ryol, it was hard to ignore that their treatment of the neffaler bordered on cruelty. Over the centuries, the Federation had evolved stringent guidelines to distinguish between the legitimate employment of domesticated wildlife and the willful exploitation of minority species; she suspected that, under close examination, Ryolanov would not qualify for Federation membership.

That was not the issue at hand, however. For better or for worse, the Prime Directive meant that the relationship between the Ryol and the neffaler was none of her business. *And yet,* she thought, *I would never dream of working my dog the way the Ryol work their pets.*

Her path led her to Varathael's private chambers, located at the dead center of the pyramid. Only a hanging curtain of thick velvety fabric separated the Elder's residence from the wide corridor that led up to his door. Janeway was again impressed, as she had been the first time she visited Varathael in his chambers, by the startling lack of visible security. It said much about the peacefulness and stability of Ryol society that their leader apparently had no need of guards, locks, or even a receptionist. *The Cardassians could take over this city in an hour,* she thought, feeling vaguely guilty for even thinking in such militaristic terms. Then again, it was probably only a matter of time before the Kazon, the Vidiians, or some other hostile species stumbled onto Ryolanov. *Perhaps I should say something about this to Varathael, warn him not to be so trusting,* she thought, *or would that cause him to think of humanity as warlike and paranoid?* She sighed silently at the prospect of one more thing to worry about, but stayed resigned to the inevitability of this and future dilemmas. First contact was never easy, but always a tricky business, requiring plenty of caution and forethought.

Muffled voices passed through the heavy burgundy-hued curtain. Janeway paused before the doorway, unwilling to interrupt the Elder's business. According to plan, she was scheduled to meet Varathael here before proceeding to a ceremonial inspection of the *sotul* vineyards. She wasn't entirely sure what the ceremony involved, but she imagined that it involved a lot of newly pressed wine and long-winded toasts. She made a mental note to herself to keep an eye on her wine consumption; *sotul* wine was strong stuff, she had learned, almost as potent as bootleg Romulan ale, and it wouldn't do for the captain of the *U.S.S. Voyager* to end up tipsy in front of foreign dignitaries.

And dignitaries didn't get much more dignified, for that matter, than Varathael of Ryolanov. Janeway was grateful that, if she absolutely *had* to spend so much time schmoozing with the local authorities, that the Elder was such pleasant company. She could think of a lot of alien leaders, not to mention a few Federation bigwigs, who made diplomacy an exercise in tedium. Like that Andorian prime minister, she recalled, who once spent an endless afternoon extolling the aesthetic advantages of blue skin to her entire graduating class at the Academy. By contrast, Varathael seemed genuinely charming and intelligent. Indeed, aside from their somewhat disturbing treatment of the neffaler, and Janeway was very reluctant to make any hasty moral judgments on that issue, she liked the Ryol and she hoped that she and her crew had given them a good first impression of the United Federation of Planets. *Someday,* she mused, *other explorers will come to the Delta Quadrant. It would be nice to think that* Voyager *had, at the very least, laid the groundwork for future peaceful relations between this quadrant and our own. If some positive good can come from our long journey home, then all our efforts and hardships will not have been in vain.*

The voices on the other side of the curtain grew louder. She thought she recognized one of the voices as Varathael's, but there was a menacing tone to it that she had never heard before. She couldn't quite make out the words, nor was she really trying to, but the Elder sounded extremely angry. Janeway was puzzled; it was hard to imagine what on this tropical paradise of a planet could have upset Varathael enough to make the benign Elder raise his voice in rage.

The second voice struck her as familiar as well, but she couldn't place it right away. That voice seemed less angry than desperate. It sounded pleading, even frightened. *Frightened of Varathael?* Janeway wondered. That seemed unlikely, and yet . . . she found herself remembering what Chakotay had told her of his recent nightmarish vision-quest, of the malevolent unseen presence haunting his inner landscape. Could there in fact be a dark side hidden behind the sunny face of Ryolanov? She didn't want to believe that, but it would be foolish to ignore the possibility.

Wait, what was that? She wasn't certain, but she thought she heard the word *Voyager* among the heated words coming from beyond the curtain. Uncomfortable about eavesdropping on their hosts, she stepped away from the curtain. *Perhaps I should come back later,* she thought, *or simply turn off my Universal Translator.* Instead she walked softly up to the curtain and placed one ear against it. *Good manners be damned,* she thought. *If this affects my crew, I need to know about it.*

Now that she was concentrating on the discussion in the adjacent chamber, she identified the second voice as belonging to Naxor. *Oh, Tom,* she thought, *what have you gotten into now?* Somehow she knew, even though she hadn't heard his name mentioned, that Lieutenant Paris had to be involved in whatever matter was vexing the Elder and his most obnoxious underling, which probably meant Harry Kim was deep in this mess as well. *At least I know Neelix is busy fixing lunch right now,* she consoled herself, *and that B'Elanna is busy with her engines . . . I hope.*

Janeway's body was coiled like a spring, ready to leap away from the doorway if anyone approached. Her hand hovered over her commbadge, just in case she needed to beam up fast to avoid an embarrassing scene. She was not prepared, however, for the ear-splitting scream that suddenly erupted from the chamber beyond the velvet curtain. Her heart pounded at the sound of unremitting fear and suffering in the cry she heard. *My God,* she thought. *That doesn't even sound sentient!*

Adrenaline raced through her system as the scream awakened her body's primal fight-or-flight response. Janeway knew she had to act; there was no way she could ignore the torture she heard. Phaser drawn, she yanked aside the curtain and beheld a shocking tableau:

Amid the lush furnishings of the Elder's chambers, beneath the mirrored chandelier and in front of his polished wooden desk, in the center of a complex multipatterned carpet that tastefully matched the brightly dyed fabric on the couch and handmade chairs, Naxor writhed in torment beneath Varathael's hands. Naxor was on his knees before the Elder, who stood behind the younger Ryol with his reddish-brown hands gripping Naxor's bare shoulders. No obvious violence was visible, but Naxor screamed as though Varathael was yanking out his very soul by its roots. The young man's eyes had rolled upward in their sockets so that only the whites could be seen, his mouth gaped open as his agonized howl pored from his core, and his entire frame shook with palsy. Janeway could barely believe what she was seeing, but the Ryol began to physically decay before her eyes. His cruelly handsome features grew lean and haggard. Dark shadows filled the hollow sockets that formed beneath his eyes. The rich maroon color of his flesh became tinted with gray, even as his once-muscular physique appeared to liquefy and evaporate, leaving behind a skeletal frame barely covered by stringy tendons and dry brittle skin. In a matter of seconds, Naxor looked like he'd been starved for weeks in a Cardassian slave-labor camp, and yet he kept on screaming the unending shriek of the damned.

But as horrific as the stricken Ryol became, the look on the face of his tormentor was even more terrifying. Pure animal exultation transfigured his expression, so that the wise and gracious Elder suddenly resembled some bloodthirsty demon out of Klingon mythology. His teeth were clenched together in a feral grimace that threw into sharp relief the contorted lines of his face. The graying tips of his mane grew lush and golden just as Naxor's formerly tawny fur became coarse and dry. His brown talons sank deeper into Naxor's withered flesh, drawing thin trickles of watery-looking blood. Beneath arching yellow brows, the Elder's pale green eyes had been replaced by voracious whirlpools of darkness that seemed to open upon an endless empty void. Caught up in his inhuman rapture, his ruby gemstone dangling from his neck, Varathael was oblivious to Janeway's presence.

She could not remain silent. "Stop it!" she cried out. "You're killing him!"

Varathael's empty eyes turned on her. He released his grip on Naxor, who slumped gracelessly onto the carpet. Janeway could not tell if the younger Ryol was still alive. Varathael struggled visibly to regain his composure, his features forcing themselves back into a more serene and civilized mien. His voice when he spoke was thick and guttural.

"Captain Janeway," he said. "I am so sorry that you had to see that." He took a step toward Janeway, who instinctively backed away. His eyes were still as black as the shores of Ryolanov. "Please, do not concern yourself with this. You have so many other things to worry about, so much upon your mind. You must not be troubled by things you cannot understand. Let me lift this burden from your shoulders. Permit me to deal with my people in our own way. Do not be alarmed. Do not think of this at all. . . ."

The tone of his voice was soothing, almost hypnotic. Janeway felt herself being lulled by the rhythm of his words, and by the gravitational pull of those darkened eyes. What the Ryol did to each other was not her concern after all, she thought. Surely the Prime Directive released her from any obligation to intervene. Didn't it? Varathael took another step closer, then another. Her fears seemed to dissolve in the voracious nihility of his gaping orbs. It would be so easy, she thought, just to do as Varathael suggested and forget this whole thing. Naxor couldn't really be in danger, could he? Varathael could never be so merciless.

The Elder's hand reached out toward her. She felt the pointed tips of his fingernails graze her cheek.

No! Janeway flinched and stepped backward. Snapping out of her trance, she tapped her commbadge decisively. "Janeway to *Voyager*. One to beam up—immediately."

"Wait!" Varathael shouted, lunging toward her. His calm expression slipped from his face, exposing a look of frustrated malice. "Let me explain!"

Varathael vanished from Janeway's sight as the transporter took her apart.

Janeway marched onto the bridge. A turbolift had brought her straight from the transporter room. Chakotay stood up and surrendered the captain's chair to Janeway. "Captain," he informed her. "The Elder is hailing you."

"I'll bet he is," Janeway said. "Commander. Mr. Tuvok. I want to see both of you in my briefing room at once. Mr. Paris, you have the conn."

Tuvok walked away from his console at Tactical. "Actually, Captain," he said, "I suggest that Lieutenant Paris join us. He was involved in an incident you should know about."

Taking a closer look at the young pilot, Janeway noted the purple bruises on Paris's face and neck. He looked like he'd been in a fight, and she had a pretty good guess who the other combatant had been. "Naxor?" she asked Paris. He nodded.

Naxor again, she thought. *Perhaps this was why Varathael was punishing him.* "Very well," she said to Tuvok, directing a relief officer named Zon Kellar to take Paris's place at the conn. "I have a lot to tell the rest of you as well."

"Captain, what should I do about the Elder's hails?" Kellar asked.

"Stall," Janeway said.

Less than five minutes later, Chakotay, Tuvok, Paris, and Janeway were seated around the conference table. She gave them a quick description of her encounter with Varathael, then listened carefully as

Tom Paris summarized the fight on the beach. Comparing notes, she determined that Paris's violent confrontation with Naxor and his allies had taken place shortly before she witnessed the Elder's horrifying attack on his aide. Now that she knew the whole story, or at least more of it, she couldn't blame Varathael for disciplining Naxor. Even so, however, Naxor's offense hardly seemed to justify the brutal, possibly fatal assault that Varathael had subjected Naxor to. "It's hard to imagine," she said, "any crime that warranted such dreadful torture." *Nor the obvious joy,* she thought, *with which Varathael administered the punishment.*

"For myself," Tuvok commented, "I am less concerned about why both Varathael and Naxor took aggressive action than with the manner in which the attacks were implemented. The Ryol clearly possess abilities beyond those of most humanoids."

"And a dark side," Chakotay added, "that they have taken pains to conceal." Janeway knew he had to be remembering the ominous nature of his recent vision.

"As do most intelligent species," Tuvok said, "particularly when encountering an alien civilization for the first time."

He has a point, Janeway thought. *I would not introduce humanity to another species by telling them about, say, the Eugenics Wars or the Spanish Inquisition.*

"All I know," Tom Paris said, "is that these people are a lot more dangerous than they let on. Naxor nearly sucked the life out of me, not to mention Harry and Susan."

"How are the other two?" Janeway asked, afraid that Naxor might have harmed Kim and Tukwila as badly as Varathael appeared to have damaged Naxor. The thought of Harry having all his youth and boyish enthusiasm drained from him made her sick.

"They're in the sickbay," Chakotay reported, "but The Doctor isn't too worried about them. Both of them are exhausted, and somewhat anemic, but The Doctor expects them to recover. There doesn't appear to be any permanent injury."

"That's good to hear," Janeway said. She looked around the table at the solemn faces of her officers. "The question, then, is what do we do next? How many of our people are currently down on the planet's surface?"

Chakotay consulted his padd. "Approximately fifty crew members are on shore leave at this moment."

"Fifty-seven, to be exact," Tuvok said, "all of whom are potential hostages. I recommend that we beam them all back to the ship immediately."

"Very well," the captain agreed. "Let's not jump to conclusions, though. As far as we know, Naxor is the only Ryol who has attempted to harm any of our people and he appears to be an aberration. Indeed, the Elder appears to have gone to . . . drastic . . . lengths to ensure that Naxor will no longer pose any threat to us." She paused, remembering Varathael's desperate lunge at her when she attempted to beam away. Could she be sure that the Elder meant her no harm? She kept remembering the sadistic glee on his face as he tortured Naxor. What else might the venerable Elder be capable of?

"Cancel all future shore leave," she decided. "Let's not send any more of the crew down to the planet. Start quietly recalling our people to the ship. Make it look like their vacation time has expired, not like an emergency pull-out. Got it?"

"Understood," Chakotay said. "The next duty shift begins in a few hours. Several crew members were due back anyway."

"Perfect," Janeway said. "With any luck, we'll get all our people back on board before the Ryol catch on to our suspicions."

"I don't get it," Paris said. "What kind of creatures are they anyway? What do they really want from us?"

"I may be able to provide some answers shortly," Tuvok stated. "With The Doctor's assistance." He addressed the small computer monitor mounted in the center of the table. The Doctor's saturnine features appeared on the screen. "Excuse me, Doctor," Tuvok said. "Have you completed your analysis of the sample I provided?"

Sample? Janeway wondered what Tuvok was referring to.

"Not yet," the holograph replied. "As you may or may not recall, I have several other duties to occupy my time, not the least of which is monitoring the recovery of Ensigns Kim and Tukwila."

"Of course," Janeway said diplomatically. "How are your patients, Doctor?"

The Doctor's image stepped aside, revealing the unconscious bodies of Tukwila and Kim resting beneath silvery sheets on adjacent biobeds. "Oh, they'll live, no thanks to whatever debilitating alien force you've run afoul of this time. Their bioelectric fields were down fifteen percent from the recommended human level, while their metabolism and general blood chemistry showed signs of advanced energy depletion. My replicators are working overtime to manufacture all the vitamin supplements they're going to need for the next few weeks. And don't get me started about the cellular strain. . . ."

"We appreciate your efforts, Doctor," Janeway said. She looked at Tuvok. "You said something about a sample?"

The Vulcan nodded. "After subduing Naxor, I took the liberty of extracting a sample of his DNA."

"Why would you want to do that?" Chakotay asked.

"Previous attempts to gain biological information about the Ryol had been met with polite but persistent evasion. My experience has always been that the harder secrets are to obtain, the more significant they usually are. When Mr. Paris had his altercation with Naxor, the opportunity to uncover these secrets presented itself."

"I'm just glad you showed up when you did," Paris said. "I still don't understand, though. What were you doing on the beach in the first place?"

Good question, Janeway thought. She wouldn't mind hearing the answer to that one herself.

"Kes had previously called my attention to the shore," Tuvok began, then explained about the disturbing psychic echoes that Kes had sensed emanating from the harbor. "I was walking the perimeter of the beach in an attempt to confirm her experiences when I came to the assistance of Lieutenant Paris and the others."

"And did you sense anything?" Janeway asked, leaning toward Tuvok. "Before you ran into Naxor and Mr. Paris?"

"No," he declared, "which simply means that the data is inconclusive. As I explained to Kes, Vulcan and Ocampa telepathy differ in qualitative ways. It is entirely possible that she could be sensitive to psychic phenomena that would not be detectable by me."

Janeway shared a meaningful look with her first officer, who nodded grimly. *First Chakotay and now Kes,* she thought. Too many of her people were picking up bad vibes from Ryolanov; perhaps it was not at all the welcoming oasis it had originally appeared to be. "What do you think?" she asked Tuvok. "Did Kes really sense something down there."

Tuvok paused before answering. "Despite her relative youth and inexperience," he said finally, "I have not known Kes to be the victim of an uncontrolled imagination. If she insists that there is a frightening psychic presence beyond the shore, then there must be more to that beach than meets the eye."

"The beach?!" The Doctor exclaimed. Upon the screen, his usual sour expression gave way to a look of concern.

"What is it, Doctor?" Janeway asked. "What's the matter?"

"The beach," he said. "That's where Kes and Lieutenant Torres said they were going, right before Mr. Tuvok had Kim and Tukwila beamed to the sickbay. They're at the beach right now!"

CHAPTER

11

AFTER DARK, A COOL WIND BLEW OFF THE HARBOR, chilling Kes. Shivering, she hugged herself tightly and wished that she had thought to bring a jacket on this nocturnal expedition. Her usual shipboard attire provided little protection against the breeze, which seemed several degrees colder than it had been the first time she visited the beach at night.

"Here, darling," Neelix whispered. "Wear this." He slipped out of his motley jacket, revealing an even more garish tunic underneath, transferred his commbadge from his suit to his shirt, and draped his jacket over Kes's trembling shoulders. The Ocampa took the garment gratefully, although she suspected that the chill she was experiencing was as much psychological as physiological. She was not looking forward to hearing those excruciating telepathic screams again.

"Sssh!" B'Elanna Torres gave Neelix a withering look. "We're not supposed to be here, remember?"

The unlikely trio crept through the dense underbrush at the top of the beach, trying to keep their distance from the lamps posted along the path. Green and purple tendrils, looking almost black in the dim light, brushed against Kes's face as she crawled among the swaying fronds. The heavy fragrance of the blossoms overpowered the ginger scent of the Ryol sea. Occasionally she felt small insects run across the backs of her hands and prayed that the bushes did not conceal any snakes or lizards as well.

Neelix took the lead, creeping ahead of Torres and Kes. "You know," he began, "this sort of reminds me of the time I evaded an entire squadron of Tzuni guerrillas by escaping through the famous Floating Gardens of—ouch!"

Kes watched as Torres grabbed on to Neelix's ankle and squeezed. "I said, be quiet!" she hissed through clenched teeth. "I still don't see why you had to come along on this mission."

Neelix lowered his voice—slightly. "Surely you didn't expect me to let my dear Kes face the unknown alone? Besides, you couldn't find a stealthier ally aboard *Voyager*. It is a well-known fact that Talaxians have excellent night vision, plus the silent tread of a *vustoorsyl* on the prowl." Kes heard Torres grinding her teeth together only a few centimeters away.

She looked at Kes. "What *do* you see in him?" asked the exasperated engineer. "I have never understood that."

Kes wondered how she could explain their bond in a way that B'Elanna could comprehend. "It's his independence," she said softly. "He's traveled among the stars, surviving by his wits alone, making his way on a hundred different worlds. You have no idea how appealing that is to me. Where I come from, where I spent most of my life, we knew nothing of the universe beyond our underground city. Our lives were safe, sheltered, sequestered. The Caretaker tended to all our needs, until we didn't know how to exist without Him. Neelix is the complete opposite of that cloistered life I ran away from. He's everything I've ever wanted to be."

"Oh," Torres said weakly. She seemed taken aback by the passionate intensity of Kes's avowal. She peered through the tangles of vines and tendrils at Neelix's creeping form, as if seeing the familiar Talaxian for the first time. "Well," Torres admitted eventually, "I didn't care much for your hometown, either." Kes recalled that B'Elanna had nearly died when the Caretaker infected her with His own alien DNA. "Compared to that place, I can see where life with Neelix might not seem so bad."

There is more to us than that, Kes thought. *Far more than you may ever understand.* She wondered briefly if B'Elanna had ever loved anyone as much as she loved Neelix. Did Klingons love? She would have to ask The Doctor someday. There had to be plenty of information about Klingons in *Voyager's* medical files.

Footsteps slapped against the nearby walkway. Kes froze, as did her two companions. Would the lush foliage be enough to conceal them? She wanted to lower herself even deeper into the scrub, but she was afraid to move. She held her breath, hoping that the footsteps would walk on uninterrupted. *Please,* she thought, *keep on going. Don't see us!*

The footsteps stopped. "Hello?" Came a deep voice with an unmistakably Ryol accent. "Is anybody there?"

Caught! Kes's spirits sank. As a child, she had played many games of hide-and-seek amid the numerous nooks and crannies of the Ocampa's subterranean habitat, but never before had she wished so fervently for the ability to turn invisible. *Maybe,* she thought, *if we all stay very, very still. . . .*

Leaves rustled faintly ahead of her as B'Elanna Torres began to creep toward the path, stalking forward like some nocturnal predator on the prowl. Alarmed, Kes could do nothing but watch as her half-Klingon colleague risked exposure. *What is she up to?* Kes wondered. *Is she out of her mind?*

A beam of incandescent light began to sweep over the underbrush. Kes remembered the light-projecting crystal the lifeguard had employed the last time she and Neelix had attempted to visit the shore at night. There was no way they could hide from that penetrating illumination; it was only a matter of moments before they were all uncovered. Whatever dubious plan Torres had embarked upon, she could not possibly carry through with her strategy—unless the guard could be distracted.

"Here I am!" Kes blurted, standing up suddenly amid the waving green and purple fronds. The foliage came to just below her hips. She turned to face the oncoming beam. Beyond the blinding glare of the spotlight, she glimpsed the silhouette of a Ryol lifeguard. Was he carrying a weapon? Kes could not tell, but she doubted it. It dawned on her that she had never seen any evidence of weaponry on any of her excursions to Ryolanov. *Could the Ryol truly be so peaceful?* she marveled. *It's possible, I suppose.*

Then why was her heart pounding like a frightened animal's? Neither she nor Neelix had thought to carry a phaser. She wasn't so sure about B'Elanna, although she'd noticed earlier that the engineer had brought along a tricorder.

"Who's there?" the guard demanded. His tone was colder than she had come to expect from the Ryol. "Identify yourself."

"My name is Kes," she said. "I'm from the starship. *Voyager.* Perhaps we've met before?" *Where is B'Elanna?* she thought desperately. *What is she doing?* "I'm with Captain Janeway's crew."

"Are you alone?" the guard asked. The beam of light slid away from her, shifting its focus to the surrounding underbrush, exposing the empty spaces between the branches and vines. The light fell on the very spot that Torres had vacated mere seconds before. Panic gripped Kes; she knew that Torres—and Neelix—could not be very far away.

"Yes!" she insisted, taking a step toward the guard with her least-threatening smile frozen upon her face. She raised her arms slowly above her head and tried to look sheepish and embarrassed. Anything to divert his attention from the foliage.

"Don't move," the guard barked. His beam continued to search the bushes and living coral. *We're sunk,* Kes thought. She tried to convince herself that the lifeguard didn't really mean them any harm. *What's the worst the Ryol can do to us? Turn us over to the captain for a stern reprimand?* Although a reasonable assumption, the prediction did not reassure her. There was more at stake than some temporary embarrassment. The voices had convinced her of that.

Branches snapped and tendrils shook as Neelix noisily climbed onto his feet. "No need to trouble yourself, my good man," he called out to the guard. "You've found me." He looked over at Kes. "Thanks for trying to cover for me, sweetie, but there's obviously no point in hiding any longer. Our friend here is too shrewd for that."

"Stay where you are," the guard said, inspecting Neelix by the light of his crystal. With the glare out of her eyes, Kes got a better look at the man. He might have been the same lifeguard that had halted them before, but she wasn't sure; the Ryol were practically uniform in their physical attractiveness. At the very least, this guard was equally tall and imposing. The Ryol male wore an armless silken robe over his skimpy beach attire: a concession, Kes assumed, to the breezy evening. Sandals protected his feet from the cooling sand. A scowl marred his otherwise handsome features. "The beach is closed," he said. "What are you doing here?"

"I don't suppose you'd believe me if I told you that we were looking for a lost dilithium crystal?" Neelix suggested. "No, I didn't think so. What if I told you it was of great sentimental value?"

The guard looked skeptical—and none too amused. *If this is the same man as before,* Kes thought, *then he might well assume that Neelix and I are here on our own, as we were last time. B'Elanna could still have a chance to escape.*

"Don't blame Neelix," she said quickly. "This is all my fault. I begged him to bring me here. It seemed like such a beautiful night for a midnight swim. I couldn't resist."

"The tides are dangerous," the guard said. His spotlight bounced back and forth between Neelix and Kes. "You shouldn't be here."

"I know," Kes said. "I'm sorry. We'll leave now." *And try again the first chance we get,* she thought.

She slowly lowered her arms as the guard appeared to mull over her words. For a few hopeful moments, she thought they might actually be able to talk their way out of this unwanted encounter. Then the guard shook his head grimly. "I'm afraid you'll have to come with me," he said.

To where? Kes wondered. Visions of prison—and worse—flashed through her mind. She remembered the unrelieved torment in the cries of the bodiless voices. She suddenly wondered if she would ever see *Voyager* again.

The rational part of her brain kept telling her that she was overreacting, that the peaceful and hospitable Ryol would hardly execute someone for trespassing on a beach, but another part of her, something deeper, perhaps, and more primal, was shouting out a frantic warning in a voice impossible to ignore or disregard.

For the first time, she found herself assessing the muscular lifeguard as a potential foe, and wondering if she and Neelix together were enough to overpower him. *And won't I have a hard time,* she thought, *explaining that to the captain!*

The Ryol seemed to read her mind. "Come over here," he said. "Slowly. You, too," he added to Neelix.

She exchanged an uncertain glance with her companion. *What do we do now?* Her hand hovered above her commbadge as she considered calling *Voyager* for an immediate beam-out. *If necessary,* she decided, but maybe they could still talk their way out of this situation. Neelix was good at that. Brushing aside the coral and anemone plants surrounding her, she began to tread hesitantly toward the walkway. Neelix moved to intercept her as the guard looked on, peering at them with his milky green eyes.

Those eyes widened suddenly as he went falling backward, his legs yanked out from beneath him. B'Elanna Torres pounced out of the shrubs directly in front of the Ryol, growling in fierce triumph even before the man's head connected with the pavement. Kes heard his skull bang against the fused black sand and winced in sympathy. Torres leaped astride the fallen Ryol, her clenched fists poised to strike, but the guard did not rise. He lay where he fell, sprawled atop the path. Despite her natural empathy, Kes felt a surge of relief.

"B'Elanna!" she exclaimed anyway. "What have you done?"

"Me?" Torres replied, stepping away from the supine figure. "I didn't do anything. He slipped on the sand." Turning her back on the guard, she strode toward the beach, a phaser tucked neatly into her belt. "Well?" she asked, looking back at Kes and Neelix. "Are you coming or not?"

I guess so, Kes thought. She changed course and

headed after Torres, away from the lighted walkway. "Neelix?" she called.

"Just a minute, honey," he said. Hurrying onto the walk, he bent over the unconscious guard and extracted something from the man's fingers. Kes was confused by his actions until she saw the white radiance emanating from Neelix's grip. *Of course,* she thought, *the light crystal.* "I thought it might come in handy," he said.

With the aid of the crystal, they easily caught up with Torres, who, tricorder in hand, continued to advance toward the shore. Leaving the path and its bordering foliage behind, the trio trudged across the sandy beach in search of the land's end. Their footing was uneven; Kes stumbled more than once over tiny dunes of rounded pellets. "Here, sweetie," Neelix said, taking her arm. "Let me help."

The farther they went, the more they depended on the beam of light scouting the terrain before them. The night was dark and silent. As her heartbeat gradually slowed to normal, Kes could barely hear the waves lapping against the shore. They sounded very far away.

So did the screams. She could sense them again, wailing at the periphery of her awareness, but she did her best to keep them at bay. She had heard these same cries before; there was nothing more they could teach her. This time she had to go beyond the screams, to find the unknown horror at the heart of their pain and fear.

Keep on going, she told herself. She hung on to Neelix's arm as if it was anchoring her to reality. "I don't understand," she said. "Shouldn't we have reached the water by now? I don't remember it being so far from the path."

"The tide's out," Torres said, only a few meters ahead. "The Ryol weren't lying about that." She marched on resolutely, following the lead of the spotlight. No sign of hesitation or doubt was displayed on her half-Klingon features.

Tides were a new concept to Kes, but she understood the basic idea: the section of beach they were crossing now was underwater during the day. Indeed, now that she thought about it, the sand felt moister and muddier the farther they walked. Her boots sunk into the watery sand, which burped squishily each time she pulled her boots free of the muck. *Surely,* she thought, *the sea could not be much farther away.*

"Er, what exactly are we looking for again, sweetie?" Neelix asked softly. He glanced down at the sticky mud clinging to the bottom of his trousers. The shiny chartreuse fabric had turned black around his ankles.

"Antimatter," Torres answered for her, "though what it's doing out here under all this dirt and water I can't begin to imagine." She scowled at the readings on her tricorder, evidently finding them difficult to believe.

Am I looking for antimatter, too? Kes wondered. It seemed reasonable to assume that there was a connection between B'Elanna's mysterious sensor readings and her own strange feelings about the beach, but she still couldn't see how any technological conundrum, no matter how surprising, could have anything to do with the anguish she heard in these bodiless screams. In truth, she didn't really know what she was looking for, only that the answer waited somewhere in the darkness ahead of her.

Torres halted abruptly, so quickly that Kes and Neelix almost bumped into her before they stopped as well. "What is it?" Neelix asked.

"Look," Torres said, pointing to the far end of the spotlight. Neelix raised the crystal to give them all a better look.

About ten meters ahead, at the outer limit of the incandescent beam, the muddy surface gave way to . . . nothing. The spotlight illuminated nothing but blackness beyond the edge of the beach. Kes listened for the sound of the ocean, but the water still seemed quite distant. There was nothing ahead of them but empty air.

"A drop-off," Neelix realized aloud. "An underwater cliff."

"Not so underwater now," Torres said. "Good thing you brought along that light. We could have walked right over the edge."

"Thanks," Neelix said, looking a bit smug. "It always pays to be prepared. You never know when you might need something you almost left behind. Like my father used to tell me, right before we ran out of double-plaited meteorite renderers—"

"I *said,*" Torres said brusquely, cutting him off, "it was a good idea." She looked at Kes. "What's next?"

Kes took a deep breath. Carefully, cautiously, she lowered her psychic shields by a few degrees. Almost instantly the screams came streaming through the cracks in her defenses, deafening her. They were louder and more frenzied than ever before. Wherever the screamers were, it was like she was standing right on top of them, feeling the vibrations rise up through her body, shaking her bones from her feet to the top of her skull. It was more than she could bear. The screams filled her up, drowning her, until they came pouring out of her lungs, erupting from her throat and out between her lips.

Her psychic shields slammed into place in self-defense, evicting the alien screams from her mind. With a violent shudder, she found Neelix's arm wrapped around her. He held the palm of one hand tightly over her mouth. "Sssh," he hushed her, and Kes realized that she must have been screaming for real.

She nodded, signaling him that she was all right again. Caring yellow eyes searched hers, looking for confirmation and finding it. He lifted his hand away from her face. Kes sighed and slumped against him, resting her weight upon his reassuring solidity. "Kes," he whispered, "what was it? You nearly scared me out of my wits."

"Not that far to go," Torres muttered. Kes ignored her.

She marshaled what remained of her strength and pulled away from Neelix. She walked to the very brink of the cliff and looked out over the darkness. "They're down there," she said.

"Who?" Torres asked.

"Them," Kes said. "The victims."

The captain's commbadge chirped, interrupting the conference in her briefing room. She stood up at the head of the table and tapped her badge impatiently.

"Janeway here. What is it?"

"Transporter Room Two, Captain. The Elder's daughter is here for her tour."

Oh hell, Janeway thought. She had completely forgotten about Laazia's planned tour of *Voyager.* This was the last thing she needed now. "Is she alone?" she asked, afraid that Varathael himself might have decided to accompany his heir.

"No," came the voice from the transporter room. Janeway identified it as belonging to Lieutenant Zon Kellar, a veteran technician and enthusiastic amateur musician. "She's brought along about a half-dozen companions."

"Including the Elder?"

"No, Captain. They all seem to be about her age."

Thank heaven for small favors, Janeway thought. She wanted to delay her next meeting with Varathael until she had a better idea of what the Ryol were really up to. In the meantime, however, what to do about this tour business? She glanced around the faces at the table; she could tell by their expressions that Chakotay, Tuvok, and Tom Paris had all heard Lieutenant Kellar's unfortunate announcement. Paris looked particularly uncomfortable. Amused, it occurred to Janeway that she might have enjoyed the young officer's embarrassment if the overall situation had been less dire. "Any suggestions?" she asked the assembled officers.

"I recommend caution," Tuvok said. "Until we know more, we must consider the Ryol to be a potentially dangerous life-form."

"I'm inclined to agree," Chakotay said, "although I'm not going on much more than a hunch. A *strong* hunch, granted."

The kind of hunch you get from your spirit guide, Janeway thought. She knew better than to dismiss his more mystical insights out of hand. "Your points are well taken," she said, sitting down in her chair. "On the other hand, we've already conducted a couple of earlier tours for various Ryol dignitaries without any negative results. More importantly, our relations with the Ryol are at a touchy-enough juncture without completely snubbing the Elder's only heir. Let's not start circling the wagons just yet, gentlemen. Aside from Naxor's unauthorized attack on Tom and the others, we still have no firm evidence that the Ryol mean us any harm. To the contrary, they have decisively punished the only Ryol to assault one of us, punished him even more severely than we might like."

We have enough enemies in this quadrant, she thought, *without making any more.* It bothered her sometimes that they had yet to make a lasting alliance with any of the advanced races and societies inhabiting the Delta Quadrant; Starfleet was about meeting new civilizations, not running away from them.

"Besides," she said, "if we do have to sever our association with the Ryol, let's get all our people to safety first."

Are B'Elanna and the others in danger down at that beach? Maybe so, she decided, but she was reluctant to call them back before they had their chance to unravel the mysteries they'd discovered. In the end, all of *Voyager* might depend on the information that those three crew members managed to track down. *Find out what you need to,* she thought to the missing crew members, *and get back here pronto.*

"Your analysis is quite logical," Tuvok conceded. "Still, I cannot recommend permitting any Ryol to have access to the ship while their true nature and intentions remain in doubt."

"Agreed," Janeway said, "but let's be diplomatic about this." She turned her attention toward Paris. "Lieutenant," she addressed him, "the rest of us have bigger fish to fry. I'm afraid that sticks you with the task of greeting Laazia and her friends and inventing some plausible excuse for postponing their tour indefinitely. You have any problem with that?"

If Paris had any qualms about his assignment, he did a good job of hiding them. He only hesitated for an instant. "No, ma'am."

"Very good," Janeway said. "I know I can count on your judgment—and discretion." She rose from her seat. "I think that concludes this meeting for now. Chakotay, take command of the bridge. Tuvok, you're with me. Let's head for the sickbay and see if The Doctor has learned anything about that Ryol DNA. With Kes off the ship, he might be able to use a couple extra pairs of hands."

"Captain," Paris said as they headed for the door. "What about Kes and the others?"

A very good question, Janeway thought. She hated to put any of her crew at risk, but took comfort from the fact that none of them had called for help just yet. "For now," she said, "we have to assume they can take care of themselves."

Be careful down there, she thought privately. *And come back soon.*

"I'm not sure," Neelix said, "but I think I see some sort of cave entrance."

The cliff dropped roughly twenty meters to the muddy harbor floor. Neelix dangled headfirst over the edge while Torres and Kes, kneeling side by side in the moist sand, each held on to one of his legs. The cuffs of his trousers were wet and slippery, but Kes kept a tight grip upon her companion's leg. There was no way she was going to let him fall, even if it took all the strength she had.

"I don't know how I let you two talk me into this," Neelix commented. "The way we Talaxians are designed, our heads are supposed to be *above* our feet."

"Stop babbling," Torres said. Kneeling in the cold damp sand had not improved her disposition. "Can you see anything else?"

"Not really," Neelix answered, "just a lot of muck and rock. The cliff face looks pretty solid, though. There must be a firm foundation of rock underneath all that sand up there."

I knew it, Kes thought. There was definitely more beneath them than just the bottom of the harbor. The screams came from down there . . . somewhere. She could still hear them, their faint voices drawing her onward.

Working together, she and Torres pulled Neelix back onto the safety of the sandy beach overlooking the cliff. His face was flushed and ruddy at first, but gravity quickly drained the excess blood from his features. Long black streaks, left behind by the muddy cliff face, stained the front of his clothes. Kes took a moment to catch her breath after the exertion of dragging Neelix up and over the brink. Her legs were soaked all the way up to her knees. Chilly black mud coated the bottom halves of her legs. Even wearing Neelix's jacket, she still felt cold.

"So," Torres said to Neelix, glancing again at the readings on her tricorder, "I guess the next step is to check out that cave you think you spotted."

"Yes!" Kes insisted, surprised herself by the urgency in her voice. She crept to the edge of the cliff and looked at the exposed sea bed so far below. It was a long way down. "But how are we going to get down there?"

"I don't know," Neelix said. "I wish I'd thought to bring a rope."

"I thought Talaxians were always prepared," Torres said dryly. Kes found herself growing annoyed at B'Elanna's sarcastic attitude, especially when it was directed at Neelix. She resisted the temptation to snap at B'Elanna. *It's this mission,* she thought. *We're all on edge.*

"Do you think all that mud is soft enough to cushion our fall?" she asked the others.

Neelix shook his head. "I wouldn't want to risk it. There could be more rock only a few inches beneath the muck." He scratched his chin thoughtfully, leaving muddy fingerprints upon his jaw. "Maybe if we formed a humanoid ladder—"

"Frankly," Torres interrupted him, "I've always preferred more high-tech solutions." She rose from her knees and tapped her commbadge. "Torres to *Voyager,* requesting an immediate site-to-site transport. Three to beam to the following coordinates."

Kes heard Torres specify a site approximately five meters ahead (and twenty meters below) of their present location, then felt the familiar tingle of a transporter beam scanning her body. A golden radiance appeared before her eyes, a hum filled her ears, and Kes found herself kneeling at the base of the cliff, looking up at the sheer rocky expanse of mud-slick stone that loomed before her. Torres and Neelix stood and sat, respectively, beside her. "Look!" Neelix shouted, jumping to his feet. "There it is!"

Just as he'd informed them, the cliff held the entrance to what looked like a cavern of some kind. Beneath a jutting arch of rock, a shadow-filled opening penetrated the high stone wall before them. It looked large enough for two standard-sized humanoids to enter the tunnel simultaneously. Neelix shined the light of his borrowed crystal into the gap, but the bright white ray revealed only the first few meters past the entrance. What lay beyond that remained cloaked in darkness.

Torres pointed her tricorder at the cave, then checked the readout. "We're on the right track," she announced. "I'm detecting a concentration of subspace ripples far above the statistical average for ordinary matter."

Shivering, Kes climbed to her feet and contemplated the ominous threshold in front of her. Wrapped in Neelix's motley jacket, she hugged herself to stay warm. They were getting closer to the secret of the screams, she knew. *We're almost there.*

Anticipation of whatever horror awaited her nearly unnerved Kes completely. She had to force herself to take the first step toward the opening of the cave. *We're coming,* she told the voices in her head. *Your long wait is over. I'm going to find you at last.*

The mud was about two meters deep where the three of them now stood. They waded through cold black sludge until they reached the entrance to the cave. The scent of ginger in their nostrils was overpowering. Kes held her hand over her mouth and felt like gagging.

"I'll go first," Neelix volunteered, raising the crystal to eye level. He stepped beneath the rocky ledge, then looked back over his shoulder. "Say, it just occurred to me: do either of you know when the tide comes back?"

Kes had no idea. All she knew was that, by the time the beach opened at dawn, this entire area—the towering cliff and much of the muddy terrain before and beyond it—would be several meters beneath the water. It was a frightening thought, especially for someone who was just learning how to swim.

"I don't know," she confessed. Neither did Torres.

"I was afraid of that." Neelix sighed. "C'mon. We'd better hurry then."

The cave turned out to be a tunnel, leading downward at a steep incline to somewhere below the base of the cliff. A thin trickle of silty golden water ran down the path ahead of them. Kes wished it were fresh enough to drink from; her throat felt dry and sore from all that screaming earlier. At first the tunnel looked like a natural formation, but the deeper they descended the more the tunnel betrayed signs of deliberate technological artifice. The muddy uneven cavern floor gave way to a polished black surface complete with vents to drain away the remainder of the sea water. Smooth obsidian walls rose at perfect right angles to the floor, meeting in a graceful arch above their heads. Someone had obviously carved this corridor on purpose, Kes realized, while taking pains to make its exterior look like nothing more than a natural crevice. But why choose such an inaccessible location for the entrance, especially one that was submerged for large portions of the day? Where did this tunnel lead?

"This is more like it," Torres commented as she walked beside Kes, scanning their surroundings with the tricorder. "This looks like a place where the Ryol might actually store antimatter."

Maybe, Kes thought, but she knew there had to be much more hiding down here. Antimatter didn't scream.

Eventually they discovered the door: a sheet of solid metal blocking their way. The silver sheen of the door contrasted vividly with the polished black walls of the corridor. Only a handle located halfway up the metal sheet suggested that in fact it was a door and not a barricade. Neelix tugged on the handle with his free hand. The door didn't budge. He handed the light crystal over to Kes so he could use both hands, but his strenuous efforts proved futile. The door remained firmly in place. "Locked," he said, wiping the sweat from his speckled forehead with a muddy paw. "A dead end."

"Duranium," Torres clarified, consulting her tricorder. "Three centimeters thick." She inspected a faint tracing of reddish rust around the edges of the door. "From the look of things, no one's used this door in a long time." She drew the phaser from her belt.

"Wait!" Kes exclaimed. "What are you doing?"

"You have a better idea?" Torres asked. She raised the setting on her phaser and aimed it at the door. A beam of glowing red energy sizzled through the air, striking the door just above the handle. The silver metal turned red where the beam hit it, then blue, then white-hot. Tears of melted metal ran down the length of the door, pooling upon the floor in front of their feet. Kes stepped backward instinctively. Torres switched off the beam with a flick of her finger. A hole about the size of a humanoid's fist had formed above the door handle. "Give it a few minutes to cool," Torres told Neelix, "then try it again."

Kes swallowed hard. This felt suspiciously like breaking-and-entering to her. B'Elanna was right, though: there weren't any other options, not if they wanted to find out what the Ryol were hiding down here.

It took several minutes, actually, before the door cooled sufficiently to touch it once more. Neelix blew upon the silver handle nervously, then placed his hands lightly on the metal bar. A grin broke out on his mud-covered face as his flesh declined to sear upon contact with the door. Tightening his grip, he yanked hard upon the handle.

With an ear-piercing shriek, the massive door swung open. Torres kept her phaser aimed straight ahead, just in case there was something hostile on the other side of the door. Kes held her breath, unsure of what to expect.

What they found was wreckage. Beyond the door was an awesome display of torn and twisted metal—and the silence of a tomb. The door opened onto a narrow ledge from which Kes and her companions looked down upon the sundered remains of a broken starship.

Huge curved pillars supported the rough stone ceiling above them, creating a vast artificial cavern to hold the ruins below. The alien vessel was enormous, nearly twice the size of *Voyager,* but it was clear at a glance, even to such an inexperienced eye as Kes's, that it would never fly again. The hull, made of a reflective green material that still gleamed brightly here and there, was breached at over a dozen locations. Great gaping fissures opened all along the ship's metallic skin, revealing glimpses of the devastation within. At one time, Kes guessed, the ship had been essentially cylindrical in shape, but now its frame was so bent and distorted, with huge chunks of debris jutting out from the hull at unlikely angles, that it was difficult to visualize the vessel's original contours. Scorch marks and charred, blackened metal provided evidence of long-quenched fires while gigantic patches of rust and corrosion hinted at the length of the ship's entombment. Cobwebs the size of holodecks stretched across the ragged gaps in the hull. The dust of years, maybe even of centuries, lay upon the grimly breathtaking scene. For an Ocampa such as Kes, to whom eight or nine years constituted a lifetime, the sheer age of the ruins was even more impressive than its size.

"Of course!" Torres exclaimed, scanning the wreck with feverish excitement. "I should have guessed. The ship's trashed, but there must be reserves of antimatter locked away in the warp engines. Maybe even some dilithium crystals, too!"

"Do you think we can claim salvage rights?" Neelix asked, sharing Torres's enthusiasm. He probed the broken starship with his spotlight, the incandescent beam darting back and forth over the twisted length of the wreck.

Torres rolled her eyes. "I think the Ryol can reasonably claim that they knew this was here. After all, *somebody* carved that tunnel, not to mention reinforcing the ceiling up there."

"Oh," Neelix said, his bubble only slightly burst. "I'll bet we can still make a good deal for whatever we need. Trust me on this. I was bartering used and abandoned spaceships while you were still going to Klingon Kiddie School . . . or whatever."

At the moment, Kes didn't care about the salvage rights or the dilithium. She gazed down upon the ancient ruins. *Is this what happened to you?* she thought. *Did you all perish in some long-ago crash? Is that why you scream?*

"Do you recognize the design?" she asked Neelix. "Can you tell me who they were?"

"Hmmm. I'm not sure." He used the light crystal to pick out the details of the wreck. "Not Kazon, not Trabe, not Haakonian, not a modern design at all. It bears a slight resemblance to the ships of the old Pahkarpian Empire, but only a little. To be honest, it's such a mess that I think you'd need an historian, an archaeologist, *and* an expert engineer to figure out its origins."

"I see," Kes said. She couldn't tear her gaze away

from the broken ship. She tried to imagine what the crash must have been like. "Do you think there were any survivors?"

Compassion filled his eyes as he responded to the sorrow in her voice. "I don't know, sweetie. Maybe the Ryol can tell us. That ship's been here a long time, though; if there were any survivors, they must've died out years ago."

No, she thought. *That's not true.* She didn't know how she knew that, but she was certain of it. There was more here than she could see now, a tragedy even greater than that implied by the sight of the ravaged spacecraft. The crash was just the beginning. . . .

"I need to get closer," she said. "I need to go inside that ship."

Transporter Room Two was only a turbolift away from the captain's conference room. Tom Paris spent the brief ride wondering how to cope with his swiftly arriving encounter with Laazia. *It should only take a minute or two to send them back home. No problem. I can handle this,* he thought—until the doors slid open and he found himself staring into the captivating green eyes of the Elder's daughter.

"Tom!" Laazia called out, the vibrato in her voice rippling through the air. She was even more stunning than he remembered. She wore an indigo velvet cape over a flowing gown of turquoise silk. The cape fell to her ankles and was held on by a silver clasp about her slender throat. The gown, cut low in the front, shimmered when she moved, attracting his eye to the curving lines of her body. Elegant sandals, dyed the same turquoise hue as her gown, adorned her feet. Silver jewelry glittered on her ears, fingers, wrists, and ankles. Her short blond hair had been streaked with black tiger stripes; it looked good on her.

"Dear Tom, I didn't dare to hope that you would be the one to meet us," Laazia said. "What a pleasant surprise." With a graceful flourish of her cape, she gestured toward her entourage. "These are my friends and associates. You remember Romeela and Sitruua, don't you? I'm sure your friend Harry does."

Paris tore his gaze away from the exquisite vision Laazia presented and scoped out the rest of her party. To his relief, he didn't see Naxor or any of his cronies from the ambush on the beach. Six Ryol had accompanied Laazia to *Voyager,* three men and three women. Paris thought he recognized most of them from his various excursions to Ryolanov, including the two women from the dance club. Lieutenant Kellar, along with two security officers, stood by at the transporter controls. Paris was glad they were there. *Who am I afraid of?* he thought ruefully. *Laazia or myself?*

"Welcome to *Voyager,*" he said in his best tour guide's voice. "My name, as most of you know, is Tom Paris. The captain and the first officer are busy right now, but Captain Janeway sent me to welcome you aboard—and to apologize for having to postpone your tour of the ship."

"Postpone?" Laazia looked surprised. The other Ryol made disappointed noises.

"I'm afraid so," he said. "I'm afraid *Voyager* has been contaminated by an unexpected cosmic ray fluctuation. It's nothing serious, but we have to conduct a complete baryon sweep of the entire starship and you might be exposed to some trace radiation if you stayed." He sighed. "I know, it's terrible, but what can we do? I'm sure we can reschedule your tour as soon as we're sure the ship has been completely decontaminated."

Are they buying this? Paris wondered. He hoped Laazia hadn't brought any physicists or radiation experts along on this outing.

He addressed the entire group, but the other Ryol seemed to defer to Laazia. "But we have been so looking forward to this," she objected. "Surely, this procedure can't be that hazardous."

"I certainly hope so," Paris said with a grin, "but the captain refuses to take any chances with guests of your stature, especially since we know so little about your physiology. You might have a lower tolerance for baryon particles than the rest of us."

His improvised explanation sounded convincing enough to Paris, but Laazia would not give up that easily. "Please, Tom, can't we see just a little of the ship? Perhaps just a quick peek at the control center? That is the heart and mind of the vessel, is it not?"

Not a good idea, Paris thought, *until we figure out exactly who and what you people are.* "I'm afraid that's not possible right now," he explained. "First Officer Chakotay is performing some delicate flight simulations and can't be disturbed." He shrugged his shoulders. "To be honest, there's really not much to see there, just a lot of boring people hard at work on their jobs. It's not exactly a spectator sport." He hoped he sounded sincere.

"I see," Laazia said. She stepped closer to Paris, almost enveloping him in the swell of her cape. Her perfume went straight from his nostrils to his brain, sending a thrill up and down his spine. He could feel the heat radiating from her body. "In that case," she whispered, "perhaps we should go directly to your quarters?"

"Oh," Paris muttered, caught off guard by Laazia's frontal assault. *Thank goodness I'm not the blushing type,* he thought, stealing a glance at Lieutenant Kellar and the security team. *Did they hear her?* he wondered. *What would the captain think?* He looked past Laazia at her assembled companions. "Don't you think it might get a bit crowded?" he asked her.

"They can wait outside if you like," she intoned, lowering her already husky voice even lower than he would have ever guessed possible. She laid her bare hand upon his chest. Beneath her long black lashes, malachite eyes seemed to probe his very soul. He couldn't look away. Her pupils, like miniature wormholes, exerted some sort of gravitational pull on his thoughts, sending them spiraling on a dizzy course to an unknown quadrant of his brain. "They're very discreet."

As if to demonstrate, she snapped her fingers with her free hand. Instantly the other Ryol formed a protective circle around Paris and the Elder's heir. She snapped her fingers twice more, and the six men and women turned their backs on Paris and Laazia, facing away toward the walls of the transporter room. "Lieutenant Paris?" Kellar called out, with an edge of anxiety in his voice.

"Everything's under control," Paris reassured him, staring into Laazia's pale green eyes. *I think.* Her pupils seemed to be growing larger and more black. That was bad news, he remembered, but he was past caring. It felt like her eyes had forged a direct connection to his nervous system. "You have your friends pretty well-trained, I see," he said, struggling to keep his tone light and breezy. His own voice sounded strange to him, like a stranger's.

"Of course," she said. Laughter bubbled up from the depths of her elegant throat. "No one ever says no to me for long."

"No one?" he asked, half-afraid of the answer. "Ever?"

She did not waste any more words. Still holding on to him with her eyes, she lowered his mouth to her lips. The kiss hit him like a phaser set on stun. He had to grab her to steady himself. All his resolution and better judgment, along with the better part of his strength, nearly evaporated in the heat of her kiss and the promises it bestowed. He felt his defenses crumbling. *What am I doing?* came one last dwindling voice at the back of what remained of his mind. *Why can't I stop her?*

Laazia withdrew her lips. Paris gaped at her like a fish plucked abruptly from the water that sustained it. "Now," she said, "your quarters."

"Yes," he murmured, confused and disoriented. Hadn't her eyes been green before? They were almost entirely black now.

Cobwebs, dusty white and clingy, hung like curtains along the twisted corridors of the broken ship. The air felt musty and old. A heavy layer of dust lay over every exposed surface while small six-legged vermin, resembling a cross between a spider and a mouse, scurried into the shadows whenever the light of Neelix's crystal fell upon them. Kes heard their tiny feet scuttling beneath the floor and within the walls.

Beneath the webbing and the dust, strange hieroglyphics decorated the walls. Not even Neelix, who was fluent in most of the major languages of the Delta Quadrant, recognized the symbols. Torres recorded the inscriptions with her tricorder; in theory, the ship's computer could translate the symbols using the same algorithms employed by their Universal Translators. *Probably just directional signs,* Kes guessed, but it couldn't hurt to decipher them later.

Dead insects, along with miniature scraps of bone and fur, clung to the webs, but Kes did not spot any larger remains, humanoid or otherwise. "No casualties," she said. "Do you think they all survived the crash?"

Who were you? she thought. *What happened to you?*

"Hard to say," Neelix answered her. He tore through a wide sheet of webbing, clearing a path for the others. "If there were survivors, they might have removed the bodies of any casualties for burial or cremation or whatever their customs required."

"From the look of things," Torres said, scanning the

surrounding wreckage with her tricorder, "there's been some attempt to salvage technology from this ship. I'm detecting serious gaps in the communication and energy transfer systems. Somebody cleaned this place out, and probably a long time ago."

"Except for the antimatter," Neelix pointed out.

Torres nodded. "Antimatter is dangerous to transport without the proper equipment. It may have been safer just to leave it where it is." She checked her tricorder again, then pointed toward the rear of the ship. "I think I've located the engine room," she said. "This way."

"No," Kes said. "I mean, not yet." She felt something pulling her in another direction, calling to her from the bowels of the ruined spacecraft. She walked past Neelix with one hand held up in front of her to keep the cobwebs away from her face. Sticky strips of gauzelike webbing fastened onto her uniform, trying to impede her progress, but Kes pushed her way through the webs, following the path of Neelix's spotlight. Her footsteps echoed down the lifeless hallway. *Just up ahead,* she thought, although she couldn't say why. *That's where we have to go.*

"What is it?" Torres asked impatiently. She clearly trusted her tricorder more than Kes's psychic intuition. "What exactly are you looking for?"

"Here," Kes said. She got down on her knees and brushed away the dust covering the floor. The spotlight fell upon a crescent-shaped gap in the metal tile. She stuck her hand into the gap, feeling the curved edge of a steel plate approximately two centimeters thick. It was a circular hatchway, she realized, only partially open. She tugged on the plate, but it wouldn't budge. She gritted her teeth and tried again, straining her muscles against the ancient inertia of the hatch. At first it refused to move, but then the hatch slipped just a sliver, sliding under the surrounding tiles and opening a slightly larger crescent in the floor. Kes let out a sigh of satisfaction; it wasn't much, but at least she'd proved that the hatch could still move.

"Hang on, sweetie," Neelix said. "Let me help." He looked around for a place on which to rest the light crystal.

"Never mind," Torres told him. "I'll do it." She squatted in the dust beside Kes and handed Kes her tricorder. Gripping the hatch with both hands, she tried to pull it all the way open. A low growl escaped her lips as she fought to overcome the hatch's years of disuse. Rusty metal shrieked in protest, hurting Kes's sensitive ears, but the hatch yielded to B'Elanna's demi-Klingon strength. A circular portal, roughly three meters in diameter, appeared in the floor.

Neelix stepped forward and shined his light upon the portal. Peering through the circle, Kes saw a spiral staircase leading to lower and lower levels of the ship. Voices from below, silent to all but Kes, seemed to rise up along the stairway, growing ever louder in her head. "They're down there," she announced.

"Who?" Torres demanded, wiping her dust-covered hands off on her uniform. "Are you hunting for ghosts or what?"

"Maybe," Kes said, suspecting that B'Elanna would prefer a more scientific explanation. "I've told you what I feel. How would you describe it?"

Torres hesitated before answering. "Maybe it's just the psionic residue of a past event so devastating that it continues to send psychic ripples through the space-time continuum. I'm an engineer, not a telepath, but I know that psionic energy can have measurable effects on the physical world."

Kes thought that explanation sounded as good as any other. "All I know," she said, "is that the screams are coming from below, so that's where we have to go next."

Torres mulled over Kes's words for a few minutes. "Well," she said eventually, "you're obviously on to something, or we wouldn't have gotten this far." She reclaimed her tricorder from Kes and tucked it into her belt. "I guess that antimatter isn't going anywhere soon." She lowered her legs into the open hatch and starting hiking down the stairs. "Let's go," she said.

The spiral stairs led to the next level, then onto the level below that. Each step consisted of a metal grille that easily supported the weight of a Klingon, an Ocampa, or a Talaxian. Kes counted the ship's levels as they descended: one, two, three, four. . . .The air seemed to grow colder and damper the farther they went down. Torres led the way, with Neelix's light shining past her and Kes, casting long distorted shadows on each floor they passed.

Finally, thirteen levels down, they came to the end of the stairs. The trio found themselves in what looked like the remains of a large empty cargohold. Broken support beams hung like stalactites from the vaulted ceiling of the cavernous chamber; small winged creatures, like frogs but with webbed sails stretching from their fingers to their toes, flapped and glided overhead. The floor of the holding compartment appeared to have partly disintegrated on impact. Sand, rock, and coral carpeted the ground beneath their feet. Jagged formations of stone jutted through what little remained of the ship's outer wall. Purple moss coated the surface of the boulders.

Neelix searched the chamber with his spotlight, exposing nothing but debris and empty space. "There's nothing here," Torres said, scowling. "We're wasting our time."

Kes ignored her. Indeed, she was barely aware of anything except for the incessant wailing of the agonized voices crying out to her from the past. Now that she was heartbeats away from the unknown climax of her quest, the screams reached an eerie crescendo, urging her onward. Kes rushed past Torres and Neelix toward a swelling of sand and rock at the northern end of the hold. She felt driven, possessed. It frightened her; she hadn't felt this out-of-control since she was gripped by her premature elogium.

But there was nothing she could do to resist the compulsion that had seized her. As Neelix and Torres looked on, caught by surprise, she dug her hands into the mound of dirt and started digging feverishly through the gritty sediment covering the fractured floor of the ship. Clumps of sand and gravel went flying as she threw them to the side in her frantic search for . . . what? Kes wasn't certain, but she knew she had to keep digging. "Don't you see?" she called to her companions. "They're not at the bottom of the ship. They're *beneath* the ship!"

Then she saw it: a weathered stick of bone protruding from the newly exposed sand. It could have been an arm or a leg or even a rib for all she knew, but the sight energized her even more. She tore into the ground with new ferocity until she had uncovered the upper half of a skeleton lying on its side amid the rubble. A cracked brown skull, smaller than her own but seemingly humanoid, rested only centimeters away from her fingertips. Empty eye sockets, disproportionly large for the dwarfish skull, gazed up at her. *I've found you,* Kes thought triumphantly, sucking down deep gasps of air. *Tell me who you are.*

"Well, I'll be a Gristakean gutter-snail!" Neelix exclaimed. He and Torres hurried to catch up with Kes, even as her fingers touched the skull—

It was a peaceful sunny afternoon. The sky was a radiant pink, just right for this time of year. Loowo watched her children play in the field while she grinded the sweet roots to powder for their evening meal. They were healthy and strong. Her mate, Fleat, hunted for fresh mushrooms amid the swaying filaments of the tall grass, his glossy red fur brilliant beneath the noontime sunlight. Occasionally the wind brought the faint tantalizing aroma of the sea, many miles away. Birds chirped overhead and Loowo sung to herself as she worked. In the distance, she glimpsed other families, her friends and neighbors, all taking advantage of the warm afternoon. Loowo smiled, content with her life and her world. Perhaps, she mused, she and Fleat should have another child this summer.

Suddenly the birdsong ceased. Loowo heard a thunderous roar that sounded as if it were coming from the sky itself. She looked up in time to see something huge and black pass between her and the crimson glow of the sun, blotting out the very sky and throwing all the world into shadow. Loowo screamed and ran for her babies but she was already too late. The darkness crashed down upon them all, burying them forever, so that all that remained was endless suffocating blackness stretching on for year after year, century after century, trapped in the dark and forgotten. . . .

—Kes yanked her hand back as if shocked by an electrical current. Tears ran streaming down her face. "All dead. All gone," she said, sobbing. "The ship smashed them all. It crashed right on top of them, carving out the harbor and burying them all beneath the waves. It was horrible!"

"Who was buried?" Neelix asked her. He hugged her against his muddy chest, comforting her and trying to understand. Kes was glad to feel his shaggy arms around her. She couldn't have faced this nightmare alone. "The Ryol?"

"No," Kes said bitterly. "Not the Ryol." Reluctantly, she pulled herself away from Neelix's warm and soothing presence, approaching the skeleton once more. Torres stood above her scanning the ground with the tricorder.

"Amazing," Torres said. "I'm detecting partially fossilized organic remains beneath us in every direction. There must be dozens of bodies buried here, maybe hundreds."

"A whole community," Kes explained. "Wiped out in seconds." She was afraid to touch the bones again, but she blew carefully upon the tiny stones and sediment covering one of the skeleton's hands. She puffed the dirt away until they could see all *six* of the specimen's delicate finger bones.

"Not the Ryol," she said again. "The neffaler."

CHAPTER

12

"FASCINATING," TUVOK SAID.

"Remarkable," The Doctor agreed. "There can be only one explanation."

"Indeed," Tuvok said. "The logic appears unassailable."

"Well then," Captain Janeway said. "Spit it out. What have you learned?"

Janeway stood waiting in the sickbay between the twin biobeds tending to Harry Kim and Susan Tukwila. She was relieved to see that both crew members appeared to be recovering nicely, and was glad that she'd had the opportunity to spend a few minutes with each of them. Music wafted through the sickbay as Kim sat up in the bed, practicing his clarinet, while Susan was concerned about missing her upcoming shift on the bridge. Morale problems or not, Janeway felt a lot better about her crew. *Maybe the crew's in better shape than I feared,* she thought. *Like Harry and Susan, we can take everything the Delta Quadrant has to throw at us and still come out fighting.*

While she'd paid a call on her injured crew members, Tuvok and The Doctor had devoted themselves to analyzing the Ryol tissue Tuvok had extracted from Naxor. Now they emerged from the attached medical laboratory with the sample in hand and a padd full of answers she was anxious to hear. *What's the real story about our newfound "friends" on Ryolanov?* she wondered. There was still no real proof that the Ryol had hostile intentions regarding *Voyager,* but Janeway was getting more suspicious by the moment.

Tuvok and The Doctor glanced briefly at each other, apparently unsure who should speak first. "Go ahead," The Doctor said. "You snatched the DNA, you do the honors."

"Very well," Tuvok said. "Captain, the evidence strongly suggests that the Ryol are not native to this planet. Their genetic structure bears no resemblance to that of any of the other life-forms present on what we have come to call Ryolanov. They are clearly the product of an entirely different evolutionary process."

"Are you sure?" Janeway asked.

"Observe," Tuvok replied. He guided her into The Doctor's laboratory, where a large viewscreen displayed two-dimensional models of three different segments of DNA, with colored markers indicating the various amino acids involved. "The pair of segments on the left belong to, respectively, a small winged mammal and a flowering shrub; the segment on the right came from the ill-tempered Mr. Naxor. As you can clearly see, the first two samples have several sequences in common, which they share with all the other life-forms we have tested. In contrast, the Ryol DNA lacks these sequences, as well as including a few distinct nucleotides that are missing entirely from the other flora and fauna of the planet." He pointed toward a series of amber-colored symbols upon the Ryol double helix.

"Yes," Janeway said. She was more of an engineer than a biologist, but she could spot the discrepancies herself.

"Either the Ryol have come here from somewhere else," The Doctor said, elaborating on the hypothesis that Tuvok had presented, "or everything else did, including the plants, insects, birds, monkeys, bacteria, and assorted varieties of fungus." He glanced at his padd. "Frankly, I lean toward the former theory. The Ryol are immigrants."

"Or invaders," Janeway said, considering all the implications of this new discovery. She took the padd from The Doctor and inspected the data more closely; as she quickly scrolled through Ryolanov's vast animal kingdom, the assembled data confirmed everything she had heard. "There's nothing inherently wrong about colonizing an uninhabited planet—the Federation does it all the time—but why should they conceal this fact from us? What are they hiding?"

"It is possible," Tuvok pointed out, "that the Ryol first arrived on this planet so many generations ago that their ancestors have long since forgotten their true origins."

"Or," The Doctor proposed, "they may simply regard it as none of our business."

"I see what you mean," Janeway said. Both explanations for the reticence of the Ryol struck her as equally plausible. While intriguing, the secret revealed by the Ryol DNA was not necessarily alarming. In light of recent events, however, she couldn't help looking for a more sinister ulterior motive behind the secrecy of the Ryol. Were they afraid, she wondered, that *Voyager* would try to stake a claim on the planet if we knew that the Ryol had not originated here? That seemed unlikely; nothing she had done or said could have given the Elder and his people the idea that she and her crew had any sort of expansionist agenda. *We said we were just passing through,* she thought. *If they didn't want us to stay, why invite us to sample all the diverse pleasures of their world. Not exactly the best way to discourage a potential conqueror.*

Genetic data continued to flash by on the padd in her hand; Tuvok had been exhaustive in his cataloging of the planet's wildlife. As she glanced down at the padd, a sketch of a semi-humanoid figure appeared on the screen. "Wait a second," she said, freezing the illustration.

A new idea occurred to her, along with the mental image of a small reddish primate carrying a tray full of hors d'oeuvres. "What if," she suggested, "the planet was not uninhabited before the Ryol came along?"

"I'm not sure what you mean," The Doctor said. Janeway realized that The Doctor was probably the only member of the crew who had not been exposed to the ubiquitous "pets" of the Ryol. *Perhaps the true inhabitants of this world,* she thought, *have been under our noses all the while. Serves us right not to pay better attention to the room service.*

Tuvok had no difficulty following her reasoning. "The neffaler?" he said. "An intriguing supposition, although it is unclear to me how that would change the nature of our relations with the Ryol. The Prime Directive argues against us interfering with the established social order, no matter how unsavory its possible origins."

"I know," Janeway said, "and yet I'm getting a very bad feeling about all this. How much have the Ryol not told us, and why?" *If they can exploit one species,* she thought, *why not another?*

Her commbadge chirped, distracting her from her suspicions. "Chakotay here," came her first officer's voice. "I have a transmission from B'Elanna on the planet's surface. She says it's urgent."

"Put her through," Janeway ordered. A second later she heard Torres speaking. The transmission was faint and full of static, as if Torres were trying to send the message through several layers of shielding. Janeway wondered just where B'Elanna was calling from.

"Captain," the engineer said, "you won't believe what we've discovered down here!"

"Try me," Janeway said.

"Alone at last," Laazia said with a throaty chuckle. Her velvet cloak was draped over her shoulders, concealing her body within its capacious folds, as she inspected Paris's quarters. In the dim lighting selected by the young officer, Laazia's eyes appeared to shift from green to black to green again. Paris sat upon the edge of his bunk, transfixed by those eyes.

His mind still felt foggy, confused. On some level he knew what he was doing was wrong, that Laazia wasn't supposed to be here, but he couldn't bring himself to defy her. He felt like a passenger in his own body, unable to halt this chain of events and break free from the disastrous path the Elder's daughter was leading him along.

As promised, her entourage had waited outside during this unplanned detour to his personal quarters. *How long had he been with Laazia?* he wondered. Ten minutes? Thirty? He found it hard to remember his original mission; it felt like ages since the captain sent him to turn Laazia away. *I failed again,* he thought. *Just like I always fail.*

"Alone," she repeated, "and far from prying eyes.

Perfect." She swept her cloak back over her shoulders, then knelt down in front of Paris until her eyes and lips were only centimeters away from his face. "Now then, I want you tell me everything you know about the bridge and its defenses."

Huh? Whatever Paris had been expecting to happen here in his quarters, this wasn't it. "The bridge?" he asked. Despite his surprise, his thoughts felt mired in the haze that had enveloped, his mind like each idea was traveling through his brain at far less than impulse speed. A momentary spark of alarm flickered weakly amid the haze.

"Yes," she said, speaking slowly as if to a child. Her eyes were as black as the cores of dying suns. "Start with the security systems in place on the bridge, then proceed to the shipboard communication network. Tell me everything, Tom."

No! his mind protested, but his lips refused to speak the word. A terrible weariness descended upon him with the force of a phaser blast. Every muscle felt drained of vigor. Gravity seemed a hundred times stronger. It took all his strength just to keep from collapsing backward onto his bunk. He tried to look away from Laazia's mesmerizing black eyes, but she took hold of his chin, her sharpened nails digging into his flesh, and kept his gaze aimed directly at her. *I should stop her,* he thought helplessly. *I should call Security.*

"Emergency phasers," he began, "are located at four convenient locations on the bridge, including Tactical, Security, Science, and Engineering. The phasers are kept set at stun, but can be adjusted by . . ."

Stop it, he thought. *Stop it.* But the words slipped past his lips, betraying both *Voyager* and himself. Despair overcame alarm, then sunk back into the numbed recesses of his mind.

Tilting his chin upward so that his eyes remained fixed at hers, Laazia rose confidently from her kneeling position. A predatory smile materialized on her face. "Tell me more," she said.

Flying frogs flapped overhead while Torres informed the captain of their discovery. Kes and Neelix looked on as she spoke. "The ship must have crash-landed here generations ago," she said, "completely destroying a neffaler community in the process. According to Kes, the original neffaler were definitely sentient, although probably pre-industrial."

The captain didn't sound too surprised, although her signal was frustratingly faint and choppy. Several layers of subterranean starship, not to mention the shielding the Ryol had put in place above the harbor, weren't helping the transmission get through. *Once the tide comes back,* Torres thought, *it will be a miracle if we can get through at all.*

"The ship definitely belongs to the Ryol," the captain said. "That fits in with some other data The Doctor and Tuvok have uncovered. It's all starting to make sense now. The Ryol must have been stranded here when their ship crashed."

Until we came along, Torres thought. A chill ran through her. *You don't have to be half-Klingon,* she mused, *to know a dangerous situation when you see one.* "Captain, I think we had better get back to *Voyager* as soon as possible. Can you beam us out of here?"

"I'll see," Janeway answered. "Tell Neelix to bring back some of those bones for testing."

Torres was turning toward Neelix when she heard the sound of a bone snapping somewhere behind her. She spun around, drawing her phaser, as gravel rattled in the shadows, several meters away. *More vermin,* she wondered, *or something more serious?* Her eyes strained to penetrate the gloomy recesses of the cargohold. "Neelix," she called out. "Over there!"

The Talaxian directed his light crystal in the direction she indicated. The beam fell upon three tall figures standing at the base of the stairway. Golden manes framed their faces. Bronze skin covered muscular bodies. One of the men stepped forward. A multifaceted red gem glittered upon his chest, suspended by a silver chain. Torres heard Kes gasp when she recognized the Elder.

"You shouldn't have come here," Varathael said. "There was no need for you to see this just yet." Two younger Ryol males flanked him. Torres thought that one of them looked like the beach guard she had toppled earlier. *Hope he's not holding a grudge,* she thought. "I'm afraid we can't allow you to leave now," Varathael said.

"Stay back," Torres commanded, aiming her phaser at the Elder. "Captain, we have a situation here."

"What is it?" Janeway asked through the commbadge. "We're having trouble getting a lock on you. Are you underground?"

"And then some," Torres said, remembering the shielding over the harbor. The Elder and his guards advanced toward her, seemingly unconcerned by the phaser pointed at them. *Maybe he doesn't know what a phaser is,* she thought. "This is a weapon. Keep back or I'll fire."

Varathael smiled cruelly. With a languid gesture, he tapped the ruby gemstone upon his chest. A crimson glow appeared around the Elder and his associates, outlining their bodies against the towering walls of the wrecked cargohold. The glow moved with them as they came within a few meters of Torres and the others. *I don't like the looks of this,* she thought.

Torres fired. A beam of destructive force leaped from her phaser, only to splash against the crimson radiance surrounding the Ryol. The glowing force-field absorbed the phaser beam, diffusing its power. "Damn," Torres cursed. She upped the setting on her phaser, switching it to maximum power, but the brilliant red shield continued to resist her phaser's efforts.

"Fine," she said, switching off her phaser and returning it to her belt, "we'll do this the hard way." She raised her fists in front of her. "Three of us, three of you. Sounds like pretty good odds to me."

Frankly, she would have preferred Chakotay and some of the other Maquis at her side; neither Neelix nor Kes had struck her as very threatening fighters. She wasn't about to mention that to Varathael, however. *Besides,* she thought, *when was the last time any of these pampered Ryol fought anything tougher than a bunch of undernourished monkeys?*

Thank goodness none of the Ryol had brought along a weapon of their own!

"Torres!" the captain called via the commbadge. "B'Elanna! What's happening? Report!"

Varathael raised an eyebrow. "Is that Captain Janeway?" he asked. "We had an unfortunate misunderstanding a few hours ago. Please give her my regards."

"Torres here," she said, keeping her eyes on the Elder. "We've encountered some Ryol, including Varathael, and are taking defensive measures."

"Is that what you call this?" Varathael said, sounding amused. His unworried confidence was unnerving. Torres tensed her muscles, hyped on adrenaline and poised to strike the instant Varathael or any of the other Ryol took action against her. She glanced quickly at her companions. Neelix had one arm wrapped around Kes's waist while his other hand held the light crystal aloft. Both looked apprehensive, but ready to defend themselves. *Too bad,* she thought, *that Kes didn't know how to employ her psychic gifts offensively.* She recalled that the delicate-looking Ocampa had once almost incinerated Tuvok with a burst of psionic fire; unfortunately, that had turned out to be an isolated incident beyond Kes's powers to repeat. *We could really use a telepathic zap or two now.*

She waited for Varathael to make the first move, but to her surprise the Elder stopped short only less than ten centimeters in front of her. The crimson shield pulsed around him. Torres backed up involuntarily, nervous about coming into contact with the unknown energies of the forcefield. Varathael did not pursue her. He merely glared at her with his strange green eyes. Torres watched him, puzzled and on edge, as his pupils dilated with incredible speed, blacking out his eyes instantly. *What the devil?* she wondered.

Fatigue attacked her like a blow to the stomach. Torres gasped, choking, as she felt her life-force yanked from her body. She had never experienced anything like it. This was no ordinary weariness, brought on gradually over the passage of time; instead the debilitating effect of the Elder's eyes robbed her of energy at what felt like warp speed. *Some sort of bioelectric conduction transference,* she guessed even as her knees went weak and she collapsed to the rubble-strewn floor, coming to rest atop the buried remains of the Ryol's first victims. Through blurry eyes, she saw both Kes and Neelix succumb as well to the parasitic influence of the Elder and his allies. Kes's eyes had rolled upward so that only the whites of her eyes could be seen. Neelix struggled valiantly to hold her unconscious body erect, but his strenuous efforts lasted only a heartbeat or two; they fell, side by side, onto a pile of bones and sand. Torres could not watch them any longer. Her mouth felt as dry as a Vulcan desert; her arms and legs were numb. She barely noticed when Varathael bent over to pluck the commbadge from her uniform.

"Hello, Captain?" he spoke into the badge. "Lieutenant Torres and her friends cannot answer you. I believe we have much to discuss."

Don't listen to him, Captain! Torres thought furiously. *Get* Voyager *away from here!* Pure primal rage kept her conscious for a few seconds more, as she silently vowed bloody revenge on the Elder and all his kind.

Then she blacked out.

CHAPTER 13

DESPITE HER RECENT INJURIES, SUSAN TUKWILA REported to the bridge exactly on time. *Good for her,* Chakotay thought, hoping *Voyager's* morale problems were now a thing of the past. *Nothing like a common threat,* he thought, *to pull a crew together.* Now if only they could get all their people off that damn planet safely!

Sitting in the captain's chair, he opened a link to the transporter room. "What's the story?" he demanded. "Do you have Torres and the others yet?" According to Captain Janeway, B'Elanna and her party had run afoul of hostile Ryol down on the planet.

"No luck, sir," the transporter chief reported. "We got the rest of the crew earlier, but there's some sort of shielding over the harbor area where Lieutenant Torres and the others are. We upped the frequency ratios on the phase transition coils, but all we managed to get was their commbadges."

Frustrated, Chakotay smacked his fist against the armrest of his chair. This was sounding more and more like a hostage situation. *Exactly what the captain wanted to avoid,* he thought. "Understood," he told the transporter chief. "Chakotay out."

The relief officers currently manning the bridge, a mixture of Starfleet and Maquis personnel, waited silently for his next orders. He felt their eyes upon him, wondering what he could do to rescue their crew mates. "Ensign Tukwila," he said. "Activate the long-range sensors. See if you can locate Lieutenant Torres and her party."

Without the commbadges to indicate their location, it was like searching for a needle in a planet-sized haystack, but maybe they would get lucky. *We have to do something,* he thought.

The turbolift doors at the rear of the bridge slid open. Chakotay swung around in his seat, expecting to see Captain Janeway coming to take command during the present crisis. He stood up quickly, ready to surrender her chair to the captain. He was anxious to hear what she had learned from Tuvok and The Doctor.

He hadn't anticipated a Ryol boarding party pouring onto the bridge, led by none other than Lieutenant Tom Paris. Half a dozen Ryol men and women fanned out across the bridge, assuming standing positions near each of the major control stations. A striking Ryol female, her furry dome striped like a tigress, approached the command platform. Paris followed after her, a dazed look upon his face.

At the tactical station behind the captain's chair, Lieutenant Assink, a human of Aleutian descent, reached for a phaser, but another Ryol female moved even faster. Knocking Assink's arm away from the phaser compartment, she locked her gaze on Assink, who instantly crumpled behind the station, gasping for breath. Although he kept his face impassive, Chakotay was shocked at the suddeness of Assink's collapse. *All she did was* look *at Assink,* he observed with alarm. Apparently that was all the Ryol needed to do.

"I am Laazia," the lead female declared, approaching the seat Chakotay now occupied. Unlike her companions she wore a large velvet cloak whose hem swept the floor of the bridge. "Heir to the Elder. I claim this vessel for the Ryol." Her eyes scanned the bridge, checking the deployment of her agents. "Remember the plan," she instructed them. "Strike anyone who even touches a control panel. Don't give them a chance to beam us away." She turned to Paris. "Confiscate every phaser, then seal off the bridge manually."

"I might have something to say about all this," Chakotay responded, placing himself between Laazia and the captain's seat. Years of Starfleet training went into effect and he tapped his commbadge. "Chakotay to Janeway," he said, a determined expression on his face. "Ryol have boarded the bridge. Go to red alert. Repeat. Ryol have—"

A vicious slap across his face cut off his warning. "Silence!" Laazia snapped, plucking Chakotay's commbadge from his chest. His cheek stung where Laazia had struck him, surprising him with her strength, but at least he had alerted the captain to the crisis on the bridge. Out of the corner of his eye, he spotted Susan Tukwila tensing to leap to his defense.

"Nobody move," he ordered the crew. "Hold your positions." Chakotay quickly evaluated the situation. None of the Ryol appeared armed, but obviously the Ryol didn't need weapons to immobilize their foes. Their alien powers were all they required to overwhelm the crew on the bridge.

Chakotay shook his head at Tukwilla. Until he

knew the extent of the mysterious powers of the Ryol, he did not want to sacrifice any member of the crew just to find out how deadly those powers could be. Laazia and the other Ryol were certainly acting like they had nothing to fear from the bridge crew. *A bad sign,* Chakotay thought.

Moving like a zombie, Paris moved across the bridge, handing off an armful of hand phasers to one of Laazia's lieutenants, who in turn distributed the weapons among the Ryol. Then Paris headed for Tuvok's security station, which was currently unoccupied. Chakotay glowered at Paris, trying to look the junior officer in the eyes, but Paris's glassy expression remained unchanged by his commander's gaze. "What's this all about, Lieutenant?" he demanded.

"The Ryol have need of this vessel," Laazia began, her chin held high in an imperious manner. "Consider it payment," she said with a smirk, "for our hospitality."

"I wasn't talking to you," Chakotay interrupted her. Beneath his tattoo, his face was grim. "Lieutenant Paris, I asked you a question."

Paris stared at Laazia as if hypnotized. "I'm sorry, Commander," he mumbled softly. His hands moved deftly across the security controls. Chakotay could guess what he was doing there, raising forcefields all around the bridge, and he didn't like any of it. "I can't help myself," Paris said.

Laazia wandered over and stroked the young man's cheek absently. "You have no more authority over him," she informed Chakotay. "I have placed him entirely under my control. Trust me, Commander, there's no point in appealing to his duty to Starfleet. He's too far gone. Isn't that right, Tom?"

Laazia scanned the bridge. "Where is Captain Janeway?"

Stony silence greeted the Ryol's demand. Chakotay wasn't about to give Laazia any extra advantage. He wondered how and when the captain could get a security team past the forcefields cutting the bridge off from the rest of the ship. *And then what?* he worried, imagining an all-out battle between the crew and the Ryol. How many phasers would it take to overcome the preternatural abilities of the Ryol? *Good thing I got through to her before the shields went up,* he thought.

Laazia grabbed on to Chakotay's chin and yanked his face toward hers. Pointy nails jabbed into his jaw. "Tell me what I want to know or I will drain the life from you. You know I can do it. I can tell."

"You know, Tom," Chakotay said through gritted teeth, "I never did think much of your taste in women."

Laazia's nails dug deeper into his flesh, but she did not respond to his taunt. "My father was right," she said coolly. "He said I would have to destroy one of you as an example to the rest." She grinned mercilessly at Chakotay. "Guess who just volunteered?"

Just as Paris had described, the eyes of the Elder's daughter darkened. Chakotay tried to look away, but Laazia held his skull in place with inhuman strength. He squeezed his eyes shut, hoping that would spare him, but a chill began to spread through his body nonetheless. The heat was being leached from his body through a million invisible punctures. His legs began to buckle. His heart pounded in his chest. He knew that he was finally in the presence of the same inhuman predator that had stalked his vision. *Akoocheemoya,* he prayed, *great spirit of my grandfathers, preserve me from this unholy demon.*

"No!" came an anguished voice. He opened his eyes in time to see Susan Tukwila lunge from her station. The Ryol standing guard over her grabbed her by the shoulder in hopes of restraining her, but the former Maquis freedom fighter flipped him using a textbook anbo-jyutsu move, clasping the Ryol's hand with both of hers, then executing a forward roll that sent him flying through the air while Tukwila somersaulted back onto her feet. He landed flat on his back only a few centimeters short of the curved divider separating the command platform from the aft station consoles. Chakotay heard the man's skull crash against the sturdy duranium floor.

Shouting a Maquis war cry, Tukwila came at Laazia, whose head snapped around to face her attacker. Chakotay felt the force of Laazia's energy-sapping eyes diverted away from him. His depleted strength was not restored to him, but the constant drain on his resources ceased for the moment. He wobbled unsteadily on his feet, and Paris, acting on instinct, perhaps, hurried away from the security station to prop up his debilitated crewmate. Chakotay rejected Paris's attempt to support him, yanking his arm away so vehemently that he nearly toppled over onto his side. He threw his body upward, fighting to keep his balance. His vision blurred; he thought he saw a strange black aura surrounding Laazia, like the silhouette of an enormous beast.

Laazia appeared oblivious to the drama going on behind her back. She fixed her eyes, fully dilated to an inhuman degree, on the charging figure of Susan Tukwila, whose battle cry turned into a strangled choke as the Ryol's eerie powers literally halted her in her tracks. "Laazia, wait!" Tom Paris exclaimed, but the Elder's daughter showed Tukwila no mercy. Susan convulsed, the muscles of her face twitching erratically, while Chakotay looked on in horror. Staggering across the command platform, he tried to seize Laazia, but the Ryol knocked him aside with but a wave of her hand, never removing her gaze from the stiff and jerky body of Susan Tukwila.

Stunned, his head ringing from the unexpected strength of Laazia's blow, Chakotay watched Tukwila wither away before his eyes. Her face grew gaunt and haggard, her frightened eyes disappearing into their sockets, her lips receding to reveal pallid bloodless gums. Her Starfleet uniform hung loosely on her newly emaciated limbs; she seemed to shrink within the pressed black-and-gold costume. Unable to stand, she collapsed onto the floor of the bridge, falling not far from the supine form of the Ryol she had flipped so effortlessly mere minutes before. She gasped for breath for a heartbeat or two, then fell silent. Chakotay raged inwardly at the Ryol, vowing to avenge Susan Tukwila's death. *You didn't deserve to die like that,* he mourned.

Her body, with its skeletal limbs and agonized expression, reminded him, oddly, of a neffaler's. They both looked as though they had wasted away in the service of the Ryol, their vital energies drained from their bodies—just as the shadow beast had ripped out Chakotay's heart in his vision.

"That was almost too easy," Laazia purred, a satiated smile upon her elegant face. "She'd already given us so much, been tasted so many times over the last few days, that there was little left to feast upon." She licked her lips.

She turned to confront Chakotay, towering over the fallen first officer like some bloodthirsty pagan goddess. Her dark aura flickered around her, casting a bestial shadow over her deceptively refined features. *I know you now,* he thought. *My ancestors showed me your true face days ago.*

"Now," she demanded, "tell me where the captain is."

He barely had enough breath to respond. "Never!" Chakotay said, determined to deny the Ryol anything they craved. *The longer the captain stays free,* he reasoned, *the better our odds.*

"Idiot," Laazia cursed him. Her blacked-out eyes widened ominously. "Do you think that I cannot kill another so soon? If so, you are very wrong. The more

I consume, the greater my power. So it is with us all. Your people cannot resist us."

"We'll see about that," Chakotay whispered, defiance written on his face. *That's just what the Cardassians thought back home,* he thought.

"Oh no," Laazia said. "You shall not be around to see anything beyond the next few seconds—unless you tell me where I can find your captain." Bending over, she put her hand upon Chakotay's chest. Chakotay felt his heart flutter within his breast. Despite his stubborn determination, an involuntary gasp escaped his lips. A chill came upon him like an Arctic storm; all the warmth in his body seemed to rush out through a sucking hole in his chest. Once more he stood upon the desolate mountain of his vision, while an unclean beast feasted upon his heart. "Ah." Laazia sighed, an ecstatic expression on her face. "This is much better, Commander. You have so very much to give. . . ."

Chakotay knew he couldn't last much longer. *I have to stay conscious,* he thought. *Someone has to deactivate those forcefields.* But he couldn't lift his hands, let alone speak the necessary command. *I'm dying,* he thought, *just like poor Susan.* He winced at the memory of her ravaged body. *Akoo-cheemoya, receive my wayward spirit. Do not let this foul creature cast me into darkness forever. . . .*

"Stop it," Paris blurted. Chakotay had almost forgotten Tom was there. "The captain's in the sickbay." He grabbed Laazia by the wrist, pulling her hand away from Chakotay. "You don't need to do this."

The Elder's daughter looked as surprised as Chakotay. "What's this?" she asked Paris, sounding slightly intrigued "One last flickering flame of rebellion? Or are you merely jealous?" Laazia fixed her gaze upon Paris, who backed away obediently. "Very well then," she said, straightening her back and turning away from Chakotay. "There will be time enough for such refreshments later." She addressed those Ryol still standing; none of the invaders had shown any interest in tending to their unconscious comrade, still knocked out cold near the almost unrecognizable remains of Susan Tukwila. "You there," Laazia said to the two Ryol nearest the turbolift entrance. "Go to this 'sickbay' and apprehend Captain Janeway. Deal harshly with anyone who tries to interfere, but waste no time feasting on your foes. We may indulge ourselves freely once *Voyager* is truly ours. Go."

The designated Ryol, a man and a woman, both bronzed and athletic-looking, bowed their heads to the Elder's daughter, then stepped promptly into the turbolift, taking with them just one of the captured phasers. Chakotay watched the doors slide shut. "You see, Commander," Laazia said to him, "I don't need your cooperation to capture this ship. Two Ryol are more than a match for your paltry defenses."

Good thing I alerted the captain, Chakotay thought. Sickbay was only four decks below the bridge. The turbolift would take the Ryol there in a matter of minutes. His throat was dry, but he summoned up enough saliva to speak a little. "This ship will never be yours," he announced to Laazia. "The captain will—"

Laazia didn't allow him to finish. Shod in a sandal, her foot connected with his jaw, kicking him hard enough to loosen a few of his teeth. *I hope The Doctor's been programmed to perform dental surgery,* he thought wryly, *assuming I get out of this alive.* Her pointed nails left a jagged gash along his cheek, mere centimeters beneath his tattoo. His mouth filled up with blood, which he spit at the tiled floor in front of Laazia's feet. *The captain will take back the bridge,* he thought. He wasn't exactly sure how, but he had to hold on to that idea. He couldn't give up hope.

"Don't say another word," Laazia said. "Don't even breathe or I'll finish my banquet here and now." She stepped over Chakotay's sprawled figure and lowered herself leisurely onto the captain's chair. "Tom," she said, resting her bare arms upon the arms of the chair, "please take control of the helm."

Paris hesitated for a minute. His gaze darted back and forth between Chakotay's bloodied face and the regal vision of Laazia upon her newfound throne. The young navigator seemed uncertain, confused. *Maybe there's still a chance for him,* Chakotay prayed. *Come on, Paris. Remember whose side you're on.*

"For me, Tom," Laazia entreated him.

"Okay," he muttered, looking away from Chakotay. He crossed the bridge to his usual station, where Ensign Krevorr, an apprehensive-looking Ktaran, sat nervously beneath the watchful gaze of an imposing Ryol invader. "Give me the conn," Paris instructed her. Krevorr appeared to briefly consider her options, then realized she stood no chance of keeping the helm controls from Paris and his powerful new allies and surrendered the seat to Paris. *Thank heaven,* Chakotay thought, observing the episode from the floor of the command area. He didn't want to see another crew member throw away her life uselessly.

"Excellent," Laazia declared. "That's more like it." She slid back in her seat, relaxing against the back of the captain's chair. "Lieutenant Paris, prepare to land this vessel on the surface of Ryolanov. At last," she proclaimed, "our long exile is over!"

They found the sickbay easily. The turbolift delivered them straight to the entrance of the ship's medical facilities. Sitruua was impressed by the efficiency of the visitor's technology; for a people who were, in essence, little more than a new breed of neffaler, they possessed some undeniably useful skills. A stolen phaser rested comfortably in her grip, and she looked forward to operating all of *Voyager*'s systems. *To think,* she thought, *that we are finally going to escape that backwater planet!* She wondered if she would ever miss Ryolanov after they had regained their rightful place in interstellar civilization. *Probably not,* she decided; she wasn't the nostalgic type.

Nalec, her companion and lover, strode beside her. His claws were fully extended, she noted, knowing how eager he must be to confront the aliens and devour their essences. Sitruua shivered. Compared to the sunny warmth of Ryolanov, the ship's air-conditioned climate struck her as a bit chilly. She was definitely underdressed, she decided, for the current temperature. *We'll have to get the heat turned up,* she resolved, *after we've assumed total control of the ship.*

No Starfleet guards were posted outside the sickbay. Sitruua looked up and down the admirably clean, well-lighted corridor, but did not spot any of the visiting aliens. *Good,* she thought, signaling Nalec to advance. *That makes our job easier.* She was eager to return to the bridge with their prize. Such an easy victory could only increase their standing in Laazia's circle. Already, they were numbered among the Heir's favorites. "Now," she whispered to Nalec. "Show no mercy."

"No mercy," he echoed her, baring his teeth. She admired the keenness in his eyes, the controlled ferocity in his voice. *Not even Naxor had ever looked so fierce and rapacious,* she thought proudly. *I chose well.*

She expected the door to the sickbay to slide open at their approach, as all the doors on *Voyager* had appeared to do. Instead it remained steadfastly shut. Sitruua hunted for a lock or handle, but found nothing that might fit that description. Perhaps, she concluded, the ship's design was a little too streamlined. She contemplated her new phaser, tempted to try out the weapon's power on the obstructing door. She was reluctant, however, to inflict too much damage on a starship that would soon belong to the Ryol. "Open up!" she shouted to whoever was on the opposite side of the door. "Let us in at once!"

Nalec declined to waste time or energy on vocalizations. A snarl building in his throat, he pounded on the enemy's door. His talons left long vertical scratches in the polished surface of the door. He kicked at the barrier with all his considerable might. Smiling, Sitruua saw the door shudder in its frame. A few more such blows, she judged, and the alien's defenses would surely fall before the power of the Ryol. The visitors deserved punishment for such resistance, she knew; what a pity there would not be time to administer their torment with care. Proper discipline would have to wait until *Voyager* was safely on the ground and its former inhabitants prepared for training. She wondered how long it would take to convert them to proper neffaler. *I hope they learn quickly,* they thought. The old neffaler had been worn out to the point of near uselessness. It would be good to have able servants, and fresh sustenance, once more.

His fists locked together, Nalec delivered a two-handed blow to the battered metal door. The impact of the strike echoed down the empty hallway. His handsome face contorted with rage, he drew back to come at the barrier again when, with a *whoosh* of released air, the door unexpectedly slid open.

"That will be quite enough vandalism for the time being," came an acerbic voice. Stepping quickly through the portal before the door could close again, Sitruua and Nalec discovered the source of the voice: a singularly unimpressive-looking humanoid in a blue Starfleet uniform. "I am the emergency medical program," he said calmly. "How can I assist you?"

His skull was smooth and nearly hairless—*like a female's,* Sitruua thought scornfully—and his eyes appeared distinctly out of focus. Sitruua decided he was about the most pathetic specimen of alien life she had encountered yet. *Odd,* she thought briefly, *I don't remember seeing him down on the planet.*

"We've come for your captain," she announced in a tone that disavowed any possibility of defiance. She scanned the medical facility, searching for the human called Janeway, but could not locate their prey. Sickbay looked deserted—even the sickbeds were empty—except for the laughable human physician standing in their path. "Give her to us."

"I'm sorry," the human said, "but Captain Janeway has left the sickbay. There's nobody here but me."

Sitruua scowled. Something about the physician's manner irritated her. He seemed remarkably smug for a creature so beneath her on the food chain. "Where is she?"

"I'm sorry," he said again, "but I'm afraid I only dispense medical advice. Missing persons are an entirely different department." He lifted a shiny metallic instrument from a tray on a nearby counter. "Perhaps you'd care for a vaccination? I hear there's a bad Talaxian flu going around."

"Drop it!" Nalec growled. His reflexes were even faster than hers. He wrapped his fist around the human's wrist and yanked the medic's arm upward so that the strange instrument pointed at the ceiling. "Neffaler!" Nalec cursed him.

"That's *Doctor* Neffaler to you," the balding human said, sounding curiously unperturbed, "and I can't say I much care for that as a name." Nalec refused to release the so-called doctor's wrist. The veins in his own muscular arm swelled as he squeezed the other man's arm. Sitruua wondered casually if The Doctor's wrist would break before or after he was forced to release the instrument.

"Really!" The Doctor said indignantly, rolling his mismatched eyes. "It's only a hypospray, not a phaser. You'd think you've never been in a doctor's office before."

"Surrender now," Nalec snarled, "or I will shatter every bone in your body and suck out the marrow!"

"How perfectly revolting!" The Doctor said. He glanced up at his captured wrist. "Very well," he said with a weary sigh.

Two things happened almost simultaneously. The "hypospray" fell to the floor, striking Nalec in the foot and bouncing off his other exposed foot before coming to rest, with a sharp metallic ring, upon the floor of the sickbay. And The Doctor's hand slid effortlessly out of Nalec's unbreakable grip. Sitruua blinked her pale green eyes, unable to accept what she had just seen. If she didn't know better, she would have sworn in the name of the Elder's unquenchable thirst that the bald human's hand had actually *passed through* Nalec's flesh and bone. But that was impossible, wasn't it? None of these new neffaler had demonstrated that sort of transdimensional ability.

"Carcass!" Nalec swore at The Doctor, on his foot one injured claw grew blue and swollen at its tip, the razor-sharp nail cracked down the middle. "Leftover!" Claws extended, he pounced for the human's throat.

"Be careful," Sitruua called out, suddenly wary of this strangely unsettling human. "Watch out!"

She was too late. Nalec's claws passed through The Doctor like the wind, the momentum of his charge carrying him through the immaterial form of his adversary and into the counter behind The Doctor. He crashed noisily against the counter, sending the tray of medical instruments flying, then spun around in a frenzy of frustrated rage. Foam sprayed from his lips. His eyes were wild. The golden mane framed a portrait of homicidal fury.

"Nalec, wait!" Sitruua cried, desperately trying to

make sense of the situation. "He's just an image, an illusion."

"No!" he barked. "I felt him before, he was as solid as you or I." He glanced down quickly at his bruised right foot, then back at The Doctor. "How could he hold that instrument if he wasn't real?" he wondered out loud. "His weapon is solid enough. Trust me on that!"

Nalec is right, she realized. *I hadn't thought of that.* She must have looked as puzzled as she felt, because The Doctor spoke again in an infuriatingly pedantic tone. "It's very simple," he said. "I can touch you." He reached out and tugged on Nalec's beard, pulling out a handful of stiff blond whiskers. "But you can't touch me." Acting on instinct, Nalec clawed at the offending human hand, but his talons merely sliced the air, while golden whiskers drifted slowly downward toward the floor. "Do you understand now?" The Doctor asked. "Or shall I demonstrate again?"

"I don't need to touch you," Sitruua said icily, "to consume every last spark of your being." She meant it, too; this hairless human irritant had provoked her beyond the limits of endurance. For a moment she forgot about the missing captain. All that mattered was teaching this miserable excuse for a sentient entity who the true masters of the cosmos were. Impaling The Doctor upon her stare, she unleashed her hunger upon him. The doorways of her mind opened wide, sending out psychic tendrils of desire and need to drag his puny life-force into the irresistible vortex of her own superior will . . .

"Excuse me," he said, "but there seems to be something wrong with your eyes. Perhaps you should have them looked at? Excessive dilation can be a symptom of a wide variety of disorders, including substance abuse and Rigellian brain fever."

Arrrgh! Sitruua nearly screamed in frustration. Never before, except in competition with other Ryol, had she opened her mind to feed only to have her desire denied. Her hunger quested fruitlessly for the other's essence; it was all she could do to keep the reins on her unfettered voraciousness, lest it turn and feed upon her own spirit and energy.

It was maddening. She could see the arrogant neffaler, hear his smug and patronizing voice, but as far as her hunger was concerned, he wasn't there. It was like trying to consume a vacuum. Wave after wave of insatiable need poured out of her eyes—only to crash against an equally thirsty accumulation of invisible psychic feelers. *By the savage shadows of our distant home,* she realized, *Nalec was trying to devour The Doctor as well, and failing just as badly!*

For a second, their separate hungers grappled with each other, like hounds fighting in the street, but they both pulled back just in time, before they drained each other dry. Arduously, painfully, Sitruua drew her desire back into her body. Its unfulfilled appetite ached like a physical wound within her. "Enough!" she said, gasping to Nalec. She could see from his pained expression that he, too, had suffered while trying to recall his hunger. "We have wasted too much time on this . . . idiot phantom. Search these chambers. Find Captain Janeway!"

The Doctor shook his head. "You aren't listening to me. I already told you. The captain isn't here. I'd ask you to make an appointment, but I'm afraid your friends are holding my assistant captive in a cave."

Good, Sitruua thought spitefully. *I hope we butcher him or her.* Forcing herself to ignore the bald ghost's jibes, while trying to keep one eye on his occasionally tangible hands, she decided to look around for some clue to the captain's whereabouts. "You inspect the laboratory," she instructed Nalec, approaching the humans' impressive-looking technological sickbeds. "I'll search in here."

A slender black-and-silver artifact, lying atop one

of the beds, caught her eye. At first Sitruua thought it might be another variety of exotic medical equipment. On closer inspection she recognized the clarinet as the musical instrument the human named Harry Kim had once played for her and Romeela in an entirely unnecessary effort to secure their attentions. The melody had been pleasant enough, she remembered, although both she and Romeela had enthused and applauded his little tune far more than it deserved. *By the Elder,* she thought, *these neffaler were so easy to manipulate.* She gave The Doctor a sideways glance. *Present company excepted.*

Her hunger, thwarted mere minutes before, still throbbed inside her. The clarinet reminded her of the pleasure of feasting on these creatures, making her present hunger all the more keen. She and her sister Romeela had fed upon young Harry Kim more than once in the days and nights they had just left behind. She smirked, remembering; they had kept Harry so enthralled and enraptured that he hadn't even noticed his life-force being drained away, bits and pieces at a time. Perhaps she would give Harry to Romeela as a present, once the ship was theirs and the entire crew had been domesticated.

She licked her lips, momentarily lost in savory memories of nights gone by, when she heard Nalec emit a gasp of surprise. Straightening her back, she swiveled about in time to see her consort dropping onto his knees, his head swaying, his eyes bulging from their sockets. The bald phantom stood only a short distance away, tapping his hypospray against his palm. "Give it up," he said in his usual insufferable tone. "That's twenty-five cc's of undiluted narcotrizarine. I don't care what kind of freakish Delta Quadrant life-form you are, that's enough to knock out a Horta."

Horta? Sitruaa was puzzled as well as alarmed. *What is a Horta?*

Despite The Doctor's treacherous attempt to poison him, a furious Nalec still managed to pull himself up off the floor. Sitruua's heart stirred with pride at the sheer intensity of her lover's indomitable rage. Even the self-important phantom physician seemed appropriately taken aback at Nalec's resurgence. "Oh dear," he muttered, "this is unexpected." He hastily manipulated the controls of his hypospray. "Well, maybe another thirty cc's couldn't hurt."

He thrust his wretched device at Nalec's mighty frame, brushing its head against the back of the Ryol's neck. Sitruua heard a hiss of air, then watched as The Doctor sprang away from Nalec the instant his hypospray connected with its target. In his haste to become immaterial, The Doctor fell through the wall of the laboratory, so that all but his legs disappeared from sight. Sitruua heard the discarded hypospray clank upon the floor.

Nalec roared in fury, but the second injection was too much for him. She saw his eyelids begin to droop, watched his expression slacken and his arms go limp. She stepped away from the empty sickbeds, her grip tightening around her phaser. "What have you done?" she cried out in rage.

"I should think that was fairly obvious," The Doctor replied. His head emerged from the apparent solidity of the wall as he awkwardly rose from the undignified position he had landed in. "Tell me, are all your people so resistant to sedation or was your friend just unusually hyperactive?"

"You're food," she growled at him. "That's all any of you are." She could feel the cold metal of the phaser beneath her fingers. Could this compact little device possess enough power to destroy her foe? She raised the weapon uncertainly, having never fired a phaser before, and pointed it at the ghostly form of The Doctor.

He raised a quizzical eyebrow, appearing unconcerned by the threat of the phaser. "Are you quite sure you know how to operate that thing?" he asked. "Take a doctor's advice, put it away before you hurt yourself."

"Dead food," she snarled. "Carrion fit only for scavengers." She depressed a switch with her thumb and was gratified to see a brilliant azure beam shoot across the sickbay, striking the ghostly physician in the neck, less than a handbreadth beneath his offensively impudent mouth. *Yes!* she thought ecstatically. *Die!*

"Arrgh!" The Doctor shouted, his face contorted with pain. He clutched his throat with both hands, swaying unsteadily upon his feet. "The pain! The agony! I can't see . . . everything's going black! Oh, dear god, I fear I'm bound for holographic heaven!"

Wait a second, Sitruua thought, a scowl forming upon her face. Something wasn't quite right about this.

The Doctor's posture straightened out. His face resumed its disdainful expression. "But seriously," he said calmly, "I'm a doctor, not a casualty. I'm afraid you'll have to do better than that."

Sitruua fired up, raising the phaser to its highest setting. The beam caused a slight ripple where it intersected with The Doctor's immaterial body, but he showed no sign of distress. The wall behind him, on the other hand, glowed brightly red where the beam struck it, the phaser burning a hole through the solid metal barrier until she could glimpse the laboratory area beyond the wall. A siren, triggered perhaps by the damage being done by the phaser, erupted from the walls. The shrill blaring noise pierced the air, hurting Sitruua's ears. She switched off the phaser, but the siren continued.

"That will be quite enough," The Doctor said sternly. He walked across the chamber and reached beneath the pillow of the nearest sickbed. "Medical supplies are difficult enough to come by in this quadrant without you shooting up my sickbay." He drew out a familiar-looking object that Sitruua identified as another phaser.

"I confess," he said, "that I prefer hyposprays to handarms, but I am capable of using this if necessary. I suggest you surrender."

A Ryol surrender to neffaler? Sitruaa howled in fury. This was the final indignity; she could hear no more. She charged, claws extended, for the alien, eager to rend his flesh into bloody ribbons. *If he's solid enough to hold a phaser,* she reasoned, *maybe he was solid enough to die.* The creature's features remained impassive, but she was determined to carve a scream onto his face if necessary. *There will be nothing left of you but scraps,* she thought.

She felt the phaser beam strike her before she saw the bright blue light. A numbing sensation raced through her body. She tried to resist the beam's effects, but her flesh and spirit, already weakened by her failed attempt to feed, began shutting down. As she dropped onto the floor, only a few meters away from Nalec, the last thing she heard was The Doctor's smug, insufferable voice.

"Hmmm. I suppose phasers have their uses after all."

CHAPTER
14

THE TURBOLIFTS AREN'T SAFE, JANEWAY THOUGHT AS SHE raced with Tuvok and Harry Kim through the ship toward Engineering. If the Ryol had really taken command of the bridge, as Chakotay had warned her before being cut off, then who knew what systems they may have already have assumed control over. The last thing she wanted to do was get trapped with Tuvok and Harry in a frozen turbolift until the invaders came by to take them into custody. *Damn,* she thought. *How in blazes did any Ryol get on the bridge?*

They must have done something to Tom, she thought, hoping that Paris had managed to survive the experience.

Phaser in hand, Tuvok ran ahead of her, intent on defending his captain from any opposition they might encounter, with Kim taking up the rear. "Do you think The Doctor will be okay?" he called out to her as he ran.

"The Doctor can take care of himself," Janeway replied. "He's proven that more times than I can remember." Indeed, she thought, The Doctor may have the least to fear of any of them; she'd be surprised if the strange psychic attacks of the Ryol proved to be effective on a hologram.

They reached the access port to a series of vertical Jeffries tubes. "Perfect," Janeway declared. Engineering was on Deck Eleven, six decks below the sickbay and a full ten decks away from the bridge. The tubes seemed the quickest way down to where she had to go. *First things first,* she prioritized, forming her strategy on the run. Eventually, she had to regain control of the bridge, and rescue Chakotay and whoever else was being held hostage there, but first she had to keep the Ryol from flying away with *Voyager*. Engineering was the obvious place to throw a wrench into the invader's ambitions; it was too bad that B'Elanna wouldn't be there to help out. Janeway prayed that Torres and Kes and all the others currently held captive on the planet were still safe.

Everything was happening too fast. When the ship's transporters retrieved Kes and the others' commbadges, they had also cut off her dialogue with Varathael. The next thing she knew, Chakotay was hailing her to warn her that some Ryol had seized control of the bridge. Tuvok had immediately attempted automated counter-measures against the intruders, but someone had effectively sealed off the bridge from the rest of the ship, setting up defensive forcefields to prevent them from beaming anyone in or out of the bridge. *How,* she wondered, *had the Ryol learned so much about* Voyager*'s defenses?* That hadn't been part of any cultural exchange she'd authorized!

For all she knew, she had barely left the sickbay in time to avoid the Ryol invaders sent to capture her. Tuvok had insisted she take herself out of danger immediately, and despite some initial reluctance, she had been forced to agree. It galled her to order a strategic retreat on her own ship, but the three of them weren't ready to confront the invaders just yet. *Be careful,* she warned herself. *We don't know enough about what these people are capable of.*

"This way, Captain," Tuvok said, opening the hatch to the Jeffries tube. As always, she admired his Vulcan composure in the middle of a crisis. "Please be careful of your step."

"After you," she said. Climbing into the tube, and leaving the access door behind her open for Kim, Janeway grabbed on to the top rung of the service ladder and swung her feet onto the lowest rung she could find. Tuvok's boots struck methodically against the rungs below her feet. She began to descend rapidly through the narrow tube, simultaneously activating her commbadge and requesting an emergency override channel.

"Attention. This is the captain speaking," she said, her words echoing throughout the entire ship. "This is a level-two alert. The bridge has been temporarily captured by the Ryol. Do not attempt to confront the intruders. They are extremely dangerous. All non-security personnel should take shelter within their quarters until this crisis is resolved. All security personnel, report to Engineering at once. I'm on my way. Janeway out."

Hand over hand, rung by rung, level by level, she climbed down the breadth of the ship. Her anger at the Ryol grew hotter the more she thought about how their so-called hosts had deceived them. *At least the Kazon were honest in their hostility,* she thought. *The Ryol took advantage of our trust and vulnerability.*

Prime Directive or no Prime Directive, she vowed, the Ryol were going to regret threatening her ship and her crew.

"So much for shore leave," she quipped. "Some vacation this is turning out to be . . ."

"Well, this is quite a mess," The Doctor observed, inspecting the palm-sized hole the female Ryol's phaser had burned through the wall separating his medical laboratory from the patient recovery area. He shook his head morosely. "Gunplay in the sickbay. Whatever is this quadrant coming to?"

The pair of Ryol still lay insensate upon the floor in front of him. The Doctor kept the phaser aimed in their general direction as he activated his commbadge. "Captain," he paged. "This is The Doctor. I heard your announcement. Are you quite all right?"

Captain Janeway's voice came over the commbadge, reassuring The Doctor. "We're almost to Engineering," she reported. Her voice sounded hurried and slightly out of breath. "What's happening in the sickbay?"

The Doctor informed her of the confrontation in the sickbay and its consequences, taking only a few extra seconds to emphasize his own heroic accomplishment in overcoming two deadly opponents. *I'm becoming quite the two-fisted warrior,* he thought, feeling more than a little pleased with himself. The male Ryol began to stir, raising his head blearily from the floor, and The Doctor casually zapped him with a short phaser burst. The Ryol's golden-maned head dropped cooperatively back onto the floor tiles. "Two prisoners, both under control," The Doctor told Janeway. "Shall I call for Security to pick them up?"

The captain paused a second before responding. "Not yet," she said. "I want you to subject the Ryol to a full metabolic analysis. The more we know about our new adversaries, the better chance there is of uncovering their weaknesses. Can you handle this by yourself?"

The Doctor inspected the unconscious Ryol. He wasn't looking forward to wrestling two inert bodies onto his biobeds, but he supposed he could manage. "That should be no problem, Captain," he stated. "I can instruct the biobeds to monitor the prisoners' brain activity and administer sedatives if they show any sign of regaining consciousness."

I can also lock the surgical support frames in place above both Ryol, he decided. Ordinarily, he preferred not to place his patients in restraints, but this time he was willing to make an exception. *So far,* he thought, *the Ryol have made a very bad first impression on me. I wonder why the rest of the crew seemed to find them so appealing?*

"Very good," the captain said. "Notify me if you learn anything significant about the Ryol."

"Of course," he said. "I still don't understand how the male was able to resist the effects of the narcotrizarine for so long. I gave him more than enough to render the average humanoid unconscious in a matter of nano-seconds."

"I believe we've established," Captain Janeway replied dryly, "that the Ryol are far from average. Anything else?" Through the commbadge, The Doctor heard the sound of an access hatch clanging open.

The Doctor started to sign off, then hesitated. "Captain, what about Kes . . . and the others down on the planet?" he asked.

He did not want to admit how worried he was about her. She was more than his assistant; she was the first person who had ever treated him like a true living entity. *Come back, Kes,* he thought. *This will be a lonelier ship without you.* "I'm afraid I'm feeling somewhat short-handed."

"I won't abandon them," the captain said, steely determination in her voice. "I promise you that. Janeway out."

The captain's voice vanished, leaving The Doctor alone in the sickbay with the two oblivious Ryol. He retrieved the female's phaser from where it had fallen, then placed it on a counter next to Ensign Kim's clarinet. Sighing wearily, he bent over the male and, wrapping his arms around the man's torso, struggled to lift the Ryol off the floor. He was even heavier than he looked.

"You'd think," The Doctor muttered as he laboriously wrestled the limp and unresponsive Ryol onto an empty biobed, "that Starfleet could spring for a holographic orderly or two!"

"Tell me, Tom," Laazia said, seeming quite at home in the captain's chair. "How long before we land on Ryolanov?"

"Not much longer," he fudged, glancing up at the screen in front of him. The planet, a golden globe mottled by masses of purple and black, occupied the center of the main viewer. Paris quietly rerouted the controls for the long-range sensors through the conn station. The shimmering globe expanded before his eyes, appearing to draw ever nearer. *Looks good to me,* he thought *but will it fool the others?*

His mind was his again. The shock of Susan's death, as well as Laazia's brutal treatment of Chakotay, had acted like a phaser blast through his brain, burning away the mist and cobwebs that Laazia had wrapped around his consciousness. He could think again. *She must have underestimated,* he thought, *the impact on me of what she did to Susan. Shows you how little they really understand us, and how little they must care for each other.*

But now what could he do, aside from letting Laazia and the other Ryol know that he was free of their control? He furtively scanned the bridge, swiftly assessing the situation. He fought an urge to shake his head at the sheer bizarreness of his dilemma. *How in the world did I end up undercover,* he asked himself, *at a hostile takeover of the ship?*

Tension filled the bridge. While Laazia lounged upon her stolen throne, her confederates stood guard over Chakotay and other crew members. The male Ryol whom Susan Tukwila had knocked out earlier had since recovered; a swollen bump upon his forehead, not to mention a broken lip, testified to the force of Tukwila's assault. Paris avoided looking at the aft operations station, where Susan's shriveled corpse had been callously swept into a corner. In the end, he reflected, her bravery and considerable fighting skills had not been enough to save her. *It happened so fast,* he grieved. *I couldn't do anything. There wasn't enough time!* He tried to tell himself that it wasn't really his fault, that he had been the helpless victim of some insidious alien mind control, but it didn't make him feel any better.

Not far away from Tukwila's body, Chakotay sat helplessly upon the floor, his arms tied behind his back with a strip of adhesive cloth that one of the Ryol had extracted from his robes. Even though they had already drained his energy once, the Ryol weren't taking any chances with Chakotay. Paris could feel the first officer's eyes staring into his back, accusing him, judging him. *Give me a chance,* Paris thought silently. *It's not what you think.*

Two junior officers, Ensigns Krevorr and Assink, remained seated at the engineering and science stations, respectively. Ryol guards loomed above them, confident in the ability of their inexplicable powers to keep the hostages in line. *Let's see,* Paris thought. *Counting Chakotay, that makes five of them and four of us. Not very good odds. . . .* He would have traded a year's worth of replicator rations to have B'Elanna or

Harry back on the bridge, not to mention Tuvok and the captain.

"Hurry, Tom," Laazia urged him. "I cannot wait to deliver this fine vessel to my father. I've been thinking about a change of career, too. How does Captain Laazia sound to you?"

Paris maintained an expression of intense concentration on his task. "Atmospheric landings can be tricky," he explained, "especially when you've got to deal with these sort of wonky orbital dynamics. The reverse polarized turbulence of the quantum gravity field can really foul up the approach vector of the aerodynamic principle."

Seated several meters away, Ensign Krevorr gave Paris a puzzled look. Her golden eyes, catlike like all Ktarans, revealed confusion.

Sssh, Paris hushed her, aiming his thoughts at the Ktaran crew member. *Don't say anything. I'm on a roll here.* He fought the temptation to look back at Chakotay, to see if the first officer finally understood what he was up to. Part of him desperately wanted to erase the scorn from Chakotay's features, but not if it meant making Laazia and her friends suspicious. Was she buying all this gibberish? He couldn't tell.

Laazia's smooth brow furrowed as she tried to decipher Paris's jargon-filled explanation. *I wonder if it's giving the Universal Translator a hard time,* he wondered, then felt the excitement of a new idea popping into his head. *They're depending on the Universal Translator as much as we are,* he realized. *Something to remember perhaps. . . .*

Laazia sighed and shrugged her shoulders, apparently defeated by the blizzard of buzzwords. "As you say," she said after a few seconds' consideration. "Land us as swiftly as you deem it wise. The Elder knows," she said, directing her words to her fellow Ryol, "we don't want to crash our only spacecraft again."

Again? Paris had no idea what she was talking about, except that it sounded like the Ryol had once attempted spaceflight. Was there any way to use that info against the Ryol? So far, they didn't seem to have any weak spots. He hoped that Tuvok's precious DNA sample turned up something useful. *I can only stall so long,* he thought, praying that he didn't look as nervous as he felt. A thin layer of sweat glued the back of his uniform to his skin.

A booming voice startled him out of his reverie. "Attention," came the voice, as if from on high, "this is the captain speaking—"

Paris suppressed a grin. Captain Janeway wasn't out of the game yet! Behind him, Laazia bolted out of her chair. She stood transfixed, listening intently to the captain's announcement, then hissed in fury. Yellow alert warnings began flashing upon the bridge. "She's still free? I don't believe it! How can this be?"

"Nalec and Sitruua must have failed," the Ryol with the bump on his head volunteered. Blood from his cracked lip stained his chin. Such injuries, Paris decided, may have given this Ryol a better appreciation of the *Voyager*'s readiness to fight. "Perhaps the strangers have destroyed them?"

"How?!" Laazia exclaimed, her green eyes filled with malice. Her hands hung at her sides, clutching convulsively at the empty air. "They're *neffaler.* We can devour them at will."

"I do not know, Heir," the other Ryol said. Laazia gave him a venomous look; apparently, Paris mused, the Ryol were not above blaming the messenger for bad news. The Elder's daughter sank back into the captain's seat, stroking her chin with her long brown fingernails.

"Engineering," she repeated, thinking aloud. "She means to sabotage the ship. I cannot allow that." Laazia sprang into action, commanding her followers with an imperious wave of her hand. "The rest of you, go to Engineering. Do whatever you have to, but bring me Janeway. Alive or eaten, I do not care, but bring her to me now!"

The remaining four Ryol moved at once toward the door to the turbolift. One of the Ryol, a slender woman whom Paris believed was named Romeela, paused before the exit and, holding a phaser aloft, addressed Laazia. "Heir, is this wise? Perhaps a few of us should remain to defend you?" She offered the Elder's daughter her phaser.

"From these?" Laazia laughed derisively. Her gaze swept over the bridge, alighting briefly on Chakotay, battered and bound, before moving on to Paris and the others. "The day I cannot handle these weak creatures is the day my father will need a new Heir." She accepted the proffered phaser, then tossed it casually into the empty seat where Chakotay usually sat. "Go," she ordered the other Ryol. "Get Janeway."

Paris heard the turbolift doors swish shut as the Ryol departed the bridge. *Well,* he thought, *this is certainly an interesting development. Four gone, one to go.* He ran through a dozen plans in his mind, rejecting them all. *I'm only going to get one chance,* he thought. *I have to do this right.*

But Laazia was thinking as well. "You," she addressed Ensign Krevorr. "Use your transport device to bring more Ryol to the bridge. Beam me up reinforcements from the planet." She kept her eyes fixed on Krevorr's console. "Be careful, the first sign of treachery and your withered bones will join the dead carcass behind me."

Uh-oh, Paris thought. *Here it comes.* "I'm afraid it's not that easy," he said, anxious to attract Laazia's attention away from the defenseless Ktaran. He didn't want to force Krevorr to say no to Laazia. Susan Tukwila's grisly death still haunted him; one casualty on the bridge was more than enough.

"Why not?" Laazia demanded, glaring at him. Her seductive manner was quickly evaporating as her hijacking plan started to fall apart. *Losing control of the situation?* Paris asked her silently. *Good.*

"Because, well, er—" He mentally composed another mouthful of meaningless technobabble, then discarded it. His instincts told him that Laazia wasn't going to fall for that trick again. "Well, for one thing, we're way out of transporter range."

He pressed a lighted icon on his control panel. The magnified image from the long-range sensors disappeared from the main viewer, replaced by a more accurate representation of Ryolanov as a tiny gold dot against a backdrop of stars. "What?!" Laazia shouted angrily as the truth hit home. "We're going the wrong way!"

The jig is up, Paris thought. *Time to go for broke.* Pushing the limits of the inertial dampers, he executed a sharp starboard turn that sent everyone on the bridge—except for Paris, who hung on tightly to the conn—flying from their seats. Looking back over his shoulder, he watched Laazia tumble from her chair onto the floor. He also saw Chakotay roll helplessly onto his side, smacking his temple against the nearby operations console. *Sorry about that,* Paris thought. *Couldn't be helped.* He stabilized *Voyager*'s flight path, then leaped from his seat, diving after Laazia, who was sprawled facedown upon the command platform, her indigo cloak draped over her like a rug or blanket. He slammed into her back and rammed her head into the floor with both hands. His fingers dug into the downy fleece covering her skull as he struggled to keep her deadly eyes pointing at the floor. "Don't look at me!" he shouted. "Don't even move!"

This time her unusual strength did not catch him by surprise. He put all his weight and energy into holding the Elder's daughter down. This was his only chance to recapture the bridge for the captain, and he wasn't going to waste it. For a second, he even thought he had Laazia pinned for good.

Then the body beneath him began to change. . . .

Lieutenant Carey had just brought the warp engines off-line when the ship lurched abruptly to the starboard side. Captain Janeway had to grab on to a support pylon to keep from falling. "What in blazes?" she called out to Carey, who was steadying himself against the master systems display console. "Did we do that?"

"No, sir," Carey informed her. The floor appeared to have leveled off for the time being. He stepped away from the console experimentally, looking relieved when he wasn't thrown off-kilter. He scratched his head through his curly red hair. *Voyager has been cruising at impulse since before you arrived. Killing the warp drive shouldn't have had any effect on the ship's trajectory.*

"Understood," Janeway said. She let go of the pylon and looked around for any damage the sudden turn might have caused. All she saw was several uniformed security officers scrambling onto their feet. Harry Kim assisted one of the officers to her feet while Tuvok kept a vigilant gaze upon the nearest entrance. Main Engineering looked to be more or less intact, although packed to overflowing with armed and anxious-looking personnel. "Who the devil is flying this ship, then?" she asked out loud, then guessed the answer. "Paris," she said, with a grim smile. *Whatever Tom's up to, I hoped it worked.*

She returned her attention to Lieutenant Carey and the master controls. "Disable the impulse drive next," she instructed him. "I don't want this ship going anywhere until it's back under my control. Are you sure they won't be able to restore power to the engines from the bridge?"

Carey shook his head. "Not even Lieutenant Torres

would be able to reroute the controls after the way we've bollixed them. Give me a few more minutes, and *Voyager* will be dead in the water."

I don't like the sound of that, she thought, *even under the best of circumstances.* There was no alternative, though. She couldn't let the Ryol take the ship wherever they pleased, and she wasn't ready to storm the bridge just yet. Too many hostages, she had concluded, and too much unknown about the full capabilities of the Ryol. There was no point in confronting the Ryol until they had found a way to neutralize the hijackers' lethal ability to sap the energy from their foes. B'Elanna and the others had apparently learned that the hard way.

"Tuvok," she addressed her security head, "is there anyway the Ryol can send reinforcements to their boarding party?"

"I do not believe so," he stated. "According to the latest navigational readings, we are beyond the range of conventional transporters, nor was there any indication that the Ryol possessed working spacecraft. We must assume that the Ryol intend to land *Voyager* on Ryolanov once their conquest of the ship is complete."

"We'll see about that," Janeway said. The ship had already been captured once before, by Seska and her Kazon enemies, and she wasn't about to let it happen again, not if she had anything to say about it. "They're not going anywhere near Ryolanov while we're in control of the engines."

She wished she knew what was happening on the planet's surface. She still remembered the cruel, arrogant sound of Varathael's voice instants before the transporter plucked B'Elanna's commbadge from his fingers. *How could I have misjudged him so badly,* she thought, *unless I needed some shore leave as much as everyone else?* So much conflict and warfare; it had seemed like almost every week they had ended up fighting for their lives against some hostile denizen of the Delta Quadrant. She had longed for the relative peace and harmony of the Federation more than she had realized, perhaps, and so had been too quick to accept the Ryol as the civilized kindred spirits they had pretended to be.

But there was no time to indulge in guilt or self-pity. Now that they had disabled the warp and impulse engines, she knew, it was only a matter of time before Laazia sent her gang to restore power to the engines. "All right," she said loud enough for everyone in Engineering to hear. "We know they're coming, so let's be ready for them. Assume defensive positions."

Phasers in hand, the security teams spread out through the entire engineering section. The bulk of the armed men and women took up positions in and around the main entrance to Engineering, but every maintenance tunnel, back entrance, and turbolift station was guarded as well. *None of which,* Janeway thought, *gets me back onto the bridge anytime soon.*

There was no point in setting up any forcefields around Engineering; as long as the Ryol had control of the bridge, they could easily deactivate the fields using the security overrides. Forcefields would only provide false security, so she had chosen not to rely on them in this instance. Tuvok had agreed with her assessment. "The Ryol have limited provisions upon the bridge. They might not be able to endure a long siege."

"And neither would the hostages," Janeway said, frowning. She tapped her commbadge decisively. "Janeway to Sickbay," she announced. "What's the good word, Doctor? Have you learned anything new about our visitors?"

"I can hardly be expected to master every nuance of an alien being's unique physiology in less than an hour," The Doctor said, sounding slightly piqued, "but the preliminary data is provocative."

"How so?" Janeway asked. She kept her gaze fixed on the well-guarded entrance, ready to direct the fight against the Ryol the instant it began. The muzzles of high-powered phaser rifles bobbed above the sea of heads like the tips of deadly icebergs.

"As nearly as I can tell," The Doctor said, "their basic metabolism is intertwined with their psionic capacity to an unprecedented degree. Even on a cellular level, their RNA and mitochondria are psychically reactive, and dependent on what we would consider excess psychic energy to function properly. The Ryol have a conventional digestive system, but it's rudimentary and almost superfluous; a vestigial remnant of an earlier stage in their evolution. They derive most of their sustenance from psychic energy, which they extract from other living beings. Sentient species, naturally, are the best sources of psychic energy."

"Such as ourselves and the neffaler?" Janeway prompted him. *Damn,* she thought. Tuvok was wrong; the Ryol had plenty to dine upon aboard the bridge, namely Chakotay and the other hostages.

"I assume so," The Doctor said, "although I have yet to examine a neffaler in person. I would be curious to observe the long-term effects of psychic parasitism inflicted upon a sentient species over several generations." He scratched his chin thoughtfully. "It's an intriguing topic."

"Let's hope we don't get to observe it firsthand," Janeway said dryly. "How do they do this, Doctor? Is there anyway of blocking the energy transference?" She kept her eye on the entrance. So far, no Ryol had shown his or her face at the door, but she knew they would have to come here eventually. "This is a matter of more than academic interest at the moment."

"Well, there is something else," The Doctor said, "although it's not quite what you're asking for."

"Any suggestions you have would be appreciated," Janeway said. *Just give a weapon,* she thought. *Something I can use to reclaim the ship.*

"Curiously," The Doctor began, "I became aware of this phenomenon not by examining the Ryol, but by observing myself. As you may not be aware, my own software contains several self-monitoring subroutines that provide a continual moment-by-moment analysis of my state of being. If necessary, I can provide a detailed report on my physical and mental capacities at any given occasion, past or present."

"That's very interesting," Janeway said, hoping to spur The Doctor toward the point of his little lecture. The Ryol could attack Engineering at any moment; she didn't have time to indulge the hologram's fondness for his own voice. "I'm afraid I don't see the relevance to our present situation."

"As I mentioned earlier," The Doctor continued, "the two Ryol who invaded the sickbay both attempted to employ their unique abilities against me. Naturally, they failed—my energies are quite different from any biological entity's—but my sensory functions recorded the progress of the psionic wave front generated by the Ryol. In the absence of any organic energy to act upon, the wave front grew disordered and even showed signs of reversing its direction. The readings suggest the possibility of negative feedback if the parasitic effect is unable to connect with its target."

"In other words," Janeway summarized, "holograms give them indigestion." *Interesting,* she thought, feeling a surge of hope. All sorts of intriguing possibilities occurred to her. There had to be some way to turn The Doctor's discovery to their advantage.

"Oh, one more thing," The Doctor added.

"Yes?" Janeway asked. *Now what?*

"Preliminary analysis of the Ryol DNA hints at metamorphic abilities."

"What?"

One minute, Tom Paris had Laazia pinned to the floor of the bridge, then, suddenly, Laazia wasn't Laazia anymore. The Elder's breathtakingly beautiful daughter changed into something else.

He could feel the body beneath her indigo cloak shifting beneath his grip, its slender contours expanding, its musculature growing larger and more solid. Her bare arms, extending beyond the hem of the cloak, stretched to twice their original length, their joints popping as flesh and bone reshaped themselves. Tawny golden fur, similar to that which covered her skull but more coarse, sprouted along her reconfigured limbs, even as her pointed nails devolved into long and lethal-looking talons. Paris heard the fabric of her gown tearing. He smelled a musky odor redolent of a caged animal.

He tried to hold her down despite the violent contortions of her body. Krevorr and Assink hurried to assist him. They each grabbed one of Laazia's flailing arms, but it was no good. With a savage convulsion, the transformed Laazia shook off her would-be captors. Paris was thrown from atop the bucking spine of the creature, landing on his back not far from the captain's chair.

The impact knocked the breath out of him, but he knew better than to take a second to recover. Scrambling to his feet, he saw Assink and Krevorr backing away from the fearsome monstrosity standing erect in the center of the command area. "Laazia?" Paris whispered, unable to believe his eyes.

The growl that emerged from the creature's jaws was several octaves lower than Laazia's usual husky vibrato, but more than just her vocal cords had changed. The thing before him was at least eight meters tall and covered with golden fur. Laazia's turquoise gown hung in tatters upon the beast's enormous, bearlike frame. Bits of silver jewelry glittered inappropriately amid shaggy bristles. The elegant sandals had been reduced to scraps of torn leather beneath the creature's massive paws. The velvet cape, which had once stretched nearly to the floor, now fell to just above her knees.

Despite the dyed tiger stripes adorning the monster's skull, its features were more lupine than feline. A snout full of ivory fangs protruded from what had formerly been Laazia's lovely face. Elongated nostrils flared above those ravenous jaws, while sticky strands of spittle dripped from her mouth onto the shining steel floor. Her transformed ears, larger and more pointed than a Vulcan's, pointed toward the ceiling. Only the pale green eyes, still gleaming like polished malachite, were unchanged.

I kissed that on the lips? Paris thought, feeling more than a little queasy. He glanced quickly at his comrades. Krevorr and Assink stood on opposite sides of the command platform, clearly unsure what to do next but never taking their eyes off the were-beast towering over them. Chakotay, his hands still bound behind him, stared at Laazia's new form with an unmistakable look of recognition. "The beast," he murmured softly.

Laazia growled again. Although her gown was in ruins, her voluminous cloak spread out behind her as she swung her arms at the uncertain humanoids surrounding her. Ensign Krevorr managed to duck out of the way, but a backhanded blow from the creature sent Assink flying over the conn to smash headfirst into the main viewer; for a split second, he looked like a comet silhouetted against the starry backdrop.

Paris marveled at the monster's strength. Not even Tuvok or B'Elanna could have propelled Assink such a distance with just one blow. *I suppose I should be thankful,* he thought, *that she isn't just zapping us with those evil eyes of hers. Probably not nearly as satisfying as ripping us to shreds.* Laazia glared at him with her baleful green eyes, challenging him. *Forget it,* he thought. A physical confrontation was out of the question; in her new guise, Laazia could easily tear him apart in hand-to-hand combat. *I need an edge,* he thought, *but what?*

He searched the bridge with his eyes. *Damn,* he thought. Whatever had possessed him to hand out all of the bridge's emergency phasers to the Ryol? Then he looked right at the raging beast before him and remembered exactly who and what had, quite literally, possessed him. *Never again,* he vowed.

Ensign Krevorr, at starboard forward, was edging cautiously toward the unconscious body of Assink, apparently intent on checking her crew mate's injuries while simultaneously keeping a close eye on Laazia. Good response, Paris noted; there was obviously no point in engaging the creature in hand-to-hand combat. *Access,* he thought. He had to shut down the forcefields isolating the bridge, provided he could get to either the tactical console behind the captain's chair or back to Tuvok's security station.

Turning his back hurriedly on Laazia, he vaulted over the guardrail separating the command area from the aft stations. He didn't move fast enough, though. A swipe from the monster's huge claws caught him across the back, tearing through both his uniform and his flesh. He gasped out loud, the pain from five bloody gashes blurring into one searing burst of agony, and fell hard against the aft engineering consoles, ramming his shoulder into the bottom of the rear aft Ops console.

With a howl of rage, Laazia leaped over the guardrail. He heard her land heavily on the floor a few meters away from him. Orienting himself, he realized that the beast now stood between him and the tactical console attached to the aft side of the guardrail. That left only the controls at the security station if he wanted to deactivate the shields, but could he get to it in time, before the were-thing pounced upon him?

Not very likely, he thought. He still felt his fingers and toes—the monster's claws had not severed his spinal cord—but his aching body felt like it could hardly move, let alone outrace Laazia to the security station. *I need more time,* he thought desperately.

He looked into the beast's green eyes. Was it just his imagination, he wondered, or was there actually a cruel sort of smile on the monster's wolflike face? Laazia appeared to be enjoying his distress—until something slammed into her from behind, producing a yelp of surprise.

It was Chakotay. Even though his hands remained tied behind his back, the first officer had somehow managed to climb back onto his feet, then plowed into Laazia headfirst, giving Paris just the break he needed. Half crawling, half diving, Paris threw himself toward Tuvok's usual station at the rear of the bridge. Behind him, he heard Laazia turning angrily on Chakotay, but he did not look back. He lunged into the station, then slid into Tuvok's seat, his torn back leaving behind crimson streaks. His fingers danced across the lighted control panel, hastily undoing the defenses he himself had erected less than an hour ago. *What was I thinking?* he thought angrily. He forced the guilt from his mind, concentrating on the task at hand.

A gasp from the command area diverted his attention from the controls. He turned and his heart pounded at the sight: Laazia had Chakotay, her claws wrapped around his throat, his feet dangling almost two meters above the floor. Choking sounds escaped the commander's lips, even as his face turned first red, then purple. The blue-black ink of his tattoo was barely visible against his darkening complexion. Bubbling foam dripped from Laazia's jaws as she squeezed the life from the former Maquis leader.

Paris searched for a weapon, any weapon. He didn't see anything at first, then he spotted a silver glint from beneath the first officer's chair. *Of course,* he remembered. The phaser that Laazia had so casually discarded. It must have fallen to the floor when *Voyager* took that sharp turn. He glanced around quickly; no one else seemed to have noticed the phaser.

Ensign Krevorr, Starfleet through and through, ran to save Chakotay. She sprinted clockwise around the perimeter of the bridge, briefly coming between Paris and their foe. Shouting at the top of her lungs, she executed a flying kick into the cloak-draped back of the monster. Paris heard the heels of Krevorr's boots smash against the beast's muscular torso.

It was like kicking a grizzly bear. Laazia did not even falter. Instead she swung around, using Chakotay as a club to strike out at the courageous young ensign. Krevorr landed squarely on her feet after delivering her kick, but Chakotay's swinging body batted her aside before she could renew her attack. Krevorr bounced once against the aft monitors, then collapsed onto the floor. She did not get up.

My turn, Paris thought. He dived toward the command area, rolling onto the floor, snatching up the fallen phaser, and firing it at Laazia. Her attack on Krevorr had brought her around to face Paris, so that the beam, set on stun, hit her directly in the chest. Laazia howled in rage and shock, but did not fall down. The force of the beam was enough to knock her back a few steps, and to cause her to drop Chakotay clumsily onto the floor, yet she remained standing. Paris's eyes widened in amazement. Even at its lowest setting, a direct phaser blast at this range was enough to drop a charging Klingon. *What in space is she made of?* he wondered.

"Why don't you be a good girl," he muttered, "and fall like you're supposed to?" The gashes along his back burned as though they were on fire. *Let's raise the setting,* he thought, keeping the beam fixed upon her chest while he stared defiantly into her eyes.

Her eyes, he realized too late. *Oh no.* A familiar chill rushed over him, leaching away both strength and resolve. His mind ordered his hand to up the setting on his phaser to full strength, but his fingers would not respond to his commands. He was paralyzed, unable to move or even look away from the hypnotic green eyes this creature shared with Laazia's earlier incarnation. His knees buckled beneath the awful cold that had gripped him. The blood streaming down his back felt like ice water. He could not even summon the strength to hold on to the phaser. It slipped from his fingers to land with a sharp metallic ring upon the floor. *I'm sorry, Captain,* he thought. *I tried to do my best.*

For a few brief seconds, the entire bridge seemed to take on the same greenish hue as the Ryol's eyes. Then everything went black.

CHAPTER
15

Phaser fire lit up Engineering. The hiss of a dozen phaser rifles firing sounded like a basketful of angry snakes. Captain Janeway took shelter behind a sturdy pylon while she fired her own hand phaser over the heads of the security team guarding the entrance to Engineering. To her surprise, a couple of identical beams came hissing at them from the turbolifts beyond Engineering. *Blast,* she thought angrily. *They have phasers, too. Probably stolen from the bridge,* she guessed.

Six uniformed officers armed with high-powered phaser rifles formed the first line of defense. They fired their weapons from kneeling positions so that another line of security personnel, standing immediately behind them, could fire their phasers over the first team's heads. Janeway, Tuvok, Kim, and various members of the engineering staff made up a third line of defense, directing their beams from elevated platforms and ladders and any other available perch. Crimson beams of energized light crisscrossed in the corridor beyond Engineering, forming an intricate and impenetrable web of destructive radiation. At least, Janeway *hoped* it was impenetrable.

The attack had begun minutes ago. Without any warning, a pack of unarmed Ryol—she had identified at least four of them—came charging out of a turbolift at the other end of the corridor. Her security people opened fire immediately—with mixed results.

The Ryol were clearly resistant to phaser beams, but not entirely immune. Concentrated fire from the phaser rifles succeeded in driving the assault back toward the waiting turbolift, but so far there were no Ryol bodies littering the corridor. A red-hot beam of energy missed Janeway by several centimeters, leaving a blackened scar on a bulkhead behind her. Fortunately, the inexperienced Ryol appeared to be lousy shots.

"Keep firing," Janeway ordered her troops. They couldn't afford to lose the offensive lest the Ryol put their psychic abilities into play. What was the maximum range of their parasitic effect, she wondered, and could they exert their strange powers even while under fire? She suspected she was about to find out.

"Captain, look!" Harry Kim exclaimed from his perch only four or five meters away from her.

Kim wasn't the only crew member caught by surprise. Involuntary gasps of shock and amazement escaped the ship's defenders as the Ryol discarded their humanoid facades in favor of a far more threatening appearance. Thick golden fur bristled all over the bronzed flesh of the Ryol, which seemed to absorb additional mass from the empty air, growing larger before the crew's astonished eyes. Nails lengthened into talons, pearly teeth transformed into fangs over two centimeters long. A cacophony of ferocious roars and howls assailed Janeway's eardrums, blending with the constant sizzle of the phaser beams to add an oppressive new element to the dire scene unfolding before her. She recalled The Doctor's comments about Naxor's DNA and nodded knowingly. "Metamorphic abilities" indeed.

"Interesting, Captain," Tuvok commented, while firing careful shots with his own phaser. He had taken shelter behind a pillar across the way from Janeway's. "Shape-shifting species are extremely rare."

"Not rare enough," Janeway said. Although she couldn't be sure, she guessed that she was now seeing the true form of the Ryol for the first time; it certainly seemed to suit their actual nature. Then she remembered Chakotay's description of his vision from a few days back, and she knew that she was looking upon the same malevolent entity that had haunted Chakotay's spiritual journey. *No more masks,* she thought grimly. *Now I see you as you really are.*

Scorch marks from over a dozen phaser bolts marred the walls of the corridor. The hum of the weapons assailed her eardrums. *We're driving them back,* Janeway thought, vaguely surprised that the Ryol had proved so easy to repel. Then Lieutenant Stevenson, one of the first row of defenders, toppled over, collapsing from his kneeling position to sprawl face-first onto the floor. His phaser rifle dropped from his fingers, a deadman switch cutting off the beam shooting from its muzzle. Next to Stevenson, Ensign Rodriguez's rifle wobbled slightly, as if the security officer was having difficulty holding on to her weapon. Another officer, at the other end of the row, seemed to be drooping as well.

Janeway felt as though the other shoe had finally dropped; the Ryol were obviously using their parasitic abilities at last. Looking past the stricken guards, she spotted a furry-faced Ryol peering around the entrance to the turbolift, his striking black eyes fixed upon the men and women guarding Engineering. Janeway aimed her own phaser directly at the malevolent face, feeling a thrill of satisfaction as her beam blasted the Ryol right between the eyes, sending him flying backward into the confines of the turbolift.

"An excellent shot, Captain," Tuvok observed. He coolly directed another phaser beam at the turbolift doors.

"Practice makes perfect, Mr. Tuvok," Janeway replied, glad to have struck back at the inhuman creature attacking her crew. *Let my people alone!* she thought, half-hoping the Ryol could read her mind. Her angry thoughts would burn them faster than any phaser ever could.

But her target was not the only Ryol launching a psionic attack upon her crew. As she looked on apprehensively, she saw one guard after another succumbing to the debilitating effect of the strange powers of the Ryol. Shaky security officers stood on trembling legs, wiping the sweat from their brows while they fought to keep standing beneath the unnatural exhaustion induced by the Ryol invaders. Fresher guards rushed to replace their comrades, as yet another Starfleet or Maquis crew member sank to the floor, their weapons abruptly unmanned and useless.

A groan escaped Kim. Glancing up, Janeway saw the young ensign tottering upon one of the upper railways. "Oh no," she heard him whisper. "Not again!"

"Watch yourself, Ensign Kim," she barked. "Hang on to that rail."

"I'll try, Captain," Kim said, gasping. He clung to a rail with one hand while firing his phaser with another. His face looked pale and clammy.

Looking away from Kim, Janeway saw a human technician, more accustomed to engine repairs than to combat, snatch up the rifle dropped by a Bajoran marksman and start firing at will, the scarlet beam leaping like lightning to strike the exposed chest of a snarling were-creature charging at the fallen guards. She smelled burning fur as the phaser beam seared the Ryol's shaggy coat and sent him running back toward the safety of the turbolift. More beams chased after him.

This is turning into a war of attrition, she thought. So far, her troops had managed to keep up the barrage of phaser fire despite their losses, but how much longer would they be able to hold the wolflike Ryol at bay? The *Voyager* crew had the advantage of numbers, but the ratio of defenders to attackers was diminishing every minute. Thank goodness that the ship was now out of transporter range of Ryolanov; Janeway suspected that she had Chakotay and Paris to thank for that bit of good news.

Still, the battle could not continue the way it was now going. She glanced at Tuvok; even the Vulcan's stoic expression betrayed signs of fatigue. His lips were pursed tightly together. Beads of sweat dotted his brown forehead. At this rate, the Ryol would eventually overrun Engineering after they had drained the energy of enough of the guards. It was time to add another factor to the equation.

"Mr. Carey," she called out, still targeting the Ryol with her phaser, "have you managed to rig up that apparatus we talked about?"

"Almost," Carey responded. Behind the front lines of the conflict, Carey and a small team of technicians were scurrying around Engineering, adapting preexisting equipment to an entirely new purpose. "It's a little trickier than I thought."

If only B'Elanna was here, Janeway thought, *and not still a prisoner on Ryolanov.* Still, Carey was probably the second-best engineer on *Voyager,* not counting herself. She watched as another charge by the Ryol was driven back, barely, by what remained of her defenders; this time, the invaders made it almost to the first row of guards before retreating. The Ryol were making far too much progress and far too quickly, Janeway thought.

"With all deliberate speed, Mr. Carey," she ordered. *Voyager* was running out of time.

What the hell was that? Tom Paris thought, waking slowly to a throbbing ache in his temples. He felt like a ton of latinum had been dropped on his head. Every muscle in his body felt sore and depleted, and the rest of him didn't feel so hot either. At first, he couldn't remember what had happened to him. Then slowly he opened his eyes and realized where he was: flat on his back on the bridge.

He tried to sit up, and discovered that his wrists were bound together behind his back. His restraints felt like cloth, but that hardly mattered; as fatigued as he was, they might as well be rhodinium. The floor of the bridge was a lot less comfortable than it should have been. Clearly it had not been intended for sleeping on.

"Welcome back," came a familiar voice. Twisting his neck, Paris saw Chakotay, seated on the floor only a meter or so away. The first officer was also a prisoner, Paris recalled, as all the details of Laazia's assault on the bridge came back to him. *The shields,* he remembered. Had he managed to deactivate all the forcefields? He thought he had, but glancing around, he didn't see any security teams beaming in to reclaim the bridge. Surely the captain would have taken advantage of the shields coming down, unless she were unable to. Had something happened to Captain Janeway while he was unconscious? He needed to find out.

Rocking back and forth on his spine, he managed to

work himself up to a sitting position, just in time to feel an angry hand smack against his face.

"Idiotic creature," Laazia growled at him. The Elder's daughter loomed over Paris and Chakotay, fury in her malachite eyes. She had reassumed her humanoid disguise, sort of. Glaring at her, his cheeks still stinging from her slap, Paris saw that Laazia had actually evolved into some sort of intermediate state between her humanoid and lupine identities. A thin layer of golden down, much like that which had previously covered only her skull, now spread out all over her body, which was scarcely concealed by the torn and shredded remnants of her turquoise gown. Although her elongated snout had retracted back into her usual refined features, her ears remained sharply pointed, as did the ivory fangs filling her mouth. *The better to eat me with,* Paris thought.

"You disappointed me, Tom," Laazia accused, her vibrato still more husky than usual. "I feigned attraction to you quite convincingly, I thought, and still you betrayed me. That was a very bad decision, Tom. I fear it may have a negative effect on our relationship."

"That's a matter of perspective," Paris said, anticipating another slap—or worse. He glanced around the bridge. Assink and Krevorr were both out cold, their motionless bodies littering the open area in front of the main viewer. At least he hoped they were only out cold. "I had to betray *somebody,* and I'm afraid my first loyalty is to my captain and my ship."

None of Laazia's associates, he noted, had returned from their mission to capture Captain Janeway. *That's encouraging,* he thought. Maybe capturing *Voyager* had proved harder than Laazia had anticipated.

"Neffaler!" she hissed at him, the ultimate insult, apparently. Turning her back, she stalked away. Laazia had discarded her purple cloak, he observed; the voluminous garment was draped over the back of the captain's chair. Striding past the command area, she approached the conn. Paris felt a surge of irrational anger at the sight of the Elder's daughter taking possession of *his* personal station.

On the main viewer, Ryolanov remained just a tiny speck against a backdrop of distant stars. Laazia looked from the navigational controls to the viewer and back again. Paris was relieved to see that the Ryol temptress seemed baffled by the unfamiliar controls. *Not much of a pilot,* he guessed. He wondered if any of the Ryol knew anything about flying a starship.

"Ship," Laazia announced imperiously. "Return us to Ryolanov."

Good try, Paris thought, but *Voyager*'s automated systems weren't quite that easy to operate. *You need a cooperative pilot,* he thought with more than a little spiteful satisfaction. *You need me.*

Chakotay must have been thinking along the same lines. "Good to see you're still on our side," he said quietly.

"Oh, come on," Paris replied. "You didn't really think I'd sell you all down the river for a pretty face and a nice pair of legs?"

"Well . . ." Chakotay said.

"Okay," Paris admitted. "Maybe I gave you some tiny excuse for jumping to that conclusion." He let his breezy tone drop for a minute. "Seriously, Commander, you can count on me. I was gone for a while there, but I'm back now. I promise." He lowered her voice. "What's going on with the captain? Do you know?"

Chakotay shook his head. "Laazia's boarding party took off for Engineering and haven't been heard from since. I have to assume that's good news."

"Silence!" Laazia snarled, proving that her pointed ears were fairly remarkable as well. "You!" she said, pointing an extended nail at Paris. "You spineless excuse for a male. Tell me how to command this vessel."

"Do I look like a flying instructor to you?" Paris said sarcastically. "Why don't you ask the captain . . . oh, that's right, you still haven't managed to get your hands on her." He made a production of craning his neck to look around the bridge. "Say, what's happened to your entourage? Run into a bit of trouble, have they?"

Laazia's face contorted with rage. He'd obviously hit a nerve. "Computer," she commanded loudly, "locate Captain Janeway."

It was an innocuous request, on the surface, so the ship's computer obliged her instantly. "Captain Janeway is currently in Engineering," came a friendly female voice. Laazia smiled triumphantly at this minor victory over *Voyager's* impressive technology.

Uh-oh, Paris thought. *She's getting the hang of this.* It was entirely possible, he realized, that the ship might prove far too user-friendly for their own good. *Remember,* he told himself, *we don't know how advanced the science of the Ryol really is.* There might be someone in Laazia's entourage who knew a lot more about operating starship systems. He couldn't just sit back and wait to see what happened next; he had to throw a wrench into the works somehow.

Laazia was in a hurry, too. Evidently unwilling to wait until her team returned, she walked slowly and deliberately over to Paris and grabbed him by the chin. Lifting his face toward hers, she addressed him in a low and seductive tone.

"You know that I will learn whatever I wish eventually," she said. "Why not tell me now and spare you and the others so much suffering." Her green eyes darkened ominously. Paris felt his hard-won resolve slipping away. *Oh no,* he thought. *Not again!* "You cannot resist us," she purred. "Surrender to your inescapable destiny. Show me how to command this ship the same way that the Ryol have always commanded whatever we deigned to control. Tell me now, tell me everything you know."

Paris tried to speak, but his mouth was dry. Swallowing hard, he managed to produce just enough saliva to say what he needed to say.

"Computer, deactivate Universal Translator. Bridge only."

The too-bright beams disappeared. The obnoxious humming ceased. Rolop, the chief deputy to the Heir, peeked out from behind the entrance to the turbolift and inspected the aliens' defenses. His milky green eyes widened in surprise as he saw the portal to the engine rooms lying open and abandoned. He let out a howl of victory. The neffaler had retreated at last!

Barking out a command to his followers, he loped down the scorched hallway toward their newly captured territory, holding a captured phaser in one clenched paw. His powerful body sung with all the vitality he had stolen from their pitiable opponents. After days spent maintaining the shape of a hairless simian, it felt liberating to inhabit once more his rightful form as a hunter. He sniffed the sterile artificial air of the starship; if he tried very hard he could almost smell the fear of his fleeing prey.

Manow and Shiila caught up with him, yelping and yowling at his side. They left another hunter, Paayra, unconscious on the floor of the turbolift. She had not managed to absorb enough strength from the new neffaler to resist the potency of their energy weapons. Later perhaps, Rolop mused, he would allow her to restore herself by supping on the last dregs of essence to be found in their defeated foes.

A handful of fallen humanoids littered the floor at the other end of the corridor. Rolop sensed some life remaining in the inert bodies, but he urged both his followers to pass them by. There would be time enough to feed on leftovers once the captain was captured. He pounced over the alien casualties, wondering where and when the rest of the neffaler would choose to make their last stand.

He found his answer just beyond the gateway to the engine rooms. Captain Janeway and roughly a dozen of her crew stood guard in front of the tall translucent pillar that dominated the center of the chamber. Banks of machinery surrounded the base of the pillar, while nonorganic energy flashed and flickered within its shadowy depths. Rolop, who had studied starship technology, guessed that the imposing structure played some key role in the matter/antimatter reactions powering the ship's warp drive.

A steel catwalk ran around the top of the pillar, several lengths above their heads. Rolop peered up at the scaffolding, half-expecting an ambush, but saw no humanoids upon the catwalk. The only aliens in sight were the ones standing directly in his path. He recognized Captain Janeway at once. The stern-looking female stood in the center of the assembled neffaler, flanked on both sides by armed guards in yellow uniforms.

"Turn back," Janeway said, "or we will resort to deadly force."

Rolop's lips peeled back, exposing his fangs. Was this creature suicidal, he wondered, or merely deluded? Hadn't they already demonstrated the overwhelming superiority of the Ryol when compared against the aliens' meager attempts to defend themselves? Rolop felt the strength and endurance of countless neffaler burning within his breast. He did not fear the humanoids' weapons, as annoying as they were. No neffaler could last for long against the power of the Ryol. They were nothing but food, after all.

"Surrender," Rolop said, his vocal cords straining to approximate the aliens' crude vocalizations. He would give them one chance to submit voluntarily, but only one.

"Never," Janeway said. "Now get off my ship."

Rolop could not comprehend this creature's colossal foolishness. *Very well,* he thought. He did not need his fangs or claws to reduce these arrogant humanoids to nothing more than an afternoon snack. He would personally drain every last morsel of energy from this so-called captain.

"Feast!" he barked to his subordinates. "Gorge!"

Together they unleashed their hunger upon the gathered neffaler. The humanoids fired their weapons at Rolop and the other Ryol, but their pathetic energy beams seemed, if anything, even weaker than before. Rolop let the crimson radiation wash over him, the minor pain of its attack merely egging his hunger and his fury to ever greater heights. Howling louder than all the energy beams combined, he tapped into the awesome voraciousness at the center of his being and flung it outward at . . .

Nothing?

It was as though he had hurled his hunger into a bottomless void. There was no life-force to latch on to, none at all. He saw the humanoids in front of him, felt the pang of their energy blasts, but he found no precious vitality to sustain him against their constant barrage. Unsatisfied, his hunger grew ever larger, coming to feel like a gaping wound in the center of his chest, a wound that sucked the emptiness into his body. The void rushed along his spine and spilled out behind his eyes, consuming his brain in its awful nihility. He had opened his mind to drain the life from his prey, but now he found himself unable to bar the doorway to his being against the emptiness that had invaded him. His own hunger was reflected back onto him.

His arms and legs extended, Rolop twitched convulsively. His triumphant howl metamorphosed into a shriek of agony. His eyes flashed from black to green to black over and over again, his pupils dilating and expanding at an increasingly frantic rate. He heard two more shrieks join his own, and realized that Manow and Shiila had to be suffering in the same manner. Instinctively his eyes sought out his comrades.

Mistake! The instant that his gaze connected with Manow's, he felt his uncontrolled hunger shift its focus from the empty humanoids to his fellow Ryol. At the same time, another hunger—and another—grabbed on to his soul and started tearing it apart. Rolop let out an ear-piercing scream, trapped in a destructive three-way circuit with the other two Ryol. He felt as though he were being pulled out of shape in three different directions. Unrestrained appetites tugged and tore at the roots of each hunter's essence, consuming each other in a frenzied attempt to evade the emptiness leaching away their strength.

Rolop tried to call back his hunger, but it was too late. The more energy he lost, the more he needed, and the more his lust for life-force, any life-force at all, ran wild and uncontrolled.

His vision dimmed. Everything grew darker, until he could barely make out the shadowy outlines of the humanoids and their engine rooms. His heart was pounding. He couldn't breathe. A sense of dizziness rushed over him as his legs seemed to dissolve beneath him.

He lost consciousness before his head hit the floor.

On the floor of Engineering, Captain Janeway and the security team lowered their weapons. The twitching bodies of three Ryol, still displaying the full horrific details of their natural form, rested uneasily at their feet. Janeway waited several seconds, just to see if the Ryol were likely to attack again, then decided that this battle had been won for now. She turned toward Tuvok. "They appear subdued," she stated.

"I concur," Tuvok said, placing his phaser in its holster. Not far away from him, Ensign Kim breathed a sigh of relief. Now that the psychic attack was over, color began returning to his face.

"All right then," the captain said. "Mr. Carey, you can do the honors."

Janeway and the other crew members flickered momentarily, then disappeared. At the same time, an identical assemblage appeared to materialize on the catwalk far above the defeated Ryol, *appeared* being the operative word.

In fact, Janeway knew, she and the surviving security officers had been on the catwalk all along, but the holographic projectors Lieutenant Carey had rigged up around Engineering had diverted their images to the floor below, while simultaneously providing a primitive sort of cloaking effect to conceal their actual location from the Ryol search party. *It's all done with mirrors,* she thought, a slight grin upon her face. "Well done, Mr. Carey," she said. "A successful—and effective—illusion."

"Well," Carey said modestly, "it helped that Lieutenant Torres has been experimenting with ways to bring The Doctor to Engineering, in case of a medical emergency." He inspected one of the projectors he'd mounted to the scaffolding behind him. "There are still plenty of bugs to be worked out before we can get it working on a regular basis—the power differential between the holographic resolution system and the main energy transponders is a real headache—but it seems to have worked out okay this time around."

"I'll say," Janeway agreed. She climbed down a service ladder to take a closer look at their defeated enemies. The three Ryol lay in graceless positions upon the cold metal floor. Their faces had a starved, emaciated look while most of their muscles seemed to have literally shriveled upon their now bony bodies. *The Doctor was right,* she thought. Holograms definitely disagreed with the Ryol. She still wasn't sure exactly why or how holographic images interacted with the parasitic abilities of the Ryol, but it seemed obvious that these Ryol had gotten a sizable taste of their own medicine. "Too bad," she mused aloud, "that we can't project holograms onto the bridge."

Carey shook his head. "Not without installing the necessary equipment first."

Janeway's grin gave way to a somber expression. Now that Engineering had been successfully defended, reclaiming the bridge had to be her next priority, but first there was some cleaning up to do after this fight. Moving quickly and efficiently throughout Engineering, she checked on the injuries of the fallen security officers, discovering, to her relief, that there were no fatalities among the *Voyager* crew. While Tuvok dispatched a third of the security team to check out the turbolift for more Ryol, she contacted The Doctor via her commbadge.

"Janeway here," she said. "We have three, maybe more, Ryol prisoners. They're all unconscious now, but I want them all doped up enough to stay that way until they're safe in security cells. I'm sending a team to pick up your two prisoners as well. Be prepared to assist them."

"I'm a doctor, not a jailer," The Doctor replied, "but I'll do my best. Has there been any more word from Kes and the others on the surface?"

"Negative," Tuvok reported to both the captain and The Doctor, joining the discussion from a few meters away. His voice contained no hint of anxiety or concern. "We must assume that all *Voyager* personnel still on Ryolanov are hostages, and that the Ryol remain in control of the bridge." Tuvok considered the matter for a moment before speaking again. "One salient point, Captain. Over the course of the battle, I did not observe the Elder's daughter, nor is she recognizable among our transformed prisoners. Did you detect any evidence of her presence?"

"No," Janeway answered, not bothering to conceal her own anger. "Not yet."

But just wait until I get my hands on Laazia, she thought, *and her snake of a father.* She glanced back over her shoulder at the withered shaggy bodies of the Ryol search party. *I don't care who or what you really are. I'm taking my ship—and my people—back.*

Laazia had gone berserk. Lifting Paris up by his collar, she let loose an incomprehensible string of whistles, chirps, growls, and barks. Paris couldn't make out a word she was saying. *Probably just as well,* he thought. *I don't imagine it's very complimentary.*

Deactivating the Universal Translator had left Laazia an inarticulate beast trapped in the nerve center of a completely alien environment. She could no longer communicate with the computer, translate the controls, extract useful information from her hostages, or even threaten Paris in a coherent fashion, not that she was having too much difficulty conveying her feelings about Paris himself.

She tossed him savagely against the nearest wall, so that his shoulder bounced painfully against the door to the captain's briefing room. Yellow-alert markers still flashed upon the walls, matching the spots of lights appearing before his eyes. The collision reopened the wounds on his back, releasing fresh streams of blood to stream down his body onto the floor.

In her fury, Laazia regressed to her most primal form, growing larger and more animalistic. Long curving fangs protruded from a wolflike snout while the soft golden down covering her body sprouted unruly tufts of coarse blond fur. Graceful fingers devolved into menacing claws that slashed and tore at everything that came within her reach, including the empty air. Snatching up her velvet cloak, she reduced it to shreds of purple cloth in a matter of seconds, then turned her claws on the padded backrest of the captain's chair.

Paris watched her growing frenzy, aghast. How could he ever have been fooled by Laazia's former beauty? He doubted that he would ever fall under her spell again, no matter how hard she exerted the energy-sapping force behind her eyes, now that he knew about the savagery that lurked within her soul. "Would you believe," he said, "I actually . . . danced . . . with her once?"

"I'm sure you only did it for the good of the ship," Chakotay quipped. Purple bruises mottled his face, but there was an angry gleam in his eyes.

"Of course!" Paris inched away, as much as he could with his hands tied behind his back, from the rampaging were-creature. *Boy,* he thought, *am I glad that you can't understand what we're saying.*

But there was no way to escape her for long. Crazed green eyes turned toward Paris. Froth sprayed from Laazia's deadly new jaws as she advanced on Paris, all ten claws extended, a ferocious growl rumbling from her chest. Universal Translator or no Universal Translator, there was no mistaking her intentions. Paris realized he was only heartbeats away from going the way of the indigo cape.

So long, Dad, he thought, feeling strangely fatalistic in the face of certain death. *You always said I'd come to a bad end.*

An unpleasant odor made him wrinkle his nose in disgust. At first, he thought it might be Laazia's foul beastlike breath, but then he realized it was coming from all around him. *What's this?* he thought, confused.

Laazia smelled the strange odor, too. She stopped, less than three meters away from Paris, and sniffed the air with her flaring nostrils. He heard Chakotay start to cough over by Harry Kim's usual station. Puzzled, and more than a little grateful for this odd reprieve, Paris tried to place the peculiar aroma. It was heavy and thick and somewhat medicinal. *Kind of like incense,* he thought, *or . . . anesthezine gas!*

All at once, he realized what the captain was up to. Laazia must have figured it out as well, because she lunged at Paris, intent on tearing out his throat before the gas knocked her out. Her outstretched claws, still stained with his own blood, came flying toward him.

No way, Paris thought, suddenly feeling not so philosophical about dying after all. He threw his entire body as hard as he could, so that Laazia's talons missed him by a matter of centimeters, smashing instead into the door to the briefing room. He heard her claws scratch against the firm duranium door.

Laazia tried to rouse herself for one more strike at her hated nemesis, but the anesthezine had done its work. With a final slurred snarl, she dropped limply onto the floor of the bridge, less than a meter from where Paris lay gasping.

Raising his weary head from the floor, Paris glimpsed the telltale sparkle of a transporter beam only a second before he passed out.

CHAPTER
16

THE CAVERNOUS CARGOHOLD OF THE ANCIENT SHIP MADE for a damp and gloomy prison. The temperature plummeted as the night wore on, and B'Elanna could feel the chill creeping into her bones like a computer virus spreading through a database. To her relief, though, no other hostages were brought to join them in this improvised dungeon. Perhaps they were still the only captives of the Ryol. *Stay calm,* she told herself. *Hold on to your temper. A rescue mission has to be in the works—unless the Ryol have already taken control of the ship.*

Torres squatted upon the sandy uneven floor, resting her back against an outcropping of rock that had torn its way through the bottom hull of the old starship. Tiny amphibians fluttered their wings overhead while water dripped from one of the broken support beams protruding from the ceiling. Not trusting their ability to keep an eye on their prisoners in semi-lit gloom, the Ryol had embedded several more light crystals in strategic locations around the walls of the chamber, placing Torres and the others beneath a constant white glare that was already getting on her nerves. Kes and Neelix sat nearby, holding hands and doing their best to reassure each other. Torres felt a pang of loneliness, envying her fellow crew members their close relationship.

"Of course," Neelix said abruptly, slapping a spotted hand against his forehead. Kes huddled silently beside him, seeking refuge, Torres guessed, from the psychic cries of the long-dead neffaler. "I should have remembered. The Empty Ones."

"What are you talking about?" Torres asked.

"An ancient myth," he responded. "Little more than a spooky fairy tale, really, or so I'd always thought. Millennia ago, before we Talaxians, before even the Trabe, there was an almost forgotten empire that ruled much of what you call the Delta Quadrant. Legend has it that this empire eventually spawned a race of mutants who fed upon the souls of other living beings because they had none of their own." He gave Torres a searching look. "I'm not certain exactly what they did to us before, but it sure felt like my soul was being yanked out of my body." He shuddered at the memory, then stared down at the sediment around his feet.

"The Empty Ones?" Kes prompted him.

Neelix lifted his gaze from the floor. "That's what the old stories call them. Supposedly all of the Empty Ones were finally captured, at great cost, and banished from the empire, never to be heard from again." Neelix gestured at the wrecked starship enclosing them. "I think I can guess where they ended up."

Torres snorted impatiently. "I don't suppose these legends contain anything useful, like how to destroy these Empty Ones?"

"Not that I remember," Neelix admitted.

Torres was not surprised. She had little faith in myths. The Klingons had a thousand old legends about Kahless and other great warriors of the past. As far as she could tell, they had never done her any good. *Give me hard scientific data over fairy tales any day,* she thought.

Still, she had to concede that the Ryol sounded a lot like Neelix's Empty Ones. She'd experienced first-hand the awful energy-sucking void generated by the Ryol; it had certainly felt like her soul was being devoured. *We need to get out of here,* she thought, *and warn the captain.*

Footsteps echoed in the spacious confines of the cargohold. Torres looked up to see a typically skinny-looking neffaler ambling toward them, clutching what looked like a wineskin with both hands. The neffaler uncapped the vessel and offered it to Torres, who sniffed the mouth of the skin before tasting the contents. She was thirsty, yes, but suspicious, too. It wouldn't be the first time an enemy had tried to drug her—or worse; the Cardassians thought nothing of poisoning the waterholes near human colonies in the Demilitarized Zone. *On the other hand,* she thought, *why should they bother to drug us when they can already drain our life-force just by staring at us?*

Thirst won out over paranoia, and Torres took a deep gulp from the wineskin. It was water, slightly warm but clean and refreshing. "Thank you," she said to the neffaler as she passed the water over to Kes and Neelix. The dwarfish creature watched her with its— *his,* she corrected herself—large black eyes. On closer inspection, she decided that this particular neffaler seemed younger—and slightly less debilitated—than the others she had seen. There was a cord around his neck, she noted, and something white and shiny peeked out from beneath the shaggy red bristles covering his chest. Whatever that something was, it reflected the light from the crystal nearby. "What's that?" she asked, pointing at the neffaler's chest.

The creature backed away nervously. Torres sat very still, making no threatening sound or movement, while the tiny neffaler gathered his courage. The frail frightened creature seemed like the polar opposite of a proud fearless Klingon warrior, which, perversely, made Torres like him even more. Slowly, apprehensively, the neffaler crept back toward her. "That's it," Torres said softly. "Good boy." She forced herself to smile warmly at the little creature. It felt very odd.

To be honest, she wasn't entirely sure why she was so interested in finding out what the neffaler was hiding. A fully charged phaser rifle, set on kill, was probably too much to ask for. It gave her something to do, however, which certainly was better than sitting around brooding about what the Ryol were planning to do to her.

"What's that?" she asked again when the neffaler came once more within reach. He looked down at his scrawny chest, then lifted up the object hanging from the cord around his neck for Torres to see. It was a whistle. A simple plastic whistle.

Torres emitted a puzzled grunt, startling the neffaler, who took a few steps back. What would a neffaler be doing with a toy whistle? She couldn't imagine any of the Ryol giving one of their slaves a gift; could the whistle have come from *Voyager?* There was no way to be sure, but it seemed a plausible-enough theory. Perhaps there was some way to enlist this neffaler to help them?

"Starfleet," she said, pointing at her own uniform. "Starfleet, understand?" The neffaler started at her with gaping black eyes. She had no idea if she was getting through or not. "Go get Starfleet." She spoke slowly, afraid of confusing him. According to Kes, the neffaler were sentient, or at least they used to be. How much could this being really comprehend. "Bring Starfleet here, do you understand me?"

The young neffaler peered at Torres, looked down at his whistle, then back at Torres. Her attempts at communication attracted Neelix's attention. "What is it?" he whispered, lowering the wineskin from his lips. "What are you doing?"

"Do you really think he can rescue us?" Kes asked.

"Sssh!" Torres hushed them both. She kept her gaze locked on the neffaler's wide-eyed stare. "Starfleet," she repeated. "Find Starfleet now."

A rock smashed into the sand in front of the neffaler's feet, sending bits of sediment flying. "Get away from them, you miserable vermin!" came a voice, sounding both quavery and furious. The neffaler screeched in alarm and bounded away, fleeing faster than Torres had ever seen any neffaler move before. Another rock crashed into the ground behind the neffaler's heels, barely missing the escaping creature. "Run, you flea-bitten piece of garbage! Run while you can!"

The irate voice broke off suddenly, replaced by a harsh racking cough. Torres yanked her gaze away from the frightened neffaler to see who chased him away. *Blast it,* she cursed silently. *I was getting through to him. I know I was!*

Varathael approached her, accompanied by a surprisingly sickly-looking specimen of Ryol manhood. Old and feeble, the other Ryol clutched yet another rock in his thin knobby fist. At first, she didn't recognize the man walking a few paces behind the Elder. His gaunt body, partially covered by a thick black shawl draped over his bony shoulders, was positively scrawny compared to the robust physique of a typical Ryol male. Streaks of gray tainted his stringy golden mane, matching the lifeless pallor of his once-bronzed flesh. He treaded slowly over the sand and coral-strewn floor, moving with obvious pain and difficulty. Torres wondered briefly why she had never seen an elderly Ryol before, then spotted the thin white scar running down the old man's face and remembered Tom Paris's vivid description of his enemy among the Ryol. "Enough, Naxor," Varathael said scornfully. "You are foolish to expend your remaining strength on such a pathetic and unworthy creature."

Naxor? Could this frail and pallid creature be Varathael's infamous assistant? Torres wondered. What could have possibly happened to him? The only explanation she could think of was that Naxor must have fallen victim to some ghastly form of Ryol cannibalism. Strangely, this evidence of infighting among the Ryol only heightened her sense of dread. *Even the Vidiians,* she thought, *don't prey on their own kind.*

"Please, Elder," Naxor begged. His voice was thin and whiny. Withered hands drew the shawl more tightly about his shoulder, apparently intent on protecting his trembling frame from the dank chill of the cargohold. "I need to restore myself. Please let me feed upon one of the new neffaler." Watery green eyes fixed on Torres. He licked his cracked and bleeding lips. "Just one, that's all I ask."

"Later," Varathael said curtly, dismissing his aide's entreaty with a wave of his hand. He stopped in front of Torres, looking down at her with his own pale green eyes. "I am told," he said to her, "that you are responsible for maintaining the technology that powers your starship. We shall have need of your services in the days to come."

Torres climbed to her feet, determined to confront Varathael face to face. "It doesn't look to me like you're going anywhere," she said. She kicked disdainfully at the rusty hull beneath the sediment. "I don't know what you've heard about my abilities, but I'm no miracle worker."

"Oh, I am fully aware that this ship will never fly again," Varathael said. "But once we have your *Voyager,* we shall leave this pitiful hulk far behind." He glanced upward at the distant ceiling. Cobwebs drooped from the jutting support beams like desiccated flesh hanging on to broken ribs. "You need not fear the tide, by the way. We have repaired the flood doors you burned your way through."

Torres could care less about any damage they'd done to this underground prison. "What makes you think you can take *Voyager?*" she challenged Varathael, half afraid of what his answer might be.

Varathael laughed in her face. "Even as we speak," he declared, "my daughter and several of her most trusted followers are seizing control of your ship." He put a deceptively friendly hand upon her shoulder. *"Voyager* is a bland title, don't you think, for such a magnificent vessel? I think I shall rename her once we are under way. Something more impressive. The *Revenge,* perhaps, or the *Terror.* What do you think?"

Torres jerked her shoulder away from Varathael's grip. A growl formed at the back of her throat, but struggling to keep her Klingon fury under control, she swallowed the snarl before it could escape. "Under way where? Just where do you think you're going?"

"To freedom!" he exclaimed passionately. "We have been marooned on this world for too long, forced to sustain ourselves on the diminishing life-force of the pathetic creatures we found here. There was a time, ages ago, when we prowled the starways at will, feasting on the souls of kings and emperors. A thousand worlds feared our hunger."

Varathael's lips peeled away from his smile, revealing gleaming white canines. His voice deepened as he became caught up in a spell of his own making. "That time will come again," he intoned. "Our mighty new ship will carry us throughout the cosmos, unleashing our hunger upon countless new worlds and civilizations. We shall taste the life-blood of the universe and drink deep. Who knows? Perhaps someday we will even consume the distant worlds that birthed you and your fellow travelers."

Inwardly, Torres felt a thrill of horror at the idea of the Ryol preying on the Federation and, yes, even the Klingon Empire, but she took care not to betray her true feelings. "And where do we fit in?" she asked defiantly. She heard Kes and Neelix stand up behind her, adding their support to her own paltry show of resistance. Neither Varathael nor Naxor looked at all scared.

"You and yours," Varathael promised, "will play a most important part in our glorious destiny, as both servants and sustenance to the future masters of the galaxy. History will remember you as our liberators as well." He shook his head sadly. "I fear its judgment will not be kind."

Torres had heard enough. If only she still had her phaser! Her eyes focused on the ruby gemstone hanging around Varathael's neck, the same device that had earlier protected the Ryol from her phaser blasts. Despite herself, she was both impressed and intrigued by the gem's capabilities; even after decades of research and experimentation, personal shields remained impractical according to the standards of Alpha Quadrant technology. The energy demands alone had defeated the best efforts of generations of Federation scientists, not to mention their counterparts among the Klingons, Romulans, and Cardassians. *A device like that,* she thought, *could revolutionize future warfare. Or grant the Ryol an easy victory over the Federation.*

"I see you are interested in my jewelry," Varathael commented. He tapped the gem and the crimson radiance surrounded him once more. He pressed it again and the glow disappeared. "A useful artifact of bygone days, although sadly unique. I'm afraid the knowledge behind its creation was lost in the crash. Perhaps, with your help, and *Voyager*'s vast scientific resources, we will finally be able to duplicate this treasure many times over, although I confess I shall regret losing the prestige of having the only one."

Torres felt a twinge of scientific curiosity. Part of her would have liked nothing better than to take the Elder's gem apart and see how it worked. The rest of her knew better. "Forget it," she said. "I won't cooperate with you, and neither will any of the others."

"That's right," Neelix said. "We won't help you. We know who you are. The Empty Ones."

"Ah," Varathael said, "I haven't heard that term for what feels like centuries. How nice to know that we are still remembered." His charming smile slipped away as his voice took on a darker, more ominous tone. "If you know the old stories, then you must realize that no one can defy us for long. If you are wise, you will not waste your energies trying to resist us." He glared at Neelix. "We need some of you to help us master your ship, but not all of you are essential. Do not think you are not expendable."

"Yes!" Naxor broke in. He slid past Varathael to stare hungrily at Neelix. "Please, Elder, let me feed on this ugly one!"

"Ugly?" Neelix protested. "I'll have you know that I am considered stunningly handsome among Talaxians."

Naxor ignored Neelix's words. The shrunken Ryol kept his gaze upon the indignant morale officer. Empty black circles began to dispel the teary green orbs in his sockets. Torres felt her muscles tense in anticipation of an attack upon the Ryol. All her aggressive tendencies came to the fore; she had to bite down on her lower lip to keep from growling. *What do I do now?* she wondered desperately. If Naxor really intended to kill Neelix before her eyes, was there any way she could stop him?

She quickly surveyed the potential battleground. There were only the three of them confined in the hold, being guarded by about a dozen unarmed Ryol, plus a handful of monkeylike neffaler tending to the Ryol and their prisoners. The odds were in her favor—if you didn't count the extraordinary powers of the Ryol. Unfortunately, she couldn't figure out a way to eliminate those powers from the equation. *Think!* Torres ordered herself, even calling upon her hated Klingon heritage for an answer. *What would a full Klingon do in a situation like this? What would Kahless do?*

"In fact," Neelix continued, "as a child I was considered so adorable that—" His defiant words seemed to catch in his throat. A choking noise burbled past his lips. Kes let out a cry of alarm, then threw herself between Naxor and her lover. Was it even possible, Torres wondered, to block the Ryol's attack that way? She didn't wait to find out. Springing at Naxor like an enraged panther, she knocked him to the floor, throwing up a cloud of dust and black sand. The Ryol's brittle bones snapped beneath her weight. His fetid breath escaped his lungs in one convulsive gasp.

"Stop!" Varathael demanded, but Torres was beyond restraint now. Pure killer instinct took over and she reached out automatically for a weapon, any weapon. Her fingers closed around the semi-petrified leg bone of one of the original victims of the Ryol conquest of the neffaler. Before anyone could stop her, before even Torres realized what she was doing, she drove the jagged point of the bone deep into Naxor's chest.

The emaciated Ryol let out a terrifying shriek

before dying. Viscous yellow fluid gushed from the wound, staining Torres's hand and sleeve. She froze, shocked by her own actions, her fingers still locked around the length of the bone. She heard Kes gasp behind her, heard also the sound of Neelix breathing once more. *I saved him,* she thought. *I think.*

"How dare you!" Varathael shouted. He grabbed her by the collar and flung her away with one hand. The back of her head collided with the tall stone rising up through the floor. The impact rattled her teeth and blurred her vision momentarily. For a few seconds, she thought she was about to pass out. Then she only wished she had. A throbbing pain drew her hand back to the base of her skull. Her fingers, still sticky with Naxor's blood, felt a fist-sized bump forming beneath her thick black hair.

Varathael gave her no opportunity to recover. Leaning over her capsized body, he thrust his face at hers until his bared teeth were less than two centimeters away from her eyes. The Elder's urbane expression had given way to a look of unmitigated rage. Even his features seemed different, the jaw larger and more pronounced, his teeth longer and more sharp. The tips of his ears poked out from beneath his golden mane. Torres realized she was only a breath away from being eaten alive.

Then, at the last minute, Varathael seemed to regain control of himself, at least partly. He drew away from Torres, straightening his spine, his fists clenched at his sides. His voice when he spoke, however, remained full of barely contained fury.

"Thank your barbarian gods," he snarled, "that your skills make you valuable to us. Naxor was an impulsive fool, but he was still superior to you and your kind. His life was not for you to take."

Other Ryol, male and female, came running to the scene of the uproar. Torres saw their claws extending, their menacing green eyes growing darker. *What are you?* she thought urgently, dismayed by growing horror of the true nature of the Ryol. She tried to summon the strength to fight back, but the pain in her head made it hard to concentrate.

"Stand back," Varathael called to his guards. They circled around the Elder and Torres. Peering through their looming bodies, she glimpsed Kes helping Neelix down onto the ground. The Talaxian looked shaken, but unharmed. "The crisis is over," Varathael informed the other Ryol. His features resumed their former civilized pose.

You can't fool me, she thought angrily, her Klingon temperament not yet fully doused. *I've seen your real face.* For once, she did not feel ashamed of her savage ancestry. There were worse things in the universe than Klingons.

Far worse.

"If the anesthezine hadn't worked," Janeway explained, "we were just going to beam in, phasers blazing, and try to retake the bridge using sheer brute force and surprise. I'm glad it didn't come to that."

"You're telling me?" Paris said. With a fresh red uniform over his injured back, he looked none the worse for his recent ordeal at the hands of Laazia and her bestial companions. Tuvok had used a specially prepared hypospray on Paris to counteract the effects of the sleeping gas. Janeway silently thanked The Doctor for his foresight.

She glanced around her. The bridge still showed signs of wear and tear from its recent occupation. Durafoam padding poked out from the vicious gashes that Laazia's talons had left in Captain Janeway's chair; she could feel the spilled padding brush her back every time she shifted her weight. Shreds of velvet and silk, scattered about the floor of the bridge, also bore evidence to Laazia's destructive rampage— and shocking transformation. Janeway took comfort in the fact that the Elder's shape-changing daughter, along with the rest of her boarding party, was now safely locked away in a security cell guarded by the strongest forcefield Tuvok could arrange.

Susan Tukwila's body had also been removed from the bridge, to await an examination and autopsy in the sickbay. Janeway winced at the thought; she felt personally responsible every time a crew member died on their long journey home. *I'm sorry, Susan,* she thought. *I wish I had never heard of this terrible planet.*

But there was little time to mourn. Although she had regained control of her ship, Janeway was acutely aware that three hostages remained on the planet below. Paris had brought *Voyager* back within transporter range of Ryolanov, but rescuing the trapped crew members was easier said than done.

"I don't get it," Paris said, seated at the conn station. "If the Ryol DNA is so weird, then why don't we just set the transporters to distinguish between them and our own people? That should work even if their commbadges have been taken."

"It is not that simple," Tuvok declared. The Vulcan officer occupied the starboard aft security station. "Even if our transporters can overcome the Ryol defensive shields, there will be considerable delay.

"The moment we start beaming out the prisoners, the Ryol will realize what we're up to. They might react by killing them before we can complete the transportation."

Seated in his chair alongside Captain Janeway, the first officer looked more battered than the rest of them. Although some quick first aid had stopped the bleeding from the wound on his cheek, his face was badly bruised from his battle with Laazia. At the moment, though, he seemed oblivious to his own injuries and more concerned with the safety of B'Elanna and the others.

At least, Janeway thought, *I have almost all of my*

senior officers on hand to cope with this emergency.
Even Harry Kim, fully recovered from Naxor's attack
by the shore, manned his usual station at the operations console. Janeway knew she could count on them
all to do whatever they could to resolve the crisis.

"As distressing as such a choice would be," Tuvok
said, turning around on his seat to face the front of
the bridge, "I feel obliged to point out that, logically,
Lieutenant Torres is the most valuable crew member
among the hostages. She is, after all, our chief engineer."

Janeway shook her head. "I'm not ready to start
practicing triage just yet. We need another solution.
Mr. Kim, is the Elder still hailing us?"

"Yes, Captain," Kim said. "On all channels."

"Probably expecting a message from his daughter,"
she commented dryly. "I think we've kept him waiting long enough. Mr. Tuvok, Chakotay, I'm going to
confer with Varathael, find out what his demands are,
and basically stall for time. In the meantime, I want
you two to put your heads together and find a way out
of this mess. Consult with The Doctor as well. Understood?"

"Perfectly, Captain," Chakotay said. He rose from
his chair and walked toward Tuvok. He had a definite
limp, Janeway noted, although he was trying hard to
conceal it.

"Mr. Kim," she said. "Put the Elder through."

Several minutes passed before Varathael's face actually appeared on the main viewer. Janeway wondered where exactly he was and what he was up to; she
didn't recognize the chamber behind him, although it
appeared old and dimly lit. "Captain Janeway," he
said. "As I stated earlier, before your transporter
snatched Lieutenant Torres's communicator from my
hand, we have much to discuss."

The Elder looked as handsome and regal as ever.
Janeway tried to imagine his face metamorphosing

into that of a ferocious beast and found it surprisingly easy to do. The monster was always there, she reflected, beneath a thin patina of charm and culture; all you needed was to know what to look for.

"Much indeed," she agreed. "Including your daughter, I imagine. May I assume that you were aware of her attempt to seize control of *Voyager?*"

Varathael sighed, seemingly weary but none too concerned. "I take it then that the attempt was unsuccessful?"

"Very," Janeway stated, "although her activities resulted in the death of one of my crew."

Varathael did not bother to apologize for the fatality. "More lives than one are at stake, Captain, as I think you are aware."

"Let's get straight to the point, Elder," Janeway said. "You have some of my people. I have some of yours. I am willing to discuss a trade."

"You have merely a fraction of my people," Varathael said. "I have three irreplaceable members of your crew."

"My seven include your daughter," Janeway pointed out.

Varathael scowled. "Do not mistake me for a sentimental man, Captain. You would be severely in error. My Heir knew the price of failure."

Is he bluffing? Janeway wondered. She didn't want to find out. "What exactly do you want, Elder?"

"Your ship," he said. "Nothing less will satisfy me. My people have been confined to this pretty prison for long enough. Your ship is our salvation."

It's not enough that you destroyed the civilization of the neffaler, Janeway thought angrily. *Now you want to inflict your vile appetites on the rest of the universe.* She knew there was no way she could, in good conscience, surrender *Voyager* to the Ryol. With the star charts stored in *Voyager*'s computers, it was even conceivable that the Ryol might be able to reach the

Federation in less than a century. She couldn't take that risk.

"Let me make my position perfectly clear," Janeway said. "I will destroy this ship, and everyone on it, before I let *Voyager* fall into your hands. Do you understand me, Elder?"

This was not the first time she had made that threat since entering the Delta Quadrant, and each time she had been deadly serious. She prayed that this time she wouldn't have to go through with it.

"Understood," Varathael replied. Every last trace of warmth faded from his features. "Know then that your people will die, one by one. How long will your resolve last, I wonder, when you hear your precious crew screaming for mercy? Who shall I begin with, Captain? Who shall be the first to perish? The funny ugly one who beamed down with you that first time? Or maybe one of the women? There's a delicate, fair-haired young woman here, with unusual ears. She looks like a promising victim, what do you think?"

Janeway sprang from his chair and marched straight toward the main viewer. "Listen to me, Varathael," she said. "If you harm one more of my crew, if you even scratch any of them, I will retaliate with deadly force. Don't think your psionic powers will be able to protect you. I don't need to step foot on Ryolanov to destroy you. There's enough firepower on this ship to devastate your world from orbit."

"I'm sure there is," Varathael said calmly, "but you cannot turn those weapons against us without also targeting any surviving hostages." His malachite eyes stared at her without blinking. "I want your ship, Captain. You have one hour."

The transmission ended abruptly. Janeway found herself gazing at a blank viewscreen. *And I thought Cardassians were ruthless,* she thought, amazed at the Elder's callous disregard for sentient life. Varathael made even a Cardassian *gul* look warm-hearted.

She turned to address the bridge crew. "Gentlemen, the clock is ticking. What do we have?"

"Just one possibility," Chakotay said. He looked up from the tactical console behind the command center. "A wide-dispersal phaser blast aimed directly at the harbor area, strong enough to overpower the Ryol shields. With luck, it would stun both the Ryol and the hostages, thus giving us a chance to send in a rescue team while the Ryol are immobilized."

"What about the neffaler?" she asked. Now that they'd ascertained the real history of Ryolanov, she didn't want to make the mistake of overlooking the planet's indigenous population. It seemed more than possible that the Elder and his cohorts might have some of their unfortunate servants with them.

"In theory," Chakotay said, "the neffaler would be stunned as well."

"But?" she prompted him. Years of Starfleet experience had taught her that there was almost always a "but."

"Given our meager knowledge of Ryol biology," Tuvok explained from his security station, "it is impossible to fully predict the effect of the phaser blast on the Ryol. The blast could be useless—or fatal. We risk both failure and the possibility of killing all the Ryol within range of the blast."

Janeway instantly saw the full dimensions of the ethical dilemma presented by Chakotay's plan. As depraved and treacherous as the Ryol were, she was reluctant to order a massacre, even by accident. "And the neffaler?" she asked again.

"Again, our biological data is incomplete," Tuvok said, "but I believe the risk is significantly less in their case. The neffaler are much more conventional life-forms, lacking both the Ryol metamorphic abilities and their psionic metabolism. According to The Doctor, they should react to the phaser blast as we expect, although I cannot state that as a complete certainty. I estimate the odds of accidentally killing the neffaler to be less than one-point-five-seven percent."

That's good enough for me, she thought, *but what about the Ryol? Do I dare risk slaughtering an unknown number of aliens just to protect a few stranded castaways from another quadrant? And what if it doesn't work, what if the Ryol prove immune to a phaser burst of this specific magnitude? They might retaliate by killing the hostages immediately.*

"How much time do we have, Mr. Kim?" she asked, knowing that he would be keeping track.

"Forty-nine minutes and counting," Kim reported. He watched her anxiously, clearly apprehensive about what might happen next. She didn't blame him; they both had close friends among the hostages. She couldn't imagine *Voyager* without Neelix or Kes or B'Elanna or any of the others.

"Well, let's not make this a split-second finish," she announced. "Any comments, gentlemen?"

"From a security standpoint," Tuvok stated, "the Ryol represent a potential danger to all other forms of life. Although I would regret any unnecessary bloodshed, I believe deliberate action must be taken to limit the threat they represent. My recommendation is to attempt to stun them with a controlled phaser burst."

Chakotay limped around the guardrail into the command area. "Once again, I'm inclined to agree with Tuvok," he said. "It may not be the most scientific basis for a decision, but my spirit guide has been warning me about these creatures since we first arrived here. They have to be stopped, for the sake of the neffaler if not for our own. Protecting innocent communities from remorseless invaders was what the Maquis was all about."

"Starfleet places a bit more emphasis on the Prime Directive," Janeway said, "although I share your sympathy for the neffaler." She sat down in the captain's chair and looked at the main viewer. At her command, an image of Ryolanov appeared on the screen. The planet slowly rotated beneath them, its bright red atmosphere as deceptive as the glistening skin of a poison apple. "With *Voyager* safe," she announced, "my first priority has to be the hostages. B'Elanna, Neelix, and Kes are counting on us and I'm not about to let them down. Whatever happens next, the Ryol brought this upon themselves. Mr. Tuvok, prepare a maximum dispersion phaser blast, set on stun."

"The ship's phaser banks have already been programmed accordingly," Tuvok informed her. "And security teams are standing by for immediate transport to the planet."

"Excellent," she said. "Mr. Kim, how long until the Elder's deadline."

"Thirty-nine minutes," he reported.

"That's plenty of time," she said. "Fire at will."

Tuvok responded immediately. On the viewer, Janeway witnessed twin beams of coruscating blue energy converge on the planet's equator. The beams shimmered slightly where they intersected with Ryolanov's atmosphere. The beams flashed for less than two seconds before Tuvok deactivated the phasers. "The burst has been completed," he stated calmly.

Harry Kim was more emotional. "Is that it?" he asked. "Did it work?"

I hope so, Janeway thought. Otherwise, they'd run out of tricks—and time. "Let me see what's happening down there. Full magnification!"

CHAPTER

17

"OUCH!" TORRES BARKED. "THAT HURTS."

"I'm sorry," Kes said softly. Her fingers dug beneath Torres's dark hair to explore the bump on the back of the woman's head. The injury didn't seem serious, although Kes wished she had a medical tricorder. Better yet, she wished she could get Torres to the sickbay for a complete examination. *We'd all be better off back aboard the ship,* she thought.

She considered asking the Ryol for some rudimentary first-aid supplies, even just a cold compress at least, but was reluctant to attract their attention for even a moment. Varathael was ignoring them at present; Kes saw him standing several meters away on the other side of the dilapidated cargohold, speaking into a portable plastic monitor that his aides had erected atop another moss-covered boulder. She wondered if he was communicating with *Voyager.*

Captain Janeway would never surrender the starship to the Ryol, Kes knew that much, but she was confident that her friends aboard *Voyager* would attempt some sort of rescue mission. *We just have to hold on,* she thought, *and do our best to stay alive, no matter how difficult it gets.*

She could still hear the murdered neffaler wailing at the back of her mind, like a headache that won't go away. Their plaintive cries tore at her heart, but she did her best to ignore them. The ancient neffaler were dead; there was nothing she could do to save them now, while Neelix and B'Elanna and the others still needed her help. *Forgive me,* she thought to the bodiless voices. *I don't know how to relieve your pain.*

A tiny skeletal figure shuffled toward her. Kes gasped out loud, thinking at first that one of the original victims of the Ryol had materialized in front of her. Then she realized that the figure was merely another neffaler, one of many servants, carrying a tray of food for the hostages. Unlike the youngish neffaler B'Elanna had befriended a few hours ago, this one had nearly reached the limits of his endurance. His large black eyes stared lifelessly at the ground before his feet. He moved slowly, lacking any sign of energy or hope. *Does he understand,* Kes wondered, *the tragedy that occurred here so many years ago? How much do the neffaler remember of their own history?* She forgot her own perilous situation for a moment, overwhelmed by the sheer enormity of the disaster that had befallen the innocent and unsuspecting neffaler. *Nothing the Ryol can do to me,* she thought, *can be worse than what they have already done to these poor people.*

Her prison fare consisted of a slice of black bread and a piece of fruit. She consumed them quickly, determined to keep her strength up for whatever trials lay ahead. Next to her, Neelix chewed glumly on his own chunk of bread. "Not very impressive cuisine," he stated. "Why is it I feel like a Sarayan swamp sloth being fatted for the slaughter?"

"Your keen grasp of the obvious?" Torres remarked, rather sharper than Kes liked. She tried to remember that B'Elanna had been injured, and that the pain was probably making her more irritable than usual.

Across a long stretch of sand and coral, Varathael concluded his business at the monitor. Kes watched him stride away from the makeshift communications station and confer in hushed tones with one of his lieutenants. To her distress, the Elder did not look overly troubled or anxious. *If only I knew what was going on between Varathael and the captain,* she thought, *maybe I could do something to help. There must be some way we can—*

Something happened then, cutting her off in mid-thought. Kes felt a sudden burning sensation all over her body, followed immediately by a peculiar sense of disorientation. Everything went black for a second, and Kes felt her body dropping to the floor, but when the blackness passed, she found herself standing right where she'd been and able to see better than she ever had before.

She gazed in wonder upon the interior of the cargohold. Whatever had just happened had affected everyone else, too: Neelix, B'Elanna, neffaler, and Ryol. Their captors alike lay helpless upon the ground, their motionless bodies sprawled where they fell. Only a few centimeters away, Neelix and Torres slumped against each other, B'Elanna's head resting upon the Talaxian's shoulder, a sight Kes found curiously endearing. Her companions' eyes were closed. Neelix's mouth hung open as he took slow regular breaths. They were both out cold, and so was everyone else in the hold.

But what about me? Kes wondered, confused. *Why*

am I still awake? She glanced down at her feet, amazed to see her own body stretched out on the sandy floor. Her face lay dangerously close to a puddle of brackish sea water, but had luckily remained turned toward the air. One shell-shaped ear sank deep into the sand. *I don't understand,* Kes thought, looking down on her own unconscious form. *Am I dreaming?*

If so, it was a remarkably vivid dream. She could still feel the dank chill of the sundered hold, listen to the sudden eerie silence. Even the flying frogs had stopped fluttering overhead. Looking around, she spotted dozens of small winged bodies scattered about the floor of this artificial cavern. It appeared as though every living thing in sight had been stunned instantaneously, except her . . . sort of.

The captain, she realized at once. This had to be *Voyager's* doing, part of the rescue operation Kes had been waiting for. Despite her bewilderment at her ongoing out-of-body experience, Kes experienced a moment of intense relief and optimism. They were going to beat the Ryol after all!

An angry growl caught her attention. Looking away from her own body, Kes was dismayed to see another figure lifting itself off the ground. It was Varathael, of course, his powerful body protected by a sheath of glowing red energy. He raised his arms above his head, roaring in rage. Claws sprouted from his outstretched fingers. His face was a mask of bestial hate and bloodlust, ivory fangs protruding from his transforming jaws.

Crazed green eyes searched the silenced confines of the cargohold until his baleful glare fell upon the slumping bodies of Torres and Neelix. He stalked toward them, clearly intent on exacting his revenge against *Voyager* by wreaking bloody mayhem on the hostages. "Stop!" Kes cried out, running forward and throwing out her hands to block him, but he seemed oblivious to her presence. She tried to grab on to him, but his flesh slipped effortlessly through her intangible fingers. There was nothing she could do to stop him, she realized, watching helplessly as he drew nearer to the unconscious forms of Neelix, Torres, and herself. The crimson forcefield shimmered around him like a demonic halo. Kes stood frozen in horror, an invisible witness to her own impending murder.

The wailing in her head grew louder, drowning out the sound of Varathael's fierce growls, transforming from cries of despair into a spine-chilling howl of revenge. The voices spilled out of her brain until they seemed to fill the entire vast chamber. Angry shrieks and shouts echoed off the rusty steel walls, so loudly that even Varathael seemed to pause momentarily, his lupine head looking around in apparent confusion. For the first time, Kes discerned a touch of fear and anxiety in the Elder's feral features.

She could hardly blame him. To her shock and astonishment, she saw strange apparitions rising from beneath the floor of the cargohold. The beings appeared composed of mist and shadows, passing through steel and stone as though they were as immaterial as Kes herself had become. *Were they holograms like The Doctor,* she wondered, *or something else entirely?*

They resembled the neffaler somewhat—Kes glimpsed six blurry fingers at the end of a vaporous arm—but stronger and taller somehow. Their limbs were long and supple, with a rich coating of shining fur. Their large moonlike eyes were full of wisdom and sorrow. *They're beautiful,* Kes marveled. *Was this what the neffaler were like, before the Empty Ones degraded them?* In her heart, she knew it was so.

Varathael, his humanoid features now completely supplanted by his more bestial persona, sniffed the air frantically. He appeared to have forgotten his intent to ravage the *Voyager* crew's defenseless bodies; instead, his head jerked from side to side, searching the shadowy recesses of the hold for some hidden danger. He could not see the noncorporeal entities ascending from the floor, Kes surmised, but he seemed to sense their presence. Varathael paced back and forth across a few short meters of rough terrain, his claws raised and ready to defend himself against the unseen foe. His growl devolved into a nervous whimper.

The fleshless beings, whom Kes knew to be the buried dead of this terrible place, approached the fallen bodies of their oppressed descendants. The bright white light of the crystals rendered the spirits partially transparent; Kes could see the walls of the hold through the entities' misty shapes. Their lustrous red fur was almost too bright to be real, like an illusion created by a combination of lasers and neon.

As Kes looked on, and Varathael grew steadily more agitated, the beings merged with the bodies of the stunned neffaler, disappearing into the tangible solidity of over a dozen sleeping individuals, who suddenly began to move again. Thin wasted limbs twitched abruptly, then lifted themselves off the ground.

Possessed by the long-denied wrath of their murdered ancestors, the neffaler advanced on Varathael with an energy and purpose they had never displayed before. The Elder of the Ryol could see the revitalized bodies easily enough; he barked imperiously at his former servants, dismissing them with a sweeping gesture, but they ignored his command. The neffaler surrounded Varathael, leaping up and down in their fury, baring their teeth and shrieking in fury. They snatched up pieces of bone and rock from the ground, brandishing them like weapons and hurling them at the Elder.

The projectiles bounced off the red forcefield encasing Varathael, but he stepped backward anyway, taken aback by the unexpected ferocity of the neffaler attack. Scorn turned to surprise in his eyes, closely followed by a look of unmistakable fear. He turned to flee, but found his path blocked by still more rampaging neffaler. A small furry figure threw himself onto the Elder's back, wrapping his arms around Varathael's throat. The red sheath flickered beneath the impact of the attack, but did not repel the invader. More neffaler imitated the first one's example, piling onto the Ryol leader one after another and flailing at him with their arms and legs. Varathael disappeared beneath a horde of berserk neffaler, exacting their revenge after generations of abuse and exploitation.

Every forcefield reaches its limit. Kes glimpsed the crimson glow of the Elder's ruby leaking out between the clustered bodies of the neffaler, then the bloodred light flickered once more and disappeared.

Finally Kes had to look away. The howling—and the screams—went on for several minutes, but she could not bare to watch any more.

"The neffaler saw the opportunity and took it," Chakotay suggested. He sat at the briefing table with the rest of the senior officers. The bruises on his face, Kes noted, were already starting to fade. "The other Ryol had been subdued, Varathael's power was being threatened for the first time in who knows when—the neffaler decided to strike when the iron was hot. That's what the Maquis would do."

"The neffaler are hardly the Maquis," Tuvok said, "although you may be right concerning the congruence of motive and opportunity. As for the phaser burst, I can only surmise that the unique composition of the alien hull provided the neffaler with some degree of protection from the effects of the phaser. It remains unclear, however, why only the neffaler received the benefits of any extra shielding. Nothing in their biological makeup suggests any form of immunity to phaser energy."

Seated between Neelix and Torres, Kes kept silent. She had her own theories about what actually happened while she was "dreaming," but she suspected that Tuvok would find them less than logical. The buried neffaler were finally at peace, though; she knew that much. Even before the rescue team beamed into the rotting cargohold to free the hostages and place the remaining Ryol into custody, she had felt their voices fall silent within her mind. Later she had gone back to the beach to confirm what she already believed: those anguished voices no longer cried out in torment from beyond the black shore. *Goodbye,* she had thought, feeling her eyes well up with tears and her throat ache from the emotions she felt. *Sleep in peace forever.*

Captain Janeway's crisp voice brought Kes back to the present. "I'm not inclined to look a gift horse in the mouth, or a gift neffaler, either. The important thing is that the neffaler fought back at the best possible moment. The question now is: what do we do with the Ryol?"

"With the Elder now deceased," Chakotay said, "Laazia is the new leader of the Ryol. She's demanding that she and her followers be returned to the planet, and that *Voyager* depart this system immediately." He gave the captain a solemn look. "I don't much like that idea."

"Neither do I," Janeway said. "After giving the matter some thought, I've decided that the spirit of the Prime Directive is best served by removing the Ryol from Ryolanov, thus giving the neffaler a second chance to evolve naturally."

"That certainly is one interpretation," Tuvok put in, one eyebrow raised.

Kes smiled, remembering the undeniable beauty of the ancient neffaler. With the pernicious influence of the Ryol gone, she felt sure that the remaining neffaler would be able to achieve their full potential once more. A young neffaler had joined her on the beach before, the same brave little creature who had befriended both Harry and B'Elanna. Listening to the simple melody the neffaler played upon his toy flute, Kes thought she heard the rebirth of neffaler art and culture in the haunting lilting notes that had brought grateful tears to her eyes. The neffaler of today may be more like their graceful ancestors than they first appear.

"According to the old legends," Neelix said, "the Empty Ones need to be driven away from all sentient life-forms. We can't let them spread through the Delta Quadrant again. Not even the Kazon deserve that."

"There are any number of uninhabited worlds nearby," Tuvok stated, "where the Ryol can be relocated to. With sufficient natural sources at their disposal, they will be forced to sustain themselves without exploiting another species."

"That's exactly what I had in mind," the captain said, "except that I want a warning beacon placed in orbit around the new Ryol home to alert any unwary travelers to the dangers involved in contacting the Ryol."

"We sure could have used something like that," Tom Paris said. Kes had been shocked, once she got back to *Voyager,* by the vicious wounds the Elder's daughter had inflicted on Paris. Thankfully, there had been no permanent damage to his back.

"I'll say," Harry Kim agreed. He still looked a little more worn out than was usual for him. The Doctor had prescribed plenty of nutrient supplements—and no more late nights for a while.

Indeed, the only lasting casualty, Kes had learned, was Susan Tukwila. She hadn't known Tukwila well, but she mourned the woman's death. Humans lived such an astoundingly long time, by Ocampa standards, that it seemed especially tragic when their lives were cut short this way. She hoped that Tukwila's life had been better than her death.

"What about the engines?" Chakotay said, looking at Torres. "Did you find anything we can use?"

"Yes and no," Torres answered. Kes had been relieved to discover that the bump on B'Elanna's head had produced no complications or concussion. The Doctor had relieved the swelling within a matter of minutes. "No luck with the dilithium crystals. If the Ryol starship ever used dilithium crystals, it must have degraded decades ago. There is plenty of spare antimatter, though. It shouldn't be too hard to transfer to *Voyager*'s storage facilities, and we can always use a little reserve antimatter."

Kes was glad that Torres had found some of what she was looking for. Working closely with B'Elanna had been an interesting experience, she thought; it was too bad that they seldom had occasion to work together.

"Besides," Chakotay pointed out, "we wouldn't be doing the neffaler any favors by leaving the antimatter there. It may be contained at the moment, but they're millennia away from being able to cope with antimatter in any quantities."

"Very well," the captain said. "Lieutenant Torres, proceed with the salvage operation, but let's not waste any time getting that antimatter aboard." She gave her officers a rueful look. "I don't know about the rest of you, but I've had quite enough of 'paradise' for the time being."

Kes understood the captain's feelings. She'd be glad to leave the black shore behind. She reached over and held Neelix's hand under the table. Still, despite all the dangers *Voyager* occasionally ran into, she couldn't wait to see where they were going next!

STAR TREK: VOYAGER

Captain's log, stardate 491750.9. Perhaps instead of worrying about a *Mutiny on the Bounty*, I should have been rereading *The Odyssey* instead, especially the verses about Circe's enchanted island. In the end, however, my crew valiantly refused to succumb to the dangerous temptations of Ryolanov, and I find myself departing this sector with renewed faith and confidence in our ability to cope with whatever the Delta Quadrant throws at us. We may be each of us a long way from home, but we're in very good company indeed. . . .

FOR A FEW, MAGICAL MOMENTS, KATHRYN JANEWAY FELT AS IF SHE were back home in Indiana. The air was warm and slightly humid; there was a scent of something that was almost like newly mown grass; and a gentle insect hum lulled the senses. She could almost forget that she was on an unknown, unnamed planet in the Delta Quadrant and pretend that she was hiking in the rolling hills of her home state.

Her eye fell on a bank of billowing white bushes—a fluffy mass of fronds that looked almost like pillows. It was tempting to lie down for a few moments, savoring the warm afternoon. She reached out and lightly touched one of the thick fronds; it yielded gently, promising a soft cushion.

Janeway glanced around at the rest of her away team, busy scanning for edible foodstuffs: Chakotay, the darkly handsome first officer, led a group of young ensigns who were clearly enjoying their first time on land in over a month; the sound of their laughter rang through the lush valley they were exploring. Chakotay, she knew, was wise enough to let them have some fun. A field trip on a verdant planet was just the thing to raise youthful spirits after a month of isolation on a starship.

Half a kilometer away, near the mouth of the valley, her Vulcan security officer, Tuvok, led the second contingent, which had been assigned the task of collecting foodstuffs deemed safe. That determination would be made by Neelix, their Talaxian guide, cook, self-proclaimed morale officer, and all-around handyman. Janeway smiled, imagining the interplay between the two. It had become Neelix' obsession to bring joy to Tuvok's life—an effort which the staid Vulcan greeted with a noticeable lack of enthusiasm. But Neelix was undeterred, determined to dispel what he insisted was the cloud of gloom that surrounded Tuvok.

Janeway inhaled deeply. It was so much like home—the faint scent of moist soil, a hint of floral fragrance on a gentle breeze—that she decided to yield to temptation. She fell back onto the mound of soft, pillowlike plants and closed her eyes, as if she were lying on a mound of hay. Back home.

The warmth of the planet's yellow star warmed her face. Insects droned ceaselessly; it would have been easy to drift off to sleep. But she wanted these few moments to be hers—to daydream, to pretend for this short time that she wasn't sixty-eight thousand light-years from Earth, that she wasn't carrying the extraordinary responsibility of getting her crew home safely, that she wasn't struggling to keep alive everyone's hopes that the journey could somehow be foreshortened. For just these few minutes, she would lie here and imagine that she was back on Earth, had managed to get *Voyager* home, had seen her crew welcomed as heroes and returned to the loving arms of their families and friends.

She wasn't sure how long she'd been lying there, drifting and dreaming, when she sensed that something was wrong. The smell had changed: the fragrant, grassy aroma had altered somehow—it had an *edge* to it, a—what? A metallic quality?

Janeway opened her eyes and sat up, saw that both teams were aware of something, were scanning with an increased urgency, pointing, calling to each other. She jumped to her feet, and in the same instant identified the odor: ozone. An electrical burning.

And that was the only warning they got.

Suddenly, there was a sizzling *snap!* A green arcing light pierced the air, and the ozone smell became acrid. Janeway twitched involuntarily, as though she'd suffered an electrical shock. The air itself had become charged by the bolt of—what? Plasma? She scanned quickly and detected a hot, electrically energized field unknown to the Federation database.

A hot wind began to stir, intensifying the burning smell; Janeway's nostrils began to sting. Out of the corner of her eye, she noticed the cottony white bushes begin to ripple in the sultry wind, but her mind quickly focused on her crew.

Chakotay and his young group were already on the move, heading toward her, when three or four more bolts of green sliced through the sky, crackling and smoking. This time Janeway heard herself cry out as pain slashed through her body.

Were they under attack? Or were they simply caught in an unexpected natural phenomenon? It hardly mattered— whatever these strange flashes were, they were clearly dangerous. She had to get her people out of there.

She hit her commbadge, noting that Chakotay was doing the same, as undoubtedly Tuvok was also. "Janeway to Voyager . . . We need emergency transport." She repeated the message several times before accepting what she had already suspected: that the electrical disturbance was interfering with the communications system, and it was doubtful the transporters would function through the interference.

Then the air crackled with energy bolts, sizzling and sparking. She heard a scream and saw someone fall to the ground. The hot wind began to gust violently, and the hissing sound of the arcing flashes became deafening. Janeway called out to Chakotay, but her voice was swallowed in the noise and the wind. She waved her arm at him, gesturing him to the mouth of the valley. Ahead of her, she saw Tuvok and his group already on the run. She began sprinting toward them.

But her body wouldn't behave as it should. Her legs were shaky, uncoordinated, like a newborn lamb's. She stumbled and then shuddered as another series of green flashes ripped through the air. Now it felt as though oxygen had been depleted from the atmosphere, and her lungs rasped as she drew stinging air into them. Reflexively, she began scanning again, and discovered a possible shelter: in the mountains that ringed the valley were a series of caves; if they could find an opening they might be able to escape this brutal attack.

Chakotay and his group came stumbling toward her, gasping, struggling against the wind. One of the ensigns collapsed to the ground; two others immediately pulled him up. All of them looked frightened but not panicky. Janeway pointed toward the mountains. "Caves," she yelled, but she barely heard her own voice over the roar of the wind.

Chakotay nodded; he understood. He turned and began herding his young charges to follow Janeway, who was moving toward the nearest outcropping of the mountains, scanning for a possible opening as she went.

Suddenly the tricorder disappeared from view. Janeway registered that fact, then realized everything had disappeared; she saw only a field of black punctuated by jagged green slashes. She barely had time to realize that there had been another series of energy bolts when the pain hit her.

She felt as though she were on fire, muscle and tissue seared, bodily fluids boiling. With an involuntary cry, she fell to her knees, stunned and shuddering. For a moment she was blind, desperate for oxygen, and in agony. But she forced her mind to take control. She stilled herself, locating the pain, isolating it, containing it until it began to subside. Gradually, the green slashes in her vision began to fade, the blackness receded, and she lifted her head.

The young officers were scattered on the ground like deadwood, writhing and moaning. Chakotay had already begun rising shakily to his feet, assessing their condition. One by one they began to get up, faces pale with shock, staggering, but on their feet.

We won't survive another round, Janeway thought, and she lifted her tricorder to scan for the nearest opening in the mountains. Then, ahead of her, she saw Tuvok's group crowding toward a dark slash in the cliff side. She realized they had found the mouth of a cave and she whirled to motion to Chakotay; but he'd already seen and was yelling at the group, gesturing toward the mountain, urging them forward.

The ragged group tried to run, fear of another bombardment of energy bolts propelling them against the fierce wind. Janeway's legs felt like gelatin, but she forced them to drive forward. The roar of the wind thundered in her ears; her lungs burned and streaks of green still obscured her vision. The side of the mountain seemed kilometers away, but she knew it wasn't—it couldn't be more than forty meters now. Tuvok's group had disappeared into the cave, but her Vulcan friend remained outside, moving toward them, prepared to help.

Thirty meters . . . The wind whipped dirt from the ground, making it even harder to breathe. Janeway glanced behind her to make sure the others were with her; they were, heads down, doggedly forcing their shaking legs to move. Chakotay brought up the rear, ready to help stragglers.

The ozone smell began to build again, and Janeway realized it was the harbinger of another attack; she picked up the pace, yelling at those behind her to hurry. Ahead of her the mouth of the cave yawned like a gaping maw; the figure of Tuvok swam before her, mouth moving, calling to them soundlessly as his words were swallowed in the wind.

And then she was there, Tuvok's arm steadying her, his firm grip infusing her with strength. She turned and waited as the young people lurched toward the cave opening and tumbled in. Only when they had all entered did Janeway, Tuvok, and Chakotay turn to follow them. The crackle of an energy buildup pulsed through the air; the eruption of a massive charge of bolts created a percussive wave that pushed them through the entrance, and they fell headlong into the cool darkness of the cave.

As soon as they were inside, the roar of the wind receded; the cave was a muffled haven, the air was clean and cool, and the dreadful energy of the plasma bolts, which they could hear outside, didn't penetrate the heavy rock. Janeway looked up, squinting in the darkness. As her eyes adjusted, she saw the entire away team huddled in the cave, drawing soothing moist air into burning lungs. Neelix was moving among them, comforting them, checking for injury. She turned toward Tuvok and Chakotay, who were already counting their people, making sure everyone had made it to safety.

"All accounted for, Captain," said Tuvok. She nodded and looked at Chakotay, who seemed to be counting a second time. She noted a worried furrow on his forehead, slightly distorting the distinctive tattoo he wore on his temple.

"What is it?" She moved toward him, fearing the worst. He turned to her, and his eyes told her she was right. "Who isn't with us?"

"Jerron," he answered, and they both hurried to the mouth of the cave. She spotted the young Bajoran almost immediately, a crumpled blue form in the distance, where they had all taken the first blast that had driven them to the ground. He must have been separated from the others and left behind when they were temporarily blinded.

Janeway immediately started forward, only to feel Chakotay's strong grip on her arm, pulling her back. "I'll get him," he said, but Janeway jerked her arm loose. "Commander, you're to stay with your team. Tuvok, too. That's an order."

Chakotay held her glance for a moment, not responding, but Janeway didn't wait for his acquiescence. Taking one last gulp of good air, she hurled herself out the cave opening and into the raging plasma storm.

It had mounted in intensity even in the few minutes they had been in the cave. Instantly, Janeway's lungs were burning; the air was bitter and caustic; she began to cough uncontrollably. Her eyes watered in the swirling dust. Her legs, which had regained some strength in the cave, turned mushy again, and she felt herself stagger. If she could reach him, get him back before the next round of plasma bursts, she'd make it. But she wasn't sure either of them would survive another attack.

She felt her body begin to go slack, reluctant to go farther, and she steeled herself again. Jerron was only ten meters ahead; she could reach him. One step, then another, fighting the brutal, swirling wind, dizzied by the deafening noise, each breath like breathing flames, she pushed ahead.

Jerron wasn't unconscious. He was staring at her with dull eyes, as though he were looking at something unreal, something his mind couldn't reconcile. His uniform was scorched, and Janeway realized he had taken a direct hit by a plasma bolt. How had he survived?

As she reached him, he pushed himself upright, reaching out an arm. She grabbed it, and he tried to stand, but his legs wobbled and he swayed against her. She struggled to stay on her feet until Jerron steadied himself. Then, bracing each other, they started toward the mouth of the cave.

Janeway smelled the unmistakable odor of an ozone surge. The plasma bolts would hit before they could get to the safety of the cave. She picked up her pace, urging Jerron on, hoping they could somehow outdistance the gathering plasma swell. The cave opening yawned ahead, not fifteen meters away; they could do it.

But Jerron stumbled, and they both went crashing to the ground. Without conscious thought, Janeway threw her body on top of the young Bajoran's, to shield him from the worst of the blasts.

It was the most ferocious attack yet, filling the air with snapping, arcing green bolts that clutched at the ground like the tentacles of some hideous beast. Janeway squeezed her eyes shut, but even so ragged streaks of green irradiated her lids. The fiery pain seemed to sear her from the inside out; she couldn't even hear her own scream. Her body thrashed as though in the throes of a violent convulsion, bucking and leaping uncontrollably, and the ragged gulps of air she drew between screams produced even greater agony.

And then her father lifted her up.

She felt his strong arms grip her, pulling her across the ground, his handsome, sturdy face calm and unworried, smiling down at her in reassurance. Janeway smiled back and relaxed into the journey, gliding across the terrain, feeling as though she were skimming on a cushion of air like a hovercraft. The air had cleared, and was sweet and cool; the pain was dissipating. She looked up again, wanting to see her father, wanting to look into his clear gray eyes just once more. . . .

Chakotay was staring at her, his face just inches from hers. Her eyes fluttered slightly and she tried to sit upright.

"She's all right," she heard Chakotay say, and she looked around her. She was in the cave again, Jerron at her side, Tuvok and Chakotay leaning over them, still coughing from their exposure to the plasma-infused atmosphere. They had rescued her, and Jerron; Chakotay's strong arms had saved her, not her father's.

She looked at Jerron, whose color was returning. "He has suffered no permanent damage, Captain," intoned Tuvok, "and neither have you." Janeway nodded. She took a deep breath and leaned back against the wall of the cave.

Death had been cheated once more. Everyone was safe.

When she entered the bridge from the turbolift, the faces of the bridge crew looked grim. Janeway moved immediately to Chakotay.

"We've been hailed by a Kazon ship," he reported. "He was none too friendly, and insisted we wait for them to intercept us. He didn't make an outright threat, but it was certainly implied."

Janeway felt a twinge of foreboding. Any encounter with the Kazon was potentially dangerous, although it had been some time since they had run into any of them; she had hoped that *Voyager* might possibly have moved outside the bitterly disputed turf of the various warlike sects.

"Did he state his purpose, Commander? Or identify his faction?"

"He said he was Maje Dut of the Vistik, but didn't give any clue as to what he wanted."

They had never interacted with the Vistik, but Janeway had heard of them. They were a group smaller than the Ogla and the Nistrim, which seemed to be the most powerful of the groups, but they had figured in a disastrous alliance that had threatened to coalesce the Kazon into a unified force—a catastrophic prospect for *Voyager*, which could deal with individual factions but couldn't hope to survive a massive and cooperative Kazon armada.

Options: they could make the diplomatic choice and wait for the Vistik ship, hoping there was a reasonably benign reason for the meeting. And, after all, one Kazon ship didn't pose a particular threat. What's more, they had detected a planetary nebula nearby that might warrant some investigation. These nebulae, formed when older stars began to shed their outer atmosphere, were magnificent and fascinating. Janeway had studied the Alpha Quadrant's Helix Nebula and welcomed the opportunity to investigate another of these massive phenomena. It could occupy the time while they waited for the Kazon.

But she found herself rejecting that option even before it was a fully formed thought. The Kazon had proven time after time that they couldn't be trusted. They were warlike and volatile, and any encounter could prove hazardous. She knew that they had once been horribly oppressed themselves, but freedom from their tormentors had not resulted in growth or enlightenment; it had led only to an endless series of battles among each other, battles that frequently harmed innocent bystanders. Like *Voyager*.

She wasn't going to jump to the whip of some unknown Kazon Maje; she wasn't willing to delay their journey by even a day to accommodate someone who more than likely would pose an unreasonable demand or a vindictive threat. She turned to Tom Paris, the young, sandy-haired lieutenant who was, as he had promised on their first meeting, the "best damn pilot" she could find.

"Mr. Paris, we're not waiting around for a Kazon that won't even do us the courtesy of telling us what he wants to discuss. Continue your course for the Alpha Quadrant, warp six."

"Yes, *ma'am.*" Paris was obviously pleased with the decision. He was still—would probably always be—a bit of a daredevil, someone who struggled at times against the yoke of Starfleet protocols, but whose skill and intelligence were such that he could get away with risk-taking that might undermine others.

Janeway knew, however, that she would hear something different from Tuvok, and before that thought was even completed, she heard his voice from the security station: "Captain, it is my duty to point out that the Kazon Maje will be highly insulted by this decision; we risk his enmity by ignoring his request."

"Noted, Mr. Tuvok. But I have yet to hear what might be termed a 'request' from a Kazon. They tend to make demands, and I don't feel like yielding to a demand."

"As you wish, Captain." Tuvok was imperturbable as ever, but Janeway imagined she could sense approval from him. No one liked being pushed around by the Kazon. In fact, Janeway thought she felt a general uplifting of spirits on the bridge; on an expedition where they frequently found themselves at the mercy of their circumstances, it was bracing to take a stand, to thumb their noses at the dark forces of the Delta Quadrant.

Look for STAR TREK Fiction from Pocket Books

Star Trek®: The Original Series

Star Trek: The Next Generation®

Star Trek: Deep Space Nine®

Star Trek: Voyager®

Flashback • Diane Carey